Dreamcatcher: Sacrifice

To Kay from Donna -
blessings -
KC Pearcey

KC Pearcey

ISBN: 978-1-7334071-5-1

For inquiries about the Balfour Mysteries, contact KC Pearcey at dreamcatcherkcp@gmail.com.

To the devoted readers

who have made it through the last four books . . .

I hope I've answered your questions

and solved most of the mysteries.

I appreciate all of you more than you know.

Thank you for spending time in Balfour.

Maybe someday we'll all visit again –

in the meantime,

I am always ready to share a cup of coffee

or a sweet tea with extra lemons.

When I began writing the first *Dreamcatcher*,

I thought there would be one book.

Maybe two. Or three is a good number.

But along the way, Cora and Charlie highjacked the story

and invited the rest of Balfour along down dusty country roads.

Odd times of the day and night, they'd wake me from semi-

consciousness,

and insist that they had something important to tell me.

Once I started writing down one of the stories, of course,

I couldn't refuse to listen to the others.

But all narratives eventually come to some sort of conclusion,

and this fifth book, hopefully, meets that criteria.

I thought I might be looking forward to a rest

from writing novels for a while, but then twelve sisters came

along with a telepathic dragon and . . .

well, please remember,

none of the people in ANY of my books are real.

If they were, I'd have an easier time ignoring them.

Chapter 1

The First Day: Monday

Cora opened her eyes and found herself dreaming in absolute darkness.

The odor of her surroundings and the sensation of waking sleep was all at once strange and eerily familiar.

She knew where she was.

Why? her mind screamed. *Haven't I seen everything I needed to see?*

She'd been expecting a nocturnal visit since she last saw James in August, but never one like this.

Possibilities raced through her mind. The dreams only changed their setting when there was purpose.

Cora tried to breathe but found instead that she was only able to take shallow breaths. Panic rose in her throat.

This is all wrong, she thought. *Where's James? Where's the light? I can't be here again. Please, not again.*

The doctors had told her, warned her, that someday the memory would return. That someday when she least expected it, she would remember the actual events that led up to the first dream.

But this was a memory she feared and prayed would never return—that it had been buried forever in her subconscious mind.

Cora tried desperately to calm her racing heart, to focus on what was real and what was only a vivid recollection.

But her mind refused to separate the two.

She'd expected her grandmother's kitchen, but instead, her pregnant body was trapped in the confines of the most horrifying place she'd ever known—a gruesome makeshift grave. A real location she had tried to erase from her mind, now dredged up from the hidden corners of her subconscious. A nightmare that brought back a real event full of desperation, death, and despair.

This was how it had all begun.

This was the beginning—and the end.

Her throbbing heart pounded inside her chest as she gasped repeatedly for air in terrified panic, unable to fill her lungs, unable to breathe normally.

A few scant feet above her trapped body, somewhere beyond the blackness, she could hear the muffled sounds of a scraping shovel and falling earth as it struck the wooden lid of her improvised coffin. The gravel and stones rained down, hitting and echoing like the crash of breaking glass.

Just like before.

No. She struggled for air. *No, not again. I can't be here again. Not now.*

She told herself to be rational—that she was not confined at all. That time had passed and her life had moved forward. She was married to Thomas, miles and miles away from New Orleans and Charlie Abbott and the life before.

Calm down, she told herself. *You can't be here again. This isn't real.*

But her body refused to believe she wasn't buried beneath the showers of dirt cascading down on the lid of the wooden crate.

There was absolutely nothing rational about how she felt, no reasoning with her quaking body. A pregnant body that defiantly demanded that she accept what was happening to her as truth rather than a dream, reminding her of the infant she had lost.

The darkness smothered her face and mouth like a velvet hood, sweeping away the concrete vestiges of the existing world and dissolving her fragile hold on reality.

Cora lost the will to struggle and surrendered control. She realized she couldn't hold back the torrent of emotion. And with that resignation, all but the last breath of resistance was abruptly gone. She was reliving the day she was buried alive. The day she lost Lonora.

Violently, inexplicably, she'd been transported back to the past. She felt herself falling down into a bottomless well.

Emotion drowned out logic.

She was buried. Buried again. The musty smell of freshly dug earth filled her nostrils. The restraining pressure against the sides and lid of her personalized makeshift hell seemed to press against her on all sides.

Cora tried to cry out, but her tongue was dry and clung to her teeth. A bitter, acrid taste hovered just inside her lips. Her arms and legs were pinned down, along with her pregnancy-swollen torso. Her only movement that of shaking her head slowly and painfully from side to side in an effort to clear her stampeding thoughts.

The horror was real.

She wanted to shout for help, but her lungs would not take in enough air.

Above her a cell phone resonated. She could almost feel the vibrations through the earth. Powerless to answer, bitter tears of frustration pooled at the corners of her aching eyes and cascaded down.

Charlie's ringtone.

She'd know her detective husband's ringtone anywhere.

He was trying to find her.

Against her left ear, Cora felt the slightest whiff of air. A tantalizing tickle that shifted her focus for a fraction of a second. The puff was followed by a whisper, faint at first, repeating itself. The words almost imperceptible.

Words from the past. A voice from the past.

"Close your eyes and open the door."

Cora labored to understand, but her strength to fight was gone.

Help me, her heart pled. *Help me to understand what to do. Help me.*

As though the voice could read her thoughts, the words grew louder, clearer, more insistent. A disembodied chant.

"Close your eyes and open the door."

Were the words audible or only in her mind? Did it matter?

She was drawn to the comforting sound of the words.

"Cora," the voice insisted, "close your eyes and open the door."

A man's voice. One she had once known—that she still knew.

Whose voice is that? I ought to know who this is, she thought, her mind cloudy and confused. *But what does that mean? Close my eyes and open the door?*

The words came for the third time, the kindly voice reassuring, gentle, and strong.

"Close your eyes and open the door."

Somewhere in her subconscious, her mind separated from her

body, moving into a freedom her physical self was denied.

She took a labored, shallow breath. The cell phone rang again, and she thought she might find the strength to call out, but the voice compelled her to act.

Cora closed her swollen eyes as her mind shattered.

She saw the door. A weathered wooden door suspended in a nonexistent wall.

She reached for the knob as the entry inexplicably swung open and vanished, and in the void she was met with a blast of cold air. Not unpleasantly cold, but cold nonetheless. Her constraints seemed to fall away, and she felt her body released from the near airless box and breathing freely.

She blinked hard. The walls were back, and she was standing in a room she knew well, at the kitchen sink in her grandmother's house.

Her mind readily accepted where she was, although in another dimension of memory she was acutely aware that this room no longer existed.

The voice that had been in her ear had moved and was somewhere at her back.

She turned, and the voice had taken on the form of a man.

"Come to the table, Cora," he urged. "Come sit with me for a moment. The coffee is hot, and you must be chilled."

She stumbled awkwardly to the ladder-back chair and lowered herself cautiously onto the quilted cushion, the four corners of fabric tied securely to the wooden legs.

She knew the colors of the cushions, a bright mix of calico and patchwork, but here they were black and white, and all the shades of gray in between.

Her hands trembled before they came to rest on the oilcloth

tablecloth. She knew it was a red-and-white checkered pattern, but she found herself mildly surprised that this, too, had no color.

Finally her eyes stopped searching her surroundings and rested, quite puzzled, on the well-dressed man before her.

"Take a sip of coffee," he said. "I know you've given it up for the baby, but you can drink it here."

The elderly gentleman moved the cup and saucer a few inches closer to her stiff hands. She could feel the heat coming off the vintage floral tea cup, the strong odor of the black liquid inside drifting up to her cool cheeks as she leaned over.

"Coffee?" she repeated blankly, touching the rim.

A soft bellow of amusement rippled under his suit jacket, while the tie that rested on his vested belly danced up and down in rhythm.

"I know this is confusing, Cora," he began, settling back into his chair and making himself comfortable as his cup miraculously appeared.

"Am I dead?"

"No."

He smoothed down his tie, lifting his own cup to drink, his eyes twinkling.

"Then where am I?" Her stiff fingers slipped into the handle of the cup. She knew that beyond this moment was a moment when she would know what was going on. But chasing the recollection seemed painfully futile.

She was broken. The glass shards of her mind lay about her, and she was afraid to move or think too deeply lest she open a random vein of recollections.

"How do you feel?" he said, taking a sip from his own steaming mug, studying her with intensity.

"Are you going to answer all my questions with questions?" Her voice quivered with impatience. She had no words for how she felt. She was in a place that no longer existed with a man long dead.

How am I supposed to feel?

The preacher gave a low chuckle and covered the cold hand that held the floral cup with his wrinkled palm.

"One sip," he urged her. "Then we can talk."

Uncertainly, she lifted the delicate, ornate cup and tilted the liquid to her dry lips.

Oddly enough, she *did* feel better.

Calm. Warm. Peaceful. Yet still bewildered.

"Cora," he said, "you do recognize me, don't you?"

"Of course." She felt a sudden spark of recollection. "You're my grandmother's preacher, James Cannon McArthur."

"Only my mother ever called me that," he chided, "in moments of extreme frustration."

"Yes." It was Cora's turn to smile. "Gramma called you Brother James."

She stopped, unsure about blurting out the obvious truth.

"And I *am* dead," he finished her thought and put down his cup. "I've been dead for quite some time now. Feel free to state the obvious."

"But how is that possible?"

"Now who is answering questions with questions?" He chuckled at his own feeble attempt at humor. "I'm here because I was sent for a higher purpose."

"That sounds both cryptic and ridiculous." She leaned forward until their faces almost touched. "I was in a coffin. I was buried alive."

"Are you sure? Does that look like where you are?"

Cora released the cup downward into its saucer, hot coffee splashing. "Please stop with the questions!"

"Accept the answers, Cora," he rejoined calmly.

"Answers? What answers? If I'm not dead then I'm having a hallucination."

She held her voice in check. The words were flat and resigned while her thoughts, in contrast, were whirling like a rapid, rushing drain.

"Not exactly a hallucination," he replied, patting her hand rhythmically as he spoke. "The secular professionals call this a psychotic break, which is exactly what Dr. Floyd will call it. A uniquely monochromatic, black and white psychotic break. Those of us in the field of theology have another word for what is happening—but you wouldn't believe me, so I won't use that word either."

The pupils of her eyes widened and darkened, searching suspiciously.

"I know what monochromatic means," she said, increasingly perplexed. "So, I'm buried alive and having a psychotic break in my dead grandmother's kitchen in a house that was destroyed by fire over ten years ago. Is that what you're saying?"

"That's what he will tell you when he talks to you," he said. "I'm glad you haven't misplaced your eye for details."

"He? Dr. Floyd?" Her head began to throb. "Why do I feel like this has happened before?"

"Because it *did happen*," he said. "You're inside a repressed memory."

He patted the table next to her cup, which was once again filled with steaming liquid.

"Have another swallow of coffee, sweet girl. I've come to remind you of something you've forgotten."

"James . . ."

"I know, Cora. I'm dead. What do I know?" His voice was completely serious, but his eyes held a curious spark of humor. "But *you* aren't dead. It's not your time . . . but you know that already, don't you?"

And as he enclosed her hands in his own warm, wrinkled palms, the past and the present collided.

She knew what was about to happen—what had happened in the past, what would happen in the future.

This was the first dream.

Her memory, against her will, was being restored to her.

"Focus, dear heart," he whispered. "I have a message for you to take back."

"Of course you do," she said softly, hot tears beginning to slip down her cold cheeks. She wanted to wipe them away along with any words he was about to say, but she clung to the preacher's soothing hands instead.

"There's a girl who's going to help Charlie," he said. "She's the answer to his questions."

"A girl? What questions? Does she have a name?"

James released her hands and picked up his cup, draining the liquid in one long satisfying swallow.

"That's not for you," he said softly, sad for what he knew she must still endure. "The past, the present, the future . . . where I am, they are all one. I know this is confusing, sweet girl, but there are some things you must leave to Charlie."

"You're giving me a terrible headache, James."

"It's the carbon dioxide, dear." He pushed his chair back from the table. "Your brain thinks it needs oxygen. You're overwhelmed with remembering the first time. Your mind is fighting to forget, but you must remember if you want to be free. The sensation won't last much longer."

The corners of his mouth turned up, wrinkling his entire face as he tilted his head sideways. An image of the Cheshire cat dressed in black and white prison stripes from *Alice in Wonderland* flitted through her mind.

"So you've come to tell me something," she said, cradling her unborn child with both hands. "Something about Charlie?"

"Yes," he said. "Tell Charlie it's time to find the girl—the girl and the candy bar."

The faint sound of thunder shook the earth, and Cora's gaze snapped back to James's face.

The old man's voice trembled.

"She won't be coming with you, Cora." His voice broke, and there were tears streaming down his weathered face like rain. "I wish I could take the memory of the pain away, but I can't. It's time to heal."

The crashing storm grew louder above her head.

"My baby?" she shouted. "Are you talking about my baby?"

Her skull throbbed, and her lungs burned. The booming drew closer and closer, centered above her torso, as she heard the muffled sound of someone calling her name.

"Cora, I don't decide these things," he whispered. He became darkness and a breath in her ear. "I only know you need to remember. Tell Charlie to find the girl and the candy bar. And Cora, when the time finally comes, you will have to deal with the professor yourself."

The walls began to shake.

The cups began to rattle inside the saucers on the tabletop. Black liquid spilled out, overflowing and splashing in hot, diminutive rivers onto the oilcloth. The table itself began to shudder and quiver under her hands.

A blast of cold, fresh air hit her squarely in the face.

For a twinkling of a second, she knew it was Charlie calling out her name from the past. Charlie standing over her.

But when she opened her eyes, there were only agonizing sparks of bright white light and stabbing pain.

And Cora was awake.

Chapter 2

The walls of the concrete block hallway seemed to grow wider the further he walked, the fading beige paint and the florescent lights adding to the illusion.

There was no sweeter music in the world for Ed Brackett quite like the sound of multiple magnetic locks resounding in a chorus of brittle notes at his back. The melodic metallic doors slammed shut behind him as the soles of his brown loafers shuffled across the tiled floor with unsteady deliberation.

The disgraced professor of Victorian literature had waited five years, two months, and three days for this moment, and he had no intention of hurrying along.

He'd come too far already not to appreciate the last rituals that signaled his release from Angola State Penitentiary.

The grizzled, unsmiling guard at his elbow was in no great hurry either.

Another day. Another justly or unjustly incarcerated inmate, except that to his ears they all seemed to *claim* that they'd been falsely accused and wrongfully detained.

The guard had heard most of the stories and had grown deaf to the telling and retelling.

Ed hugged his faded messenger bag to his chest. Inside was a battered wooden box containing his cardboard chessboard and mismatched pieces.

In addition to the classic game, tucked inside the bag were a weathered leather journal and the stub of a number two yellow pencil. Nothing else.

The guard slowed his pace, glancing over at the nondescript man at his side.

Won't be seeing this one again, he thought absently. *Not sure why he was even here in the first place. Mousey, quiet, flaccid, passive.*

The truth was that Brackett had learned the lessons of prison well, taking on the guise of a wronged academic caught in technological crossfire. His behavior and attitude changed as soon as the prison gates slammed at his back.

Fronting as meek-mannered and mild, he'd let his anger simmer and boil in the recesses behind his thick lens spectacles and non-descript expressions. No one was the wiser.

Not even the most observant of guards.

They'd watched him meekly turn over a new leaf. His writing stopped completely. Almost overnight, he shed the air of haughty arrogance from the trial and took on the persona of a cooperative, mild-mannered chess player. His quiet, patient confidence exuded his firm belief in his own innocence of wrongdoing. Even the guards were taken in by the change in his attitude and his behavior.

The chess master became the master actor.

Ed Brackett had learned his lesson well.

Hate is a powerful motivator in the hands of a skilled manipulator.

He'd lost his job, his reputation, and the adoration and attention from his circle of minions. He'd lost—forced to play a different match by the system's rules.

No one could have suspected the monumental self-control and skill it had taken to hide his mocking hatred and desire for revenge.

He'd deceived them into thinking he was a harmless old man, content to carry his chessboard and books away to a quiet life.

He'd waited a year before he attempted the first appeal. Long enough to establish his new temperament with the penal system and read volumes in the prison library about cases of libel and slander.

Armed with numerous precedents, he'd slyly begun to contact various lawyers, suggesting that they might make names for themselves by taking up his cause.

The innocent professor whose works were misinterpreted. Facts twisted by a system that needed a scapegoat. The process was slow and tedious, moving with an agonizing crawl through the court system.

Of course, these same lawyers who helped secure his eventual release, vultures in search of carrion, had strongly suggested he sue psychologist Cora Stone for punitive damages. More money for them. More notoriety. She'd left law enforcement, but she was writing best-selling books in some godforsaken small town—and that meant she would make a high-profile target. It was convenient and perfectly legal.

Those were the plans they brought to him. Lawsuits and publicity. The court of opinion and public relations. He agreed. And why not? He had a cause they could rally around, and all he had to do was keep his head down and let them work.

But he had other plans.

He didn't care about the money.

He cared about the past five years of his life—the loss of his comfortable office and his teaching position.

Let the others around him profit. He signed the rafts of documents they put in front of him and let the lawyers work their plan.

The distraction they provided would keep everyone busy while he played the chess game of a lifetime.

"He's paid his debt to society," the disinterested, underpaid attorney had so blandly but succinctly put it to the judge at the final hearing.

He was of no further danger to the world or his fellow man. So he was free to go.

As if anyone could prove I've ever been a danger, he sneered to himself. *As if that gumshoe detective and his sidekick profiler had ever proven anything at all.*

The FBI had railroaded him, pure and simple. He knew it. They knew it.

Led by the upstart profiler Cora Stone, they'd made the shaky arguments against him seem plausible.

His reputation as a lofty intellectual had played against him. His appearance and demeanor in the courtroom cost him dearly in the eyes of the jury. Too late he realized they saw him as being arrogant, egotistical, overconfident, and smug.

The five men and seven women jurors found it perfectly reasonable to believe that he was a man with the power and the personality to inspire others to kill. They reached the conclusion that he'd been an integral part of the mindset of the serial killers. That he had provided blueprints for their vicious behavior.

That not only did he know, but he encouraged.

He was too proud, too arrogant, to defend himself with a truth they wouldn't believe. That when he wrote the first story, he didn't know what would happen. That he was stunned when the first killer contacted him and told him what he had done.

That admission would have meant admitting the rest—that hearing his fiction had become fact made the author giddy with pleasure.

That he liked that feeling of power and so he wrote more. Never knowing for certain. Never really knowing how many others would take his words and use them.

But he knew that an accidental beginning wouldn't matter to any of his accusers—because he didn't stop when he knew what was happening.

He couldn't betray his loyal followers.

The FBI and that woman convinced the jurors that he'd been the mastermind at the center of a team of deranged murderers, loosely organizing the deviants into a sick society of brothers with gruesome initiation rites.

They hadn't been wrong, but the proof was still circumstantial. He'd seen to that.

Only damaging innuendo and tenuous connections forming a web that his counsel insisted shouldn't have trapped him, but it did.

A temporary interruption in his life, but one that left him changed in a way they could not possibly anticipate.

Ed Brackett no longer cared if he lived or died as long as he punished Cora Stone for what she had done to him.

The officer behind the plexiglass window made a comment, but just as Brackett had ignored his escort officer, he pretended not to hear her well-wishes for his future.

She pushed the final paperwork out for him to sign, adding his wallet, key chain with its two lonely keys, and his watch. He slid his meager possessions into his pleated pants pockets and pushed up the sleeve of his rumpled suit coat to strap the useless watch to his wrist, the battery long dead from disuse.

His street clothes felt understandably alien after the coarse fabric of the orange jumpsuit he'd worn for too long. He wanted a lingering hot shower and a real bar of soap, not a hotel-sized sliver. A full-size bottle of expensive shampoo with conditioner and a soft towel, maybe two, in a bathroom he didn't have to share and where he wasn't being watched.

He'd written his final plans for the next four days in his journal in the form of chess notation. A one-sided game in which he both planned his moves as well as anticipated the moves of his opponent.

A seldom-used, unorthodox strategy involving a pawn, a white bishop, and a lone white knight.

The best part was that he had started the match, sacrificing the first pawn in a secret move only he knew—an opening to a chess game he'd now rehearsed many times over in his head on those infinite nights, staring up at the bottom of the bunk above him. Practiced in the moments before he fell into a fitful sleep at night and as he woke for the roll call in the morning.

It was time to restart the match.

The moves were prudently planned, the countermoves of the opposition were carefully anticipated. His strategy was simple and yet beautifully obtuse.

They'd never see this coming.

And if they did—well, he'd anticipated that too.

Daylight winked through the gray clouds as the last door swung open and he stepped out into the expectant October air.

He was finally free.

Pieces were gathering on the board. The timer was at his elbow. His opponent would soon be duly notified and distracted by his lawyers, and the seat across from him was only temporarily vacant.

She would soon see what it was like to play chess with a grand master, and in the final checkmate she would understand why everything had happened the way it did.

Because of her. All because of her.

Chapter 3

Senator Stewart Wilton pulled back the lace curtain from the Rose Room of the Balfour B&B and watched the chilly rain roll in criss-crossing patterns down the windowpane.

From this particular vantage point, he could look out over the town square toward the courthouse and watch the citizens darting around in the early morning, preparing for another day in the sleepy little Georgia town.

Patrons danced between the puddles up to the door of Sam's restaurant, forming a patient line under the awning, shivering as they anticipated Bill's famous bacon grease biscuits and hot coffee. The court clerk, bailiff, and several secretaries gingerly maneuvered the wet marble courthouse steps into the main lobby of the impressive building. Hanson and his enthusiastic son unlocked the double glass doors of the pharmacy soda shop, the younger holding the door for the elder in a gesture of respect and appreciation.

Several cars had already taken the parking spaces that surrounded the square, and there was more to see, but the Senator was growing hungry and turned away from the entertainment to consider his own breakfast waiting downstairs.

He'd often avoided the daily humdrum of the locals, staying with a wealthy couple on the outskirts of town. They had supported him financially in his many campaigns for office, offered consolation when his wife died, and sent frequent messages that kept him up-to-date with his young son, left in the company of well-paid caretakers and nannies.

When his son Steve died, this same couple turned over most of the third floor of their multibedroom mansion along with their two-person staff, a devoted housekeeper and a gifted cook.

But since the opening of the Wilton House in the spring, the Senator oddly found himself more at home in the B&B. His daughter-in-law Katy had proven herself to be a radically different person than he'd believed her to be when she was married to Steve. In a rare moment of self-criticism, he wondered if she'd changed or if he just really hadn't known her at all.

His granddaughter Elizabeth, too, surprised him. She had taken to calling him Papa, climbing on him whenever she saw him and slipping her arms around his neck, sweetly nuzzling his suited shoulder. More and more he found himself looking forward to his weekend private flights to Anson's, and less and less he missed the backroom deals and cutthroat politics for which he'd become both notorious and respected.

He found himself reminiscing about the quiet life he'd once shared with his long-dead wife and their infant son.

At first he'd felt a need to make excuses for coming home so frequently. Insisted that he was only watching over the finances and endowments, supervising the spending and the decisions of the board of directors.

But once the project began, they hadn't really needed him at all. Wilton House took on a life of its own, and he was able to look at his former home with considerable pride and a sense of accomplishment.

His stomach rumbled, bringing him back to the cool October day and his current reason for returning to Balfour.

Dan McInnis, his son's brother-in-law and murderer, had been incarcerated at Atlanta State Penitentiary since almost this time last year. The trial date had finally been set, and he'd come to discuss the situation with Katy, to ask what he could do for her and see if she needed anything from him. He'd also planned to mention his concerns about the trial and discuss a new will with local attorney Thomas Stone.

Inspecting his clean-shaven face in the ornately framed bathroom mirror, Wilton made another attempt to smooth down the obstinate part in his thick white hair with a comb and another dollop of sandalwood-scented pomade.

You like it here, he told his smiling reflection. *You love that granddaughter who pats your face and pulls at your ears just like your son used to do when he was a toddler. You miss the neighborly way people greet each other during the week, especially on Sunday mornings on the way to church.*

His eyes misted over and he fought down a wave of regret for wasted years.

Maybe you're just getting old, he chided himself. *Maybe you're old and tired, but you're finally coming around to realizing just how much you love this place and these people. It's about time, grandpa.*

Dredging up the past hurt, and facing the future without his son was still brutal.

There was a sharp knock at the door, and a sweet Southern voice called out from the other side.

"Senator," the girl said, trying to find a balance between sounding like a petulant child and a scolding mother. "You left a wake-up call, sir. Miss Darcie said I should come up and remind you that you wanted to be up and out before seven thirty. It's seven now."

"Thank you," he said, his eyes never leaving his reflection, forcing a pleasant expression from his grim lips. "I'll be right down."

His leather suitcase was already packed and ready at the foot of the bed, his garment bag zipped and hanging in the open closet.

His regular pilot would be waiting at Anson's at ten, and he'd already asked AJ to pick him up from the B&B at eight thirty.

After a brief stop to speak to Stone, he'd be back where he once thought he belonged, walking the halls of the Capitol and the Senate chambers. His aides would be hovering about him with papers to read and sign. He'd spend a day or two hobnobbing with other equally intense men and women, making deals for which he'd become an icon to his local community.

The following week, the trial would begin in Atlanta, and he'd leave his apartment in Washington to travel to a courtroom there. He'd find a place on the back row to watch the proceedings, uncharacteristically out of the limelight and depending upon others to take charge.

He wanted the disgusting process over, and yet he dreaded reliving the details.

For the first time in a long time, Stewart Wilton admitted the truth to himself. So much had changed over the past year, and not just for him and his family. His son's murder had become a stone thrown into placid water that had altered the town itself.

Revenge and hatred had been replaced by vacant, unrelenting loss.

His only son died in an empty, lonely mansion, trying, to all appearances, to make overdue amends for his wayward, wasted life.

And that mansion should have been an infamous site of shame—an eyesore and symbol of disgrace. But it had been resurrected, rising out of the ashes of scandal and dishonor like a phoenix, reborn to purpose and filled with eager anticipation.

Wilton longed for that same second chance for himself. To belong. To come home again. Here, close to his roots. Close to family and friends.

Which brought a second, more serious revelation.

He had no idea how to begin this new way of life.

But he was a determined man, ready to put the past behind him and try.

Chapter 4

The sky was slate gray and dull, the late October air oppressively heavy as it weighed down the attitudes of the few random, scowling people Charlie passed on the metro streets.

The weather also suited his mood for the duration of the half-hour jaunt from his efficiency apartment—it was as dreary and empty outside as he felt inside.

He'd seen the five a.m. early morning news report, a blurb between the traffic update and the giddy weather girl with her extended Halloween night forecast for scattered showers.

He'd been about to have a bowl of cereal, but at the sight of the smug, smirking face on his television screen, he'd lost his appetite.

After a quick shower, he decided he needed air and an early start at the station. His fellow officers would make some snide comment about his eagerness to come into work, but he didn't care. If he could pull one more criminal off the street, maybe he'd feel a little better about what he'd just seen.

He turned the corner onto Royal Street where the green and white awning of Café Beignet came into view. The pungent smell of chicory and dark roasted coffee beans enticed him inside, past the white wrought iron chairs and potted ferns.

The teenage girl behind the counter brightened at the sight of his face, and he gave her a forced smile.

"The usual?" the girl said cheerfully. "The beignets are hot, and we just ground the beans."

"Absolutely," Charlie agreed, placing a twenty carefully on the counter. "Three beignets and a black coffee—large."

"No chicory, though, right?" she said, opening the cash drawer. "You always call it a burned weed."

"That's because it tastes like a burned weed," he said, forcing himself to match her cheerfulness. "Keep the change."

The young man working behind her placed the messy powdered beignets into a paper bag and handed them over the register to Charlie, then motioned him down past the display cases to take the filled disposable coffee cup.

"Cream and sweeteners there." The employee gestured to a small table on the left. "You know the drill."

"Yes," Charlie said more pleasantly than he felt. "I know the drill."

He took his napkins, bag, and cup to his right and into the garden patio area that divided the café from the portico of the Precinct Eight police station.

He had no intention of eating the sugary confections, and he could have gotten free coffee a few steps away at the station, but he wanted the peace and calm of a quiet place where he could think.

He settled himself into a chair at the back of the garden, facing the black iron fence and the street. Over his head, a broad magnolia tree shaded the corner, and potted plants, ferns, and variegated marigolds were scattered on the stone floor around his feet.

He closed his eyes.

Ed Brackett had been released from Angola State Penitentiary.

The blurb had been brief and to the point.

Civil rights lawyers had railed at the professor's prolonged imprisonment. They called his conduct merely reckless. His stories mildly provocative. The FBI prosecution excessive and overly complicated.

They called the trial a witch hunt and discounted Cora's testimony as biased and puritanical. The heavy hand of government censorship, denying a man his rights. All circumstantial.

The men who had committed the murders were still in prison, they argued, and there was nothing to prove that Brackett himself had ever killed anyone—or intended for anyone else to murder. No concrete evidence that there was a drop of blood on Brackett's hands.

After what happened to Cora after the trial, Charlie had been briefly obsessed with linking Brackett to her attack, but he had failed. Failed miserably and completely.

He hated the man, but there was no proof he was behind it.

In the end, Charlie had to drop the investigation. He accepted the possibility that Ed Brackett's case had been a catalyst for the worst imaginable moment in his marriage to Cora but that Ed himself hadn't made it happen.

Charlie knew in his gut that Ed Brackett was responsible for the string of deaths that sparked his initial investigation. He knew that the notoriety from the trial had put Cora in danger—and that her stress and distraction had cost him his child, his marriage, and his future.

But his gut wasn't admissible in a court of law.

And Ed Brackett had played the system and won release.

"Why, Detective Abbott!" A disembodied voice came from the archway into the café. "What a pleasant surprise to find you here!"

Charlie reflexively jumped, bumping the table and sending his coffee splashing in every direction outward. He rose to avoid the rolling hot liquid.

A quick glance up revealed the owner of the voice, and Charlie's stomach dropped.

"Brackett," he said hoarsely, pressing his lips tightly together, struggling with the whirlwind of emotions he was feeling—confusion, suspicion, and concern.

What's going on? he thought, his mind frantically trying to explain Brackett's presence and coming up empty. The detective felt an irrational anger—an irritation with himself as much as the man before him. As though he'd left the front door unlocked and found himself face-to-face with an unwanted intruder who had taken advantage of his carelessness.

Charlie hated surprises, and this was a doozy.

Ed Brackett, cradling something small and white in his fleshy hands, stood mere feet away.

Whatever was happening, it wasn't good.

"My lawyers checked into it and found you'd been transferred to the Eighth Precinct," the old man continued. "I was going to leave a message with your captain, but I can't believe how fortunate that you are here so I can tell you in person."

"What do you want?" Charlie said shortly. His heart was

pounding under his rib cage like winter thunder, and his face was hard as chiseled ice.

Brackett looked down at his own hands, and Charlie could clearly see that he was holding a chess piece, gingerly rolling it between his palms.

"Oh come now, don't look so suspicious! You should be glad to see me. The least you can do is acknowledge my part in your success," Brackett said, his pale lips stretched against his yellowing teeth in a near-maniacal grin. "I made you and your wife famous!"

Charlie could feel his blood pressure rising and the tips of his ears growing hot, a furious heat that flowed down his arms into his clenched fists. He flexed his fingers and thrust them into his pockets.

Brackett was mocking him now. The arrogant villain was laughing at him—and Cora. Charlie was furious with himself that he hadn't seen this visit coming.

"You were never a good chess player," Brackett said absently. "You'll never be a master until you learn to control your emotions."

Charlie bit the inside of his lip until he tasted blood, refusing to prove his accuser's point. Charlie shifted his weight, bones crackling along his spine, as he decided how to handle this very unexpected turn of events.

He decided on a direct approach.

"Say whatever you came to say," the detective spat. "I've got work to do."

The heavyset man leaned against the top of a nearby chair, his belly shaking in grotesque amusement.

"Of course you do, Detective Abbott," he taunted. "Catching bad guys. Crawling inside their minds and anticipating their moves, their motives. You're morbidly interested in my mind and how it works. Admit it. You *want* to understand."

Charlie's face blanched, his patience wearing thin. For reasons he chose not to explore, this man pushed his buttons like a hyper-active child pounding the keys of a piano—reveling in the resulting cacophony.

Brackett's body, clothed in a mottled brown and tan tweed suit, resembled an enormous rotting pumpkin ready to explode with raucous glee.

The professor put his head back and gasped, choking with hilarity.

"I came all this way, and you don't even seem interested in why!" Brackett mused. "Charlie, I'm a changed man, and I wanted you to know. I've stopped all my writing, thanks to you. It's regrettable, as I enjoyed it, but I'm playing a new game now. Things will be different this time. I've seen the error of my ways."

Charlie felt a wave of revulsion come over him, disgusted that this man had been released back into the public. The detective willed his hands more deeply into his pockets.

"We're done here, Brackett," he finished coldly. "You're nothing special. You didn't have to tell me any of that."

The folds of skin crinkled around the professor's eyes and the glee escaped again, like air gushing from a burst balloon. He licked his tongue against his thick, fleshy lips as if anticipating a triumphal checkmate.

"Cora thought I was special. I've read some of her books, you know. The prison library had quite the collection."

The mention of Cora's name should have sent Charlie into another fit of anger and frustration, but the detective had anticipated this move. His eyes widened and the pupils grew dark, the one reaction he could not control.

"Admit it, Charlie boy," Brackett taunted. "Without Cora, you and the FBI would never have won that little chess match we played. And since she's profited from the fame I provided, she owes me, don't you think?"

Charlie glared.

"Well, it doesn't matter what you think," Brackett continued, briefly inspecting the chess piece before he put it into his pocket. "The lawyers say I have a case. Quite a lucrative case. So the game is on again, you see. But this time I'm the one who is ready."

Charlie picked up the brown bag of beignets and his empty, overturned cup, turning away toward the portico of the police precinct.

"I had hoped we could have a civilized conversation," the man's grating voice continued, bouncing off the detective's back. "I hoped you had become a worthy chess opponent, but you still don't understand the whole point of a match. The act of sacrificing to win—to capture the king."

But Charlie had already stopped listening.

So that's *what this is about,* Charlie thought, turning Brackett's revelation over in his mind. *He plans to sue Cora. Makes sense . . .* s*he's the reason the jury convicted him, after all.*

He walked briskly past the front desk, waving casually at the uniformed clerk.

What does Brackett expect me to do about it? Cora's with Thomas. He'll know what to do if Brackett's vultures come after her for money. Brackett obviously thinks I'm more a part of this than I am, but he couldn't be more wrong. I'm out of this now.

As he slowed his pace and ambled past Captain Hymel's office door, a nagging sense of dread ran up his spine and tickled the back of his neck.

Marcie's rabbits on my grave again, he thought, a vision of his Plott hound bringing Balfour to his mind. *Yes, Elvira. I miss you too.*

And outside in the street, it started to rain.

Chapter 5

Thomas argued twenty minutes with Cora, explaining that he didn't actually have to go to work, but nothing could persuade his diminutive wife that he should stay at home with her for the day.

He knew she'd had a dream, but what it was about, as usual, she wouldn't say. He only knew what having a dream meant.

Charlie.

She knew, however, that her husband was expecting a call from a judge in Savannah that might move along the process of adopting Jane. Even the prospect of being with him when the call came didn't seem to influence her resolve to have him out of the house.

"I know you're concerned," she said, biting the inside of her cheek and listening for the sound of the front door opening to signal Marjorie's arrival. "But Jane and I are expecting Katy and Elizabeth this afternoon. As much as I love you and want to hear any news about Jane, you're going to be underfoot."

Her husband knew when she was teasing him, but her rejection still stung a bit.

"Well," he pouted, "I'm certainly not as cheerful as Marjorie or as energetic as Jane, but I do know how to make myself useful."

She reached up and pressed an index finger upward on his face between his eyes, smoothing out the furrow that had formed there.

"You're giving yourself wrinkles," she said. "Stop scowling."

The grating sound of the key in the front lock signaled an end to the discussion.

Once again, Cora's patience had waited him out.

"If you insist," he said, picking up his coffee cup and a plate with the remnants of his breakfast. He carried them to the sink to rinse them before drying his hands and rolling down the sleeves of his dress shirt.

"I hope you know I'm going to file a future appeal."

Cora crossed the floor to meet him and buttoned his cuffs before helping him into his suit jacket.

"We'll talk when you call at lunchtime," she said, patting down the lapels and straightening his tie with practiced ease.

From the sunroom came the sound of Jane's giggling as Solomon chased a dangling ribbon around the tiled floor followed by the sound of Marjorie singing down the hallway.

"Let me know if you hear from Savannah, and I promise not to call you-know-who without talking to you first," Cora said, standing tiptoe to plant a kiss on her husband's chin. She hadn't made up her mind at all to call Charlie.

Painful as the memories were, none of the three clues seemed to have any bearing on the present.

No, she thought firmly. *James will just have to give me more to go on than some nameless girl and an out-of-date candy bar before I'm going to open up old scars that will only hurt Charlie with memories of our baby. Especially not now when I'm expecting again and he doesn't even know. I can't be that heartless . . . no matter what James says.*

The baby inside her kicked.

Maybe I'm only remembering because I'm pregnant again, she thought. *That's probably it—just a natural fear after what I've been through before.*

Marjorie marched into the kitchen, depositing a damp plastic bag of groceries unceremoniously on the center island.

"Oh good grief!" she exclaimed, unashamed of eavesdropping as she pushed her glasses up her nose with a quick thrust. "Now I know it's almost Halloween—you're having nightmares, and I hear that you-know-who is coming to Balfour."

"Now, Marjorie . . ." Cora began, but the housekeeper put her hands on her ample hips and snorted.

"Don't you *now Marjorie* me," she said, staring pointedly at Cora's round midriff. "You're in no condition to put up with his shenanigans."

The housekeeper appealed to Thomas for support, but he'd been watching the shifting expressions on his wife's face and knew there was more that she wasn't sharing.

"And what do you have to say about this? You surely don't approve!"

The beleaguered husband knew not to take anyone's side against his wife, despite the fact that Marjorie was making the same arguments he himself had just made. He kissed soundly on the top of Cora's head and gave her expanded midsection a gentle pat.

"I'm going to work and leaving this problem to the professionals," he said. "Cora, I'll call at lunch. Marjorie, I was hoping for chicken pot pie for supper, but I'm learning to live with occasional disappointment."

And with that, he was gone.

Marjorie, however, was intent on picking up where Thomas had left off.

"Maybe you should rest this morning," she said, bustling around the room with her usual efficiency, emptying the grocery sack of its contents and shaking off the excess rainwater over the sink. "Go on into your office and put your feet up. That baby is due in less than six weeks."

"Lisa said my vitals are fine," Cora countered. "My weight is on track, except for normal water retention around my ankles. She checks on me every week now."

Marjorie held a thick glass jar of marshmallow fluff midair, shaking the container as she spoke.

"I cannot believe you're still determined to have the baby in this house," she said. "Could you at least consider going to Griffith for a second opinion?"

"I understand your concern," Cora said. She wanted to tell Marjorie that the only thing that made her tired was arguing, but she didn't. "I've been practicing breathing exercises, and Lisa's made all the necessary preparations for an at-home birth. You'll be with Jane the whole time, and Thomas says he's looking forward to helping."

"We'll see," Marjorie said, putting the jar on the countertop with a thud and picking up a box of rice cereal in its place, shaking it with equal irritation. "As if that man has any idea at all what he's getting into."

Cora sighed.

"You're a dear friend," she said. "But the years with you have taught me well. I'm learning to trust. Isn't that the theme of the songs you've been singing? Nothing in life is without risk."

Marjorie found herself unable to argue the point, so she changed the subject and went back to putting away the groceries.

"I'll make a cup of tea. Do you want to talk?"

A cold chill shot up Cora's spine, and she hesitated.

I can't tell you the dream was about being buried and losing Lonora, she thought. *No, I can't worry you like that. I can't even tell Thomas the whole truth.*

Still, Cora knew the housekeeper was not likely to drop the subject without some sort of answer.

"Not really," she said, trying to sound lighthearted. "I *can* tell you that it involved a nameless girl and a candy bar. There isn't much more to tell."

Marjorie laughed out loud.

"Now that's a new one," she said, her mood lightening to match Cora's. "Maybe it's your sweet tooth talking. I'm going to let the girls help me make marshmallow treats this afternoon, and there will be plenty to go around."

She searched the younger woman's face for any sign of distress, but Cora had made up her mind to keep her thoughts to herself. And maybe Charlie. She'd have to tell Charlie eventually.

The baby shifted inside her.

"I'm going upstairs to shower and dress for the day," she said.

"And I'm going to make tea and put a chicken on to boil for pot pie for supper."

Cora slid from the stool and waddled to the double French doors of the sunroom.

"Morrie's here," she announced to the giggling girl and the massive black cat.

Solomon's sharp claws clicked against the hard surface as the strip of red satin fabric eluded his grasp.

He and the child paused in their game of ribbon chase.

"Morrie's here," Cora repeated. "I'm going upstairs, but I'll be back down in just a few minutes. Elizabeth is coming this afternoon too."

Jane obediently rose and ran to hug her foster mother, her arms encircling the woman's legs just above the knees.

"Come back soon," she said innocently. "We miss you."

Cora disengaged herself and knelt, supporting her belly with one hand, balancing the weight of her unborn baby carefully while she embraced Jane with her other arm.

Jane's bouts of separation anxiety, along with her nightmares about the blue-eyed man who was responsible for the deaths of her family members, were less frequent, but the birth of the new baby had added another layer of stress for the child. Cora knew this was not uncommon under the circumstances.

"And I will miss you," she said, kissing the tip of Jane's nose affectionately. "I love you very much."

"I love Baby too," Jane added, resting her face against the obvious bulge under Cora's robe. "Hello, Baby."

In response to the external pressure, the unborn child inside pushed back.

This was not the first time the three of them had felt the sensation, but for Jane the experience was novel every time it happened, and her dark eyes lit up with wonder.

"Baby loves me," she said, turning to the cat. "Baby loves you too, Cat."

Solomon rolled over onto his back indifferently and yawned, exposing rows of bright white sharp teeth and protruding canines, his rough pink tongue curling.

Cora wasn't sure how much the baby was going to affect the cat. She'd given it little consideration. He'd taken all of the other children who'd come into the house in his padded stride, and another one would probably not make much difference one way or the other.

She was happy he had been remarkably partial to Jane.

Marjorie, who'd continued her eavesdropping, stood on the threshold and saw the pregnant Cora struggling to stand. She gripped her friend under an elbow, helping her to rise.

"There now," the housekeeper said, holding tightly to Cora's upper arm until the young woman steadied herself. "I'm going to need help putting away the rest of the groceries. Who do you suppose might help me with that?"

Jane threw up her hands.

"I can!" she volunteered. "I can help!"

"Why," Marjorie said, rolling her eyes comically, "what a lovely idea!"

The two women exchanged a perceptive glance, and Cora disengaged her arm.

Jane skipped into the kitchen, suitably distracted.

"Take your time," Marjorie said. "I'm here if you need me."

Chapter 6

Darcie Jones couldn't quite put her well-manicured finger on what had caused the change in her most influential and eminent boarder, but her well-honed Southern intuition was electrified.

He had not only come down to breakfast with all the other patrons, but he had greeted and exchanged pleasantries with each and every one of them as though he were campaigning for office for the first time and needed their support.

He'd even gone into the kitchen to compliment the stunned cook on her rendition of redeye gravy and broiled boneless pork chops with homemade applesauce.

The combination of outgoing geniality and eager appetite was more than the innkeeper's mind could absorb. Here was a glimmer of the man who once was—the man around whom the town had rallied when tragedy left him to be both mother and father to his toddler son.

This was the Senator she had known, and his reappearance, like the splendid butterflies who emerged from cocoons, filled her with unexpected wonder.

As a further shock to her system, when AJ arrived on the porch to collect the Senator's bags, the politician insisted that the young man have a cup of coffee or hot chocolate while he waited, and the Senator brought his own belongings down from the second floor.

The inexperienced chauffeur's eyebrows rose in surprise, reluctant to sit and refusing the proffered beverage. He stood awkwardly, shifting from one foot to the other, his hands jingling the keys in his pocket and his gaze fixed on the squirrels playing tag among the brightly colored autumn leaves in the town square.

"We've certainly enjoyed having you stay with us," Darcie offered as the Senator descended the stairs, her hand resting lightly on the polished oak banister. "I hope we see you whenever you can get away from your responsibilities in Washington."

Wilton came to a full stop on the last step, draping his garment bag over the railing and dropping his suitcase to the floor.

His hands free, he grasped Darcie's wrists in an unexpected gesture of warmth and leaned down into her spellbound face.

"Miss Jones," he said, "I thank you for your exceptional service both to me and to this community. As always, your skills as a hostess have exceeded expectations."

Flustered, Darcie found herself unable to formulate words, blushing at the man's closeness and making a vain attempt to pull away.

But the Senator held fast for a few seconds longer than absolutely necessary before planting a quick kiss on the woman's flaming cheek.

Then, just as suddenly as he had moved toward her, he moved away, releasing her as he picked up his bags.

AJ averted his adolescent eyes, awkwardly uncomfortable as he followed the Senator to the waiting car.

Five minutes later, Darcie was still standing, an unsteady palm pressed to her cheek, when the teenage maid came down the stairs with the linens from Wilton's room.

Wisely, the girl avoided any comment on her employer's behavior, but there was no denying that something of great consequence had just taken place in the foyer of the Balfour B&B.

Chapter 7

As she pulled into the gravel driveway of the law office, Susan noted the black car parked beneath the massive southern red oak, its leaves brilliant with red and yellow among the green and mottled brown, its roots like giant bark-encrusted pythons. Most houses-turned-businesses within the city limits had converted the backyards into paved parking using pebbles and crushed stone rather than asphalt or concrete in an effort to preserve the root system of as many of the shade trees as possible.

Likewise, the sidewalks and walkways were paved with rustic bricks to maintain the authenticity of the town, and shop owners took particular pride in the time-honored appearance of their businesses.

The preservation was costly but, to the minds of the citizens of Balfour, well worth the time, effort, and money.

As a descendent of one of the founding families, Thomas took his responsibilities to the town seriously, and for that he was highly respected.

Susan, too, had benefited from her association with him, making her transition from city life in Atlanta to the country much more pleasant than it might have been.

Sometimes, however, the urban and the country collided.

Susan dragged her eyes away from the burst of fall color on the magnificent tree and reluctantly pulled her car beside the expensive black Mercedes.

The driver sat stiffly, eyes forward, in the driver's seat, and she could detect the shadow of a passenger through the tinted windows.

The Mercedes engine hummed on, and as she approached the car, a quick rush of air escaped as the back window came unexpectedly down.

"Good morning, Susan," a disembodied voice came from the back seat.

Momentarily startled, she dropped her keys.

"Hello," she answered, peering into the open back window in an attempt to identify the speaker. "Were you waiting for Thomas?"

The chauffeur, a tow-headed young man that Susan recognized from church but whose name she could not recall, popped out of his seat and stood at attention, waiting.

An arm extended from the window and gestured. The youth quickly bent down and picked up Susan's keys, placing them politely into her palm. With another gesture from his employer, the driver returned to the car, but not before opening the door behind him.

Stewart Wilton stepped out and straightened the cuffs of his Italian-made suit, beads of perspiration dotting his high forehead.

"I do wish October would decide if it's going to be fall weather or not," he said in an attempt to make polite conversation. "I'm ready for a cool spell."

Susan nodded, shaking her keys to remove the moisture from the ground and checking her watch to see the exact time. Thomas was late.

"That's Georgia weather for you, Senator," she said unsympathetically. "All four seasons in a single day. Come into the office. I expect Mr. Stone shortly."

"I'm on my way to Anson's," he explained crisply. "I need to speak to Thomas before I go back to Washington."

"Certainly." Susan tried not to sound impatient. She was feeling the heat of the morning sun clearing the air of the early rain and slicing through the branches of the oak like bright orange arrows into the earth. "I can take a message, if that's acceptable."

Wilton wiped at his forehead with his handkerchief, clearly agitated by the delay.

"I suppose that will have to do," he said, tapping pointedly on his Rolex. "I'm on a strict schedule. I have appointments in Washington."

"Of course," Susan said, tingling defensively at the implied criticism of her employer and the Senator's pompous attitude. She straightened her sequined shoulders and adjusted her purse strap. "I'm sure he'd have been here if he'd known to expect you."

"Well," he began, ignoring her jab and taking a confidential step closer, "I came by to talk to Thomas about changes in my will, but I've also heard a disturbing rumor that I felt I needed to share. Reliable sources tell me that Ed Brackett is being released from Angola Penitentiary. He's already attracted a pack of ambulance-chasing attorneys who want to make names for themselves. Brackett's made it pretty plain that he's intent on suing Cora for defamation of character and intends to collect damages for the loss of his position at LSU."

Susan drew in a quick, short gasp of air.

"I remember that name," she said. "Five years ago."

Wilton nodded his head, frowned, and gave his forehead an animated swipe.

"The incumbent senator from Louisiana is an old friend of mine," he said. "He called me late last night with the news, since he's aware of my connection to Balfour."

Cora, Susan thought. *He means the connection to Cora and Thomas—and Charlie. The secret everyone knows but no one talks about.*

"The Brackett conviction made national headlines," he ran on as if she didn't know, "because of the FBI's high-profile involvement. He can't go after the government and he knows it, so Cora is the next soft target. The senator called me last night with confirmation of Brackett's release. I came by to talk to Thomas about the new will, and I felt I owed it to him to give him a heads-up about a possible lawsuit against his wife, but apparently Mr. Stone is late to the office."

So many words! Susan thought, peeved. *You're such a politician!*

He gestured critically across the near-empty lot, reaching for the handle to the car door, just as the lawyer's Honda pulled past the two where they stood and neatly into his designated space.

"Never mind," Wilton said crossly. "I suppose since he's finally here I can make the time to do this the right way."

He rapped lightly on the car window for AJ to roll down the glass.

"I'll be about fifteen minutes," he said tersely. "You can turn off the engine and save gas. Let down the window if it gets too warm inside the car."

The youthful driver complied, enjoying the light breeze as he watched the Senator, the legal assistant, and the lawyer go into the building.

Chapter 8

Andrew Evans didn't especially like waiting in the car while his wife went in to see the oncologist, but she'd asked him sweetly not to hover over her and he'd agreed.

Not so much because he wanted to agree, but because he saw no point in creating additional stress. Between his increasing nightmares and her ongoing chemo treatments, they had spent more time together in the last three months than they had in the previous year.

The forced togetherness took a predictable toll on their decades-old marriage.

She'd have let him accompany her if he'd pressed, of course, but he could see from the strained look on her face that she needed her space.

Familiarity breeds contempt, he thought. *Or, at least in this case, irritability.*

Her treatments were going well and the prognosis was optimistic. The doctor was pleased with her body's response to radiation and chemotherapy, not to mention her incessantly cheerful attitude.

"Positive outlook is a major component in any recovery process," her physician had said, "as well as the support and encouragement of loved ones."

The staff of the Women's Health Wing of Griffith Medical Center found her to be inspirational, although it was rather obvious they found her husband difficult to manage.

Andrew asked too many questions. Stood too closely. He was a mother hen in ruffled rooster's feathers.

But Ginny loved him dearly, and so they tried to appreciate his effort and accept that in his desire to be helpful, he simply got in the way.

Jack had become a well-needed buffer, doing wonders both to encourage his mother and pacify his father, who accepted the intervention gracefully after Jack finally admitted that he'd enrolled in an EMT program and was pursuing certification.

Through Casey's encouragement, Jack had come to know a number of the staff at Griffith Medical, and they had to appreciate the soft-spoken, rather humble young man who was so much like his mother, eager to learn and get along.

Andy, slow to accept permanent change in his son, wondered aloud why Jack hadn't talked about his plans sooner, forcing Ginny to explain that Jack didn't want to disappoint them again after so many failed attempts to find a vocation.

That's Ginny for you, Andy thought grudgingly. *Always seeing the best in people. I guess that's what's kept her married to me.*

He was brooding in the driver's seat and feeling sorry for himself when Jack rapped on the passenger side window and the old man jumped.

"Are you *trying* to give me a heart attack?" the preacher shouted at the face pressed against the glass. "Son, have a little consideration!"

Jack tried not to laugh at the overreaction.

"Sorry, Dad," he said insincerely, swallowing his amusement. "I saw your car and wanted to see if Mom had an update."

"She's not back yet," Andy grumbled. "I had to wait in the car. Again."

Jack shook his head, gathering up his long hair and securing it into a loose ponytail at the nap of his neck.

"Come on, Dad," he smiled, opening the door and climbing into the passenger seat. "You can't blame her. You know what you're like when Mom is sick."

You know what you're like when Mom's not sick, Jack wanted to add, but he knew it wasn't necessary. He didn't want to pick a fight.

The older man knew what his son meant, but admitting his faults was out of his character, and Andy certainly wasn't in the mood to concede that his son was right.

"How are classes going?" he said. "Shouldn't you be studying or something?"

By "or something" what you really mean is you think I should be working at making money. Jack thought. *You've never been good at hiding what you really think, Dad.*

"I finished a shift at the coffee shop about a half hour ago," he said instead, brushing an imaginary crumb from his patterned scrubs.

Andy held up his watch.

"It's only one thirty," he said.

"Yes, Dad," Jack said, trying to explain without sounding rude. "The shop opens at six. I go in at five. It's a coffee shop. We do most of our work between six and ten in the morning. Most days I put in six to seven hours before classes start."

"I suppose so," Andy said, slightly ashamed of himself for jumping to conclusions. "I'm just worried about your mother."

"We both are," Jack said. "This can't be easy on her either. I mean, worrying about the two of us while she's the one going through all the cancer treatments."

Andy's eyes clouded. The ball of compromise had been neatly lobbed into his court, and it was his turn to respond with something positive. A comment his wife would want him to make. He was exhausted from so much more than Ginny's cancer treatments. The nightmares had become more frequent with every passing week, dragging him back to a past he had struggled to escape.

He was almost too tired to think at all.

He said the first thing that came into his mind.

"You look great in those scrubs, son," Andy said, grasping for anything remotely truthful. "I know your mom's proud of you. It must be hard to hold down a job and study at the same time."

"Wow, Dad," Jack said, ill at ease with the sudden empathy. "Don't go getting all sappy and emotional on me. We'll both be teary-eyed and Mom's likely to walk up and think we've been fighting again. Are you okay?"

"I'm fine," Andy lied. "I was just trying to be encouraging, that's all."

Jack refrained from rolling his eyes. "Thanks, Dad," he said. "You know, it's okay if we don't try to make small talk and I just sit here and wait with you until Mom comes out."

Relieved, the preacher leaned his head back against the headrest and closed his eyes.

"Good idea, son," he said. "Let's just do that."

Chapter 9

One of the two keys on Brackett's sparse ring opened the storage unit he'd rented the weekend before his trial began.

He was still relishing his early morning bout with Charlie Abbott and the sheer pleasure of playing mind games with the arrogant detective.

Before the trial, Brackett had known his life was about to change completely. One way or another, win or lose, he had known his professional teaching career was over and had prepared for the worst.

The university hierarchy had made it quite plain that convicted or not, he would not be welcomed back to the campus in any capacity. Whether he'd incited crimes or not, the stories he'd written were much too salacious and graphic for the alumni, much less the student body.

He would bring with him unwanted notoriety and speculation, so he prepared for a hasty exit after the trial—either to prison or to another more liberally minded location.

He'd paid some undergraduates rather generously to pack up what he wanted to keep, cleaning out his apartment and his LSU office space.

He rented a U-Haul truck and paid the same students to move the boxes of books and clothes, as well as a few pieces of antique furniture and his collection of chess sets, into a prepaid ten-by-fifteen-foot storage unit. He had enough money in his bank account for the initial deposit plus six months, then he set up automatic payments to ensure that his meager possessions would be there when he was able to retrieve them.

He'd hoped it wouldn't come to that, but Ed Brackett was not a naturally optimistic man. He much preferred to prepare for the worst.

The remainder of his possessions and the simple contents of his two-bedroom off-campus condo were sold or given away, while he took a duffle bag of clothes and chess pieces, moving into an economy, extended stay hotel for the duration of the trial.

The process was painful but necessary.

There was never a serious doubt in Brackett's mind that he would eventually be released. He had much too high an opinion of his own brilliant mind and his innate ability to work through the chess game of life he loved to play.

The storage unit was insurance. There because he knew he would need clothes, cash, and a weapon—but equally because he couldn't bear to part with the multiple chess sets he'd collected over the years.

The knowledge that his treasured game pieces were waiting gave him a sense of security and confidence while he was in prison. He wanted to collect a few more random pieces from each of the sets to tuck inside his duffle.

Then the sets would be useless to anyone who found them—and that thought pleased him greatly.

His work, his life, and his reputation were all gone. The trial had taken those from him. Cora Abbott's testimony had blackened his employment record forever. No legitimate publisher would touch his writings after the notoriety, and there was no living to be made on the dark web. He'd be forced into some menial job far beneath his abilities and talents.

No, he thought bitterly. *I'll finish this on my own terms and in my own way.*

He took the key ring from his pocket and ran the tip of his finger along the rough-cut edges, enjoying the cold of the metal.

Chess, he thought, *is a battle of strategies—a thousand moves and countermoves. Amateurs don't have my experience. That arrogant detective and his profiler ex-wife are in over their heads. I've got nothing left to lose. I know what happens next and they don't.*

He used the tip of the second key to slit open the brown packing tape on an unlabeled cardboard box, well-hidden under a desk in the back corner of the unit.

Inside the box was a locked fireproof safe containing a trifold wallet, his passport, a manila envelope with several thousand dollars in tens and twenties, a leather pouch filled with medicine bottles, and a handgun.

He knew only enough about the gun to know how to load it, take off the safety, and write convincingly about its use—that was enough for his purposes. He planned to fire it once. Maybe twice.

The wallet contained four fake IDs and an assortment of credit cards. Brackett was especially proud of these—the results of the last of his once considerable influence over some of his less than honorable graduate students.

No one knew better how to create false identification and one-use credit cards that would pass casual inspection. No one knew better how to use technology to its best illegal advantage, or could be more easily persuaded using grades and gratuities.

They'd been amused when he asked them, one by one over a period of three months—beginning almost as soon as the FBI came to New Orleans and began their more serious inquiries—to do him a few small favors, but not one had asked him why he wanted fake IDs, credit cards, and his own supply of narcotics and illegal drugs.

He liked to be prepared. It's what made him such a master player—anticipating the next move.

He knew if he went to prison, it would be years before he needed to use any of the items and the suppliers would never tell anyone what they'd done, even if they remembered. The cards, even if they worked only once, would get him what he wanted and where he needed to be without the paper trail of his own identity.

The drugs—well, those had their own unique purpose.

And as it turned out, he had been right to prepare for the worst. In Angola, he'd given quite a lot of thought about what to do once he was released. So many details he'd had to consider. But now he was congratulating himself for all his advance planning.

Plane travel was definitely out. He knew the fake cards might be more easily challenged at the airport, and a faster trip to Atlanta wasn't worth the jeopardy. He didn't want the possibility of being easily tracked.

He also didn't want to risk renting a car with a fake license and credit card, or chance the possibility that he could be pulled over and some overzealous officer would find the gun or the pills in the car.

On the other hand, there was always the old-fashioned option for travel.

A ticket from New Orleans Union Terminal on Loyola Avenue to the Amtrak bus station on Peachtree Street in downtown Atlanta was less than a hundred dollars. The security was less stringent, the atmosphere less regimented, the pace more relaxed.

He could easily secure himself an anonymous seat on the nine a.m. passenger train out of New Orleans and arrive in Atlanta by eleven that same night.

Before he could secure his train ticket, however, he hitchhiked from Angola to Baton Rouge, and traveled from there to New Orleans by way of one of the frequent Greyhound buses.

He found a clean, cheap hotel near the train station, bought himself a large pizza, and used the first of his fake IDs to secure a room and enjoy a hot shower.

There were only two other details to attend to before morning.

The first was to select three chess pieces from his collection, wrap them in one of the hotel's plain white washcloths, and put them into a small cardboard box.

The second was finding the nearest post office.

Chapter 10

Katy sent a bouncing Elizabeth into the kitchen to find Hannah and went upstairs to let her sister Amy know she was home from her weekly appointment with Cora.

Amy was rocking baby Anne in the nursery, and as Katy paused in the doorway to watch, she thought about Cora and the changes that would soon be coming in Cora's life too. Keeping the secret of Cora's pregnancy had been easier than she expected.

Elizabeth was too young to ask questions, caring only about playing with Jane, and Katy had too many secrets of her own to betray Cora's trust.

She could understand Cora's point of view. Amy had felt much the same about her own pregnancy, albeit for a drastically different reason.

Neither wanted to spread the news to nosy, well-meaning neighbors who would insist on baby showers, gifts, and unwanted advice. For Cora, there would be clients who would want to talk about the baby with Thomas and ask about future plans. Plans the couple did not feel comfortable sharing. Cora's desire for her own privacy was added to the instinct to protect shy Jane from even more public scrutiny. Besides, once the baby was born everyone in town would know—and that wasn't going to be long now. When the baby was here and healthy, that would be the time for the avalanche of questions and answers that were certain to come.

The muted light coming through the pink sheer curtains cast a warm glow over Amy as she cradled her infant, cooing and singing to the sleeping bundle. The pang in Katy's heart was deep, but in recent weeks and months, she had come to understand and accept her mixed feelings toward the baby, with Cora's unwavering guidance.

Katy did not blame Amy, of course, for what had happened. They knew Steve far too well for that. Keeping the secret of his attack from the masses and coming to grips with the consequences, however, had taken an increasing toll on the sisters' relationship, mainly because Amy steadfastly refused to seek counseling herself.

The handful of others who also knew the truth protected the sisters from local gossips with unfailing loyalty, so completely that there was not so much as a whisper of speculation that Dan was not Anne's biological father.

Katy's therapy, as well as her involvement with Deborah's Daughters and the day-to-day running of the Wilton House venue, had given her life added meaning and purpose. She found herself growing more confident every day in her relationships and her roles as mother to Elizabeth and valuable community member to the town.

On the other hand, Amy had grown more and more introspective and sad. She opened the well-meaning inspirational and self-help books that were brought to her before putting them aside to gather dust. She pretended to listen to persistent advice from Katy and Hannah, but for the most part she'd withdrawn into the upper rooms of the house, spending her days with her baby and turning over the day-to-day workings of Dan's business to his foreman.

Katy had hoped that the situation would change with time, but Anne's birth only seemed to give Amy more reason to stay home-bound and isolated.

Katy knocked on the frame of the open door.

"How are you feeling?" she asked, as if she hadn't already asked the question twice since she got up that morning. "Would you like a cup of tea or maybe some soup? Hannah's made a fresh pot of vegetable beef and a skillet of cornbread—your favorites."

Amy looked up, dark circles under her bright eyes, the paleness in her cheeks reflecting a noticeable absence of makeup and lack of sleep.

"I'm not really hungry right now," she said, "but thank you."

Katy stepped into the room without an invitation.

"Amy," she said firmly, "you can say that to me if you like, but I wouldn't argue with Hannah. She's going to traipse up the stairs and treat you like she did when we were children. You remember what happened when she called us to supper and we didn't come."

Her sister's eyes misted over with childhood memory as she looked lovingly at her sleeping infant.

"So what you're saying," Amy said, "is that we can't just hide in the closet in your room and keep playing dress-up, pretending we're princesses in a tower and Hannah's the fire-breathing dragon?"

"Fire-breathing dragon, indeed," Katy said, shaking her head. "She's going to tell you that you're nursing a baby and you need to keep up your strength."

"I'm glad we never told her that we used to pretend she was a dragon."

"And I think that was probably your best idea ever," Katy agreed, "but dragon or not, you know she's right."

Amy sighed as tiny Anne stirred in her sleep, her delicate arms extending up and away from the cloud of pink blanket that surrounded her.

"I heard the Senator late yesterday afternoon when he came by to talk to you," Amy said, avoiding the issue of Hannah's impending wrath over supper. "I wasn't trying to listen in on the conversation, but he was standing in the foyer of the house and he has that booming voice that just naturally carries."

Katy was relieved. The Senator had left it up to her how she wanted to update Amy, and she hadn't known quite how to start the discussion.

"Then you know the trial begins next week," Katy said, looking directly at the baby in her sister's arms. "Stewart didn't want to bother you with details."

"Do we have to go?" Amy struggled, her hand stroking her baby's sleeping face. "Are we—am I—required to go to the trial? To testify?"

"My understanding is that they can't force you, as Dan's wife, to testify either for or against a man who is still legally your husband," she said, twisting the narrow wedding band of assorted rainbow stones she still wore around her left finger. "I don't understand how all of the legal system works, but I suppose either the defense or the prosecution could subpoena us."

"I'm sorry. I don't want to see him," Amy said, quivering with repressed emotion. "I know he's my husband, but I don't want to talk to him or see him. I can't leave Anne, and I can't take her either."

"I'm not the person to tell you how to feel," Katy said, leaning against the corner of the four-poster bed.

How times have changed, she thought. *You were once the one who gave me advice and I wouldn't take it. I wish you'd get help. Maybe not Cora, but there are plenty of other counselors. I've said this over and over, and I know you're as tired of hearing it as I am of telling you. Life is hard. We all need help.*

There was another knock at the door, and Hannah's form filled the entrance.

"Just took the cornbread out of the oven," she said, one hand on the knob and the second waving a crocheted pot holder. "The iron skillet is cooling on the counter, and I'm about to ladle out the soup. Elizabeth has already washed her hands and is sitting at the table. Tuck that little one in the crib and come along."

The sisters exchanged knowing looks.

Neither had the energy for a futile skirmish with the determined housekeeper, the fiery dragon of their childhood.

"Yes, Hannah," Amy said meekly. "Thank you so much. Let me settle Anne in her crib, and we'll be right down."

Chapter 11

Cora had successfully avoided thinking about Ed Brackett for years.

Her recent vivid dream combined with a noon call from Thomas about the man's release from prison had opened long-standing wounds.

She had been sure she'd dealt with the memories of the trial, the last week of her life before Lonora's death, and the hazy details of her divorce from Charlie.

She'd blocked them securely from her conscious thoughts.

The only period of time still missing from her memory was the two hours or so before she was miraculously found. She still couldn't remember who had called her to the abandoned house or why she had gone in the first place.

She knew she'd been no help to Charlie in finding out what had happened, and she knew he wanted to punish someone for what had happened, but she simply did not know who was to blame.

So Charlie punished himself.

Her marriage to Thomas and Marjorie's music had woven a blanket of peace over her subconscious mind that had been violently pulled back, making her aware that she'd been lulled into a false sense of security.

Her well-built defenses didn't matter, and hiding at home was futile.

The door had been kicked down and barriers had fallen, followed by a flood of every vivid, nasty detail of the case and the weeks that followed it that brought Cora more than her fair share of unwanted notoriety and pain.

Cora had no idea how the clues of the dream were linked—or even if they were linked at all. A girl, a candy bar, and a professor.

She dismissed the first two clues and concentrated on the third.

Maybe the professor was Brackett. His case was the last big event before the events of the dream, and apparently now he was going to sue her. It made sense that James would forewarn her.

Like a ghostly specter, Brackett's image had appeared before her all morning.

Every time she closed her eyes, she could imagine his hateful, smug face, vile eyes sunken beneath bushy brows, unkempt, shaggy, graying hair, his portly body filling and spilling over the chair where he sat. His posture as if he fancied himself one of the celebrated Victorian poets and authors he so envied and emulated.

She could visualize every excruciating detail of the trial.

Especially the chess pieces.

Brackett was as passionate about chess as he was teaching graduate level classes at a prestigious university and consuming calorie-laden gourmet meals.

His obsession with his own self-importance had been clear in his testimony and his conversations with reporters, lawyers, police, and even the judge, both in and out of the courtroom. He spoke in monologues littered with obscure references to literature and exotic food, but especially the chess matches he had played and strategies he used or admired.

There were always random chess pieces in his pockets too. One or two in his hands or out on the table during the lengthy days of the trial.

As for the chess pieces, he did not seem to have a bias. Cheap plastic sat proudly beside antique ivory. Light and dark pieces carved from hardwoods and yellow pine shared the same board. Molded crystal that sparkled confronted shades of Oriental jade on the cardboard battlefield.

Brackett used each individual piece like a child playing with a fidget toy.

That immature behavior, in addition to his unkempt appearance and haughty demeanor, did not endear the defendant to the jury and made Cora's work the easier.

None of those thoughts reassured her now.

Brackett was free.

Between the time Katy left and Thomas came home from work, Cora sat alone in her office, mulling over the details of the trial, reviewing the facts as she remembered them.

So if James really was warning me about Brackett when he mentioned a professor, she thought, *maybe I'm supposed to remember all the details of the trial because I'm supposed to defend myself in court. How else would I be the one to take care of the problem?*

If the Senator was right and Brackett did indeed intend to file suit against her, she would *have* to remember.

Brackett's case hadn't been her first testimony in a courtroom, and as she considered her previous actions and words, the confidence that she had done what was right grew.

Once the initial shock was over, her professionalism reasserted itself, and she found reviewing the information was not as emotional as she had expected.

Brackett was guilty. There was no question in her mind.

By the time she heard Thomas turn the key in the front lock, she was ready to put the topic aside and talk about the other news her husband had shared in his call.

"So," she said as she followed him up the stairs to their room, "you heard from the judge in Savannah."

"Judge Mayer returned my call around three thirty." Thomas took off his dress shoes and rummaged around the closet floor looking for his loafers. "He spent the majority of the day in court."

"You sound pleased," Cora said, climbing awkwardly onto her side of the bed.

He found his shoes and joined her on the bed.

"Well, there's apparently some precedent for what we want to do. He's willing to walk us through the process."

The unborn baby fluttered like a kaleidoscope of butterflies. Cora had been reluctant to get her hopes up, concerned with the unusual nature of Jane's family tree and the fact that there was no birth certificate.

"Is the process difficult?"

"Research and paperwork," he said, smiling as he put a strong arm around her shoulders. "About the time I had the house cleaned and closed up last fall, I contacted a local attorney in Savannah to look into the import business that Jane's grandmother and uncles owned. He was able to sort out the legalities and transfer the holdings into a trust fund Jane will receive when she comes of age."

"But what does that have to do with the adoption? We don't want her money."

"Of course we don't," he said. "And I'm staying out of that part of the legalities as much as I can, but she has an inheritance we should protect, and that means getting her a birth certificate. We already knew the Chens never registered her birth."

"As far as we know, no one registered her mother's birth either."

"True," Thomas said. "Making the whole process rather complicated."

He saw the concerned look on his wife's face and wondered if he should have said anything at all until the matter was settled.

"But not insurmountable," he added quickly. "That's why I've been talking to Judge Mayer and Detective Maclin. I've also had two paralegals going through the boxes to sort the vital information and documents on the rest of her family in order to establish who Jane is."

"You didn't tell me any of this," she said, trying not to sound hurt that he'd left her out. "How long has that been going on?"

Thomas hugged her more closely.

"I wasn't keeping secrets," he said. "There hasn't been much to say. Everyone in Savannah has been working since August, and there's finally progress."

Cora leaned her head back into her husband's shoulder.

August, she thought. *When we first began to talk about Jane's birthday. When Miss Bessie's died and that horrible woman pretended to be her daughter. Is that what triggered this latest push to get Jane's birth certificate? Was Thomas thinking about lost inheritances and baffling identities?*

"Aren't most of the documents in Mandarin?" she asked.

He sighed. He'd opened this discussion, and Cora deserved to know.

"Well, that's part of what is taking so long," he said. "The paralegals found a number of documents in both English and Mandarin, so I gave them permission to hire a translator."

You're working so hard, she thought. *You are always thinking ahead.*

"So the bottom line is you think we'll be able to legally adopt Jane?"

"I happen to have a famous wife with impeccable credentials in child trauma and psychology," he said. "Judges and courts like those qualifications, so I hear."

Cora's frown deepened in spite of the compliments.

"What do we need to do to finalize everything?"

Thomas looked at the top of his wife's head and realized that her gaze and her attention had wandered away.

She seems nervous, he thought. *Is she thinking about the new baby and the dreams—wondering how long this will take? Is this concern about Brackett and his threat to sue her? There's so much uncertainty in our lives. Should I have shared so much information? Maybe she can't handle this right now.*

"Judge Mayer seems to think it will be reasonably straightforward since the Chens were prominent business leaders. There are a number of legal documents to establish their identities," he said, stroking her dark hair. "I need to go to Savannah sometime soon to meet and share documents the paralegals have found so far."

"Documents?"

"Passports, residence history, birth certificates, business licenses, immigration and naturalization records for the rest of the family."

"Will that be enough?"

He hesitated. The process sounded so complicated when he explained it out loud, but he'd begun and couldn't stop now.

"Well, Maclin's also working with a private investigator to locate the midwife who was present during Jane's birth. He found a man who's assisted the police in Savannah on some difficult cold cases, so he's hopeful."

"That's kind of him."

"Maclin's a good man. He remembers Jane."

"Won't there be a bigger problem?"

His jawline hardened. He knew she meant the blue-eyed man, the convict serving time in prison.

Jane's biological father, who'd drugged her with tainted milk while thugs tortured and murdered the rest of her family.

"Her birth certificate is only required to list the mother's name," he said. "Besides, parent rights can be permanently forfeited due to abandonment, neglect, and ongoing criminality. You don't have to worry."

Cora shifted uncomfortably as the baby inside her moved to readjust and roll. She trusted Thomas, but until they stood together in a courtroom and heard the judge issue his ruling, her heart would be unsettled.

"Does this form we need have a name?"

"DHA-288," he said, "along with documentation and Judge Mayer's involvement. It won't be quick, but Jane needs a birth certificate, and this is our best way to secure one before the adoption can be legal."

"Then our names will be on the birth certificate as Jane's parents," she said.

"Yes," he said, standing and slowly pulling her up beside him. "The original certificate from the DHA-288 will be sealed, and no one will be able to look at the new birth certificate and be able to tell she was adopted."

"This is all beginning to feel real," she said, her hand at her throat. "I haven't even considered what we should do about her name. What will she want for her name?"

"There's time for that," he said. "And not to change the subject, but can you hear my stomach growling?"

Cora laughed and patted her husband's chest.

"Actually," she teased, "I can."

There was a timid knock at their bedroom door.

"Come on in," Thomas said.

The door opened a fraction and Jane's dark head appeared, followed by the tantalizing aroma of Marjorie's famous chicken pot pie, full of new potatoes, Vidalia onions, fresh peas, and carrots.

"Morrie says our dinner is done," the child announced shyly. "She said I should come and tell you."

"Thank you," the man said, picking up his shoes in one hand and crossing the short distance across the room. He easily swept the little girl up with his free arm and onto his hip. "I'm so happy to see you!"

Cora watched as Jane's face lit up with joy, her tiny arms wrapping themselves tightly around the man's neck.

"Lizzie's having a party," she said brightly, babbling into his ear. "And Morrie says I can dress up like anything. I want to be a princess, I think, or a pirate. I want to dress Cat too, but Morrie says I shouldn't. She says he wouldn't like it very much. There's going to be pumpkins and games and apples and candy and friends."

"That sounds exciting," Thomas agreed. "Can I come too?"

Jane gave him a stern look and patted the knot in his tie.

"No, Daddy," she said seriously. "The party is for *children*. Not daddies and cats. No daddies and cats at the party."

"Well," Thomas said, equally serious, "I don't see how you can have much fun without daddies and cats, but there you go. What do I know?"

She giggled and squeezed his neck tighter.

"Oh, Daddy," she said. "You are so silly!"

"And hungry," he said, dropping his shoes to the floor and slipping his feet inside them. He extended his hand toward Cora. "How do you feel about it?"

The baby inside Cora kicked in agreement, but she said nothing, taking her husband's hand as they went down to supper together.

Chapter 12

The Second Day: Tuesday

Her grandmother's kitchen was uncommonly warm. Sunbeams crisscrossed the floor, warming the worn linoleum and the faded rag rug in front of the sink and another, larger rug next to the cushioned window seat.

Cora was relieved to find herself in the familiar, friendly place—overwhelmed by a feeling of peace. She was sitting in her grandmother's rocking chair, surveying the monochromatic room.

Dressed in one of her husband's discarded shirts and her own stretchy maternity pants, she was at peace. The unborn child inside was, from all appearances, sleeping. There was gentle movement in her midsection and an almost imperceptible heartbeat.

From her left she heard a rustling sound near the table, and her intuition told her who was there.

"Brother James," she called softly, reluctant to rise from the comfortable rocker, her pregnant body satisfied. "Should I make the coffee?"

The pastor chuckled.

"I'll take a turn, Cora," he said, unbuttoning his suit jacket and shuffling gingerly toward the gas stove. "The kettle's already boiling and ready for pouring."

Cora leaned back and watched the old man, examining her emotions and failing to find a rationale for her calm.

She had nothing else to do but to rock contentedly back and forth and allow her visitor to wait on her.

The preacher scooped the fragrant grounds into the stainless-steel basket of the drip pot, tapping the side against his open palm to level it before adding more.

When he seemed pleased with the amount, he took the crocheted pot holder and lifted the copper kettle, pouring the steaming water slowly and deliberately.

The sweet scent of strong coffee filled the room as he patiently poured, waited, poured again, waited, and listened for the persistent drip of the water as it made its way through to the container below.

When he'd finished the procedure, he dragged a ladder-back chair from the table across the linoleum floor, placing it beside the rocking chair, before returning to the counter to fill their cups.

"So, how are you doing, dear?" he said, handing her the floral cup she knew so well, the cane bottom creaking beneath him as he sat. "You've got quite a lot on your mind, haven't you?"

"I suppose I have," she admitted, sipping the steaming liquid, "and I don't think I can lay all the blame at your feet."

"That's good to hear," he said. "The world will become more and more real to you when I'm not."

She tilted her head.

"When you're not what?" she said, puzzled. "I don't understand."

"Ah," he said, lifting the milky white mug to hide the bottom half of his face. "We'll get to that another time. For now, I've come with news and reminders."

Cora rocked back and forth as the edges of her peace began to evaporate.

"Well, at least you're consistent," she said, enjoying the taste of the coffee and accepting that they'd come to the reason for the dream. "I suppose you're here to tell me that someone is going to die and that Charlie needs to know."

He drank almost half his mug before he answered, as if he knew what he was about to say demanded her full attention and he wanted her to finish her drink too.

"First, let's deal with the unpleasant," he reprimanded her. "You've forgotten what I told you to tell Charlie."

Cora realized that she'd been focused on Jane's adoption and Brackett's release, avoiding thoughts about the last dream simply because it *was* unpleasant—no, more than that. It was the worst experience of her entire life.

Of course I haven't thought about it, she thought crossly. *I'd like to forget the whole horrible experience and every gruesome detail. And in case you haven't noticed,* her thoughts ran on, *I'm almost eight months pregnant and counting down to Thanksgiving. I'm a trifle overloaded here.*

"I know you're overwhelmed, Cora," the old man said, taking the near-empty cup from her hands. "It's always darkest before the dawn."

"Seriously?" she said, recognizing the lyrics to one of Marjorie's favorite songs. "You aren't going to start singing again, are you?"

His eyes twinkled, and he burst into a raucous belly laugh.

"Sweet Cora," he said, trying to control himself, "I'm going to miss you. No, I'm not going to sing. That's Marjorie's forte. I'm here to remind you about the candy bar."

"The candy bar?"

The moment the words were out of her mouth, she knew what he meant. James had told her to tell Charlie about a candy bar and a girl. Borderline absurd. No wonder she didn't remember. She had no context.

What could a candy bar and a nameless girl have to do with a murder?

"So you want me to call Charlie?" she said, looking for some logic, some clue, some connection. "Not that I expected the dreams to be any different from the usual, but I really don't have the least idea what I should tell him."

"Tell Charlie that he needs to find the girl first," he said bluntly, "and then he'll find the candy bar."

"The girl? What girl?" Cora repeated.

"You'll know soon enough," the old preacher said, smiling, "but you don't have to worry about calling Charlie. He doesn't know it yet, but he'll be in Balfour tomorrow. You can tell him then."

And Cora was awake, staring at the red lights of the ceiling clock.

She slipped from the bed without waking her husband, wondering what Thomas would say if he found her in the kitchen at four in the morning, rummaging through the cabinets and refrigerator, looking for something sweet to eat to get the bitter taste of coffee out of her mouth.

Chapter 13

Charlie rubbed his blurry eyes, lifted his cell phone from its charger, and stared at the stark white numbers that displayed the current time.

Almost eight in the morning.

He hadn't set the alarm, but he was awake anyway—had been awake off and on for hours.

This was his day off, and he'd looked forward to sleeping in after the last week. He should be sleeping. He wanted to be sleeping.

His mind and body refused to comply.

He'd tossed and turned through the night, unable to relax and yet unwilling to get up. The bed felt lumpy and empty without Elvira. His T-shirt and cotton pajama pants felt itchy and uncomfortable even in the late October cool spell.

But how he felt physically was only half of his frustration.

He was wrestling with whether or not to call Cora with the news about Brackett.

Does she need to know? His mind turned the question over like a roasting chicken on a rotisserie. *If this is important, wouldn't she know before I do? Wouldn't she have a dream? What would I say if I called her?*

He knew what he'd say. The cold, hard facts.

Ed Brackett had been released from Angola State Penitentiary, and there was absolutely nothing to be done about it. At least, nothing he could do. Lawsuits were someone else's headache. There was nothing speedy or urgent about courtrooms and trials. Those could take weeks and months of preparation. Did she need to know now that the professor meant to sue her? How would that be productive?

But despite the logic, his mind kept returning to Cora and how she'd managed to put Brackett behind bars in the first place. All her hard work. Her masterfully researched testimony. The extended hours of grueling preparation for court and the strain on her and their marriage during the actual weeks of trial—all those erased and discounted. She'd worked so hard, and for what?

Five years.

Brackett should have served his whole ten-year sentence and not a day less.

But no one cares what I think, Charlie thought bitterly. *I watched how much she sacrificed to bring that scum to justice, and no one cares.*

The powers that be made up their minds that, with or without his input, the man was going free.

Free to pursue a new life, a life that apparently included suing Cora for her role in putting him behind bars.

No matter how hard he tried, the sniping voice and the professor's pasty, gloating face haunted him and dragged him back to the past.

He couldn't erase the memory of Brackett's hands, which played carelessly with a solitary chess piece as he sat between his court-appointed lawyers, rolling the ever-changing piece between his palms, caressing it as though it were a living thing.

Charlie pictured the glint in the man's narrowed, hooded eyes. The hint of a smirk on his puffy face. The movement of his hands drawing attention away from the tense drama in the courtroom, the tiniest hint to suggest that Brackett considered the entire procedure only a game—a game of skill, patience, and experience.

And though he'd lost the battle in the courtroom, five years of appeals and countless lawyers later, the professor's persistence had won out.

He had gained the right to be released.

The detective knew from the beginning they couldn't keep Brackett in prison forever. They'd been lucky that the man had been imprisoned at all.

Well, the detective told himself. *I was lucky, Cora was brilliantly perceptive, and the FBI was darn skillful.*

Which brought his mind, as it often did in the sleepless hours, back to Cora and the life he'd abandoned.

The life he'd delivered to Anson's airfield on the outskirts of Balfour, Georgia.

He closed his eyes and let his troubled mind drift to the gory headlines from six years ago. The news reports that blared every night from every local station in the South warning about the danger.

Details of crimes committed on young women along the Gulf Coast.

A string of violent murders, eerily dissimilar and yet impossibly linked to each other by some unforeseen common denominator found by the experienced white hat hackers of the FBI on a dark web encrypted address.

The FBI became involved, but they remained frustrated in the search for a pattern.

After a time, they uncharacteristically appealed for help to solve the unsolvable.

From the beginning of their relationship, even before their marriage, Charlie and Cora worked together. She had been a rising star profiler called in on a complicated case involving a kidnapping and murder in New Orleans. He was the brilliant detective assigned to the case.

They argued. They fought. They fell in love. They married.

Without a doubt, they complemented each other in style and ability, and their whirlwind marriage was alive with excitement, made even more joyful at the discovery that after a scant six months of matrimony they were expecting their first child.

Charlie urged his wife to slow down. To cut back on her hours. Spend more time at home. Rest. But in the early months of her pregnancy, the FBI's search had drawn closer and closer to home, culminating in the discovery of yet another mutilated body in the bayous between Baton Rouge and New Orleans.

Cora grew restless with the need to be useful, to be productive.

Against Charlie's wishes, she volunteered her services as a profiler, a second set of eyes. One of many second sets of eyes. And the FBI looked at her credentials and agreed to let her have access to what they knew.

Pouring night after night over the accumulated files of gut-wrenching crime scene photographs and seemingly unrelated murders, she began to piece together a profile.

She was the one who saw the controversial connection first, although her theory was met with skepticism.

The FBI doubted her. They'd never heard of or seen the scenario she suggested, and certainly not the personality nor profile of the person she declared to be at the center of the crime spree.

But she could see what they didn't, and she pushed them to consider it.

A single deranged mind. A single unifying source. A single leader orchestrating the behavior of the others.

Cora suggested the radical profile—not of a lone serial killer but an organized pseudo gang of murderers inspired by the twisted heart and mind of a demonic mentor.

She handed the FBI her profile of a mentor who could inspire others to kill while he drew blueprints for the murders, relishing in the details of the executions without getting actual blood on his own hands.

Find him, she insisted, *and you find the head of the snake.*

That would amount to conspiracy, the agents argued, *and not much more.*

But when they ran out of time and conventional leads, they finally listened to her, setting in motion a massive search that led the agency to Brackett.

The evil author of a deep web virtual library of sadistic literature.

Details of the murders showed clearly that many of the stories had been acted out in horrific detail by a wide assortment of brutal killers—all linked inexorably to Ed Brackett's writings.

After that, it was the state's word against a tenured but extremely unpopular LSU professor. The proof of intent was found in manuscripts on the dark web and on the bodies of the victims of a band of serial killers. Killers who had terrorized the coastline from Corpus Christi through New Orleans, Gulfport and Mobile, all the way to

Tampa and Miami.

Proof was found in the minute details and specifics of the murders, which were carefully choreographed, each one planned on paper and executed in person.

The crackerjack computer wizards at the FBI followed a cyber trail through the twists and turns and were able to trace the virtual fingerprints Brackett had left in his mutual contact with the killers both before and after the stories appeared.

The professor knew without a doubt what they were doing. He knew how his words were being used. He encouraged the killers by writing more.

More salacious, suggestive stories with more readers who responded with details and comments and words of their own.

Nothing else, the defense had insisted. *Just words. Just words between people who had never met. Just an author of literature doing what an author does.*

But the FBI had found their man—they investigated, accused, and arrested Brackett and a number of his deadly literary fanatics in a nationwide search involving multiple local and state agencies as well as high-profile federal agents.

From the list of names who had responded to his stories, six of the actual killers were tracked down in their respective states, convicted on the basis of their contact with Brackett and blinding forensic evidence.

Cora had helped to uncover a poisonous spider's web of devious serial killers the likes of which the FBI had never seen.

None of the men had ever seen or met Brackett, only via correspondence on the dark web. So while the six found themselves sentenced to life imprisonment or on death row in multiple

Southern states, Brackett was sentenced to ten years behind bars for his involvement in conspiracy to commit murder.

The whole case was a long shot, a one of a kind, and the FBI kept both Cora and Charlie's names out of the fray until the last moment.

In the end, though, they needed her on the stand.

Cora was the FBI's key witness, alongside the taped video confessions of the killers themselves. Only she, the agency said, could take the videos and combine them with the complicated electronic evidence to convince the jury that Brackett had written the stories *knowing* what would be done with them. *Knowing and understanding* that he was inciting, inspiring, and impelling them to commit the most horrific of crimes.

The agents asked her to crawl inside his head and explain so the jury would truly understand the mind of the monster.

Her testimony was impeccable, her calm, professional demeanor in sharp contrast to the weasel-faced egoist in the defendant's chair.

Her testimony was powerful, articulate, and convincing—and her artfully tailored maternity clothes drew sympathy for the slight woman who dared to face evil.

After the jury returned the guilty verdict, the FBI gave both Charlie and Cora unprecedented credit for solving the multiple homicides as the husband-and-wife team rocketed to nationwide exposure.

But the exhilaration was short-lived.

A scant two weeks after the cell doors at Angola slammed behind Brackett, Cora was buried alive, losing their child mere weeks before her due date.

He wanted to blame Brackett, but the man's alibi was airtight.

Charlie Abbott, guilt-ridden, resolved that police work was not for anyone he loved, not even Elvira. The morning after he found Cora's buried body using her cell phone GPS, he confronted her as she lay in the hospital bed, delivering an ultimatum.

Cora was in shock, too weak and too traumatized to resist.

Three days later she was released from the hospital and a private charter plane with an attentive nurse was waiting to take her to his grandparents' home in Georgia.

Charlie sat stone-faced and watched her sleep on the flight.

The following week, he drove his battered blue Volkswagen to deliver Elvira to Marcie's care and sign the legal papers that dissolved his marriage and surrendered his inheritance to Cora.

With that, he believed he'd cut off that part of his life and separated himself from his ex-wife and his faithful Plott hound.

At least, they were separated until the damned dreams started.

The cell phone screamed at him from its charger on the nightstand, dragging him from his self-pity and back to the present.

Just as well, he thought sourly, welcoming the interruption and the jolt back to reality. *Only so much of the past I can handle at one time.*

"Abbott," he answered briskly without bothering to look at the caller ID. "You do know this is my day off and—fair warning—I don't care who you are, I'm not in the mood."

Chapter 14

Thomas unlocked the front door of his recently renovated law office and noted that while he was late to work, his legal assistant appeared to be even later.

Turnabout is fair play, he thought. *She had to deal with the Senator yesterday all by herself. At least no one was waiting to ambush me when I got here this morning.*

He leaned back in his leather swivel chair, staring out his office picture window at the foliage, reflecting on the conversation with Wilton about his new will, and with it Dan's upcoming trial in Atlanta and the news about Brackett's release from prison.

Cora's dreams and Jane's adoption proceedings weighed heavily on his mind.

The law firm had been steadily busy for months. His clients, as predictable and regular as the planting and harvesting seasons, continued to buy and sell land, forming trade partnerships with neighbors in their own and the surrounding counties.

The elderly of his clients prepared to distribute the gains of a lifetime to their offspring, and the younger prepared to begin new businesses and seek their inevitable fortunes. As had his father and grandfather before him, Thomas was a primary source of legal knowledge and financial security.

Far away from the hectic, fast-paced life in Atlanta, and the frustrating commute to and from on I-85 and 285 through Spaghetti Junction, as it was fondly known, the uncertainty in the lawyer's life had drawn to a virtual standstill. Traffic was nonexistent in his sleepy hometown. Simple two- and four-lane backcountry roads lined with trees and rowed fields of soybeans, corn, cotton, and truck-farming crops made commuting scenic, not to mention the absence of concrete dividers, pillars, and overpasses.

Not that Thomas had always felt that way.

He'd spent years imagining himself in Italian suits, arguing world-changing cases before renowned judges. Once or twice he came perilously close to having scorn for his humble heritage.

Then came the prolonged illness and death of his grandfather. Thomas had agreed to come back with the understanding that he would temporarily take up his grandfather's practice as the elder's health declined.

Susan, quite graciously, came along as his legal assistant, serving as his crucial right hand as he transitioned the clients through his grandfather's descent into dementia and the heart condition that claimed his well-lived life.

What happened was what his wise grandfather had intended all along.

Two long years of reconnecting with his roots changed Thomas.

Or maybe brought him back to the man he'd been all along.

He resisted his feelings at first. Told himself that he needed to think of Susan's future. She'd been dragged away from a cosmopolitan world. But the legal assistant settled into the country life long before he did and relished the peace and tranquility.

He tried to tell himself that he could always reenter the cut-throat, urban world, keeping in touch with his former colleagues, and they with him.

Thomas had been a rising star expected to occupy the coveted corner office at the top of the corporate high-rise in Buckhead. He lied to himself that he could always return. Tried to convince himself right up to the minute he saw Cora descend from the plane at Anson's with Charlie Abbott gripping her elbow.

Cora made him think about Charlie.

Their grandfathers had been fast friends and confidants. He and Charlie had been thrown together as teenagers, becoming unlikely friends.

Charlie wanted to leave Balfour for the big city even more than Thomas.

He could barely wait to leave and enroll in the police academy in Atlanta after his grandfather died. With no intention of ever returning, he'd contacted Thomas and asked if the lawyer could draw up legal papers to take over the management and care of his grandparents' house until further notice. Until there was time to clear out the house of the furniture and sell.

Taking care of one of Balfour's most valuable properties seemed both reasonable and prudent.

They had been teenage boys with different backgrounds and temperaments, but both had solid morals and the drive to succeed.

Thomas was the dignified, mature captain of the baseball team and president of the student body. Charlie was the charismatic new student who was the class clown and cross-country track star. In an odd way, they were two sides of the same coin.

Maybe, Thomas thought, *Charlie knew that he could trust me to handle the details—with the house and then with Cora. I wonder if he knew what would happen.*

Thomas realized it didn't matter. Once he saw Cora, his fate was sealed. The thought of leaving Balfour left his mind forever.

And Charlie's plans, harebrained and impulsive as they seemed when he descended the plane, seemed perfectly logical and rational in light of the results.

Balfour wasn't without an underbelly of Southern scandal and gratuitous gossip, but the town was close-knit and caring. Whole families of skeletons surely inhabited the cherrywood armoires of the folksy populace, put there by well-meaning folks, but Faulkner himself would have envied the unique, curious stories each one had to tell.

Everyone had a secret. That was how things were.

Thomas thought about all the secrets he himself knew, ones he'd been forced to share and the ones no one would ever know.

And Cora's pregnancy, that even now only a handful of Balfour's community knew for certain. Marjorie, Lisa, Katy, and Susan had all pledged to keep the news of the baby to themselves until the infant was actually born.

Jane knew, of course, but her understanding was limited. The fact that Cora loved to wear oversized clothes, seldom came to the front porch, and didn't venture out of the house made everything easier.

Easier? Ha! Thomas thought to himself. *Nothing this year has been easy. Divorce and murder, suicide and kidnapping, assassins and imposters. And Charlie ricocheting in and out of town like a manic ping pong ball with Cora's dreams the pivot point for the chaos.*

Beyond the window, a storm of multicolored oak leaves swirled and rose like a mini tornado up from the damp ground, lifted by the gusty wind.

The lawyer picked up Caleb Stewart's last will and testament from the corner of the desk. He needed to proofread the typed copy, but his mind rejected anything so mundane with all the other pressing matters on his agenda.

A scuffling outside caught his eye, and he was distracted again.

Two irritated chipmunks were waging hand-to-hand combat over a handful of acorns that one or the other had hidden and returned to claim as his own. Their chattering was pleasantly entertaining as the tiny creatures wrestled and bickered over the prizes.

October, he thought, trying to bring order to his feelings, *the time for gathering and preparing—but I feel as though there's no time for either. The baby will be here soon, and I don't feel ready at all.*

For the first time in his life, his faith felt strained by the onslaught of changes.

The antique chiming clock Susan had added to the outer office in her latest redecorating frenzy began to count out the hour.

I wish Susan would get here, he told himself as he settled in to proofread the document in his hands. *Maybe a cup of coffee would be just what I need to get down to business. It already feels like it's going to be a long day.*

Chapter 15

Susan's morning had also been less than serene.

As she was leaving for work, her inquisitive Siamese cat, Mr. Jones, made a mad dash between her feet and escaped. Darting into the front yard of her modest ranch style home, he sprinted straight for the row of hedges lining the sidewalk that ran through the subdivision.

For weeks, a scurry of territorial squirrels had been taunting Mr. Jones from beyond the safety of the decorative glass door and front windows.

Normally solitary creatures, they had banded together for the express purpose of tormenting the Siamese cat.

In addition, the cool autumn weather had given them a burst of extra energy as they cavorted back and forth, chattering and twitching, pausing occasionally to chase each other up and down the lower branches and fence top in enthusiastic games of tag.

The bored, housebound Mr. Jones wanted nothing more than to join them.

Susan had tried to ignore the tom's distinctive yowls of frustration, and perhaps she should have known, or at least suspected, that he was intent on joining the party outside at the first available opportunity.

So, despite her best attempts, Susan's fifteen-minute head start on the day quickly dwindled and disappeared. She spent a full fifteen minutes pleading and chasing the elusive feline around the front yard. At one point she would have been willing to swear under oath that she could hear the squirrels laughing at her from the branches of the trees.

Finally, she resorted to extreme measures to lure Mr. Jones back into the house.

She opened her last can of albacore tuna.

Spooning a generous portion of the fragrant fish into the cat's personalized dish, she opened the front door and placed the bait a few feet inside. Within minutes, the frazzled owner was rewarded with a purring Mr. Jones.

She scribbled the word *tuna* on her refrigerator shopping list and dashed out.

Disheveled and out of sorts, Susan was about to call Thomas when, in her haste, she turned the corner down Broad Street into a fender bender with Ginny Evans.

Ginny was in a matching hurry to get to the Emmanuel Baptist Church office to finalize plans for the annual fall festival the following weekend.

After a quick and almost unnecessary exchange of insurance cards and phone numbers, they cleared the intersection themselves in their freshly dented cars and set out again.

Ginny insisted that Susan needed to get on to work, and that she, on the other hand, had plenty of time to call Ben with details. That way if they decided to file, they could get always get a formal police report for their insurance companies, although they agreed that each should pay for her own repairs.

Determined to salvage the morning, she was a stone's throw from the front door of the office when she heard a shout from behind. Quincy the postman was striding purposefully across the parking lot, his white hair flying out from under his official postal baseball cap, waving a bulky certified mail envelope.

The daily canvas mailbag was slung carelessly over his uniformed shoulder, and he was breathing heavily.

"Hold up there!" he called out. "Need a signature so I can get on with deliveries."

"Come along inside and have a cup of coffee," she offered, hoping Thomas had not taken matters into his own hands. "You don't usually walk the route, do you? Where are those new mail delivery people you just hired?"

"Humph," he snapped, gesturing wildly with his free hand. "They both called in sick at the same time. Some nonsense about allergies and the change in the weather. Darned inconvenient, if you ask me. Somebody needs to suggest an antihistamine."

"Oh," she said, not knowing what else to say and a bit taken aback at the force in the man's rushed tone. "Give me a minute to get an ink pen from my desk. Are you sure I can't get you a bottle of water or something?"

"Got a pen right here." He pushed aside the lower edge of his snowy beard and pulled a ballpoint pen from his front pocket, clicking it before handing it to her. "Thanks but no thanks. Had my coffee early, and that gets me through the morning. Not much real mail for downtown today. Circulars go out on Friday. I'm off to Sam's as soon as I'm done. Most people use the post office boxes anyway. Don't know why we hired two when there's only work enough for one."

Susan took the package, signed the return receipt so Quincy could tear it off, and handed back the pen. Her head was beginning to spin trying to follow the conversation.

"Well, have a good day," she said, hugging the package closely. She felt a strong desire to mollify the agitated man. "I hope that your workers feel better soon."

"Humph!" He turned on his booted heel, sending a tiny spray of gravel flying as he hefted the mailbag up. "Have a day yourself there too."

Thank you, she thought, watching the crotchety postman stomp away, ready to explain why she was late to Thomas and quite looking forward to the predictability of her own day at work. *I think I've already had quite a day!*

Chapter 16

"Well, Detective Abbott," Inola Walker said formally, adjusting the phone against her ear and leaning back into her office chair. "I'll try not to take up too much of your valuable day off."

Charlie ran a hand through his unruly hair and sat bolt upright in the bed.

Someday I'll learn to check the number before I answer the phone, he thought disagreeably.

He debated whether or not to hang up the phone and pretend they'd been disconnected, but Walker sounded a bit more peeved than usual.

"Hello, Agent Intimidation," he joked. "I mean, Special Agent Walker. How are things in Memphis? Need help catching arsonists, assassins, and fortune tellers? Sorry, my dance card's full."

There was the slightest icy pause before he realized that Walker would never have called him on a whim, and his mood sobered when she didn't answer right away.

He began to have an eerie feeling—one he couldn't quite explain but that fit with just how many times the man's name had already come up for Charlie in the past twenty-four hours.

Ed Brackett, he thought. *His release has to have the FBI in a snit.*

"I'm out of line," he admitted. "It must be important, or you wouldn't have called. Brackett, right?"

"I hear you've seen him since he's been released," she said matter-of-factly. "Give me a firsthand reading of Brackett's state of mind."

He considered asking her how she knew his business, but he didn't want to listen to denials and the runaround. She was an FBI profiler. She wanted information.

"I saw Brackett," he admitted. "He's slimy as ever."

Inola suspected his flippant, clipped answer hid a deeper meaning.

"Look," she said, "don't ask me to read your mind. I've spent the last twenty-four hours talking to the warden at Angola, the head judge who presided over the final hearing, and a baker's dozen dubious attorneys—everyone seems to agree that Brackett is harmless. I'm asking *you* if *you* think Brackett is harmless."

"You called me because you want *me* to tell you about Brackett's state of mind?"

"I'm asking you for a reading," she retorted. "I didn't look into his face and see his expression. But you did, so I'm asking for your help. I need to know if there's any reason to expend FBI manpower on this piece of rotten humanity when there are so many other carcasses on my radar right now. Do we need to keep tabs on Brackett?"

"Let's regroup," Charlie said, swinging his bare feet over the side of the bed and standing. He needed to fully wake up. The conversation was getting too intense for an empty stomach. "Why did you call me?"

"Brackett's about to launch lawsuits, and the FBI is likely to be caught in the crossfire. Any time an inmate is released like this from an FBI case, they get flagged. We don't want further issues from him. It's bad for PR."

You and your precious image, he thought. *Since when is the FBI's embarrassment my problem?*

"Agent Walker," he said, more restrained than he felt, "if you're worried about Brackett becoming violent, I never found evidence that Brackett ever actually committed acts of violence himself—though God knows, I tried. He's a chess player. He fancies himself as one who controls the game. You could keep tabs on his online presence, I suppose . . . try to make sure he doesn't start putting out stories again. But I don't see him needing agency resources beyond that."

He could imagine Inola taking notes as he kicked aside his tennis shoes and discarded clothing to make his way across the efficiency apartment to the refrigerator. He surveyed the meager contents, pushed aside the nearly empty pizza box, and grabbed a half-full container of orange juice, taking a long swallow.

This doesn't make sense, he thought, and then the truth hit him.

The first time he'd spoken to Inola Walker, she had used him to get to Cora. He was feeling used again. If this involved his ex-wife, he wanted to know right now.

"Does this urge to protect the FBI also extend to protecting Cora?" he said, cutting straight to the point.

This situation felt all too familiar, and he was tired of it. Beyond tired. He polished off the juice.

"Bottom line," he said, "do you want my opinion or do you need Cora and you think I'm your go-between?"

"I'm reasonably certain Mrs. Stone is already involved," she said coolly. "There are verifiable rumors that Brackett's going to sue her for defamation of character. He contacted attorneys while he was in prison. Started almost the moment he was incarcerated."

"You're not answering my questions," he said.

He could almost hear the wheels grinding as they turned in her head.

"I heard that you'd had a conversation with Brackett, and I wanted your read on him," she said politely. "I'm not asking you to *do* anything. In fact, what I need you to do is nothing. Stay where you are and do nothing."

"Really?" He tossed the empty orange juice container into the sink with a sharp and audible thump, his fury building. "You call me to ask if you should keep tabs on a recently-released inmate, and that's it? Something's not right. You can't order me to sit on my hands."

"I have a slightly different recollection of our last encounter," she said smoothly.

Charlie's face flushed at the memory of surveillance in the hot car in the Holiday Inn parking lot in Balfour. She'd treated him like a green recruit, and the memory of her high-handedness still rankled, leaving him without appropriate words.

"What's that noise?" she continued. "Are you throwing things, detective?"

He came perilously close to tossing his cell phone against the wall, restraining himself with a muffled curse and looking around for another target for his frustration, glad that no one was there to document his temper tantrum.

She was using him. That's what she did. He didn't have to like it.

She was mocking him too. And that reminded him of his encounter with Brackett.

His labored breathing told her that he was struggling to regain at least a superficial control.

"That's what I thought," she said with a patronizing tone. "Now, back to your impression of Brackett's state of mind."

His voice was hoarse, strained through clenched teeth. "You're an FBI profiler, and I'm a humble grunt-work subordinate. I don't know why you'd bother with me. You've got your information. *You* do something with it."

"Don't be so modest," she countered, ignoring his self-deprecating sarcasm. "You have excellent instincts—and I *do* want your opinion."

Charlie closed his eyes and saw Brackett's smirking face.

"He hasn't changed," he said directly, putting his anger temporarily aside for Cora's sake. If he could give them answers, maybe they'd leave her alone. "If anything, he seemed more devious, more dishonest. I know he was a model inmate, but he's a gamesman, a chess master. He thinks he's a genius so he's destined to outsmart us all."

"Speaking of chess," she said, as though she'd been waiting for him to bring up the topic. "Was Brackett holding a chess piece when you saw him?"

That's an interesting detail, Charlie thought. *Why would she focus on that?*

"Yes," he said. "Like the trial."

"Do you remember which one he had when you saw him?" she prodded.

Charlie really wasn't following her train of thought, but that was not unusual in his experience with profilers. Early on in most of his investigations with Cora he was perpetually confused by the questions she asked and the details she thought were useful.

He could put the pieces together once they were all on the table, but Cora and Inola were the ones who were skilled at finding the pieces he needed.

His insecurities needled him then, as they were needling him now.

"Do you remember which one," she repeated. "King, pawn, knight?"

"None of those," he said, retrieving the carton from the sink and tossing it into the recycling bin next to his trash can. He was exhausted and still no closer to knowing why Walker had called. "It was a white bishop."

He wanted to ask why they were wasting time talking about chess pieces. Really he wondered why they were talking at all, but he'd been caught in that cycle before. She wasn't going to tell him anything she didn't want him to know. He cleared his throat.

"You still haven't told me what I'm supposed to do in New Orleans," he said. "I mean, while I await your further omnipotent instructions."

"That's all, detective," she said shortly. "And your assurance that I'll know where to find you when I need you."

The line went dead.

Charlie Abbott let himself go and kicked the recycling bin across the kitchen floor, scattering the colorful contents in a broad swath of orange juice containers, Styrofoam take-out boxes, empty chili cans, and assorted cereal boxes.

Feeling remarkably unsatisfied, he decided he'd clean up the mess later after his shower.

Less than an hour and a half later he was standing in Louis Armstrong Airport, boarding pass and paperwork in hand for Hartsfield-Jackson International Airport in Atlanta, replacing a cooperative federal air marshal who was willing to take another flight. He would feel better when he could ask Cora directly whether she knew what was going on.

If Brackett was suing her, he wanted to tell her to her face. See her reaction. Know that she would be okay with dealing with things. Maybe he'd even tell Thomas first so he could be ready to help her defend herself.

Hang Walker, he thought, shifting his backpack. *I'll see Cora when and where I want to. The FBI is not my boss, and neither is Walker. She can't fire me. I can be in Balfour and back before she even knows I've gone. Maybe next time she'll answer my questions when I ask them.*

Chapter 17

Ellie Sanderson plopped down happily on the bench just outside the hospital's front entrance where they often met on Casey's breaks from the ER.

Her engagement was the talk of the town, eclipsing all conversation about the annual Halloween costume night at Balfour Elementary School and the Fall Harvest Festival, held jointly by the United Methodist Church and Emmanuel Baptist on the street that ran between the two main buildings.

October festivities came every year, the highlight of the month, but they paled in comparison to the Sandersons' news. A late spring wedding of the only child of two of Balfour's most prominent citizens—well, that was a once-in-a-Georgia-blue-moon kind of celebration.

No one could tell who was more excited about her impending marriage to Casey, Ellie's father or her mother. The couple set the date—a week after Ellie's graduation from nursing school. Both parents insisted that they needed much longer to prepare for the upcoming nuptials, but the couple stood firm.

"I'm glad you agree with me about a spring wedding," Ellie said. "I was afraid my dad would convince you to wait until Christmas."

"I'm just glad your parents approve of me," Casey said, playing with the fingers on his fiancée's left hand, tracing the scar along her palm where she'd cut herself the day they'd first met. "Let's discuss what kind of ring you'd like so we can make everything official."

Ellie wrinkled her nose and snuggled closer to him on the bench.

"Mom's had her heart set on giving me my grandmother's antique wedding rings," she said. "An engagement ring and a wedding band, but they're—well, ostentatious."

"Define ostentatious," he said. "I'm not sure what you mean. Do you like them?"

"Put it this way," she said, "if I sold them instead of wearing them, we could use the money for a down payment on a house, buy a new car outright, pay off the balance on our student loans, and still have money left over to pay for food and utilities for six months after we get married."

"No honeymoon?" he teased. "Maybe you're exaggerating just a smidge."

She blushed.

"Okay," she said, "you win. Maybe just a smidge."

"You didn't answer my second question," he persisted. "Do you like the rings?"

"Mom got them out of the safety deposit box at the bank once when I was younger and showed them to me," she said thoughtfully. "I slipped the engagement ring on my finger. I felt as though I'd put a headlight on my hand."

She saw his look of disbelief.

"Okay," she admitted, "maybe I'm still embellishing a little, but not much. The engagement ring was made specially for my grandmother—a one of a kind design in platinum with a two-carat, multifaceted center stone surrounded by diamonds in all shapes and sizes. There's a matching band littered with more diamonds all around. I can't imagine wearing either of those rings on a regular basis, if I wear them at all."

Casey tried to visualize the enormity of the rings and failed.

"We could use them for the ceremony and your mom can put them back in the deposit box," he suggested. "I guess I'm selfish, but I'd like for you to wear *my* ring—one you pick out from Copperfield's that we look at together. I've got some specialty catalogues for first responders so you can find one you like for me too. There are all sorts of silicone rings to pick from so I can wear it while I'm working."

"Speaking of working," she said, checking her practical watch, "your break is almost over, and I'm taking double shifts at the nursing home all next week. My parents have asked if you can come over this weekend to discuss who to include on the invitation list."

She stood up and pulled him up beside her, his slightly taller frame matching her willowy form. A sudden breeze dislodged several dead brown leaves from a nearby magnolia tree, and they swirled and crackled around the couple's feet.

"And," Ellie said, "while we're on the subject of making plans, my mom's made an appointment for us to talk to Vicki at the florist's shop on Thursday to discuss the kinds of flowers we want for the ceremony."

It was Casey's turn to wrinkle his nose.

"Flowers?" he said. "Isn't it a little early to be discussing what flowers we want for a wedding in May? That's seven months away."

Ellie wagged her finger teasingly at his chest.

"I told you not to underestimate my parents!" she laughed. "Besides, according to etiquette—and my mother does everything according to etiquette—it takes six months to a year to properly plan a wedding. She said the groom is supposed to pay for the flowers, so if you're paying, you might need to show up and express your opinion."

"Well," he said, "I suppose if we're not surprising your father, then we ought to show the same respect to your mom. I'd already asked for Thursday off, so we'll make a day of it and look for your ring at Copperfield's while I'm in Balfour. Would that work?"

"That's wonderful!" she said, taking his hand again. "You may not realize this, but I'm thankful every day that you were there at the Christmas bazaar when I needed you. Do you ever think about that? Two people in the right place at the right time—how life changes completely because of one simple action, however crazy it might be?"

"All the time," he said, pulling her hand through his elbow and drawing her protectively against his side. "I think about that all the time."

Chapter 18

Charlie was on the first flight to Atlanta's Hartsfield-Jackson Airport from Louis Armstrong International Airport, seated next to the emergency exit, and in the sky before he had time to reconsider his decision to defy Special Agent Inola Walker's order to remain in New Orleans.

Not that there was a snowball's chance that he would have changed his mind.

Hitching a ride on the plane was too easy, and defying Walker felt too satisfying.

His go bag and backpack were always ready and stored in his battered blue Volkswagen. He traveled all the time for the seminars anyway, often at the last minute, and to places much farther away than Georgia. His certification as a substitute federal air marshal had its perks.

As soon as he boarded, he sent a terse text message to his New Orleans superior, the wiry, leather-faced Cajun Captain Hymel, letting his boss know that he had urgent business and was taking the rest of the week.

In an odd way, Charlie could almost thank Brackett for that ability.

After the successful arrest and conviction in the high-profile case, Captain Hymel rarely questioned Charlie's choices about where he was going or what he was doing. Much like the Balfour PD, Charlie's fellow officers didn't care one way or another whether he showed up for work at all.

He was a lone wolf and a royal pain in the backside, but he took risks that his fellow officers would never dare attempt. Many of them openly resented him for his privilege and his attitude.

But that didn't bother Charlie.

Over the last few years he'd established himself traveling about the country doing interviews, making presentations, writing manuals, and teaching training seminars. That kind of publicity was, in almost all instances, also to the department's advantage when the time came for the city council to vote on the next year's budget and funding.

Charlie's books and connections kept him front and center in the news, and the mayor of New Orleans liked having a quasi-celebrity for his own PR purposes, especially one who could solve high-profile crimes and close stone-cold case files.

Hymel, too, learned early on that it didn't hurt to have a star player on the team, even if the star player was something of a prima donna.

The New Orleans captain acknowledged Charlie's most recent message with a noncommittal thumbs-up emoji and reminded himself that picking which battles to fight was a major part of managing his rogue detective.

As for Charlie, he was grateful for the extra legroom his seat by the emergency exit afforded. The flight attendant had already passed by twice trying to persuade him to have a snack or something to drink. His stoic silence stung her pride a bit, so she reluctantly gave up and went to offer her help to a stressed young mother soothing a crying baby in the back of the plane.

Charlie didn't mean to snub her. He was too deep in thought to care about food or flirting or being overly friendly or whatever it was she thought she was doing.

Charlie didn't notice most of the women who noticed him.

Why would she call me and be so cryptic? Charlie thought, his concerns back where he'd started at Inola's early morning call.

He stared out the window at the fluffy white clouds and piercing blue sky.

Surely if something were really wrong, even if it's just a lawsuit, that preacher of Cora's would tell her—and she'd tell me if I needed to do something, he thought. *What help will I be with a lawsuit? And what does any of this have to do with chess pieces?*

The whole mess reminded him of Cora's dreams—bits and scraps that made no sense and made his head hurt.

The baby's crying dwindled into sniffling, so the flight attendant made yet another pass by his seat, but this time she refused to look his way.

It didn't matter. Charlie didn't notice her either.

He took out two pieces of gum, his ears popping uncomfortably, and stuck the sticks into his mouth in rapid succession.

Then, as a matter of habit, he slid his hand inside his jacket under his arm and discreetly felt for his shoulder holster, assuring himself that everything was in order. He'd taken his yearly trip to the firing range to requalify the week before, passed with his usual flying colors, and cleaned and serviced his gun.

Hoping, as he always hoped, that he wouldn't have to use it.

Chapter 19

Once she finally made her way inside the office, Susan found that Thomas had not taken care of any of the general morning duties that came with beginning the workday.

The blinds were still closed, as was the inner door to his office. There were no donuts on the corner of her desk, and the pot for the coffee stood coldly empty.

She was especially grateful her boss had neglected the last item on the list. Thomas made terrible coffee, and everyone knew it.

She called out her arrival before she placed the unopened priority mail in the center of her desk and set about her duties.

Ten minutes later the scent of brewing hazelnut breakfast blend brought the lawyer out of his seclusion.

"Coffee," he said unnecessarily. "I forgot the donuts."

"You did indeed," she said good-naturedly. "And I'm late, so we're even. There's a priority for you. It's labeled *personal* so I didn't open it."

"Savannah?" Thomas took three long strides to where she sat. "Are you sure?"

"Reading is part of my job description," she said, lifting the heavy envelope to his extended hands. "You're obviously expecting it. From a law firm."

"Yes!" he exclaimed, uncharacteristically animated. "Where's your letter opener?"

Wordlessly, she opened the long drawer and handed him a miniature sterling silver sword in a tiny purple velvet sheath, one of Harry's latest quirky gifts. Thomas eyed it suspiciously for only a moment before he took it gingerly and slit into the edge of the envelope.

"That's ridiculously sharp," he said, handing it back hilt first, taking great care with the blade. "Where does your gentleman friend find these things?"

"Same place he buys my sequined sweaters, I suppose," she said, shaking her shoulders to illustrate, the irregular pattern of multi-colored reflectors sparkling under the fluorescent lights. "He brought it back the last trip he made to Memphis to finalize his half-sister Dinah's estate. I don't ask because I don't need to know."

"Fair enough," Thomas said, removing a leather-bound notebook and a sheaf of typed papers from the envelope, dropping the wrapping neatly into the trash can. "Just promise me you won't ask for workman's comp if you happen to cut yourself."

"And bleed on one of my sweaters?" she said, fluffing at her short hair before she tucked the letter opener back into the drawer. "What *are* you thinking?"

He didn't answer, absorbed in the notebook and papers in his hands.

Susan watched him as he read. The pleased expression grew on his face until it reached his eyes, and then his whole face was smiling.

"Boss," she said, trying not to disturb his obvious joy, "can I get you a cup of coffee? Would you like for me to get Cora on the phone? Better yet, do I need to cover the office while you go home?"

"All excellent suggestions," he said. "Let's begin with coffee. If you'd like, you can raid the petty cash and get bacon or sausage biscuits from Sam's for the both of us. Or a salad. Or a piece of pie. Entirely your choice. Those donuts I forgot are good too."

"Okay," she said, mildly bewildered by his erratic behavior. "Can I assume that we're celebrating?"

Thomas finally looked up.

"We are," he said, beaming. "We most certainly are. I'm going to call Cora right now. And when you get back, I'll be happy to explain to you exactly why."

Susan didn't have to be asked twice.

She opened the drawer to get the petty cash box as the cell phone in the lawyer's inner front pocket began to ring.

She waited while he answered.

"Hello, Charlie," he said stiffly, making no attempt to turn away from his stunned legal assistant.

Susan watched as the color drained from her employer's face, his mood sobered with the tightening of his jaw.

She picked up her purse to go and couldn't help overhearing.

"To be blunt," Thomas said, "I'm a little surprised you're calling, but maybe it's a good thing. Do you know what's going on with my wife?"

Chapter 20

Alice's husband dropped her off in the usual spot at the end of the sidewalk on the office side of Emmanuel Baptist Church. He was making his weekly pilgrimage to see his mother in Griffith, and Alice was pleased to have him go.

Since his full retirement in August, he'd been spending entirely too much time looking for ways to occupy himself. Even when she went to the church to work every morning, he was always making excuses to drop by around lunchtime and check on how things were going.

"I think it's rather sweet," Donna had ventured one day after Andy had brought his wife homemade meatloaf sandwiches for lunch and insisted that they eat together in the break room just off the main office.

Alice frowned.

"Wait until it happens to you," she warned. "You'll see what it's like. Even AJ can find something to do to keep himself busy. And he does his own laundry now too."

AJ, their only child, had graduated from high school and was living at home and saving to go to veterinary school. He'd managed to take over and keep the lucrative position as the Senator's designated driver after Wilton lost patience with Tipton's slothful son.

AJ had worked hard to make himself virtually indispensable as the go-to driver whenever the politician flew in to Anson's. In addition, the teenager also made special arrangements with a local rental car company in Griffith, with the aid of his parents, to rent a limo to drive on other occasions. He'd already created a profitable side business driving for the Wilton House guests, high school proms, homecomings, fancy birthday parties, and anniversaries in the neighboring towns, as well as an almost daily shuttle service for the Balfour B&B.

His quiet manner, meticulous appearance, and reasonable fees brought him a steady income. Those same qualities also garnered him hefty tips.

This morning Alice was feeling particularly proud of her son after he'd made a sizeable deposit into his savings account, and she was looking forward to another opportunity to brag on him. Unfortunately for her, Donna cut her fellow worker off before Alice could even put her purse away in her desk or hang her sweater over the back of her chair.

"What is the matter with the preacher?" Donna began, her strident voice carrying across the room from behind her computer screen as her artificial fingernails continued to click away at the keyboard. "He's an hour early one day and forty-five minutes late the next. Long lunches to who knows where, he hasn't asked to edit the bulletin in weeks, and he's taken to closing his office door almost every day."

"Can I sit down first before we start analyzing Pastor Evans?" Alice complained. "I mean, I've got plenty of my own opinions to share, but can you please wait until after I've made the coffee and cut the apple walnut bread for the deacons' business meeting this morning at ten?"

"I didn't want to talk about him when he was in the building," Donna sniffed. "But if you don't mind if the preacher overhears us talking about him . . ."

She let her voice drift off meaningfully.

Alice sighed.

"You know I don't mean that at all," she said. "I'll admit he's had some dark circles under his eyes lately, and he's been crankier and absent-minded, but that could just be worry and loss of sleep. His sermons are about the same. Not really any better but certainly no worse. You've got to remember that Virginia's been sick. That'll take a toll on any man who loves his wife as much as the preacher loves Virginia."

Donna had the decency to blush under her carefully applied makeup.

"I take your point," she said, "but the fact remains—"

The security buzzer notifying the women that the outer entrance had been opened sounded, and in a moment Andrew Evans appeared from the hallway, slightly disheveled but dressed, the women noticed, in coordinating colors.

They knew what that meant.

Ginny must have laid out his clothes, Alice thought kindly. *As if she doesn't have enough on her mind. Poor color-blind man! What a daily chore to keep him from embarrassing himself.*

"Good morning, ladies," he said cordially. "Ginny said to let you know she will be running a bit behind, but she'll be in later to help with the festival preparations."

"Coffee or tea this morning?" Alice popped up from her cushioned office seat, feeling a wave of guilt at the gossip he had almost heard. The preacher waved her back down.

"Had a good breakfast," he said. "Nothing for me, thank you. I don't want to add to your duties, but I'd appreciate it if you'd let me know when the deacons get here."

Alice gave her coworker a pointed smile as the door closed to the inner office.

"See," she whispered, "that doesn't sound so grumpy now, does it?"

"It's early yet," Donna responded. "You never know what the day may bring."

Chapter 21

Cora finished her morning shower and rescued another one of her husband's shirts from the donation box. Marjorie insisted on ordering a couple of flowery, feminine maternity blouses, but they lay still folded in their shipping box at the back of the closet. Cora explained that she was grateful for the thought, but since she never went out, she had no need for fancy clothes and they could be donated to the local women's shelter where they would be truly appreciated.

She was perfectly content to be enveloped in the soft perma-pressed cotton that still had the light scent of her husband's cologne.

This morning she was glad for time alone with her thoughts.

Both Thomas and Marjorie had been taking turns hovering over her, and the recent dream about Lonora had made her question whether they had good reason to be concerned about her state of mind.

She'd picked up the phone more than once with the impulse to call her psychiatrist Dr. Floyd for his advice, especially since the dreams were coming now on a more or less regular basis. They hadn't really had a therapy session since just after Marjorie came to live with them and, against Floyd's recommendations, Cora stopped taking prescription antidepressants.

Cora still didn't want to leave the house, and she still had bouts of sadness from time to time—she just had different reasons for what she did and how she felt.

Different coping skills. Different habits.

She'd been more or less content with her progress, but now Cora was concerned about what her lack of sleep and stress might do to her unborn child.

Lisa was a capable physician, and Cora trusted her with the birth of the baby, but she was a general practitioner. Cora hadn't confided anything about her dreams and didn't plan to share.

She valued her privacy and her husband's reputation, especially in a town the size of Balfour. Her self-enforced isolation was enough by itself to wag tongues.

This morning, Jane and Marjorie had decided to go grocery shopping for BOGO Halloween candy sales at Sanderson's Piggly Wiggly. Marjorie had also decided that they should go on to Griffith to check out accessories at the thrift store, because Jane needed a suitable Halloween costume for the annual street celebration and her first holiday party at a friend's house.

If the housekeeper and her tiny companion added a stop to Marjorie's sister-in-law's house for a quick visit, Cora knew they could be gone most of the day.

She was on her way down the stairs to revel in her limited solitude when Cora was taken aback by persistent knocking on the front door.

She recognized Charlie through the frosted glass.

Oh, darn, she thought. *I've had two dreams. I should have known. James warned me Charlie was coming today—why didn't I believe him?*

She unlocked the door, buttoned the top button on the shirt, and stepped back to let her unexpected visitor inside.

"I wish you would've called first," Cora said, searching for the stair railing with one hand and balancing precariously on the bottom step of the staircase. Stepping up one step brought her almost even with her ex-husband's chin. She would have gone higher, but she was unsteady in more ways than one.

Charlie exhaled heavily, staring at her midsection.

"I should have prepared you for this," she offered.

Damn, Thomas, he thought. *We talked for twenty minutes, and you didn't think to mention Cora was pregnant? What's wrong with you?*

"Not sure it would have been possible to prepare me," he said, trying not to sound overly dramatic as a dark stain of color rose up his neck toward his forehead. "Would it be polite to ask when you are due?"

"I meant to tell you, but we just don't talk very often," she offered lamely, glad that Marjorie and Jane were gone and there were no witnesses to another awkward episode of her life. "Three or four weeks. Probably around Thanksgiving."

"I'm not sure what I'm supposed to say next," he said, sliding his hands into the top of his jeans pockets. He managed a crooked half smile. "I *should* have called first."

"Charlie . . ." she began, but he threw up a hand to stop her.

"Why don't I say what I came to say and leave?" he said. "That way we avoid all this uncomfortable small talk. We aren't good at small talk."

You're right, Cora thought. *As long as our lives are tangled up with crimes and clues and dreams, our talks will be uncomfortable no matter what kind they are.*

"Of course," she agreed. "You wouldn't be here without good reason."

He nodded, debating whether or not he should tell her to sit down first. The sight of her pregnancy evoked feelings he'd thought were dead and gone, and he was having difficulty clearing his head. He felt suddenly vulnerable himself and protective of her.

"Charlie," she said, full of concern for the shock she'd given him, her therapist's training rising to the surface, "are you okay? Do you want coffee or something to eat? Marjorie left lemonade and chicken salad in the refrigerator. There's plenty."

He looked away, and she suspected he was thinking about the last time Thomas walked in and found them talking in the hallway.

That was a side of her husband she hoped never to see again.

"It's okay if you eat," she said coaxingly. "No one will mind, I promise. You look like you could use food, or at least a drink of water."

I may never be comfortable looking at you again, he thought. *All I can think about is Lonora and how beautiful you looked the morning I left you. By nightfall our child was gone, and I was to blame.*

His stomach rumbled loudly. He suddenly regretted his haste to get to her and his refusal to accept snacks on the plane.

"Follow me into the kitchen," she said. "You might as well say what you've come to say—only I can't hear you over that noise your insides are making."

"I'm not hungry," he protested, finally finding his voice. But he followed her down the hall and took a seat at the island anyway, watching her as she poured two large glasses of lemonade and prepared salad plates and crackers.

"Take a bite, and then we can talk," she said, handing him a fork and looking up at the kitchen wall clock. "Thomas calls around noon every day, and I'll tell him you're here when he calls."

Oh, Lord, Charlie thought. *Here we go.*

"He already knows I'm here," Charlie admitted, the fork poised over a piece of chicken. "I called him after the plane landed in Atlanta and talked to him an hour ago."

Cora put down her fork and glared.

"So you talked to Thomas *before* you came to see me?" she said, her voice rising. "I'm the *second* person to know what you have to tell me? Since when do you check in with Thomas before you talk to me?"

There was nothing to do but blurt out the truth.

"Ed Brackett's been released from Angola," he said in a vain attempt to pacify her growing irritation. "I wanted Thomas to know first because he's a lawyer. I came to you because I wanted to tell you in person."

She picked up one of the crackers and crumbled it deliberately over her plate.

"Well, I don't know what to say." The words came out between stiff lips.

He wanted to reach over and take her hand, but he pushed away his need to comfort her. He picked up his fork again, taking a substantial bite.

"Marjorie makes great chicken salad," he said, chewing thoughtfully, saying the first thing that came into his head. "The lemonade is homemade too, right?"

His attempt at defusing the situation was almost comical, and Cora could not disguise her irrational reaction. She covered her mouth with her napkin as she dissolved into unexpected mirth, tears trickling down her face at his goofy attempt to lighten the tension between them.

"Oh, Charlie!" she said, mopping the tears from her eyes. He was such a paradox. A child and a man. "You really *don't* have a clue how sweet you are, do you?"

He gave her his most innocent stare.

He didn't want that from her. Not the compliments. Not the affection. Not the warm kindness of her heart. Those weren't his to accept. Not anymore.

"I'm glad you find me amusing," he said, emotion drained from his voice, his tone even and controlled. "I got a call this morning from the FBI in Memphis. Special Agent Walker thinks Brackett is planning lawsuits against you. Thomas is a lawyer. I called him. That's all. I've been missing Elvira, and I was planning a trip anyway."

"Oh," she said quietly. "I had a dream. I guess I thought you were here because of that."

"I had no idea you had a dream," he said, lying smoothly. It was bad enough he'd talked to Thomas first. If she thought they'd been discussing her dreams, she might not speak to either of them until she calmed down—and that could take quite a while in her present pregnant state. Besides, Thomas didn't have any details. As usual.

He polished off the salad and picked up the glass.

"What was this dream about?"

"Well," she said, stirring her salad around with her fork, "James said something about a professor. Could that be about Brackett?"

"You're the one with the clues, Cora," he said. "Am I *supposed* to do something about this professor?"

She had no intention of bringing up their dead child.

"No," she said simply. "You're not supposed to do anything

about a professor. James said I could handle that. You're supposed to find a girl and a candy bar. That's all—a girl and a candy bar."

Charlie shook his head.

"And I thought the dream about gypsies and licorice was crazy," he said. "Are you sure you didn't go to bed hungry?"

"According to James," she said, shrugging her shoulders at the skeptical look on his face, "I'm supposed to remind you about a girl and a candy bar from the past. You know very well I don't know what it means any more than you do."

"Okay." He stood up. "I guess James will have details when it suits him. I hope I don't have to take this one to Walker. Candy bar, indeed."

Her curiosity got the better of her tongue.

"Charlie, did you really call Thomas? What did you say?"

"I told you. I asked him about lawyer stuff," he said. "How to protect you from being sued. The kind of things he understands and is good at."

And I'm not, he added silently in his head. *I wasn't good at protecting you. Or the baby.*

Cora tilted her head and studied him, biting her lower lip.

Suddenly he seemed like a stranger. A disinterested stranger who'd come to deliver a message and was waiting somewhat expectantly on the front porch for a tip and to be told his job was done so he could be on his way.

"Well, thank you for letting me know," she said.

He took his empty plate and glass to the sink, rinsing them before turning them upside down in the drainboard.

"You still don't have a dishwasher?" he said, indicating the soap dispenser and the striped cotton drying towel. "I can't believe

Thomas hasn't convinced you that you need one. Do you still wash dishes by hand?"

"I've gotten used to standing at the kitchen sink." Cora went back to picking at her chicken salad. "The warm soapy water helps me think."

He couldn't tell her that he understood, because he didn't.

"Don't get up," he said much too politely, glancing at the kitchen clock, his words tripping over each other in his haste for the time with her to be over. "It's eleven forty-five. Thomas will be calling you soon. Thank you for lunch. I'll see myself out."

Cora waited until she heard his steady footsteps fade away and the front door close before she put her uneaten salad and drink in the refrigerator.

Then she waddled down the hallway to turn the dead bolt and go into her office, waiting more or less patiently for her husband to call.

She hoped Marjorie was successful in her shopping trip.

While she wasn't hungry for the chicken salad, she did have the most impulsive, irrational craving for a candy bar.

Chapter 22

Charlie decided to forego a visit to the Balfour Police Department in favor of the Piney Woods and an afternoon with his Plott hound. Jim Smith was the only one who would miss him if he didn't go by the station. Even Ben Taylor had seemed a bit distant after the whole episode with Bill and the general upheaval Charlie had caused the last several times he'd been to town.

The rogue detective knew he'd stomped on more than a few sensitive local toes. The same way he stomped on toes in all the precincts in New Orleans, where they'd passed him around like a bad penny. He happily admitted that his attitude was arrogant and high-handed, but he got the job done and that was what counted.

He didn't really care who got the credit, and he thought he'd proven it.

His part in solving the grocery store shooting, Miss Bessie's murder at Beulah Land, duping the would-be assassin, and ultimately arresting the arsonist-killer Beth Brown had been downplayed in favor of elevating Smith and the FBI. Only a few people in town knew how much he'd been involved in solving the simultaneous cases, and Charlie wanted to keep it that way.

To the Balfour folk who didn't know better, he looked like a meddling, interfering outsider, which to his mind was best.

The less they link me to local crimes, he thought, *the less likely they are to link Cora to me, and she'll have the peace and quiet she deserves.*

He parked the rental car in an empty space in front of his apartment building and decided to walk around to find Marcie.

Unlike the last time he was here, he'd come on his own recognizance, and that would count for bonus points with his landlady.

There were several other cars he didn't recognize parked in both the lots, and he was glad for the added income to Marcie's pocketbook.

The burst of color in the mountains generally brought tourists in, and the busy Christmas holiday shopping season in Dahlonega and Gainesville was just around the corner.

He frowned at the memory of the last Ladies Auxiliary Christmas Bazaar.

One holiday at a time, he scolded himself. *Halloween, then Thanksgiving, then Christmas. Why does everyone have to be in such a gosh-awful hurry?*

There was no sign of the cheerful proprietor of the Piney Woods, who was often outside cleaning, planting, or making repairs. Her car was parked in its usual spot outside her ground floor apartment, so he knocked politely on the door.

Inside he could hear Elvira's whining greeting, her sensitive nose detecting his scent long before he'd turned the corner of the second building.

Marcie embraced him with honest enthusiasm.

"Well if it isn't the prodigal son come home for a visit! I've just made tuna salad, and, as your luck would have it, I'm all out of celery. Come inside and sit down. You look hungry."

Charlie discreetly brushed a random cracker crumb from the front of his shirt.

"Oh, I'm ravenous," he lied, releasing himself from her maternal bear hug and kneeling down to his dog. "Tuna sounds delicious. I can't wait to hear what's been going on since I've been gone."

"Then you've come to the right woman!" his landlady exclaimed, dishes clattering as she removed them from her cupboard. "How long are you planning to stay? Let's start with Ellie Sanderson's upcoming nuptials and go from there."

Chapter 23

Despite the skills he'd acquired from his courtroom experiences and his own natural self-control, Thomas was finding it difficult to rein in his erratic feelings about Charlie's phone call. He'd considered himself an even-tempered man, but the current emotional rollercoaster was testing his limits.

He was at once furious that Cora was being drawn back into the dangerous life she'd left behind and grateful that his old friend had called him first to let him know before visiting Cora unannounced.

Thomas stared at the worn notebook journal and typed papers on his desk.

He'd planned a special lunch call to let his wife know his news—that weeks ago the two paralegals he'd hired in Savannah had found a handwritten journal among the legal documents in a filing cabinet in the mansion. The leather-bound book was written in Mandarin by Jane's great-grandmother. With his permission, the paralegals located a translator from a nearby university to transcribe the contents and then sent the English version as a hard copy for Cora to read.

He hadn't wanted to get his wife's hopes up, waiting until the journal could be fully translated before he gave it to her.

Beyond the legal papers, Thomas had hoped the diary would provide clues to tell them about Jane's extended family. Personal and private thoughts from a woman who'd ruled her business with an iron fist. Maybe even important dates and family history.

He hadn't read it, of course. He wanted Cora to be the first.

Now his happy news was dwarfed by Charlie's dire warnings.

I'm being petty, he told himself. *I'm feeling petty and angry and childishly jealous.*

In the outer office, Susan was also emotionally torn.

She had been watching her employer's attitude with increasing concern.

She knew him well enough to know that Charlie was a serious problem, but she hadn't been prepared for the rollercoaster of emotion—from the elation of receiving the package to the nosedive that followed Charlie's phone call.

She also knew from experience that what he needed was a healthy lunch, whether he felt like eating it or not.

While Thomas went over the estate papers, Susan excused herself and made a beeline to Sam's, enjoying the quick walk through the town square.

Once in Simmons' Restaurant, she artfully dodged the restaurant owner's barrage of nosy questions and brought back two dinner garden salads with grilled chicken, minus the Vidalia onions, in clear plastic take-out bowls with low-calorie house vinaigrette dressing on the side and two large unsweet teas with extra lemons.

Thomas rolled his eyes at her selection, but she knew he was secretly grateful.

"Eat first," she said firmly, putting the salad, dressing, tea, napkin, and a plastic fork in the center of his desk. "Talk after."

"Of course," he said. "Are you sitting at your desk?"

"And closing the door to eat my own lunch," she said briskly. "How else am I going to keep you from talking?"

Fifteen minutes later, Thomas had to admit that he did feel much better.

"Can I come out now?" he asked, standing in the doorway of his office, empty bowl in hand. "I'd like a cup of coffee too."

Susan swept her lunch debris into the trash can, checking her watch.

"Have you called Cora?" she asked. "It's almost noon."

"Not yet," he said, depositing his own trash with hers. "Charlie's at the house right now. Remind me to take this out later so it doesn't reek."

"Sure thing." Susan fluffed at her hair and folded her arms across her chest, waiting for the clarification she was certain would be forthcoming. "I'm ready to listen. It's been an eventful morning for both of us, but you go first."

"Well," he began, propping himself on the outer corner of her desk, "the priority mail is from paralegals in a law office in Savannah. I contracted with them to go through the Chen family papers. They found a diary written by Jane's great-grandmother, and I asked them to have it translated for Cora."

"That's great news," Susan said, deliberately inspecting her recently painted nails and curbing her natural impulse to ask questions. "Anything that helps with the adoption process is great news. Go on."

"Then you were here when Charlie called to tell me what we already knew from the Senator this morning. Ed Brackett is out of prison and is considering legal action against Cora."

"That's a little out of character, isn't it?" she asked. "For Charlie to call you?"

"I'm not sure what's out of character for Charlie anymore," Thomas admitted. "I didn't bother to tell him that I already knew about Brackett. He said he'd flown in from New Orleans to tell Cora personally."

"I thought you were going to do that at noon when you called her."

The words were out before Susan could contain them, and she would have cheerfully bitten her tongue to take them back. Thomas frowned, a thundercloud forming on his face, and Susan hurried to try to forestall the impending emotional storm.

"So Charlie is at your house telling Cora about Brackett?"

"That's what he said," the lawyer said. "He wants me to look into the legal ramifications. I thought I'd let them talk and then I could call Cora with the news about the diary."

"You're a better man than the vast majority of men," she said admiringly. "You do know that, don't you? Any other man would have punched Charlie's lights out years ago and bragged about it."

"Don't take any bets on that," he said, tapping the corner of her desk as he stood. "Why don't you get the files for the Evans vs. Dodd property suit ready? We can go over the case as soon as I've talked to Cora. Or you could tell me about your morning. Either way, I could use some normal for a change."

Chapter 24

Special Agent Walker looked across the room at the hulking, muscular man stuffed into a formfitting three-piece black suit and striped silk tie. His polished dress shoes tapped lightly from time to time, but otherwise Jim Smith sat ramrod straight on a metal office chair against the far wall of the busy office space.

The snug vest beneath the unbuttoned coat might well have been an armless straightjacket judging by the man's posture. A thin veneer of perspiration dotted his dark forehead, and the FBI agent thought she could detect a hint of fatigue on his handsome face.

The weeklong process had been necessarily grueling, but then the means by which an individual became a special agent for the bureau was geared to select only the best. Her recommendation carried substantial weight, but the rest had been up to the officer, and he had not disappointed her expectations.

His background check, education, work history, and credentials were spotless.

She'd known that long before she considered asking him to come to Memphis for the interviews. She could vouch for his artistic skill in drawing sketches from the vague descriptions of witnesses as well as his calm demeanor and professionalism during the course of investigations.

If nothing else, his ability to spend prolonged time dealing with Charlie Abbott without strangling the man was another feather in the officer's proverbial cap. How he would deal with the pressures put on him by her superiors and whether or not they would see what she saw still remained to be seen.

She wanted Jim Smith on her team. Period.

But now there were complications that delayed the decision.

The news of Ed Brackett's release had spread throughout the agency corridors like a raging brush fire. Agents who had been directly involved in the initial investigation scrambled to check the status of the convicted killers who were still serving time, some of them on death row in their respective states.

The fact that he intended to sue Cora Stone for defamation of character could quite possibly call into question the validity of her previous court testimony.

Agent Walker had studied the case in depth, as had most of her colleagues, and they all knew how tenuous and complicated it had been to prove Brackett's connections to the serial killings in the first place.

Many of the inmates who had been associated with the professor heard of his impending release, and the dockets were already filling with multiple appeals intended to fight their convictions on the grounds that the evidence linking them to Brackett was mainly circumstantial.

Time had blurred the intensity of their crimes, and there was no longer urgency or the fresh fear of more serial killings. The public and the media had moved on.

If Brackett succeeded in dragging Cora back into the limelight, all the cases that hinged on his guilt might also be called into question. Another bona fide circus.

Cora would be trapped in the center ring surrounded by the twin lions of publicity—the press and public opinion.

I'm glad I got to Abbott before he had some idiotic notion to run off to Balfour, Inola thought. *He needs to stay as far away from his ex-wife as he can right now. If she is going to have to defend her testimony against Brackett, she doesn't need anyone digging up the cases she's worked in the last few months. That's all she'd need—someone finding out she's been dreaming impossible clues. A skilled lawyer could investigate her past. Open up the details of the last year. Tear her apart on the stand, or at the least make her look irrational and mentally unstable.*

A shadow fell over her desk, and she looked up to see that Jim had crossed the room and was standing at attention in front of her.

"Special Agent Walker," he said formally, "I know you've got all this under control, but you'd mentioned an evaluation at the gun range and I was wondering if that had been scheduled yet, or if there's more paperwork."

"There's always more paperwork," she said dryly. "Have you had lunch yet?"

Jim looked around the room to see if she might have been talking to someone else, but everyone else seemed busy with other concerns.

"Not really," he said, tilting his head down slightly and lowering his voice. "I'm not complaining. Breakfast at the hotel was great, waffles and all, but that was a couple of hours ago."

"Then we need to take care of that, don't we?" she said, standing up and tugging down her gray suit jacket, an idea germinating. "I'll go by my office and get my car keys and we'll go together."

"Oh," Jim stammered. "I didn't mean that you needed to do anything. I can take an Uber or Lyft and find a place close by to grab something and come back."

"Nonsense," she said crisply. "This isn't a social lunch, Officer Smith. There's a matter of some concern I'd like to discuss with you. An issue that's just come up and for which your skills would be particularly suited."

"A case?" he said curiously. "But I'm not an agent."

"We're going to try to prevent our little problem from becoming a case," she said, heading for the elevator and gesturing for him to follow. "And it's actually much better that you aren't an agent. In this situation, Officer Smith, I much prefer that you just be yourself."

Chapter 25

Jane skipped into the house and down the hallway to the kitchen, plastic bags from Sanderson's swinging from her arms and dress-up treasures from the thrift store clutched in her hands.

A hymn-humming Marjorie followed close behind, also laden with packages and plastic shopping bags, her oversized quilted purse hanging from her forearm.

"Come see!" the little girl called out as she passed the office. "Morrie's going to help me make cookies and then a costume! I'm going to be a princess pirate!"

Cora got up as quickly as she could manage, maneuvering carefully around the dozing Maine coon cat who had joined her after Charlie left.

"A princess pirate?" Cora repeated, sitting down at the island to watch the pair unpack their purchases. "Sounds fascinating."

Marjorie looked over the top of her spectacles, her eyes twinkling.

"She wanted to be pretty, and she wanted to carry a sword," the housekeeper explained. "We found some peel-and-stick jewels still in the original wrapping and a plain wooden sword at the thrift store."

"And a princess dress!" Jane declared, pulling out a filmy pink mass of fabric with swirling layers of glittering net and lined with wrinkled slipper satin. She held it up proudly for inspection. "Morrie says it's too big, but she can make it fit me—and tennis shoes will match perfectly!"

"Ah," Cora said. "A princess pirate wearing hot pink high tops with a bejeweled sword. Is there a tiara in there somewhere too?"

"Of course there is," Marjorie said. "Not sure which bag it's in though."

Solomon, who had followed Cora, ambled in the kitchen and lifted his head, his whiskers twitching. Failing to detect the scent of anything edible, he flopped under Jane's stool, exposing a massive black fur belly as the pair of shoppers emptied their plastic bags and dropped them to the floor.

Too lethargic to bother with swatting them away, he began to purr.

When she'd finished, Jane hopped down to his side and rummaged through the bags a second time to make certain she hadn't overlooked anything.

Marjorie was in her element, humming and arranging the multiple packages of assorted Halloween candy into piles, separating the costume pieces from the cooking supplies on the countertop.

"I'm still looking," she said. "It's in one of those silly bags somewhere. I forgot to take the recycle ones, so we're stuck with too many plastic. We were temporarily torn between a bejeweled crown and a feathered pirate hat, but the sparkles won, as well I think they should."

"The feather was pink and big," Jane said as she continued to sort her new possessions. "But I like the jewels. Morrie said she'll make my sword match my crown."

The little girl pulled out a stack of brightly colored board books, which she loudly deposited on the floor beside the cat's head. Solomon opened one eye, refusing to flinch, purring louder.

"We found these too," Jane said proudly. "They can go on the bookcase in my room, and they match each other too."

"What she means," Marjorie interjected, "is that we found a set of some of the Eric Carle books at the thrift store, on clearance no less."

"Of course." Cora smiled, following the child's logic. "I like books too. Especially grouchy ladybugs and hungry caterpillars."

The baby inside had begun to kick in what felt like protest, and Cora wondered if perhaps she should have eaten something at lunch. She reached into Marjorie's neatly stacked pile of candy and opened a bag of miniature chocolates.

"Have you eaten your lunch?" Marjorie asked accusingly. She picked up a quart of milk and opened the refrigerator, spotting the salad and glass of lemonade.

The housekeeper made soft clucking noises of disapproval.

"I'm not your mother," she said, "but why did you make a salad if you weren't going to eat it?"

Cora unwrapped the chocolate and put it in her mouth, pointing over the top of Jane's head at the solitary clean dish and drinking glass drying on the rack.

"Well, someone else enjoyed your chicken salad very much," she said cryptically. "He said to thank you. He loved the fresh-squeezed lemonade too."

"Oh, good Lord," Marjorie gasped, half-joking. "Don't tell me you-know-who showed up while I was gone. I'm all for Southern hospitality, and I'd certainly feed a stray puppy too, but did you even know he was coming? Why does he persist in popping in and out of town like a crazed jack-in-the-box?"

"I'll take that salad now," Cora said, ignoring the comments and opening another chocolate, "but only if you promise not to ask me any more questions about you-know-who. Thomas called about thirty minutes ago and knows all about it anyway, so you needn't fret over me."

"I'll get your food out," Marjorie said. "But you know very well that I'm not going to stop fretting over you, and I certainly do not intend to stop asking questions."

"Then I'm having another chocolate," Cora said. "And don't worry, I'll be eating my lunch all the same."

Chapter 26

Mildly unnerved by the morning's fender bender with Susan, Ginny Evans arrived at Emmanuel later than she wanted but in time to see her husband disappear into the conference room with the quorum of deacons at his back.

She'd hoped to be there to tell him about her auto adventure before he heard from someone else, but the call to Ben Taylor had taken longer than she'd expected.

Ben's such a stickler for details, she thought. *No one was seriously injured. I don't know why he wants to make such a production over a simple accident. Balfour's a small town after all—and Susan works for a lawyer. It isn't as though there's going to be a dispute over who pays for the repairs.*

She told herself she didn't have the energy to dwell on Ben's stubborn attention to detail when she was more concerned about Andy's business meeting.

She'd wanted to get to the church in time not only to forestall the news about the dent to her front bumper, but also to show her husband that she supported his work at Emmanuel. He'd been spending considerable time and energy supporting her at her doctors' visits and treatments even though she knew he was struggling himself.

He hadn't been sleeping soundly for months, his dreams about his days in the military becoming more frequent and troubling.

Adding to his lack of sleep and concern for her well-being, Ginny knew that the monetary situation at Emmanuel was heavy on his mind too.

The beginning of October signaled a new fiscal year for the church's financial planning, so Andy and the deacons would be busy for several hours at least, going over the proposed budget, negotiating, and evaluating. Tithes and offerings were down for the year, and making determinations about how to divide the limited resources in the coming year caused untold friction.

The process was stressful to all concerned.

The committee chairmen and women who weren't present for the initial meetings had made their priorities and plans widely known, putting Andy in the position of playing mediator to them all.

Tight money often made for even tighter fists.

Alice and Donna, whose husbands were on the current roster of deacons, had discreetly excused themselves to the kitchenette off the main office when the men arrived and went into the larger conference room down the hall.

They'd busied themselves making sandwiches, turkey with cheese and glazed ham, for the anticipated late lunch break in the meeting.

In addition, Marcie had already delivered a giant Tupperware container of potato salad, and Marjorie had promised chocolate chip cookies for dessert to be delivered sometime later in the day.

Everyone could agree on food, even if they argued about everything else.

Both the secretaries were overjoyed to see the preacher's wife appear carrying a cake container of her famous vanilla pound cake cut into generous slices.

They took turns hugging her gently and offering compliments on the style of her hair and her homemade, flower-print dress.

Ginny knew they'd been concerned for her health over the past months, and she appreciated their sisterly effort to encourage her.

"What can I do to help?" Ginny said, soaping her hands and thrusting them under the faucet, washing them with eager cheerfulness. "Are you ready to make the coffee? Put ice in the glasses?"

"Just making the sandwiches so they'll be ready," Alice said. "We're going to put them in the fridge until the menfolk want to eat."

Donna covered the first platter with plastic wrap, handing it to Alice.

"Well, I came to help," Ginny said. "Please put me to work."

Alice gave Donna a doubtful look.

"How are you feeling?" Alice said. "Didn't you have a follow-up in Griffith this week?"

"Did you bake this cake from scratch?" Donna said, studying Ginny's pale face with increasing alarm. "The container still feels warm. You shouldn't overdo it."

Ginny felt a tingling in the tips of her fingers, and the room began to turn at the corners. Her stomach did a flip-flop under her rib cage.

"I'm fine," she said, unexpectedly lightheaded and swaying as she put out a hand to steady herself on the edge of the counter. "Really, I'm fine. I shouldn't make sudden moves, that's all."

"You're a terrible fibber," Alice said, hurriedly placing the platter in the refrigerator and taking Ginny's upper arm in a firm grip, guiding her to a chair at the old-fashioned dinette table. "Donna, can you get some water, please?"

The other secretary had already filled a small glass and slipped it into Ginny's trembling hand.

"I'm calling Lisa at the clinic," Donna announced flatly. "She'll know what to do."

Ginny took a sip of water and waved her free hand in the air.

"Don't think that will do you any good," the preacher's wife said, trying to catch her breath. "She's gone for the week to a medical training seminar in Atlanta."

Ginny didn't want to tell them that calling the doctor was the first thing Susan had suggested after the accident. She also did not want to confess to having an accident at all. She knew the two worried secretaries would ship her off to the hospital in Griffith to be checked out, or home to bed, and there was too much to do for that kind of time wasting.

"I'm curious how you know for certain that Lisa is gone for the week," Donna said suspiciously. "But if that's true, then I'm sure our good doctor left someone equally competent in charge. She's too responsible to go off and leave Balfour unattended."

"Call the fire department," Alice insisted. "Or the ambulance service out of the emergency room in Griffith."

Heavens! Ginny thought. *This is getting completely out of control! I don't want Casey to show up and word get back to Jack. Or Andy to come out of his business meeting to find out I've been carted off to be checked out for who-knows-what at the hospital.*

She forced down the rest of the water and set the glass on the table. "I'm perfectly fine," she insisted. "You are both being mother hens, and it isn't necessary at all. I'm just a little faint since I haven't eaten lunch yet. A lovely slice of Alice's walnut bread and a half a sandwich will have me right as rain."

The secretaries exchanged unconvinced glances.

"I'm still for calling the fire department," Donna said. "Alice had an excellent idea."

"I agree," Alice said. "Maybe that nice paramedic engaged to Ellie Sanderson is there. Or David. David's good too."

"I've got the final vote," Ginny said, giving the table an audible and resolute slap. "I'd like some sweet tea, please, and one of those turkey and cheese sandwiches. The least you can do is let me eat before some well-meaning EMT or a volunteer fireman hauls away the best help you have for planning the fall festival."

Alice exhaled and picked up the glass, refilling it at the sink.

"She does have a point there, Donna," she said gently. "Ginny's the best volunteer we have. I say let's respect her opinion about how she says she feels. I'm willing to wait for a few minutes to see what happens. What do you think?"

"I don't like it one bit," Donna said disagreeably, "but we'll say an extra blessing over the turkey to see if the food helps. But mark my words, Virginia Evans, if your cheeks don't have some color in them after you've eaten, not only will I call the fire department, I'm getting the preacher out of the deacons' meeting to talk some sense into you."

"I hear you," Ginny said meekly, "but I really am hungry. Why don't you two take a quick break and join me? At least have a glass of tea. The only thing worse than eating with an audience is eating alone."

Chapter 27

Marjorie put away all the shopping as Cora choked down a little over half the chicken salad, then she sat down across the island, watching her charge intently. After several minutes, Jane's gentle pleading to work on the princess costume overtook the housekeeper's desire to make sure Cora ate.

"Gather up all the plastic bags, sweetie," she said to Jane as she draped the pink fabric nightmare over her forearm. "My sewing machine and pins are upstairs in my bedroom. You and I can go up and get started on your dress while the grown-up here finishes her lunch."

"I ate my lunch," Jane said proudly. "I was 'bedient."

"Obedient," Marjorie corrected absently, bending to help the little girl stuff the accumulation of bags into one and tying the top together. "You're an excellent helper. We'll take these back for recycling the next time we go to the store."

"Can I hug?" she said innocently.

"Of course you can," Cora said, struggling to stand, but Marjorie's firm hands pressed her shoulders back down.

"Come over here and hug Baby. Be gentle," the housekeeper said.

Jane stepped around the snoozing cat and pressed her tiny hands against the smooth cotton just under Cora's rib and was rewarded with a sharp kick.

"Baby loves me," Jane said happily. "Can we make my sword now?"

"Let's work on the dress first," Marjorie suggested. "Then we'll tackle the sword. We may decide we want to spray-paint it silver or gold before we put on the jewels."

"Yes, Morrie."

The housekeeper turned to her other charge.

"Do you need help getting to the den?" she asked. "I can take the rest of your salad and lemonade in there."

Down the hallway, the phone in Cora's office began to ring.

"It could be important," Cora said, rising slowly. "I've been consulting with the publisher about the new book coming out in the spring, and I'm expecting a call."

"Well," Marjorie said, "we've already established that you aren't listening to me. Answer your phone, and I'll clean up the kitchen when we've gotten a good start on the princess costume."

The phone was still ringing when Cora reached her office, closing the door behind her as she entered.

"Hello," she said, a trifle out of breath. "Cora Stone speaking."

"Hello, Cora," a man's voice said. "I must admit I didn't expect you to answer. What a pleasure to hear your voice, although I need to get used to your new married name."

"Who is this?"

"Ah," he said, "I'm not surprised you don't recognize me, but then, you did most of the talking at the trial, so I guess that's to be expected. It's been over five years."

Cora dropped into her office chair, indigestion and irritation rising in her throat. She knew that voice.

Brackett, she thought, her mind reeling. *Why is Ed Brackett calling me?*

"Professor Brackett," she said, slowing her breathing. "I'm not sure what you hope to accomplish by calling me."

"Don't underestimate the satisfaction of competition," he said, "especially between two master players and a game of skill like chess."

Chess? she thought. *Competition? Is he talking about suing me?*

"I know nothing about your games," she said. "Certainly not chess."

"Oh, you might know more than you think," he countered. "I always had that impression of you, you know. I'm sure you could master chess if you put your mind to it. You are the epitome of a white bishop."

"Are you suggesting we are in a chess game?" she asked.

If he wanted to play chess with someone competent, he couldn't have chosen a more ignorant partner.

Cora felt a cold chill creep up her spine. She wished she'd paid closer attention when Charlie tried to explain the intricacies of chess and the cryptic analogies that Brackett used during the trial. All she could remember at this moment was that the pawn was the least valuable piece on the board, and that white pieces made the first move.

"So, changing the subject, I was wondering about your opinion on Halloween," he said, taking on a playful, conversational tone, almost as if they were old friends. "As a child psychologist, I mean. What do you see as the advantages? Disadvantages? Don't most children enjoy a fright every now and then? They're all gruesome little monsters themselves."

"Halloween?" she said carefully, her thoughts whirling. "We were talking about chess."

"But how do you feel about Halloween?" he insisted. "Your opinion as a child psychologist. Let's talk about something that interests you."

"Why did you call me?" she said bluntly. "What is it you really want?"

"Ah, little bishop," he said, returning abruptly to his chess analogy. "I'm playing with you. Isn't it obvious? And the lovely part of this chess game is that it happens in October—a Halloween gambit as it were."

"I'm confused," she said. "What do you mean?"

"I'm tired now," he said, yawning in her ear. "The clock timer's gone off, and I need to review the board for tomorrow's match. You will excuse me, won't you, little bishop? We'll talk again soon."

The line went dead and Cora stared at the phone, her hands trembling as she reached for her notebook and a pen.

Oh, Thomas, she thought. *I don't know if you can help me with this. I may have to call Charlie again after all. I'm so sorry.*

Chapter 28

Sam was enjoying the fall weather that had brought in an influx of tourists along with her usual clientele.

Beyond serving delicious Southern food and Bill's gourmet concoctions, Sam also prided herself on being the hub of chitchat and shared information.

Simmons' Restaurant was Balfour's front porch.

The biggest stories, most outrageous gossip, and all noteworthy announcements made their way to and through Sam's front doors.

Ellie Sanderson's engagement to Casey and every new juicy detail about plans for the nuptials had become weekly staples.

Jim Smith's interview trip to Memphis with the lady FBI agent was riveting news, although Sam especially missed Jim. The handsome officer could be depended upon to deliver the latest updates from the police station on his morning visits for biscuits and coffee. He'd been gone for most of the week, and she was having to pump a less-than-informed Officer Jenkins, whose best answers were wide-eyed stares and mumbled denials about traffic tickets and dubious DUIs.

Judge and Linda Candler were on a two-week cruise in the Bahamas, so trial dates and court cases had either been moved to the courthouse in Griffith or postponed. Traffic to and from the seat of county business had dwindled to a trickle, and tables that were normally crowded midweek were sparse, but a number of customers still came from force of habit.

But Sam's attitude was far from rosy. Thomas hadn't come in for lunch for over a month, and Susan darted in and out today as though she thought she'd come into a fast-food diner—not so much as a pinch of information about where the lawyer was or why he was so obviously avoiding her.

Other rumors were swirling just out of Sam's reach too. She knew they were.

Bill steadfastly refused to gossip, so she was agonizing alone.

There was a moment of promising potential when a grumpy Quincy wandered in for lunch, empty mailbag over his shoulder, and let slip that he'd delivered a priority mail package from Savannah to the Stone Law Firm. But when Sam asked the first simple question, he stopped talking and went back to eating, saying something silly about postal privacy.

She'd also heard from one of the delivery boys who brought the latest order of yeast rolls that Susan and Ginny's cars had collided in front of the bakery that morning. The young man said both cars drove away and no one seemed hurt. But when Ben came in to get a takeout for his lunch and she asked him about the accident report, he insisted that police business was confidential.

She'd never seen so many tongue-tied people in her life.

There was an outlandishly juicy yarn from the cook by way of a college student, claiming she'd witnessed Senator Wilton kissing Darcie Jones in the lobby of the bed and breakfast. A rumor that sounded incredibly scandalous and totally improbable.

To Sam's extreme displeasure, no one on the staff was willing to confirm or deny, ostensibly out of fear of retaliation from the B&B's notorious matron.

Of course, there *were* other events to talk about. Dan's murder trial was beginning in Atlanta, but that was too serious, painful, and far away to merit consideration. Sam could have gossiped with authority about Katy or Amy, or even the Wilton House Estate's current dispute over the name of the next executive director, but those topics were completely off limits.

As was Ginny Evans's cancer scare and treatment and, by association, her husband's increasingly morose behavior in the pulpit.

Even Sam had standards.

She vented to the silent Bill, who hid in the kitchen, insisting he needed peace and quiet to come up with a menu for the upcoming holiday season.

Her last avenue of communication gone, she decided to take matters into her own hands.

If the gossip won't come to me, she thought, *then I'll just go in search of gossip.*

That was when, crossing the town square on her way to Henson's Pharmacy on a quest for a bottled root beer, jelly beans, and fresh informants, she caught a glimpse out of the corner of her eye of an unfamiliar car driving past the courthouse.

A car she didn't recognize at all, but a driver she would have known anywhere and under any circumstances.

Why Charlie Abbott, you handsome rascal, she thought, rubbing her palms together in satisfaction. *What in the world are you doing in Balfour—and who else knows you're here? This is an exciting news story if I've ever seen one! Who can I call who would be as interested as I am?*

Chapter 29

"I'm not at all sure what you expect me to do," Jim Smith said, his athletic form turning the heads of impressionable young women as he walked through Memphis International Airport. He'd changed from the restrictive dignity of his best suit into business casual—a long-sleeved, dark green dress shirt and khaki slacks. His muscular arms dangled deliberately at his sides, a carry-on canvas suitcase in one hand and his backpack in the other. "Explain what we're doing again, please."

The head-turning pair stopped momentarily at the checkpoint.

Inola Walker offered her FBI badge and a handful of official-looking papers to the homeland security guard. The first guard kept one eye on Jim while he checked the proffered information, and another guard inspected his meager luggage for contraband. Finally, the guards gave cursory nods and escorted both the agent and the officer through the metal detector on their way to the gates.

Once clear of security, Inola picked up her pace.

"Keep walking, Smith," she snapped, "or you'll miss the plane."

"But I still don't quite understand why I'm flying to New Orleans," he said, his wide stride matching her strident march. "You said I'm babysitting Charlie? Why?"

"Have you *met* Detective Abbott?" She threw the words over her shoulder, a tart mixture of amusement and sarcasm. "You must be joking, Smith. Why don't you ask me a question you can't figure out on your own?"

They darted in and out of the flowing pedestrian traffic so quickly that Jim began to feel a bit like a patrol car with flashing blue lights in hot pursuit of a suspect.

Walker didn't even slow down when they reached the escalator, taking the steps up as though they weren't moving on their own, barking to be excused as startled but cooperative passengers moved aside to let them pass.

When they reached the C concourse, Jim slackened his pace at a newsstand to gaze longingly at the racks of chips and cookies and the cooler filled with bottled drinks, but the stern FBI agent's intensity never slowed.

"They'll give you snacks on the plane. Flash your winning smile, and I'm sure they'll give you double of whatever you want," she said. "Otherwise, you can eat when you get to New Orleans. Wasn't that large supreme pizza enough to tide you over?"

He knew better than to answer, even if he could muster the breath to speak.

He galloped on, keeping up with her speed, wondering how she could manage to talk, run, and breathe at the same time.

"Final instructions," she said when they arrived at the departure gate.

Jim dropped his bags and decided he needed to get in better shape. Soon.

All he could do at that point was listen to her talk.

"You're on the exit row. It's all arranged." She thrust the handful of papers, a boarding pass, and a white business envelope at his broad chest before she continued.

"There's a room reserved at the downtown Drury Hotel on Poydras in your name. I've convinced my superiors that this little expedition is part of the interview process, so they've agreed to send you with a limited credit card to cover necessary expenses. I've added some petty cash for tips. Don't eat it all in one place."

Jim looked at her chiseled face to see if he could tell if she was making some sort of joke, but her face was a poker-faced mask of ice.

She had a deadly serious look that came close to frightening him.

"Officer Smith," she said, "this is the first, last, and only time I'm going to explain myself to you. I'm a profiler. That's who I am. Most of the time I do extensive legwork and research. *Most* of the time I have standard operating procedures. Sometimes, however, I follow gut feelings, intuition, and hunches. In this particular circumstance, every bone in my body is screaming at me that Ed Brackett is up to no good—serious, dangerous no good—and I should put you on a plane to be with Charlie Abbott. That's it. That's all. Call when you get there and leave a message."

The steward at the desk announced that first class passengers and people with small children or who needed extra time could begin boarding the plane.

Jim turned his head to look. When he turned back, Inola Walker was gone.

He'd expected nothing less.

Chapter 30

Brackett found it difficult to remember getting on the train at nine that morning, perhaps because everything, including the trip itself, seemed to be happening in slow motion and viewed from a great distance. Even the passengers seemed unhurried and unperturbed by the easygoing pace of both their fellow travelers and the agreeable Amtrak employees.

He'd never really been in a train station before, nor traveled any length of track on a train. He was pleased that the New Orleans terminal was spacious and clean. To one side was the waiting area for bus riders, and on the other, in the train waiting area, there were matching multiple rows of metal seating.

A gigantic clock hung on the wall as if resting on the silver Amtrak sign.

Over the entrance to the tracks was a brightly colored mural of sorts. He could make out historical references to groups of people who were depicted in Picasso-like fashion. Native Americans,

Aztecs or maybe Incas, Catholic priests in cassocks and nuns in exaggerated black and white habits, French, British, and Spanish soldiers in their respective uniforms, African Americans. A choir of multiracial children with a small angelic being.

He was intrigued and distracted until the time came to board.

Not that he hadn't been looking forward to the trip for the sake of the trip alone.

Any time he heard someone mention trains, he always thought of the scenes from *North by Northwest.* The legendary Cary Grant on a sleeper car. Dining in a formal dining car with linen tablecloths and silver. Or another Hitchcock train favorite, *The Lady Vanishes.*

He chuckled to himself.

I'd like to think I'm pulling that one off, he thought. *I'd call it* The LSU Professor Vanishes. *Let them all puzzle that one out.*

He'd always promised himself a trip, although he'd never imagined that these would be the particular circumstances.

He liked the atmosphere.

For the most part, everyone seemed content to be left alone.

There were a few chatty people—there always are—but since the seats on the train were assigned, they could not seek each other out. There were some curious children, but he discouraged those with a scowl.

Not surprisingly, Brackett found himself seated all alone in the center of the second coach car. He didn't have a full window to himself, but once the train started, he was able to lean his seat back and have a reasonably comfortable view of the scenery.

Just as he thought the train was finally underway, the cars slowed and came to a gradual stop. Brackett's view from his partial window was boring—a slanted concrete embankment with a black chicken wire fence on top. At the base were assorted weeds and discarded trash. Over the top of the wall, he could see the tall heads of palm trees, telephone lines, and various hardwoods towering over the scattered houses below.

With a jolt, the train began to move again, lurching gently forward and picking up speed.

From time to time he could see the bare concrete footprint of a house mixed among the rebuilt and reconditioned homes, a tangible scar from the ravages of Hurricane Katrina. Just outside the dust-coated window, he watched as the concrete walls turned into a grass-green covered levee. The levee that had been breached.

And then they were over water and crossing the gray, choppy waves of Lake Pontchartrain. He tried not to think about the narrow bridge and the tracks below the speeding train, or the two narrow bridges out in the distance and the ant-like traffic that danced back and forth along them.

The train's whistle sounded in muffled announcement and warning as the conductor announced that the lounge car was open for the breakfast service.

Passengers around him rose and made their way toward the back of the car, but he turned away from their laughing faces and closed his tired, swollen eyelids. He had his own life, what was left of it, and he couldn't be bothered, not right now. He was caught between enjoying the leisure of the trip and his anxiety to arrive at his destination and continue the game.

The name of the upcoming stop blared over the intercom, and Brackett inwardly groaned. It was scheduled to be an ambling fourteen-hour trek through the seemingly endless stops, boarding and deboarding the masses one by one and two by two—Slidell,

Picayune, Hattiesburg, Laurel, Meridian, Tuscaloosa, Birmingham, then Anniston just before they reached Atlanta.

There were much faster ways to get to Atlanta and he knew it, but this one still carried the fewest risks to his plan and was the most likely to evade detection.

Those were his only concerns before he laid his head against the back of his seat and drifted into a fitful, restless sleep.

Several hours later, he awoke to the aroma of a kosher hot dog and the fizzling sound of a soda can being opened and poured over a cup of ice. The seat beside him was still vacant, although when he sat up and glanced up and down the aisles, it looked to him as though most of the other seats had been filled.

Slips of paper, most of them white, extended from the edge of the luggage rack above each seat, indicating the passenger's destination. Most had the letters *ATL*. The conductors regularly checked them as they walked up and down at the appointed stops and in between stations to ask for a show of tickets.

The overly friendly female conductor and her cheerful red cap had checked his ticket when he boarded, and he'd been left alone since then. Except for the prattling on the intercom, he was blissfully ignored.

Almost halfway through the trip, he realized that several of the people who had been sitting in the assigned seats across from him had changed. He surmised that while he'd slept, they must have gotten off at one of the numerous stops along the way and had been replaced by other travelers.

Not that he cared, but the fewer people who saw him, the better. No sense in calling attention to himself or getting friendly with someone who might identify him if there was some trouble with the authorities.

The authorities, he thought bitterly. *What a polite word for the FBI thugs who persecuted me and locked me up like some rabid dog. They made it sound as though I've been on vacation and not deprived of everything I love in life—satisfying work, easily manipulated students, chess games, and good food.*

The train crawled to another stop, but this time there was no station. From his window he could see groves of trees and bunches of orange and black daisies dotting the ground. Then came the whir of another train on the parallel tracks, sweeping by outside his window, clicking with a soft roar of passing as the passenger train rocked gently from side to side.

The intercom announced that the train was waiting for traffic as the matter-of-fact voice apologized for the inconvenience caused by the delay.

He reached inside his jacket pocket and retrieved the apple he'd taken from the breakfast bar that morning. There wasn't much there that he could take with him, nor did he want to bother. He'd eaten his fill of scrambled eggs and biscuits before he checked out.

He'd purchased a few more snacks and two bottled waters from the vending machines at the station, placing them in the top of his duffle bag, not knowing how much or what kind of food to expect on the train.

The apple would suffice for the moment, and then he would sleep.

There was time. There was so much time.

It was only three forty-five in the afternoon, and Atlanta was still hours and hours away.

Chapter 31

After supper, Marjorie took Jane upstairs for yet another costume fitting before her nightly bath and story time. As was their routine, Thomas helped his wife wash and dry the dishes, cleaning the kitchen together in congenial silence.

Tonight instead of going to the den to sit together and talk when they finished, he insisted that Cora go into her office and call Charlie about Brackett's phone call.

"Charlie's the detective," Thomas said more calmly than he felt. "Ask him if he thinks this professor is a real danger to your safety. One way or another, he needs to know that you got a phone call this afternoon on your office phone."

"I hadn't thought about that," Cora admitted. "Brackett must know where I am."

That's all I've been thinking about since you told me he called, Thomas thought. *The idea that a man like Ed Brackett might come to our home is truly terrifying.*

"Just ask Charlie what he thinks," Thomas said instead. "He's the professional. I'll be upstairs waiting when you're done."

Charlie answered his cell phone immediately.

"Hello, Cora," he said, smacking his chewing gum in her ear. "It's almost seven o'clock. Elvira and I were just about to sit down to a canned chili-cheese supper with extra cheddar and crackers. Did you nap and have a dream in the middle of the day?"

"Not exactly," she said. "Ed Brackett called me on the office line."

The sound of smacking stopped.

"Let me turn off the stove and get my notebook," he said. "Hang on."

She could hear him put down the phone, a gentle complaining whine coming from the Plott hound in the background, and she waited patiently until he came back.

"What did he say to you?" Charlie flipped to a blank page in his notebook. "Be specific."

"Well," she began, "the whole conversation was confusing, mainly references to chess. I didn't understand most of it."

"That's not surprising. He lives and breathes chess. Not much else to think about during his prison stint, and who knows how many other inmates would be interested in carrying on chess conversations."

"But why tell me things I won't understand? It almost sounded like code."

"Brackett enjoys playing games. He likes feeling smarter than other people."

Charlie sat down on the sofa, and Elvira climbed up to snuggle closer to him, pressing herself against his legs to keep him from moving. Seventy pounds of dog was considerable incentive to stay put. Charlie gave her ears a playful tug with one hand while he took notes with the other.

"What exactly did he say about chess?"

"He said I was a little bishop—a white one."

"Interesting." Charlie spit his gum into the foil wrapper and tossed it artfully into the trash can across the room. "The white bishop represents the church, and it's the third most powerful piece on the board, after the king and queen."

"Really? I still don't understand."

"Maybe you weren't supposed to," he said. "Did he talk about anything else?"

"Well, he asked me my professional opinion of Halloween celebrations."

"Halloween," he repeated. "That's odd, but then, it *is* October. Maybe he just wanted to keep you talking for some reason."

She couldn't argue with Charlie's logic, but her training and intuition insisted that there had to be a deeper, darker meaning.

She had no idea why, but Charlie's words gave her an opening to say what had been on her mind off and on for some time.

"Has it ever occurred to you that over the last year we've had mysteries centered around holidays?" she said. "Christmas, Easter . . ."

"I'm flattered you think my birthday is a holiday."

"Be serious, Charlie. Have you noticed?"

She could hear the almost imperceptible rustling of paper and knew he was putting in another piece of gum.

"There's a holiday in almost every month, Cora."

Her suspicions were confirmed when the soft popping sounds began in her ear.

"The months that don't have holidays, well, someone simply makes up one or two or three so they can say there's a holiday. The greeting card companies, florists, and jewelers love it. People like to celebrate. There's always more stress and conflict around those times of the year. Do you have a point?"

"No," she admitted. "Just an observation."

"For the time being, can we try to stick to the actual subject?" He struggled to keep the irritation out of his tone. The weight of Elvira's body was cutting off the circulation in his feet, and despite the fact that he'd had two lunches he was getting hungry. "Did Brackett say anything else about chess?"

"Not really. He said he was tired and setting the pieces up for a match tomorrow." She paused, remembering. "Oh, and he also said something confusing about a Halloween gambit."

There was a long pause and Cora could hear Charlie's measured breathing, the steady, soft smack of his chewing gum matching the inhaling and exhaling.

"What are you thinking?" she said. "Do you have any idea what he means to do?"

"That's the real question, isn't it?" he said. "Are you sure that's what he said? A gambit is a plan for an opening move, but what it has to do with Halloween, I don't know. I don't know if *anyone* has an idea what he intends to do, I mean, other than your preacher friend and those attorneys Brackett's hired to come after your reputation."

Cora had nothing else to say.

Charlie looked down into the dark brown eyes of his Plott hound.

"I'm in town for another day or two," he said. "Elvira insists. Call when you have a dream or Brackett gets back in touch. Other than that, maybe Thomas can help you plan some legal maneuvers."

Cora turned off her cell phone and laid it on a charger beside the desk.

Then she went upstairs to see if Marjorie had already read Jane a bedtime story.

The housekeeper hadn't. She and Jane had been arranging the new Eric Carle books on the bookcase in the little girl's room, so Cora joined them.

An hour later she changed into an oversized T-shirt and leggings to climb into bed beside her long-suffering husband.

"Jane's finally asleep," she said. "I talked to Charlie and told him what Brackett said. He said to call if I had another dream or Brackett called again tomorrow."

"Is that all?" Thomas asked, slightly miffed. "No concern for your safety?"

Cora gave him a condescending smile.

"I thought you said to talk to the professional," she said. "He said to talk to *you* about lawsuits and lawyers."

Her husband mumbled something under his breath she couldn't hear, but she had a pretty good notion it was about Charlie and that it wasn't repeatable.

"Thomas," she said, reaching for the lamp beside her bed. "It's early, but I'm tired and going to sleep. Can we talk about this in the morning?"

She could tell by his stony silence that something was wrong.

"Okay," she said, struggling to sit up again. "I'm listening. What's bothering you?"

"Aren't you going to look at the journal transcription?"

He was staring across her at the unopened manila envelope on the nightstand by her side of the bed.

"I thought you'd want to begin reading."

She followed his gaze and realized that she'd deeply hurt his feelings. Without another word, Cora pushed back the covers and slid off the mattress, making her way around the foot of the bed and coming to stand on the opposite side.

She took her husband's hands in hers.

"I'm sorry, Thomas," she said. "I apologize. I've been insensitive. The journal is one of the most precious gifts anyone has ever given me. I cannot begin to tell you how much I love and appreciate you for all the effort it took for you to get it."

"Cora," he began, "I didn't mean to criticize—"

"Hush, Thomas," she said, pressing an index finger against his lips. "Let me finish, please."

He kissed the tip of her finger and leaned back into the pillows.

"You're going to Savannah tomorrow, and I'm certainly not complaining," she said softly. "I understand why. It's important to talk to the judge face-to-face about how to get Jane a birth certificate and legally adopt her."

"That's the only reason I'd go," he said, his grip on her tightening. "I wouldn't go if it wasn't absolutely necessary. I don't want to leave you."

"I know," she said, "but do you realize that in all our years of marriage, we've never spent the night apart?"

He nodded. He hadn't stopped thinking about it all afternoon, especially after the call from Brackett.

At first he felt ridiculously reassured because Charlie was in town. Charlie would know what to do if something happened. But now from what Cora said, Charlie didn't seem to care that she might be in danger. Charlie didn't even *believe* there was a danger.

He hadn't felt so angry or so conflicted in years.

"Thomas." She interrupted his thoughts as though she knew

exactly what he was thinking. "I won't be alone. Marjorie and Jane will be here. I'm not afraid. Brackett wouldn't dare come to the house. He's full of hot air and empty threats. He's words, Thomas. Just nasty words. I am going to miss having you beside me. I want very much to read the journal, but I'm saving it for tomorrow night. If you won't be here, at least I can take my mind off missing you by reading. You need to know that the whole time you're gone I'll be thinking about what a precious gift it is to be married to you and have the opportunity to adopt Jane. Do you understand?"

He kissed the top of her head and tried to swallow the lump that was threatening to close his throat.

"And what will I be reading so I don't miss you?" he said, rubbing his chin against her forehead. "Any suggestions, counselor?"

"Oh, I'm sure Judge Mayer will have some legal mumbo-jumbo forms to keep you busy—or at least occupied until you fall asleep," she said, laying her head on his shoulder. "And I'll take notes to share with you when you get back. There's no telling what secrets Jane's great-grandmother kept in that journal that can help us adopt Jane."

Chapter 32

Somewhere just north of Mobile, Alabama, the Amtrak Crescent sped over the train tracks into the gathering night toward Peachtree Station in Atlanta.

Ed Brackett tucked his prepaid cell phone in the front pocket of his lightweight hoodie and readjusted his substantial form into the window seat. He turned off his reading light and closed the curtains before he slid his duffle bag under his feet, using his worn backpack for a lumpy pillow.

For a long time, until the gathering darkness turned the trees and passing scenery into ominous black outlines, the former professor stared out at the landscape and let his mind wander, enjoying the expansive view and replaying classic chess games in his mind.

After the years of confinement, he was grudgingly grateful for the view from the window, grateful for the clean air, grateful for the snacks he'd brought along—but more than anything else, he was thankful he'd planned ahead for this particular day.

The day the ultimate chess match finally began with an unsuspecting Cora Stone.

Then, reluctantly, he drifted into a fitful sleep, an elegantly carved white marble bishop clutched in his sweaty palm.

Chapter 33

The Third Day: Wednesday

Cora turned from her grandmother's empty sink and looked around the room for James, but the old preacher wasn't there.

His usual ladder-back chair was empty, pushed completely under the edge of the plaid oilcloth, and his translucent mug was turned up-side down in the drying rack beside a still-damp rose-handled spoon.

It was as though he'd been there already, had his coffee, and left without waiting to talk to her.

Her own floral designed cup was resting serenely in its place on the countertop beside the cold stove. Beside it was a cup she'd never seen before. A metal cup that reminded her of camping and the outdoors—rough and battered, well-used but clean.

Whose cup is this? she thought absently. *What's it doing in the kitchen? Am I expecting someone? Who? What am I expected to do?*

There was no water in the kettle on the stove and no coffee grounds, either fresh or used, in the metal basket of the coffee pot.

The muted sunlight coming through the windows gave no hint

of whether it was morning, noon, or evening.

The rocking chair was empty and motionless.

Everything was clean and waiting. But waiting for what?

If there's a message, she thought, *it needs to be a little clearer than a cold stove, an empty chair, and a metal cup.*

As her eyes searched the kitchen for anything else that might be odd or out of the ordinary, her attention returned to the table, and she saw something she hadn't seen before.

At her place at the table was a sheet of plain stationery, the edge tucked under the pine cone sugar bowl.

Moving closer, she could see that it was embossed across the top edge with a scrollwork pattern, and on it was written what appeared to be a single-column list.

Cora picked it up and recognized the spidery script.

Her grandmother's distinctive calligraphy, fountain pen ink dark against the stark white of what felt like expensive cotton parchment.

What do the cup and the note from my grandmother have in common? Have James and Gramma been here and gone? Are they avoiding me?

Cora went back to the paper in her hand.

The list was brief and to the point, a delicate box drawn to the left of each line.

She could almost hear her grandmother's voice reading with her as she read the list aloud.

☐ *Send Charlie home*

☐ *Remember the candy bar*

☐ *Find the girl*

☐ *Let Marjorie take Jane*

☐ *Call Andrew Evans*

There was a postscript at the bottom, written not in her

grandmother's hand but in the preacher's distinctive cursive: *Breathe, dear heart. You aren't the only one with dreams.*

An unexpected tremor shook the wooden floor under the linoleum, and for a split second Cora thought she heard a clap of thunder or what might have been a rifle shot in the distance.

Where is everyone, she thought, *and why am I all alone?*

Then she was awake, scrambling for her notebook while the items on the cryptic to-do list were still fresh on her mind.

Chapter 34

Thomas got up before Marjorie or Jane and was waiting when Cora padded into the kitchen for her now-customary cup of herbal tea.

"You're up early," Cora said, wrapping her robe around herself as best she could against the early morning chill. "I didn't think I woke you when I got up last night."

"You didn't," he said, placing a cup of tea in front of her at the island. "I've been thinking about what's going to happen this afternoon when I go to Savannah."

"Oh," she said, sipping at the tea. "Do you want me to call Lisa in Atlanta and ask if I can come with you? Marjorie can stay with Jane."

"We already decided the trip wouldn't be the best for you or the baby," he said, taking his own seat beside her. "You're reading the journal tonight, and I'm going to be busy with the judge, Maclin, and the paralegals. That's not what I'm thinking about."

"Oh," she said again. She could clearly read the concern on his face.

"Do you know how long Charlie is staying in Balfour?"

"No," she admitted, thinking about the dream list. "I'll probably talk to him today. Why do you ask?"

"Just thinking," he said.

She waited for him to explain, but he didn't.

"I'm going upstairs to get ready for work," he said. "I'll come home after lunch and finish packing for the trip."

"Okay," she said, confused. "You aren't leaving until after lunch? I thought you might get an early start."

"I've got plenty of time," he assured her. "There are a couple of things I need to do first."

He rose and kissed her lightly on the forehead.

"Don't fret," he said. "Just take care of yourself and the baby. Won't take me long to do what I need to do this morning, then I'll have a bite of lunch and be on my way."

"You're acting rather oddly," she said. "Do you realize that?"

"These are odd times."

He took his breakfast dishes and cup to the sink and rinsed them as Marjorie came down the hallway, a laughing Jane in her wake.

"See you after lunch," he said. "I'll talk to you then."

And he was gone before Cora could ask any of the dozen questions she had on her mind.

Chapter 35

Susan had pulled into a parking space behind the law office when she saw the postman Quincy striding toward her, a book-sized parcel in his hand.

"Another special delivery," he announced in his crusty voice. "Need you to sign for this one too."

The legal assistant got out of the car and gathered up her purse.

Thomas had already parked in his usual spot, and she was feeling a little frazzled since she'd hoped to get there before he did at least once this week. But in another act of defiance, her Siamese had tried to escape to be with his squirrel friends, and she had to resort to extreme measures to lure him back inside—yet another can of expensive albacore tuna.

"Good morning to you too," she said, self-conscious at the fishy smell of her hands and wondering if the postman could smell the pungent aroma too. "I see your fellow postal workers are still out with their allergies."

Quincy tugged down his official cap and made a noise of disgust, his nose twitching as he thrust his pen at her, much like an aged wizard with a magic wand.

"Follow me," she said, ignoring his grumpy mood and his outstretched arm. "I need a minute to get settled and let Thomas know I'm here, please."

"Oh, all right," Quincy said, his patience stretching to the point of evaporation, "but I want that cold water you offered me yesterday."

Thomas swiveled his chair to face the inner door when he heard his legal assistant arrive, but he didn't get up. He was reorganizing the paperwork he needed to take with him to Savannah, and his desk was covered with sticky notes and half-filled manila folders.

He needed to hurry to get to Sam's before the time he'd set with Charlie.

"Hello, Susan," he called. "Hello there, Quincy. Another special delivery? From where?"

She took a pen from her desk and the package from the crotchety postman.

"Looks like New Orleans," she called back, signing the return receipt. "Water's in the refrigerator, Quincy. Get one from the top shelf, they're cooler."

Susan used the letter opener to slit the edges of the tape on the box, lifting the flaps carefully. She had no idea what she expected to find, but the standard white priority box looked harmless enough and she wasn't much for hesitation, especially not when she was already late starting her day.

"New Orleans?" Thomas called back. "Did you order something for decorating?"

"No," she said loudly. "Come in here, please. This is the strangest delivery I've ever seen. There must be some mistake."

Thomas finally got out of his chair.

"What's the matter?" he said. "What's in the box?"

Susan held out her cupped hands in answer.

Thomas could see three chess pieces, from different sets but all white. He wasn't quite sure from where he stood, but they looked like pawn, a bishop, and a knight.

"Well, if that doesn't beat all," Quincy said, twisting off the cap of the water bottle and poking his head over Susan's shoulder. "It's not even a full set. Who does that?"

"I agree," Susan said. "Only three pieces. That's crazy."

"Is there a note inside?" Quincy asked.

Thomas picked up the box, flipping the container over to inspect the neatly printed shipping label as a plain white terry washcloth fell to the floor.

"There's no name," Quincy observed, pointing.

"I thought you were busy," Susan said dryly. "Don't you have deliveries?"

"Taking a break," the postman retorted. "Besides, I'm curious. Only people I know from New Orleans are Charlie and Vicki the florist—do they play chess?"

"Charlie does," Thomas muttered under his breath, a scowl darkening his face.

Cora said Brackett talked to her about chess. Are these from him? Does that mean he's in New Orleans? This settles it. I can't go to Savannah without talking to Charlie.

"Boss?" Susan said as she watched the color ebb and flow from her employer's face, the crow's feet around his eyes deepening. "Are you okay?"

"I'm just puzzled," he reassured her, shaking the washcloth to see if there might be anything else wrapped inside. "There's probably a perfectly reasonable explanation."

"Seriously, boss." Her voice had taken on a sharp tone of sarcasm as she rolled the pieces between the palms of her hands. "You are a terrible liar. I can get Ben Taylor on the phone if you don't want to call him. This certainly qualifies as suspicious."

The lawyer reached over and scooped the chess pieces out of his legal assistant's hands, clicking them together before putting them in a neat triangle on the far corner of her desk.

"No, leave them right there where we can find them later," he said, turning back into his office and thinking about Brackett's phone call. "I'm sure it's nothing important, but all the same you should take the rest of the day off and I'll lock up. No reason for you to be here. I've got a meeting this morning, and I'm leaving for Savannah after lunch."

"You heard him," Susan said, affectionately turning the postman around by his broad shoulders and giving him a gentle push. "Take the water with you so I can finish up before my boss leaves. I hope your new hires get back to work soon. Have a good day."

"Have a day yourself," Quincy said, pocketing the receipt and re-capping the bottle, hitching the mail bag up. "I know when I'm not wanted, but if you ask me, I'd call the Chief. People who don't put their names on packages can't be trusted—and that's the truth."

Chapter 36

Cora took her morning tea into her office and sat down at her desk, rereading the dream list for the umpteenth time since Thomas left for work.

Marjorie and Jane had decided to decorate the dozen small pumpkins from their shopping expedition and had commandeered the kitchen island, which was littered with construction paper, markers, school scissors, white glue, and glitter.

Jane had balked determinedly at cutting the tiny gourds, so knives and any sort of cutters were out of the question. Marjorie was disinclined to argue.

Solomon sat under Jane's stool, content with batting away the various pieces of colored paper as they fell to the floor.

Cora left her office door open so she could hear the muffled laughter and remind herself that the world was still turning in spite of Brackett's return to her life.

The list seemed straightforward enough, even if she had no idea what it meant.

Sending Charlie back to New Orleans shouldn't be a problem, but telling him to find a nameless girl and a candy bar just might be. Especially since she had no other clues to offer him.

Sending Jane with Marjorie seemed even more complicated.

Send her where? And why? Cora pondered. *And when? After I've done the first three items or at the same time? Will I know when the time is right?*

And what in the world was she supposed to say to Andrew Evans? She hadn't spoken to him in almost a year. Not since Steve Wilton's murder.

The postscript concerned her most of all.

What could that possibly mean? Someone with dreams like her own? Who could that possibly be?

A tension headache was beginning at the base of her neck, and the baby rolled restlessly inside.

And those thoughts brought her right back to Charlie, chess, and candy bars.

She knew that whether she understood or not, she needed to call Charlie. She didn't expect him to help with any of her confusion, but she called anyway. Charlie answered immediately.

He'd just hung up from a cryptic conversation with Thomas and the cell phone was still warm in his hand.

"Hello, Cora," he said. "Had a dream?"

"Yes," she said, slightly surprised. "You're awfully upbeat."

"I've got an early lunch meeting at ten thirty," he said. He wondered if she knew Thomas had just called, and decided not to bring it up. It wasn't his place. "Then I'm spending the rest of the afternoon taking a hike with Elvira and going back to New Orleans in the morning. What do I need to know?"

"Well, there were three clues specifically about you," Cora began, hesitating. "I'm supposed to remind you about the candy bar."

Charlie scratched his unshaven chin thoughtfully.

"Can't help you there."

"And then there's a girl you're supposed to find."

"Strike two," he said. "And the third item on your list?"

He'd already said he was packing and going home, so she didn't think that telling him he needed to leave was relevant. She was feeling foolish for calling him at all, but she decided she should follow all the instructions.

"Well, for some reason, you're supposed to leave Balfour," she said. "I know you said you were going, but the dream was specific. I'm supposed to tell you to go."

"Haven't your dreams always asked me to do something?" Charlie said, his detective senses tingling unpleasantly. "Why would they suddenly tell me to go away? It doesn't make sense."

"I don't know why," she said. "Maybe this time is different."

"Well, I'm going to agree with you," he said. "This time is certainly different. And I don't like it. I don't like it one little bit."

And he hung up.

Cora tucked her dream notebook back into the drawer of her desk, cradled her unborn child with the palms of her hands, and waddled upstairs to shower.

Chapter 37

Andrew Evans was already irritated when he emerged from the financial meeting with the deacons, even before he discovered what had happened with his wife.

He saw Ginny, pale-faced and unable to finish her sandwich, sitting at the table in the break room. Alice and Donna were clucking over her like brooding mother hens.

It was obvious that something was wrong.

He began by chastising the two secretaries for not immediately getting him out of the meeting. Then he gave his wife a perfunctory pat on the shoulder, assuring himself that she was capable of walking, before he took her arm possessively and helped her up and out to his car.

"Your car will be fine overnight in the church parking lot," he said firmly. "You'll be getting off your feet and into bed for a rest."

"Yes, dear," she said weakly, leaning on him. "I suppose I did overdo things just a bit."

"I'll bring by some homemade chicken soup later," Alice said, picking up Ginny's purse from the table and trotting behind them out to the parking lot. "I keep a batch in the freezer for times like this. And I can have AJ bring the car over to your house if you'll leave the keys."

"Thank you," Ginny said. "You can get them out of my purse. Right there on top. I hate to be such a bother."

"No bother," Donna said, close behind the three and feeling left out. "I can bake some fresh yeast rolls and make a garden salad."

"You're both very kind," Ginny said. "Andy and I appreciate you."

"Yes," the preacher said, his focus clearly on his wife. "Thank you."

But even after the evening meal of soup, hot rolls, and salad, a long warm bath, and unburdening her conscience with the truth about the automobile accident, Ginny still slept fitfully through the night, tossing and turning.

Andrew, afraid his own restless dreams would disturb what little sleep she might have, chose to spend the night awake in the armchair in the corner of their bedroom, reading his Bible, making notes for Sunday's sermon on his yellow legal pad, and keeping watch over his wife.

A little after eight thirty, he woke her with a cup of hot tea and buttered toast.

"Time for your medications," he said gently. "Have a little something to eat. How do you feel?"

"Weak," she said, struggling up on one elbow while he put down the tray and adjusted the pillows at her back. "I'm just a little sore all over."

"I don't doubt it," he said. "I've already called Donna. I'm spending the day at home with you. I put a call in to your doctor's office in Griffith."

"Oh, Andy!" she said. "You're making such a fuss."

"We'll see if the doctor thinks so," he retorted calmly. "I called Jack too."

"I don't need Jack standing over me," she said. "You're doing an excellent job all by yourself."

"I called him to see if he could find a body shop that does repairs in Griffith," he said. "Although if you insist on scaring me like you did yesterday, I might just ask him to help me keep tabs on you."

"Repairs for my car?" she said, puzzled.

"Yes," he said. "Since you won't be driving for a couple days, it seemed like a good time to put it in the shop. Jack's going to ask around at that coffee shop where he works to find a reputable place. Alice left a message on my cell phone that AJ will bring it by later this morning and leave the keys in the mailbox."

"That's very thoughtful of you, dear."

The phone rang in the living room.

"That's probably your doctor's office," he explained. "I told them to call the home number. Eat your toast. I'll be right back."

A few minutes later he came in to take her empty plate and cup.

"I'll make more tea for you," he said. "The nurse said you should stay in bed and see how you feel tomorrow. If you're still having pain, we'll call and they can see you."

"Sounds practical," she said, settling back and smoothing the blankets at her waist before pulling them up under her aching arms.

"Aren't you going to argue with me?" he asked suspiciously.

"No, dear," she said. "Another cup of tea with honey would

be lovely. I *would* like for you to pull the curtains so there's some sunshine in here though."

He did as she asked.

"Ginny," he said when he returned with a second cup of tea, "I'm worried about you."

"I know, dear," she said softly. "I can tell."

Chapter 38

Thomas straightened his favorite blue tie, pulling at the knot, wondering if Cora would say he was subconsciously feeling strangled by his fear. No, fear was not the right word for what he felt. He didn't know exactly how to describe it, but the emotion was darn uncomfortable.

He knew he shouldn't have called Charlie to schedule a meeting without telling Cora, but he knew she would have objected and he didn't want to argue.

His awkward anticipation grew more and more by the minute as he waited for his wife's ex-husband to arrive, and he was beginning to wonder if he would be able to swallow, let alone eat. He still felt confident about asking Charlie to meet him, and the appearance of the chess pieces in his office only added to his certainty. Thomas was not a worrier by nature.

Instead, the lawyer let his mind drift, hoping to find a topic with less emotional baggage to occupy his mind until Charlie arrived. He knew he was early, but then Charlie was always punctual too.

They'd often joked about which one was the more compulsive about time, back in a time when they were able to joke with each other.

He recognized four women from the Emmanuel choir at a front window booth, and he supposed it was some sort of celebration. There were small gift bags with pastel tissue paper stuffed around the tops and tied with ribbons, and the table itself was littered with salad bowls, bread baskets, napkins, Mason jars of tea, and silverware.

The women were chatting together, as good friends do, and Thomas envied their easy comradery. He'd had precious few friendships like that, especially after he and Charlie graduated and grew apart.

But those thoughts brought him back to confusing feelings about Charlie, so he concentrated instead on his heavily sweetened coffee and Sam's loitering interest.

On the other hand, Charlie's entrance was clear and full of purpose. He walked directly to the Stone booth, which had been assigned to every Thomas Stone since the first one had been seated there by Samuel Simmons. The unlabeled booth was as well-known and well-respected in the town of Balfour, Georgia, as the Stone family itself.

The importance of this royal summons, as it were, from Thomas was not lost on Charlie. Something earth-shattering was happening, because, except for the necessity of speaking about Cora's dreams, never in the years of Cora's marriage to Thomas had Thomas spoken to him one-on-one in a social situation.

Especially not one that required sharing a meal together.

During the most recent investigations, they'd met over business in the office, the courthouse, or the police station, once here in Sam's, even a crime scene that qualified as neutral ground. The two had a grudging mutual respect, but there was absolutely no sign of friendship, no fraternal feelings. Except for the explosive confrontation in Cora's hallway about a hidden heirloom, there had been no outward expression of emotion in their meetings.

The boyhood friendship they had shared was a distant memory, and, since Cora came into their lives, an uncomfortable one at that.

As Charlie made determined strides toward the booth where Thomas sat, it was difficult for Sam not to notice the differences between the two men she had known since high school.

Thomas was mature, classically handsome, and clean cut.

Charlie exuded shaggy boyish charm.

Sam noticed the sharp juxtaposition.

Thomas wore an immaculately tailored black suit, starched white shirt with plain silver cuff links, silk tie, and highly polished black shoes. The platinum wedding band on his left hand, the only jewelry he owned other than the cuff links, was simple and had belonged to his grandfather.

Charlie wore faded jeans and an untucked, unbuttoned red plaid shirt, exposing the mildly inappropriate logo of the T-shirt beneath. The sleeves of the outer shirt, in deference to the heat, were carelessly rolled to his elbows. His worn sneakers gave little warning of his approach.

What Sam couldn't see was that around his neck, invisible to anyone except Elvira, hung a sturdy gold chain on which he wore his own simple gold wedding ring. He'd taken it from his finger the day Lonora died and bought a chain the next day.

It hurt to wear it, but it hurt too much to leave it behind when he traveled, and he refused to examine his feelings too deeply about the reasons why.

Sam intercepted the scowling detective beside the table before he could sit down. She was carrying a Mason jar of sweet tea, the brim crowded with lemon slices, and two sets of silverware rolled in white linen napkins.

"Caesar salad, no croutons, and a double cheeseburger, medium rare with extra bacon," she announced, sliding the tea in Charlie's place. "I'll get more coffee, Thomas."

She turned without expecting confirmation and went into the kitchen. Charlie perched himself on the edge of the seat, directly across from the lawyer, glaring openly as he surveyed the room with calm calculation before he spoke.

"I'm leaving for New Orleans in the morning," the detective said flatly. "I thought that would make you happy. Exactly what else do you want?"

"Straight to the point," Thomas said, picking up his glass of water to moisten his dry mouth. He was a powerful adversary in the courtroom, but his relationship with Cora was personal and private. Involving Charlie in what he felt was his family business was almost more than he could stomach.

Charlie flipped the lemon slices into the tea, sloshing ice over the top onto the table, and picked up the jar to take a swallow only to put it down again without drinking.

"Speechless?" The detective raised his eyebrows sarcastically. "This has got to be a first."

Thomas cleared his throat, took another swallow of liquid, and summoned all his will to speak.

An image of Cora flashed through his mind, but he ignored the warning.

"I don't know how to begin," Thomas admitted.

"That is painfully obvious."

"Could you be a little less—"

"A little less *what*?" Charlie leaned back, crossing his arms defiantly, impatiently. "Is that what you want, Thomas? Less of *me*?"

Thomas sighed. This was going to be as difficult as he'd imagined. Charlie had never been an easy person to reason with, and the lawyer was sadly out of practice.

"What I want, Charlie, is *more* of you, if that is possible."

Charlie stifled a snort.

"Are you crazy? What does that even mean?"

"Maybe you should eat the cheeseburger first before we talk."

Charlie thrust his elbows firmly onto the table and leaned forward.

"Maybe you should tell me why I'm here."

Thomas opened his mouth, but Charlie bombarded him with questions instead, rapid fire and with no particular order or logic.

"Is it Cora? The dreams? The baby? Is Jane okay? Marjorie? Have you done something stupid and you don't know how to tell your wife?"

"No."

"Do you think *I've* done something stupid and I need to talk to your wife?" Charlie stopped abruptly. "Don't sit like a mute statue—I want answers."

"We don't need to play twenty questions," Thomas said, twisting his wedding ring absently. "Asking you for a favor is awkward."

"Is *that* what this is about? A favor? For you or for Cora?"

Sam appeared from the kitchen, effectively silencing the two men as she placed the filled plates in front of them. She backed away quickly, returning with a steaming pot of coffee that she gingerly placed on the table before hastily retreating to her observation post at the cash register.

Thomas bowed his head in a quick prayer, his lips moving silently while Charlie continued to stare, his elbows firmly planted at the edge of the table.

When Thomas looked up, Charlie's expression was stern, the irises of his eyes taken over by his dark pupils, his teeth clenched.

"Are you going to eat?" Thomas picked up his fork and poked at the cucumber slices and cherry tomatoes in the bowl, redistributing the dressing.

"When I see what you have to say I'll decide if I'm hungry." Charlie looked with disgust at the salad. "You go ahead and chow down on your rabbit food, though."

Thomas put his fork back down on the table.

"Okay," he said, his voice halting and hesitating. "I'm going to Savannah for a couple of days, and I need someone to take care of Cora. I want you to promise me you'll stay in Balfour until I get back and keep an eye on her."

"What?" Charlie said sharply. "Has something happened that I don't know about?"

"No, nothing's happened," Thomas said. "I can't believe I'm asking you for a favor, but I thought *you* at least would understand. I don't like leaving Cora alone."

He wanted to say *at a time like this*—but now, hearing himself say the words, he didn't know how to back up the conversation. He'd put his foot determinedly into his mouth, and there was no way to move except forward.

Charlie sensed his old friend's hesitation and embarrassment. He'd never seen Thomas like this before, and it made him uncomfortable and irritated. Why did the first time Thomas asked for a favor have to involve his own pregnant ex-wife? This was getting out of hand, and he was overfull of drama already.

"I'm not staying around to babysit," Charlie shot back.

I don't need this, he thought. *Cora telling me to leave. Thomas telling me to stay. Agent Walker demanding that I be at her beck and call. Why am I the first one everybody calls and the last one anybody listens to?*

This was exactly the reaction that Thomas should have anticipated, if he'd been thinking more like a lawyer and less like a worried expectant father.

"Charlie—" he began in his best persuasive voice, but Charlie had stopped listening.

"I don't hear from you in years. We don't talk, and we aren't friends, and I won't pretend to be back in high school!"

Charlie's voice had risen, attracting the attention of the other restaurant patrons, but he didn't seem to care. Sam lingered by the cash register, shifting from one foot to the other nervously, while Bill's bandana-covered head poked out from the edge of the kitchen door to investigate the commotion.

"Come on, Thomas!" the detective continued sarcastically. "What do you think is going to happen that Cora can't handle? Lawyers? Lawsuits? Have you even thought about how having me at her elbow would make *her* feel?"

The women at the front booth looked discreetly out the window, clearly uneasy at the outburst from the back of the restaurant—but Charlie wasn't finished with his tirade.

"I respect her. I refuse to go behind her back or treat her like a child," he continued, leaning across the table and clenching his fists. "You two need to get on the same page. She asked me to leave. She told me that's what *she* wants."

Charlie stopped at last to take a breath, still too agitated to let Thomas speak. He remembered his last conversation with Cora, where she had insisted he leave town because of her dream.

"Look, I'm done arguing with you, and I'm not the least bit hungry." He shoved the plate violently away toward the coffee pot, the hot black liquid sloshing wildly onto the tabletop, and stood up. "If you can't handle a case of nervous Nellies, find someone else who can—anyone else. Just not me."

Thomas grabbed his napkin from his lap, reaching out to steady the pot, and let the other man storm away without trying to stop him.

Within seconds, Sam appeared at the booth, tossing a dish towel into the puddle with one hand, the other hand holding two large Styrofoam to-go boxes.

"That went well," she said with artificial cheerfulness, reaching across the lawyer to mop at the mess and prevent further damage. "I'll box up the food."

"Sam"—Thomas threw up his hands in exasperation, pulling back to get out of her way—"you know Charlie, and you know I'm as much to blame as he is. I should have known better. I don't want to talk about it, and I can do without your attempt at humor right now."

She shrugged, scooping and sliding the untouched food efficiently into the two cartons and snapping the tops closed. She slid them into a plastic bag, tying the top.

"Sorry, Thomas," she apologized. For the first time in a long time, she was feeling uncomfortable with the behavior of her patrons. This was not the kind of gossip she'd wanted. Too truthful. Too deep and painful. Too many secrets exposed.

She searched for some way to lighten the mood as Thomas reached for his wallet.

"Don't bother." She waved his hand away. "Lunch is on the house."

She gestured around the room at the whispering covey of female customers at the front window, dropping her voice to a conspiratorial whisper. "See those women? When word gets out that you and Charlie had a fight in here, I won't have an empty table for the rest of the week."

A cavernous crease appeared in his forehead, and the lines rippled in his jaw.

"Don't," he growled, taking out two twenty-dollar bills and slapping them deliberately on the table before he pushed her aside to stand.

For a moment he was back in high school—defending Charlie's behavior and befriending the lonely fifteen-year-old orphan trouble-maker. Giving up his time and his energy to help a rebellious, angry boy fit in and find a place.

And this was the thanks he got for all he'd done. This was the repayment for his friendship over the years. He'd asked for one favor. Asking Charlie to stick around a few days was hardly an imposition—Charlie had a place to stay and plenty he could do in the meantime.

Thomas didn't understand. He didn't want to understand.

Sam blushed to the roots of her ponytail, unpleasant guilt increasing under the harsh rebuke. She could almost hear her grandfather's cautioning: *Be careful what you wish for, Sam. The angels are taking notes.*

Thomas strode out the front door without looking back, leaving the two unfinished lunches behind.

Chapter 39

By midafternoon, the Deborah's Daughter's grapevine was ablaze with the latest two newsworthy incidents in Balfour—Ginny's enforced bedrest and the argument at Sam's restaurant between Thomas and Charlie.

Everyone had an opinion about one or the other, and most had strong opinions about both. Katy initiated a list of those willing to provide meals for the preacher and his wife for the next week or so, and Darcie offered to send over one of her latest hires to help with the housework and laundry. Vicki made up a vase of Ginny's favorite flowers and Allison delivered them, and there was a rush on Henson's Pharmacy to purchase get-well cards.

The argument produced a totally different response.

Speculation swirled around the police department about whether or not Charlie would ever return to Balfour after the fiasco, with Burton taking side bets and the Chief refusing to get involved. Without Jim Smith to come to his defense, the talk was almost exclusively negative against the rogue detective.

The women who had witnessed the incident also took the side of the respected lawyer, finding Charlie's outburst uncalled for and bewildering. After the men left, they found Sam's steadfast unwillingness to comment on the situation equally astonishing and unlike the normally unabashed busybody.

Word spread so quickly that by the time Thomas reached home a little after noon to pack for his trip, an anxious Marjorie met him at the front door.

"I heard what happened," the housekeeper said, pulling him aside into the front waiting area. "As far as I know, Cora doesn't know. Yet."

"And you think I should tell her," he said. "Where is she?"

"Upstairs lying down," Marjorie said. "She said she wasn't hungry. That's the third time this week. The time's getting close, and she's not sleeping well—especially with the dreams and all."

Thomas knew she didn't mean to sound accusatory, but she did.

He was painfully aware that his confrontation with Charlie had added the "and all" to that sentence.

He put his briefcase on the floor and keys on the side table and went up the staircase, opening the door as quietly as he could and tiptoeing inside their bedroom.

The curtains were pulled tightly against the afternoon sun, and the air held the crisp coolness of the coming fall weather.

Cora was propped against a wall of pillows on her side of the bed, her eyes closed, her dark hair spread across the snow-white pillow. Beneath the lightweight cotton blanket, her torso was rising and falling in the steady rhythm of sleep.

Thomas went into the walk-in closet and closed the door while he finished his packing. When he came out again, Cora was awake.

"How are you feeling?" he said. "I was trying not to disturb you."

"Thomas," she said, "you were acting very strangely this morning. How are *you* feeling? Please don't be worried about me."

He put the suitcase on the floor and draped his suit bag over it.

"I'm afraid I did something that may make you angry," he said. "Actually, I know it will make you upset with me, but I did it for your own good."

"Did *it*?" she repeated. "Thomas, exactly what did you do?"

"I was a little concerned about leaving you while I went to Savannah," he began slowly, looking like a scolded puppy as he tried to avoid her penetrating stare. "And I thought since Charlie was in town—"

His voice stopped abruptly when he saw the look of stunned shock on her face.

"Oh, heavens," she said, pulling the blanket tighter around her arms. She knew the look on his face too well. "You and Charlie are oil and water. Was there an argument?"

"Yes."

"About me?"

"Yes."

"Thomas," she said, summoning all her patience, "I love you. And I know that you are concerned, but I'm fine. I really am. The dreams cause enough problems for us. I wish you wouldn't involve Charlie in our personal lives."

"I see that now."

"Then let's just move on from there," she said, pointing at the unopened journal at her bedside. "I'll be reading tonight, you'll be working on Jane's adoption, and we can talk after you've met with

Maclin and the judge."

He came over to her side of the bed and kissed her warmly.

"Please drive safely," she said. "Just a quick text to let me know you've gotten there safely."

"I will." He smoothed her hair gently and tucked a strand behind her ear. "I've got to run by the office for a minute, and then I'll be on my way. Enjoy reading tonight, but try to get some rest too. I can't wait to find out what you discover."

Chapter 40

Brackett had two choices about how to get to his next destination—he could take the Greyhound bus to Gainesville and then hire a taxi from there, or he could just take a taxi all the way to Balfour.

One way cost about nineteen dollars and took an hour and a half, and the other was close to a hundred and fifty dollars plus tip, but he could shave off at least thirty minutes from the time.

He found himself thoroughly enjoying this part of his freedom—planning his way around like the moves on a chessboard. How and when and how far to move. In what direction he should travel and which pieces he should involve.

In the end, he decided the sooner he reached Balfour, the better. He wasn't going to need the money in the long run anyway, and he knew he'd have to evaluate his next move when he arrived. He might need more time.

The taxi driver, a talkative middle-aged man, stopped talking after the first fifteen minutes when his fare seemed uninterested in idle chitchat or queries into his travel plans. Brackett clearly had other things on his mind, and the driver decided that he really didn't want to know anything about the portly, disagreeable man—at least, nothing other than whether he was going to tip.

Brackett had researched enough to know the tiny town would be easy to navigate once he was there. He'd made a hand-drawn map of the downtown area including a local venue called Wilton House. There were also primitive cabins for rent just north near Shetland Lake, deep in the Georgia woods. He'd booked one of those for the next three days and had the GPS coordinates in his cell phone.

He wasn't quite sure how he'd get there, but just like a chess match, he knew he could adjust his moves when he saw how the game progressed.

And as far as he was concerned, everything was progressing very nicely.

The weather had taken a colder turn, and Brackett was glad for the hoodie that provided extra warmth as well as a pocket to conceal a solitary chess piece and the handgun he'd purchased years ago.

Today he'd chosen a polished black marble queen.

A little after one o'clock, the taxi pulled into a parking space in front of a quaint bookshop called Dragon's Breath on the Balfour town square.

He paid the driver and added a generous tip, much to the driver's surprise, then indulged himself for a moment looking longingly into the tinted shop window at the assortment of books.

I wonder if anyone really reads the classics anymore, he thought absently. *Did any of the students I taught actually enjoy reading Jane Eyre or Wuthering Heights? Or Vanity Fair or Dracula? Such fascinating, deep, complicated tales of love, betrayal, life, and death.*

A gust of wind blew behind him, and he watched the reflection of the leaves blowing wildly in the open square among the trees and across the ground.

Does anyone write those books anymore? He frowned down into the glass. *Are all the best plots already taken? Or made into two-hour movies?*

He pulled the hoodie over the top of his head against the chill.

Well, he thought, *at least there were men who gave life to my stories. For a time I was the creator and they were my chess pieces—moving about the board and fulfilling my dreams and desires. But now, alas, I must write the final plot and fulfill it myself.*

He pulled the map from his pocket and took his bearings.

The cool October weather was pleasant and his load was light.

He admired the architecture as he walked to the south, past the confines of the town square and into the surrounding streets, taking note of his route.

Most of the buildings in downtown Balfour had been reclaimed from the turn-of-the-century houses that had once been homes. These simple but sturdy brick buildings lined the streets that branched off the center of town.

As with many early Southern communities, the Baptist and Methodist churches were just off center from where the planners began, along one of the branches. The hub included the city hall, of course, and within walking distance there appeared the post office, local bank, pharmacy, and a ring of two-story brick buildings that included Simmons' Restaurant and various other shops that came and went with the financial seasons. Many of those buildings included an overhanging balcony with wrought iron railings and French doors overlooking the park below.

But even as he enjoyed the sights, his midday walk was purposeful through the quiet, uninhabited streets toward Stone Law Firm.

Just a short walk, but the most satisfying of his life.

Chapter 41

The news about the argument at Sam's went viral in a wild game of telephone tag among the members of Deborah's Daughters and the community at large.

One of the eyewitness diners at the restaurant, a front-row soprano from the choir at Emmanuel, called Marjorie with the excuse that she was only expressing her concern for Cora and Thomas. Marjorie feigned knowledge about the incident, then she called Marcie to see what was going on. The landlady, who had gotten her own call from another of the four women at the restaurant, said Charlie had stormed up the stairs of Building B into his apartment and come down fifteen minutes later. He'd thrown an old pop-up tent and sleeping bag in the trunk of his rental car, along with fishing gear and a cheap grill, and put a puzzled Elvira into the back seat.

"I'm so glad you called," she confided in Marjorie. "At least I know you aren't just gossiping and telling tales—you want to help. I'm concerned. I tried to ask Charlie if he was okay when he came down, but he brushed past me like I wasn't even there. I've never seen him like this. He was so angry."

"That's not like Charlie. Maybe you mistook frustration for anger."

"Well, I've got responsibilities at the Piney Woods, and you can't leave Cora and Jane," Marcie continued. "He could go back to New Orleans with his stinky attitude any minute—then who knows when we'll see him again. I know everyone else has their issues with him, but that would be too hard for me. I'm open to suggestions."

"I'll handle this," Marjorie assured her. "I've been on my knees in prayer since I heard. What Charlie needs is praying-over and a stern talking-to. You and I can take care of the praying, and I know who we can trust to take care of the talking-to—Sam."

"Sam?" Marcie said thoughtfully, feeling a weight beginning to lift. "Yes, yes. I think you are on to something there. Sam would be the best one to talk to him. He can't argue with her about what happened."

"Yes," Marjorie said, warming to her own idea. "And let's not forget that at that low point in her life, Sam ran away from her problems too."

"True," Marcie said. The topic of Sam's questionable history was ground they'd covered many times before. "Thank the good Lord for Bill."

As soon as she hung up, Marjorie called Sam, who confirmed firsthand what had only been rumor—that for the first time anyone could remember, Charlie lost his temper in a public place—and with Thomas, of all people.

"Where do I find him?" Sam said, already planning her next move and scanning the near-empty restaurant. She thought about what she owed the detective for helping Bill. About how he'd stuck his neck out with the FBI and put his reputation on the line.

"Well," Marjorie said, "I asked Marcie, and we both think Fort Yargo is the most likely place. It's that state park out on Highway 81. There are primitive camping sites, and it's not likely to be too busy right now. Marcie says he's gone there before with Elvira when he just wanted some peace and quiet in the woods."

"It's a good place to start," Sam said. "I'll let Bill know I'm leaving and call in a server for the rest of the day. Luckily we're in a lull right now. Thank you for asking me."

Sam didn't have to be told how to get to the state park or what to say to Charlie.

Everyone in town knew where to find Fort Yargo on Highway 81. She'd also given a great deal of thought to what she had to say about what happened. She was eager to find a way to make up for her earlier attitude about gossiping.

She'd never thought of herself as a peacemaker, but then, desperate times.

After cheerfully paying the gate attendant the nominal entrance fee, she followed the signs on her way to the primitive camping sites.

She recalled quite clearly what Charlie's rental car looked like from seeing him driving through town. Driving the required snail's pace down the narrow roads, she checked the sites one by one until she spotted what she was looking for.

A one-man tent was pitched to one side of the gravel area, and thin puffs of white smoke were rising from the cheap charcoal grill. Charlie sat on a folding camp stool, poking at a pan on the grate with a long-handled fork. Elvira lay sleeping at his feet.

At least he's being productive, she thought. *Not just brooding. That's a good sign. And he must feel like eating, or he wouldn't be cooking.*

Reminding herself that Marcie and Marjorie were counting on her, she pulled her car next to his, trying not to notice the dark, deepening overcast of the clouds and the harsh burst of cold wind when she opened her door.

Charlie looked up and saw her, but he did not move from his seat. Elvira raised her head and stretched contentedly, opening one lazy eye and sniffing the smoky air to determine the identity of the interloper.

Her nose twitched, but since Charlie appeared reasonably calm she closed her eye and went back to snoozing.

"Don't have enough fish for two," he announced as Sam slammed the door to her car and started toward him, her feet crunching on the rocky ground.

"It's okay," she shrugged. "You're probably hungry yourself. You passed up a bacon cheeseburger at lunch, with steak fries, no less. Don't know that Bill's ego will ever fully recover."

"I'm not much in the mood for conversation, Sam—"

She cut him off briskly.

"There are people who love you and care about you."

She gave him a withering stare of cold disapproval, stopping short of entering his ring of personal space but close enough to confront him without yelling.

"People I care about. I don't care how mad you are, you don't get to go stomping off and worry your friends."

Charlie's cheeks reddened as he tightened his jaw.

"I've done my best to mind my own damn business," he began, but she cut him off again, crossing her arms and shaking her head like a parent with a rebellious four-year-old who won't eat his green peas.

"You are such a noble martyr," she mocked sarcastically.

"Shut up, Sam." He raked at the frying pan, stabbing the two carcasses of fish inside with his fork, oblivious to the spattering grease and oil. "You don't know what you're talking about."

Sam took a deep breath and another step closer. Elvira raised her head and put it down again. Charlie still hadn't moved from his stool, and despite the argumentative tone of the conversation, she seemed satisfied there was no imminent threat to her master.

"So," Sam went on, her hands moving to perch on her hips, "Thomas asked for your help and you told him no. It's none of my business, but don't you think you owe him an explanation?"

Sam took the fork out of his hands with practiced ease, ignoring what she suspected to be trembling in his fingers, and placed it to one side on a tin plate.

"Don't make a mess of things like I did once upon a time, Charlie," she said, her voice soft, steady, and clear. She put her palm firmly on his shoulder. "Don't run away and scare the people who want to be there for you. You'll regret it later."

He wanted to tell her that she didn't understand, but he knew she did. Better than most. Sam understood what it was like to leave and come back home again. What it was like to see the curious stares of busybodies and hear the muted whispers of well-intentioned gossips.

She understood because of Bill too. She'd come to him in desperation when she needed help, and he'd done what he could.

Maybe that explains why she's such a gossip herself, he thought. *And why she came to me now—to repay a debt she thinks she owes.*

"I'm not apologizing to Thomas," he said defiantly, attempting to shake off her hand and failing. She only tightened her grip and gave him a friendly pinch.

"No one's asking you to apologize," she smiled down. "Personally, I don't think you have anything to be sorry for—except the cheeseburger. Maybe you should be sorry I had to throw away a perfectly good cheeseburger."

"With steak fries," he added, trying not to smile. "Don't forget the steak fries."

"That fish doesn't smell half bad," she continued brightly, nudging him off his seat on the folding camp stool until he stood and she took his place, picking up the fork again and turning the blackening fish. Charlie studied her for a long, long moment and then knelt beside her.

"That fish is horrible, and I can't eat it," he corrected her. "And I would never feed it to Elvira."

"Well, I should certainly hope not," she agreed. "It's disgusting."

He leaned back on his heels, resigned to participating in the conversation she seemed so intent on having with him.

"Sam, don't underestimate Thomas, and stop judging me," he said. "I'm not leaving because I *want* to go—I'm leaving because I've been *told* to go. Never mind who or why. Believe me, I'd rather stay right here in Balfour. If Thomas is concerned for Cora, and I don't blame him if he is, he needs to call someone else to look after her. I need to get back to New Orleans."

Sam reached over for his hand, her own hand remarkably strong as she gripped his fingers with a fierceness that took Charlie by surprise.

"Thomas is Sir Galahad and Superman and Cary Grant all rolled into one," she said simply. "He's too perfect and too insufferably, patiently humble. You know that. I know that. Everyone knows that. He's always been the white knight—a good man with a kind heart

. . . and he's never been in a street fight in his entire life. Thomas settles his problems with pithy words and logic."

"But—"

"A man who has no demons doesn't understand how to destroy the demons." She let go of his fingers and patted his hand with a sisterly slap. "You and I, Charlie, we aren't perfect or patient—we have demons. All the legions of demons that roam the earth. We know their names by heart, and they know ours."

He retrieved the fork from her hand and the pan from the grill, exhaling loudly as he stood.

Sam knew the fight had gone out of him. She'd finally gotten through his thick head. He understood. He was ready to surrender pride to her hard-won wisdom.

"Know any place where a man and his dog can get something to eat?"

"I might." Sam stretched and flexed her knees. "I probably know a cook who wouldn't mind a special order, especially for someone who once saved his life from a crazed professional killer. Just don't push your luck and ask for another cheeseburger."

"I'm not living that down, am I?" he said affectionately. "Hey, Elvira, how does a steak from Simmons' Restaurant sound to you—medium rare? Bet Bill will let you eat in the alley with his cats."

The Plott hound twitched her ears at the sound of her name and yawned.

Charlie handed Sam the frying pan.

"Can you throw this away and rinse it out while I take down the tent?" he asked. "Won't take a minute to pack up. Elvira wasn't looking forward to sleeping on the ground anyway, and a hot meal would be great—if you're sure Bill won't mind."

"Bill won't mind," she assured him. "Bill likes dogs—and cooking—and you, Charlie. You'd be surprised to find out how many people like you, in spite of how hard you work at being a pain in the rear end."

He frowned.

"I don't know about liking me," he said. "I'm not quite like you, Sam. The demons you're talking about, they don't just know my name, they have a long history of victories with me too."

She took his chin in her firm fingers and shook it, holding the fork and pan to one side with her other hand. He thought for a minute she was going to hit him in the head with the skillet.

"Temporary victories, Charlie," she said sharply. "Don't you dare give up. Too many people are praying for you. You have no idea. Remember that. Only temporary victories."

She let go of him and looked around for the trash can.

"Now hurry up and pack the car," she snapped. "You aren't the only one who's hungry. If we hurry we can be there by two o'clock before Bill finishes cleaning the kitchen for the day."

Chapter 42

Thomas inserted the key into the office door and slipped inside, intending to retrieve the notes he'd left on his desk when he went to talk to Charlie at Sam's and be on his way to Savannah.

He was also going to call Ben. He didn't know exactly what he was going to say, but he wasn't leaving until he was sure an officer would be watching the house—and Cora—for the next two days until he got back.

Ben Taylor would make sure nothing happened. He was a dependable man.

Thomas dropped his car keys on Susan's desk and went into his office.

When he came out of his office he found himself staring into the barrel of a handgun, aimed between his eyes.

"Back up," the hooded man said. "We need to have a chat, and then we're going to take a scenic drive."

"Who are you?" Thomas asked, though he already knew.

"Who am I? Ha!" Brackett chuckled briefly before his face settled into a sneer. "Surely you know who I am, Mr. Stone. Don't pretend you don't."

"Brackett," Thomas managed, beads of perspiration forming on his upper lip.

"Yes, Brackett," Ed shot back.

"Is that really necessary?" Thomas said, indicating the weapon. He took several cautious steps backward until he bumped into his desk. "Can I ask what you want?"

"How calm and lawyer-like, Mr. Stone," the man said easily. "Just you. I only want you."

Thomas swallowed, evaluating the wisdom of trying to take the weapon away from the intruder and realizing that although he was about six inches taller, the other man outweighed him by quite a few pounds.

"Thinking about your options?" the man continued. "You're not close enough to take the gun before I shoot you, and then I'll just move on to Cora. She's a much easier target."

At the mention of his wife's name, his heart began to pound erratically and his palms began to sweat.

"Oh, nothing to worry about," the man said. "I don't want to kill you—or her. At least, not right now." He looked around the room. "Did you get my gift? It should have come priority mail this morning."

Thomas looked over his shoulder. There, clearly visible in the center of his desk, were the three chess pieces, lined up like tiny soldiers. When he turned, the man took advantage of the opportunity, striking Thomas forcefully on the back of his head with the butt of the gun.

Blood gushed from the wound and sent the lawyer reeling forward onto the desk, grabbing at his torn scalp. Nausea rose in his throat and his vision blurred.

"Just a tap so you know I'm serious," the man said. "I *will* kill you here and now if you don't cooperate. And if I kill you first, then you need to know that nothing will stop me from killing your wife. Remember that, won't you?"

"What do you want?" Thomas repeated, biting the inside of his lip to stifle a cry of pain. The washcloth was still lying where he'd dropped it on the desk, and the lawyer picked it up to stanch the flow of blood.

"Just you," the man said, "and your cooperation. The game's afoot, and there's nothing like sacrificing a willing white knight to begin a Halloween gambit."

Chapter 43

The order of events for the day was cut-and-dried—and the son followed instructions exactly to his father's specifications.

First, Jack asked around at the coffee shop and got the number for a AAA-rated body shop in Griffith that he thought might meet with his father's approval. Then he texted Casey at the ER to see if he'd have an hour or so between shifts to ride over to pick up his mother's car and get it back before the shop closed at five. Casey, whose car was a few years newer and much less cluttered than Jack's battered car, offered to drive.

"So," the paramedic began, "first things first—how's your mom doing? Chemo's rough."

Jack tossed his EMT study manual, water bottle, and his backpack, along with his lightweight jacket, into the back seat and climbed in.

"Yes. She was doing okay. I'm getting her car because she had a fender bender yesterday," he said, pulling on his seat belt with a sharp click. "She's a little bruised and battered, but my dad's made her stay in bed for the day and rest."

"Good for him," Casey said. "How are you doing?"

"Classes are hard," he said, "but I'm doing okay. There's a lot of information, but this roommate of mine is always gone, so it's quiet when I need to study."

Casey smiled at the friendly jab.

"I know," he said. "But picking up shifts means more money. Don't worry, though. It's going to be a lot quieter when Ellie and I get married next spring and I move out. Have you thought about what you're going to do?"

"Do you mean if I don't pass the exam?"

"Of course you're going to pass the exam," Casey said. His hand hesitated on the key in the ignition. "What I mean is, are you going to find another roommate and stay in the apartment, or are you going to move back to Balfour?"

"I don't know," he said. "My dad and I seem to get along better when I'm farther away, so it's probably best I stay here in Griffith. Shouldn't be hard to find someone who wants to share the apartment. If not, I hear the fire department is recruiting. I can put the studies on the back burner while I make some of that money you're talking about. I can find another place I can afford. If I can pass all the certifications, that is."

"You can do it," Casey said encouragingly, starting the car before he handed his cell phone to Jack. "Hey, put your mom's address in the GPS, okay? That way we can just talk without you having to give me directions."

"Sure."

They rode for several miles, the silence broken only by the GPS voice.

"You're quiet," Casey said, tactfully keeping his eyes on the road. "You must be worried about your mom. I would be. How are things with your dad? It's none of my business, but you did mention him."

Jack looked out the window at the passing trees, their branches growing more and more bare from the gusty winds, ominous in the darkening autumn skies.

There had been no one to confide in since he'd come back to the area except Casey, and Casey had been busy lately with Ellie. His mom had been too sick to involve her in his petty disagreements with his dad—not that he would have done that anyway. She'd been a buffer for far too long.

"Better," he said absently, glad for a chance to vent. "He called me about Mom's car and asked for my help. I guess that's a good thing. Treating me like an adult."

"You *are* an adult," Casey said. "You know, I've been going to Emmanuel with Ellie and her parents on Sundays when I'm not on duty. I haven't gone to church since I was a kid, but his sermons aren't half bad, and I like the music."

Jack's mouth curved in a wry half smile.

"I think that's called *damning with faint praise*," he said, "but you're right. Dad's sermons aren't half bad—at least the ones I've heard recently. He's taken Mom's cancer pretty hard, and I think it's softened him."

"I wonder how he decided to be a preacher in the first place," Casey said. "I mean, it's a little like being an EMT or a paramedic—trying to fix people's aches and pains. I would think the people who are good at it are called to it."

"I've never asked him," Jack said. "We weren't that close. He was the authoritarian, and I was the typical preacher's kid—always causing problems, always the loudest, the craziest, the most troublesome. Our would-be conversations often turned into shouting matches with Mom playing referee."

"Sounds familiar," Casey said.

Sensing that Jack had more to say, he decided to remain quiet and wait. They sat in companionable silence for another few moments before Jack began again.

"He was in the Army before he met my mom," Jack said. "He doesn't like to talk about it, but I found a metal pin and a gold coin in Mom's jewelry box when I was a kid. She said she'd gotten them out of the trash when he tried to toss them. Asked me to forget I'd seen them, so I'm pretty sure he doesn't know."

"That's sad."

"Yes, I thought it was." Jack shook his head and stared down at his hands. "He's always been like that. I don't know that he's got any real friends."

"A preacher's got to be careful," Casey said. "Like a lawyer or a doctor. He's got other people's secrets as well as his own. He can't afford to get too close or let anyone else get too close either."

"I guess I never thought about it that way," Jack admitted. "I know he's got a tattoo on his left forearm. He keeps it covered with long-sleeved shirts no matter how hot it gets. We don't talk about that either."

"He's left-handed, isn't he? I've seen the way he gestures in the pulpit."

"That's an odd question," Jack said, turning and looking at his friend. "Why would you ask that?"

"I don't suppose that metal pin was a bar with the word ranger on it?" Casey kept his eyes directly on the road in front of him, avoiding Jack's intense stare. "And the coin had a pair of crossed rifles?"

"It was a long time ago, but I think you're right," Jack said, his attention fully engaged. No one, not even his mother, had ever seemed this interested or wanted to talk about his father's background. "How would you know that?"

"A hunch," Casey admitted. "I've seen you notice my tattoo too, but you've never mentioned it. I got it when I finished qualifying as an Army medic. I suspect your dad got his when he qualified as an Army Ranger."

"Aren't those guys like Navy SEALs? That can't be right," Jack protested. "I can't imagine that being true. My dad hates guns. I talked about going hunting once and learning to shoot, and he hit the ceiling."

"Maybe that's because he was a sniper," Casey said, letting his words sink in. "I heard Ellie's dad making jokes about your dad's color blindness. Back in the day, a man who was left-handed and color-blind was seen as having special accuracy advantages. I know it sounds a little unbelievable, but I've met quite a few snipers, and I've heard them talk. Your dad fits the profile."

"My father?" Jack was incredulous. "You've got to be kidding me! I can't believe he'd carry a gun, much less shoot anyone!"

The GPS called out a right turn at the next stop sign.

"Suit yourself," Casey said. "You could look him up in a database by his social security number. You'd know right away because his dog tags would be black."

"Black?"

"Special operations." Casey could see that he had upset his friend, but this just seemed like the kind of information a son should know about his father.

"I could be wrong," Casey continued, "but it's not likely. All the pieces fit. If you want to know for sure, you could simply ask him."

"Now *that's* not likely," Jack said, pointing ahead. "Our house is the third one on the right. The red brick with blue shutters. That's my mom's car in the driveway. If you want to park on the street, I can grab the keys out of the mailbox and we can be on our way to the garage."

Casey checked his watch.

"Works for me," he said. "That'll give us just enough time before I need to be on duty in the ER. Double shift today. I need to have Friday off to meet Ellie—we're doing some advance wedding planning and picking out flowers and rings in Balfour."

Chapter 44

Unable to go back to napping after Thomas left, Cora went downstairs to her office to check the messages on her office answering machine and then the computer to see if her editor had sent an email with comments on her current book.

Marjorie and Jane were at the kitchen island working on Jane's wooden pirate sword, applying the peel-and-stick jewels to the hilt and down the center of the thick, dull blade. The soothing sound of singing and the scent of baking cookies drifted through the house.

Cora briefly considered asking the housekeeper what she knew about the meeting between Thomas and Charlie, but she didn't want to mention either name in front of Jane. Not that she really wanted to know from a secondhand source. Thomas could fill her in when he got back from Savannah. Life was complicated enough.

The baby was exceptionally active, turning and rolling while the rest of her body felt bloated and achy.

She hoped the journal upstairs would be a genuine distraction when night fell and she was all alone with her imagination. Maybe then she might find some answers about Jane as well as a little peace of mind.

She opened a desktop file on her computer, trying to concentrate on writing, but her mind refused to cooperate. There were several messages in the email inbox, but not the ones she was expecting, and the only message on the answering machine was from Katy, canceling her session for the next week. No reason. Just canceling.

She must be thinking about Dan's trial, Cora thought. *Maybe she wants to spend time with Amy. Maybe she thinks she'll have to testify. Or maybe something is going on at the Wilton House. I'm so out of touch with the outside world I wouldn't know.*

Marjorie knocked on the open door with the toe of her shoe and brought in a tray with a pot of hot green tea and several triangles of toasted cheese bread surrounded by bunches of green grapes.

"Just a little something," the housekeeper said. "You didn't have lunch."

"Thank you," Cora said, trying to adjust herself in her office chair. "This looks delicious. I'll try."

She put a grape into her mouth and bit down, the sweet juice giving her a tiny burst of energy.

"How's the costume coming?" she said. "Will you be finished by tomorrow? You mentioned you might go to see Marshall's sister this weekend in Griffith."

Marjorie paused in the doorway.

"Evelyn's been asking me to come for weeks now," the housekeeper said. "I went in September to put flowers on Marshall's gravestone for our anniversary, and she invited me for lunch. I think she's lonely in that big family house."

Cora thought about the empty mansion in Savannah, the attic room, and Jane's mother and grandmother. What a sheltered, restricted life Jane had led. No wonder she was so shy with crowds in church and yet so happy when Elizabeth came to play during Katy's sessions.

"I can see where she might be," she said. "What's she like?"

"Evelyn—Marshall called her Evie—was a librarian for years, first in a middle school and then the public library in Griffith. The home where she lives has walls of floor-to-ceiling bookshelves, crammed full of every kind of classic and lots of first editions. She still goes in from time to time and does story hour for the little ones."

Marjorie leaned against the frame of the door.

"We have a lot in common, I suppose. Teaching, late marriages, and then widowed. We're both active in church but all alone without living family to speak of."

Without warning, the list from her dream popped into Cora's head.

Send Jane with Marjorie. Could this be what the list meant?

Cora was too tired to ask herself questions.

"Jane's been with you before, hasn't she?" Cora asked, taking another grape and chewing thoughtfully. "Do you think Marshall's sister would mind if she came along with you for a visit? Maybe you could even make it a longer visit, stay a few days."

"What put that into your head?" Marjorie said. "I'm not leaving you when Thomas is out of town. Evelyn *has* asked me to spend the night on more than one occasion, but that wouldn't be right. I'm not leaving you alone."

"Well," Cora said, her feelings growing stronger by the minute and her intuition tingling, "I think you should go and take Jane with you for the night, maybe even two. If Marshall's sister is lonely, a visit with you and Jane would be just what she needs."

"But—" Marjorie began.

"Nonsense," Cora said, her determination showing. "I'm not an invalid. I will need you so much more when the baby actually comes. You'd be back by the time Thomas gets home. It would be good for Jane too. I think it's a lovely idea."

Marjorie tugged at the hem of her apron.

"I don't know," she said doubtfully. "I do owe Evie a visit, and she has asked me to bring Jane back to see her, but what about you?"

"What *about* me?" Cora said. "I've got plenty of leftovers, a journal to read, and nothing better to do than lie in bed and do that resting you keep touting."

Besides, she thought sadly, *I don't want Jane to grow up to be like I am—a recluse who's afraid to venture past the front door. There's been too much of that in her life already. Maybe that's what the message means—Jane needs to be with Marjorie. She needs to go out into the world—to explore. Something I'm just not ready to do.*

The housekeeper couldn't read the expression on Cora's face, but she knew there was no point in further discussion.

"You promise you'll call me tonight?" she said, torn between her loyalty to her friend and her desire to visit her sister-in-law. "And you'll call Lisa if there's the slightest chance the baby's coming early?"

Cora didn't want to remind Marjorie that Lisa was out of town.

"I'll be fine," she said, picking up a piece of toast. "Absolutely fine. There's not a thing in the world to be worried about. I'll help you pack Jane's suitcase, and she can decide which of her stuffed animals she wants to take with her. Do you want to tell her she's having an adventure, or shall I?"

Chapter 45

Jim strolled down the uneven pavement of the French Quarter sidewalk, his senses overwhelmed by all the sights and sounds of the unfamiliar territory.

Above him, the wrought iron railings that lined the balconies, some pitch black and others painted stark white, were here and there decorated with strands of metallic Mardi Gras beads in glittering pink, green, purple, and maroon, dripping down like round plastic icicles from the edges.

One side of the street was more in the scorching sunlight than the other, but the wind was blowing fiercely through the tunnel of office buildings on either side, and Jim almost didn't mind the intermittent heat of the afternoon.

He'd checked into his hotel without much fanfare. The taxi from the airport was quick and reasonable. The driver, friendly and talkative, dropped off the hulking young man at the front door to the Drury Hotel on Poydras Street.

Jim was impressed by the wide marble steps going up to the massive wooden double doors, realizing too late when he reached the top that the doors required a room key to open. A helpful clerk saw his dilemma and pushed open the lobby doors from the inside, asking politely if he was trying to check in.

The clerk at the desk immediately recognized his name when he presented his ID, handing over the room key without batting an eye and giving him a quick rundown of all the amenities the hotel offered. The helpful clerk also handed him a map of downtown New Orleans and circled several places of interest—the French Quarter, the Mardi Gras Museum, the World War II Museum, and numerous places to eat.

But in spite of his mounting hunger, Jim thought he should deposit his luggage in the room and head to the station first and check in with Charlie.

At least, that was his understanding from Agent Walker. He was being paid to babysit, and the sooner he found Charlie, the sooner they could forage for food.

From there, the finer details of his registration and the informative remarks of the clerk became something of a blur. Jim heard the words "breakfast between six thirty and nine a.m." and "dinner between five thirty and seven p.m.," along with the fact that the pool was located on the sixth floor of the building and that he needed a room key to access the elevator.

There were also some convoluted directions about how to find the breakfast and dinner serving area, but Jim felt fairly confident that his nose would guide him as long as he was on the correct floor.

He was both impressed and thankful that Inola had been so thoughtful. He had no idea there was a hotel that served two meals a day and was walking distance to the French Quarter and Charlie's precinct.

Jim had been to Atlanta several times, but he certainly did not consider himself a cosmopolitan traveler. He'd appreciated his trip to Memphis with Harry Halstein, even under the difficult and stressful circumstances of Halstein's half-sister's suicide, but that was as far as he'd ever ventured outside of Georgia.

He had all sorts of natural curiosity, but additional opportunities to travel had never quite materialized. He thought New Orleans sounded especially exciting, but the city had always seemed rather far away and exotic, and much more suitable for the Charlie Abbotts of the world.

He'd heard far-fetched tales of wild Mardi Gras celebrations and exotic French Quarter cuisine, but he had no idea what or how much to believe. At the present moment, he was feeling especially out of his small-town element.

Further, the idea of cold-walking up to another police station and introducing himself seemed odd, to say the very least, but Inola had assured him that this particular precinct would be unlike others he might have seen.

Which, he told himself sagely, *wasn't saying very much, since I've seen precious few other stations.*

Jim stopped abruptly when he reached a bustling four-lane divided intersection, dutifully obeying the red LED hand that appeared in the crosswalk sign. He looked at the crowd of people gathered around him also waiting to cross, and those moving in a wave, passing him on their way to the opposite corner.

Canal Street, he noted from the street sign. *What an appropriate name for this human river flowing around me.*

Majestic palm trees manned the center divider, and numerous brightly lit storefronts bordered the street on either side. A streetcar sang out beside the rows of passenger cars, delivery vans, and pickup trucks all patiently waiting a turn.

Jim took a moment to take in the sheer volume of people in such a small space—women with fussy babies in strollers, balding businessmen wearing tailored suits as they chatted with each other or to the clients on their cell phones, groups of teens in shorts and sweatshirts with brightly colored clothing and hair, dog walkers and their canine companions, muscular men in neon yellow safety vests and grubby jeans on their way to service the city's most pressing needs, and families making their cheerful way around the narrow sidewalks and forming patient lines to wait for trolley cars or the opportunity to sit down to a fresh seafood delight at any of several local restaurants.

The sights, smells, and sounds overwhelmed the Rookie's senses.

The light changed and everything moved at once—except Jim, who stood for several moments frozen, absorbing the scene around him.

Then he began to walk.

The streetcar tracks were embedded into the cracked asphalt, crisscrossing their pattern into the roadway and serving as a clear warning to stay well away from the path of any oncoming traffic.

When he reached the other side of the wide street, the sidewalk changed from wide to narrow. The name of the street had changed too. He was on Royal Street, surrounded on every side by the French Quarter.

Colorful seasonal flowers blossomed from window boxes and emerged from painted concrete planters. Trees of every shape and size were scattered about the yards, giving shade and ornamentation to the scenery.

Wrought iron, stone, and even wooden picket fences cordoned off the sections of parking lots, businesses, private homes, small shops, and hotels.

The sidewalk was an eclectic mixture of concrete, black slate slabs, marble tiles, and red bricks. Some sections outside businesses were painted with fading advertising logos, others were newly polished to a brilliant sheen, and many were broken and pieced together forming unexpectedly uneven surfaces.

Jim thought the walkways imitated the walkers themselves—variegated and absolutely fascinating. He was beginning to see the appeal of this French Quarter and why it was so popular and well-traveled.

He came to a sloped, still-wet driveway, having recently been meticulously cleaned of the bodies of dead insects and bird droppings, and stepped gingerly over.

The air was humid and hot, but every shop Jim passed seemed to send a blast of welcoming cold air out onto the sidewalk, inviting each passerby to come in and enjoy the air-conditioning and the offerings of food, clothing, beverages, or sundries.

Except for the major intersection of Canal, where he crossed and St. Charles Avenue became Royal Street, all the other streets seemed to be going only one way, alternating north and south. All were exceptionally narrow and lined with cars, trucks, utility vans, and buses making their tenuous routes to and from ambiguous destinations.

Jim was glad he was walking rather than attempting to drive.

Inola's directions had been confirmed by the GPS on his phone.

She had told him that once he started walking Royal Street he should specifically watch on his right for a restaurant called Café Beignet where he could find coffee and beignets. He wasn't sure what a beignet was at all, but she seemed to think it was very important that he should eat at least one.

Then she had given him that sidelong, cool smirk of hers, and he wondered if maybe she was extracting some sort of revenge for the banana Moon Pies.

The café building was obvious—a crisp green and white striped canopy under the sign, a large black and white welcome mat with the same words, and several white, heart-shaped chairs at small tables in the open storefront.

To the immediate left of the building was a black wrought iron decorative fence.

On the other side of the fence was a garden area filled with more tables and chairs, a towering magnolia tree, and multiple palm plants and ferns.

He considered briefly going in, but then he saw the massive building at the end of the adjoining fence.

Jim couldn't have imagined what he was looking for until he actually saw it, nor could he begin to imagine that the impressive stucco-covered brick building housed the Eighth District police precinct station.

He took the broad black, white, and gray marble steps up and pulled open the expansive white wooden doors, a gold-colored logo of the New Orleans Police Department star and crescent visible in the glass on each side. A dark blue rectangular sign with stark white lettering warned of *zero tolerance*, the two o's in the words cleverly joined to form a pair of handcuffs, and yet another sign that insisted there were no public restrooms.

Along the edge of the right-hand door at the bottom was another rectangular sign acknowledging the New York State Fraternal Order of Police, Empire State Lodge, in memory of those who gave their lives on September 11.

Jim felt momentarily at home, but the feeling evaporated quickly. He was completely unprepared when he stepped into the lobby and looked around inside.

The desk was elevated well over five feet above the floor, causing anyone under six feet tall to tiptoe to clearly see the officers behind the barricade.

To the left was a lower area with a vending machine that held cotton T-shirts with a wide variety of police logos and designs. In front of the machine was a clothes rack that held samples of the T-shirts that were for sale. There was a poster advertising the shirts and giving specific instructions about how to purchase them, adding that there were also NOPD caps, challenge coins, and patches available in a second machine.

I wonder what the Chief would think of selling police T-shirts, Jim thought. *I bet one vending machine costs a pretty penny, much less two machines.*

The floor itself, much like the sidewalk, was a mixture of coverings—gray carpet to one side, brown stone tiles in the center, and gray marble at the entrance.

The creamy yellow walls were lined with two-foot-wide snow-white flat columns, floor to ceiling, spaced out at six-foot intervals. Each column was topped with an ornate gold cornice. Elaborate crown molding ran around the top edge, and more gold crown molding in foot-wide strips squared off the ceiling into panels of white.

Above his head, mounted fifteen-plus feet high, were two antique wrought iron chandeliers, their six light fixtures like glowing white bowling balls nesting on the sturdy, curling arms.

There were bright posters everywhere—on the walls, perched on easels, and on the front desk.

Jim hefted his backpack over his shoulder and wondered how he was supposed to introduce himself to the NOPD's Eighth Precinct.

Agent Walker had insisted that she would call ahead and clear his path, and it wasn't that he doubted her, but everything seemed to be growing stranger and more unfamiliar with every step.

He suddenly reconsidered what he was doing.

Barging into a station cold might not be his best tactic, especially if the other officers felt the same way about Charlie that the Balfour PD did. What was he getting himself into if he introduced himself as Charlie's friend, or worse yet, his partner?

And what if Charlie wasn't there? What would he do then?

He had turned on his heel and was going back out the doors when a voice called out from behind the high counter.

"You need some help there?" A uniformed officer leaned over and squinted at Jim, who was still wearing his sport coat and slacks and looking out of place in the heat.

Another officer joined the first behind the countertop. He was also squinting.

Too late, Jim thought. *Now I'm trapped.*

"Officer James Smith from Balfour, Georgia," he said, hoping he didn't sound as awkward as he felt. "I'm looking for Detective Charlie Abbott."

The first police officer stifled a guffaw, and the second covered his mouth with his hand and snickered.

"You have my deepest sympathy," the first officer said when he regained control. "Officer LeBlanc here will check your creds"—he pointed to the second man—"and I'll let the captain know you're here."

"The captain?" Jim asked.

"Yep," the first officer said agreeably. "Just look for the guy with the upside-down badge. He's the one who's really in charge."

Fifteen minutes later, Jim was ushered into the captain's office.

The police captain rose from behind his desk and shook Jim's hand warmly before he sat back down.

"Got a call from the FBI this morning about you," he said, crossing his arms across his chest and leaning back in his chair. He seemed almost as interested in Jim's appearance as his officers had been. "Don't usually hear from one of the feds unless they need a local man to go undercover on a bust."

"Oh," Jim said, evenly distributing his weight on both feet and rolling the tension from his stiff shoulders. He was tired, but he also knew enough protocol to know he should wait to be told to sit. He did not, on the other hand, know much of anything else about how things worked between New Orleans PD and the FBI. But the relationship didn't seem cordial, and Agent Walker had apparently tainted him with the same brush.

Captain Hymel clearly showed no inclination of hospitality.

"Charlie's gone gallivanting off again to who knows where," he said indifferently, rocking the back of his chair. "Wish I had some idea when he'll be back."

"Oh," Jim said again. The curious stares and the unorthodox reception were beginning to bother him, and he wondered if he was suffering from guilt by association with the rebellious detective as well as something specific Agent Walker might have said in her phone call. He was feeling decidedly uncomfortable.

Either way, he was sweating under the collar of his jacket, and his stomach had begun to show signs of audible protest.

"Officer Brignac will be glad to see you get a good cup of coffee and whatever's in the break room, but there's not much else we can do until Charlie shows up."

"Yes, sir," Brignac said, tapping Jim on the shoulder from behind. "We're sending out for lunch, and we'd be glad to have you join us."

"I don't want to impose," Jim said, watching the amused look that passed from one man to the other before Hymel gave an abrupt chuckle.

Jim wondered if they could hear his stomach rumbling.

"I think what Brignac is saying is the department would enjoy hearing any and all of your exploits with our Detective Abbott," the captain said, suddenly animated, making no attempt to hide the curiosity in his voice. "The price of an extra shrimp po-boy is nothing compared to the value of whatever insider information you may have."

Jim had a fleeting moment of conscience and then decided that the only thing worse than talking about Charlie was not talking about Charlie. They'd take his refusal as an insult to their hospitality, and they'd also take his reluctance to discuss his friend the wrong way too.

Maybe I know some things about Charlie that they don't know, he thought. *I'm pretty sure I do, but I don't have to tell them anything that Charlie wouldn't want them to know. This may be the best place to be when he comes back. Information is a two-way street, and right now it looks as though I'm driving.*

"Sure thing," Jim said lightly. "I've never had a shrimp po-boy, but it sounds great. Thanks for the invitation."

Chapter 46

The flight from Hartfield-Jackson International to Louis B. Armstrong Airport had taken a little over two hours gate to gate.

Charlie had spent most of the flight with his eyes closed, pretending to nap even through the mild turbulence. The flight attendant made her own futile effort to rouse him, bringing him a second bottled water and additional snacks without asking whether he wanted them or not.

The water and wafers lay unopened on the tray table in front of him.

He was feeling deflated and sad.

Marcie hadn't scolded him the way he'd expected her to do when he told her that he was leaving. She took Elvira's collar in a firm hand and gave him a quick one-armed hug, telling him to come back soon. He knew she meant it, even if he didn't think anyone else in town cared one way or the other if they ever saw him again.

He'd tried to call Thomas twice on the way from the Piney

Woods, headed south to the airport, but both times the lawyer's cell phone went to voicemail, and he didn't want to leave a message that Cora might hear. He didn't know what he'd say anyway.

Thomas was a reasonable man.

If he'd left town, then Charlie had to assume that someone, probably Ben, was keeping an eye on Cora—or was arranging for another police officer to do it.

To do his job.

The last time he'd left another man to do his job, he'd left Cora in Balfour.

He'd had a random impulse to call Cora before he left, but he knew that wasn't a good idea. It was late in the day, and she was probably tired. He'd told her that he was leaving, and that's what he had to do. She would call him about one of her crazy dreams soon enough, and until then he'd just have to wonder if she knew what he'd said to her husband.

But then again, she would act like nothing had happened.

That would be like Cora—she would wait for him to bring it up. To confess what he'd done.

Not that half of Balfour didn't know by now what he'd said to Thomas.

He'd been too hard on Thomas. The man *was* a white knight who had never been confronted with true evil in his life. He'd avoided criminal law as much as any lawyer could. He was the kind of man who made peace whenever possible. Who agonized over lost friendships caused by property line disputes and broken families arguing over inheritances and painful divorces. He wrote wills and settlements and brought closure.

The pictures in Charlie's head were a far different kind.

He couldn't rid his memory of the crime scene photographs and all the mutilated bodies Brackett's stories had left in their wake. Vivid colors. Sharp focus close-ups. The stuff of horrific nightmares and gory slasher films. He could picture the grieving faces of the friends and family left behind. He could see Brackett's vacant eyes and thick lips curling in a snarl, and those cursed chess pieces decorating the top of the defense table during the trial.

His stomach threatened to heave at the images.

Charlie sincerely hoped his old friend had no such gory visions. He was sorry for anyone who had to carry the burden of knowing that sort of depravity.

The detective had turned his back on his friend.

Thomas had gotten him out of too many situations in their youth, and Charlie was ashamed that he hadn't been prepared to have the shoe on the opposite foot. When his opportunity came to repay his debts to Thomas, he'd failed miserably.

But Cora had told him to go. Cora said his leaving was part of the dream. On some damned list, of all things.

How many times had she been wrong?

Never, he told himself. *Never has she been wrong about anything in one of those cursed dreams of hers. And that Old Testament prophet James—how many times had he been wrong? Never. Never once.*

There was some reason he was supposed to be in New Orleans and, as usual, he wasn't going to be told what it was.

How was he supposed to explain that to Thomas or Sam or anyone else when he couldn't explain it to himself? The dreams never made any sense—until later.

And then they made perfect sense. Every single time.

No. Thomas would think to call Ben. Ben would take care of Cora.

That was that. It had to be enough.

The reassuring bump of the plane and the gentle strain against his seat belt told him that they'd landed safely. This trip he'd left the Volkswagen in the extended stay parking lot, so he waited patiently until all the other passengers had deplaned before he stood, thanking the pilot and crew as he made his way out and through the concourse.

His bags and his heart felt unnaturally heavy.

There was a light misting of cool rain and he turned on the windshield wipers, but they blurred the windshield more than they cleared them.

He sat in the parking lot as the rain increased, the engine rumbling, and he tried to decide which would be worse—his empty efficiency apartment or the crowded precinct station bustling with fellow officers and detectives.

In the end, he decided that his solitary thoughts and the pangs of guilt were more painful.

Besides, he told himself as he pressed the clutch and shifted the complaining gears, *there'll be work at the station and plenty of coworkers to remind me that I need to get busy and make myself useful.*

Chapter 47

Thomas had no clear recollection of how he managed to stumble into his Honda and fasten his seat belt. The throbbing pain at the back of his skull and his growing concern for his wife's safety subdued his will to fight back.

He commanded himself to drive, keenly aware of the barrel of the gun in his ribs.

Get Brackett away from Balfour, he thought. *Away from Cora and Jane and the house. Whatever it takes.*

Except for a few day trips to Griffith and Atlanta on business, he hadn't been far from home in years, and the country roads of his childhood seemed like old friends. The woods were a little denser, the undergrowth thicker, the trees themselves taller, but the twists and turns of the two-lane roads came back to him the further he drove, and his vision began to clear. Fading sunlight shot through the heavy branches that sheltered either side of the narrowing pathway, multicolored leaves rustling and rolling across the ground, and

Thomas could tell that they were headed northeast toward Shetland Lake.

In his youth, the lake area had been largely undeveloped land, too rocky and hilly to be used for agriculture or to attract businesses or subdivisions.

The original owners had allowed deer hunters on the property during the hunting season, and other hunters sporadically through the years with special permission.

The lake, ringed by forest, had never been made accessible for boating or fishing, but there were a number of popular walking trails used during the spring and summer months and local berry-picking in the many patches of wild blackberry, blueberry, huckleberry, and muscadine.

Recently the bulk of the land had been sold to a developer who intended to subdivide the area into lots. He'd already built a handful of rustic, primitive cabins for the burgeoning tourist trade and was in the process of clearing the land to open up the lake for recreational use. Construction had put a temporary stop to the hunting for the time being, although Darcie had successfully petitioned to continue harvesting the fruits, arguing that they were crucial to her local jams and jellies. The success of the Wilton House had brought renewed interest in the entire county, and she argued quite passionately that they all needed to work together if they hoped to survive.

Knowing what he did, Thomas hoped and prayed that they'd pass construction equipment or an inspector on the way to wherever they were going, but the roads remained noticeably vacant. One or two small excavators, a battered dump truck, and a grader were pulled aside into rough fire-lane clearings along the way, but apparently their crews were taking a long weekend off.

Brackett's cell phone GPS, laid on his left knee, left the criminal's hands free to hold the handgun at waist level, pointed at the lawyer's rib cage. The neutral male voice called out the turns and twists with cold, clear efficiently, and with every mile Thomas became more convinced of the seriousness of his predicament and more certain he had made the right decision to lead this man away from Balfour.

Finally, after what seemed like more than an hour, Brackett instructed Thomas to turn down a single gravel lane marked only by a crude wooden sign hung from a wrought iron frame. The number seven was burned into the rough pine surface.

Thomas recalled passing similar signs numbered five and six, so he surmised that the builder was working at the most distant sites and back toward those closest to the main roads.

Wise choice, he thought. *The builder won't have to backtrack through finished work—but not so good for me if they are trying to find me. I had no idea there was such a remote, isolated place so close to home.*

The loose gravel slid beneath the wheels as he navigated the narrow driveway. He considered driving into a tree or off the road, but he was in no physical shape to fight Brackett, who was securely buckled into the passenger side of the car, and he was in no mental state of mind to make life and death decisions.

There was a narrow, solitary parking space to the left of the log cabin, a sparse graveled clearing around the front and sides. The taller ground covering, vines, and bushes around the surrounding trees had been cleared away to expose the pine-straw-covered earth, and there was an unobstructed view down the lane.

Brackett will see someone coming out the windows, Thomas thought, turning off the ignition and trying not to feel discouraged. *He's not stupid.*

"Get out," Brackett ordered gruffly. "And hand me the keys."

Thomas obeyed, weak from blood loss and pain. He struggled up the broad wooden steps to the covered porch. The planks beneath his feet were sturdy and solid, but he felt dizzy as he supported himself against the railing.

He wished he'd eaten lunch instead of planning to get food in Savannah.

Brackett bent and produced a key from under the woven mat.

"You people around here are too damned trusting," the man observed with a snort, twisting the key in the lock and pushing open the door for his prisoner to stagger inside.

"Yes," he repeated. "Too damned trusting."

Those were the last words Thomas heard before the second blow drove him forward and he dropped to the floor and into an unconscious void.

Chapter 48

Charlie had a suspicion or two that things were off when the desk clerk gave him a deliberate smirk when he arrived at the Eighth District Station just after four o'clock in the afternoon. He hadn't expected a warm reception, but this was a tad extreme, even for the veteran Marcel, who was known for his easygoing attitude and high tolerance for the foibles of humanity in general.

When Charlie first joined the NOPD force, they'd bounced him around for a while from precinct to precinct until he finally came to settle with Captain Hymel.

Hymel, born and raised in New Orleans, was one of the more popular, experienced, and likeable captains, known to have a rather high tolerance for variety in his staff.

Variety in ethnicity, attitude, experience, and appearance.

Marcel, grizzled and garrulous, was a fifty-year veteran of combined military and law enforcement service. Threatened with mandatory retirement, he'd found a home with the Eighth as a perpetual desk clerk and greeter. He'd been the first to welcome Charlie into the fraternity of the French Quarter, and maybe the only one who expressed his honest feelings not only about the vagabond detective but about everyone and everything else.

Charlie liked Marcel immediately and found there was plenty of work at the Eighth and an array of different jobs to be done. After working his way through many of the other precincts, he was grateful to find people who were more or less willing to deal with his shenanigans.

But there was something quite stinging about Marcel's smirk today that Charlie couldn't quite identify. A smirk that sent his senses tingling and made him wonder what fresh disaster he'd stepped into. He made every effort to slip down the hall to the roll call room without being seen, but Hymel's voice calling out from his office stopped him cold.

"Abbott," the captain snapped from behind his desk. "In here. Now."

Charlie stepped inside the office and stood at parade rest.

This can't be good, he thought sourly. *I guess I'm about to find out what's up with Marcel. I wonder what I've done now. I've never heard that snap in Hymel's tone before.*

"The message you left said you'd be gone until Monday," Hymel said, taking the clipboard from his desk and scanning the pages. "I covered your shifts."

Charlie didn't know whether or not he was expected to apologize for disrupting the captain's schedule or thank him for taking care of the workload. Hymel didn't take apologies well, and Charlie didn't give them well either.

"I got back early," Charlie said lamely, shifting his weight from foot to foot, waiting for the next shoe to drop. He swallowed the gum in his mouth and cleared his throat.

Hymel looked up, his own expression surprisingly hard and his tone harsh.

"You have something else to say, detective?"

"No, sir," Charlie said, his hands clasped firmly behind his back, his shoulders squared, his uneasiness increasing as his torso stiffened. He had exactly the same gut-wrenching feeling he'd had when he first entered the police academy in Atlanta—his bravado and the thin veneer of his cockiness stripped away to expose the real Charlie.

A vulnerable boy-man with a quick wit and deeply buried insecurities.

Am I being fired? What did I do? What should I do now?

Marcel knocked on the open doorframe at his back. Charlie jumped, startled.

"There's a call on line two for you, Captain," the clerk said, finding a great deal of enjoyment in Charlie's discomfort. "Some FBI lady from Memphis. Says she talked to you this morning."

"Thanks, Marcel," the captain said, picking up the phone, his finger poised over the lighted row of push buttons. "Is our visitor still in roll call?"

Visitor? Charlie's stomach did a double-flip and dropped.

Marcel nodded, slapping Charlie agreeably between his shoulder blades.

"He's been waiting for you most of the afternoon," the old officer said cheerfully.

"Friendly, but his lips are zipped up tighter than the security across Pontchartrain. Except when he's eating. Boy, can he eat. Says he knows you from someplace in Georgia."

Eat? The Rookie? Jim's here?

"Hello, Agent Walker," Hymel said into the receiver. "I was just about to return your call with the latest."

He paused and waited, his eyes twinkling with odd amusement at the expression of confusion on Charlie's face.

Is this a joke? Charlie thought. *Are they all playing some sort of practical joke?*

"Well, yes, believe it or not, they're both at the station now," he said, winking at Marcel, who slapped Charlie's back again and went off down the hallway chuckling.

"Did you want to talk to either of them? Abbott's standing in my office."

He waited while a thin layer of sweat broke out on Charlie's upper lip.

Inola Walker is the spawn of all chaos, the detective thought. *I truly despise that woman to the core of my being. You'd think the FBI had better things to do. I feel like a puppy with a GPS chip in my neck.*

"She wants to talk to you." Hymel held the receiver over his desk, the coiled black cord dangling over the piles of paperwork. "Don't tie up my line all afternoon."

"Agent Walker," Charlie said, his backbone stiffening with resentment. "I'm back in New Orleans. Are you satisfied?"

"I asked you not to leave in the first place," she said.

Charlie pictured her sitting at her desk like a predatory barn cat, himself a mouse skewered helplessly on her claws, as she waited for the perfect time to put him out of his misery.

In an unexpected show of sympathy, Hymel discreetly swiveled his chair around and pretended to inspect the framed photos of his family on the bookcase behind him. He'd had enough fun at the detective's expense, and he wasn't particularly happy to be the FBI's messenger boy. Charlie was a pain in the posterior, but he was the NOPD's pain, and Hymel felt an impulsive sense of loyalty to his own.

He didn't like being ordered around by high-handed Agent Walker either.

"Doesn't the FBI have better things to do than interfere in my boring little life?" Charlie said, grateful for the small gesture of privacy from the captain.

"They might," she said shortly. "I don't."

He didn't want to know what she meant. The possibilities were endless, and he objected strongly to all of them.

"I understand that Jim Smith is here too," he said. "Can I assume he has more specific directions than you've given me?"

"You can assume that I expect you to stay put and wait until I get in touch with you again," she said. "I've cleared your participation with Captain Hymel."

Of course you did, he thought. *And doesn't he look just thrilled about that too.*

"Don't go wandering off again, and call when there's news about Brackett," she said. The line went dead.

Charlie leaned over the desk, carefully avoiding knocking over any of the stacks of paperwork, and politely replaced the receiver in its cradle.

"Captain," he said to the back of the man's head, "since you've already covered my shifts . . ."

His voice trailed off in expectation.

"Get your only friend from roll call," Hymel said over his shoulder without turning. "I don't want to deal with you or the FBI this week, so you just handle Agent Walker and keep me out of it, got that?"

"Got it," Charlie said. He wiped away the sweat on his face with the palm of his hand and backed out of the captain's office.

He found Jim sitting quietly in a corner of the break room, an unzipped backpack at his feet and sketchpad and charcoal pencils in hand, amusing the off-duty officers by drawing flattering caricatures. At his right elbow was a giant-sized bag of barbeque pork rinds, and someone had apparently gone to the trouble of finding a six-pack of Yoo-hoos from a local convenience store.

They've stooped to bribery, Charlie thought. *How little they know the Rookie. If there's anyone I'd trust my secrets with, it would be Jim.*

At the sight of Charlie, the room miraculously cleared, office staff and officers wordlessly scattering to the exits, off to do what they should have been doing before he arrived and leaving the two men in awkward silence.

"You know, I didn't have much say-so about being here," Jim said nonchalantly, packing up his art supplies and tucking his pencils back into their case. He carefully ripped several of the drawings from the spiral-bound sketchbook and laid them on the table. "I was in Memphis interviewing for the bureau, and Agent Walker put me on a plane here instead of back home to Atlanta."

"I've met the infamous Agent Walker," Charlie said, propping himself on the corner of the table and gingerly removing a pork rind from the bag and holding it up, sniffing at the curled crisp. "The FBI's choices are not your fault."

"So you aren't angry I'm here?"

Charlie considered the pork rind and decided he was too hungry to settle for a snack. He needed actual food.

"Not really," he said, putting the greasy skin down on a nearby napkin and wiping his fingers on his jeans. "You could say I've used up my quota of irritated, and I'm not going to borrow from next week's supply."

Jim pulled the straps of the backpack over his broad shoulders.

"What's the plan?" he said. "I mean, as long as I'm here, I'd like to help. What can I do?"

The bigger question, Charlie thought, surveying the massive officer, *is why did Walker send you to New Orleans in the first place?*

"Well, I was going to wait until this afternoon, but since you're here," Charlie said, "let's go upstairs and have them pull the files on the Brackett case. It's an old case, so it could take a while. They're probably archived in a basement somewhere, but you could turn on that award-winning grin of yours and maybe persuade the clerk to have them ready by the time we get back."

Jim nodded without understanding.

"After we put in a request, we'll grab something to eat, and we can go over the files together. It's been years for me, but you've got new eyes. Maybe you'll see something I missed."

"Sounds like a plan," Jim said. "I'm hungry."

"Glad to see that hasn't changed," Charlie quipped, checking his watch. "It's too late today for the jazz buffet at The Court of Two Sisters."

Jim's eyes widened and his brows shot up.

"Where? Is that like that voodoo restaurant in Little Five Points?"

"The Vortex is not voodoo." Charlie shook his head reprovingly. "Burton doesn't know everything. If he tried to talk to you about voodoo, he probably meant gris-gris. We've got *that* in New Orleans, but stick close and I won't let the locals put a hex on you or anything sinister like that."

"What?"

"Never mind," Charlie said, enjoying Jim's momentary confusion. "No point in getting your hopes up for a buffet. How does pizza sound?"

"New York style or Chicago?"

"Does it actually matter?"

Jim hefted his book bag again.

"No," he admitted. "I guess not."

"Pizza Kitchen it is then," Charlie said. "You okay with pepperoni bacon on whole wheat crust? Dust off your walking shoes. It's not too far to trek to the French Quarter and back, and I need some fresh air."

Jim nodded again.

"And on the way," Charlie continued, "you can give me the low-down on what kind of mysterious hold our Agent Walker has on you and what you're really doing in New Orleans."

"Don't you want to know what I told your fellow officers here?"

Charlie stopped in his tracks and turned.

"Nah, we're good," he said. "In the first place, I'd hardly call them fellow officers. And second, if you'd told them anything you shouldn't have, I'd have been fired before I got to Hymel's office. The way I see it, one way or the other, I owe you pizza."

Chapter 49

Cora settled herself in the overstuffed chair in the den, her shoulders wrapped in a loosely knit woolen blanket and her feet tucked awkwardly to one side of her swollen, pregnant form.

The cool October air outside crept in through the darkened sunroom and around the panes of glass in the kitchen windows, giving the room a clean, crisp air of autumn.

She'd lit the gas fireplace and the flames burned low, their friendly warmth accentuating the chill in the room.

She'd thought briefly about going upstairs to her own bed, but the idea of the empty rooms, their doors standing like muted, open mouths, made her uneasy.

Before she'd married Thomas, she'd spent many nights alone in the house, but now she'd come to expect family close by and the happy sounds of others. She knew she wouldn't be able to sleep anyway, not in the quiet.

She knew that she would be unconsciously listening for

Marjorie's singing as the housekeeper got ready for bed, or waiting expectantly to hear Jane calling out for a bedtime story and to be tucked into bed with the stuffed kittens and the Cabbage Patch doll.

Most of all, she'd be listening to hear the amusing noises Thomas made when he brushed his teeth in the bathroom, muttering to himself while he changed into his old-fashioned pajamas.

She loved the cotton, blue striped ones that made him look like a male character from some 1940s movie in a tastefully romantic scene with an equally classic Doris Day or Claudette Colbert or Katharine Hepburn.

Adorable. Traditional. Conventional. Smelling ever-so-slightly of aftershave and cologne.

Cora sighed, and the noise disturbed her lone companion.

Solomon had finished his smelly evening meal and was halfway through his after-supper face washing ritual.

She imagined that the feline understood how she felt and was sympathizing with her loneliness. Instead of going upstairs and taking up his station at the foot of Jane's bed, he'd curled up on the love seat across from where she sat, huddled down into one of the knitted afghans that covered her cotton blanket.

Every time Cora moved, he opened one eye and gave her a questioning glance—as if to ask if she'd changed her mind about where they were spending the night.

Cora suspected that if he could speak, he would tell her that he missed his tiny human and didn't want to go up to the vacant rooms either.

Marjorie had left choices for supper, but Cora had no appetite for food. She'd made herself a pot of herbal tea after she'd fed Solomon a dish of his canned salmon cat food and decided she could have a snack later if she felt like it.

The brown leather journal lay on top of the typed manuscript on the table beside her. Despite her desire to read, she also felt a haunting sense of dread.

A vision of Jane's great-grandmother seemed to hover just out of her peripheral vision. Waiting. Watching. Wondering what an outsider would think of what she had written.

Cora imagined the Oriental woman as she had seen her in the dream, floating up the staircase of the house in Savannah. Gesturing toward the bedroom doors that opened as she pointed toward them. Gold fish dangling from the hair sticks that adorned her sleek bun, and the ornate dragon ring curling around her index finger. Finally, the image of Madam Chen's stern face in judgment, staring down from her life-size painted portrait on the wall.

Cora wondered how much Jane remembered of her great-grandmother, and what those memories were. If one day as an adult Jane would look at the portrait that had been stored away for safekeeping with the other furniture and valuable heirlooms and feel sadness for a way of life and culture she never really knew.

Except for the pictures she drew and her nighttime fear of the blue-eyed man, Jane never spoke about her life before she came to live in Balfour. Neither Cora nor Marjorie ever pressed her for answers. Any healing that came would come from deep inside outward and could never be hurried.

Cora was thankful for the journal, hoping that if and when the questions finally came from Jane, the pages might provide the answers she wanted.

The circumstances were all wrong, but Cora could not regret her desire to adopt Jane—or her belief that she and Thomas, with

Marjorie's help, could give the little girl a good life.

Thomas.

She picked up her cell phone to check the text message again.

A simple red heart under her husband's name.

He probably doesn't want to wake me if I'm sleeping, she thought. *Or maybe he doesn't want to talk about what happened today with Charlie and he's afraid I'll be more upset. It's funny how someone who makes his living with confrontation in the courtroom avoids it at all costs at home.*

Outside the kitchen windows and past the French doors leading into the sunroom, the night increased and the long shadows of evening plunged the room into blackness.

Cora turned on the reading lamp at her elbow, picked up the manuscript, and began to read as the cat on the love seat began to purr.

Chapter 50

Thomas rubbed the duck-egg-sized lump on the crown of his head, wincing at the painful tenderness of his scalp through the crusted blood.

Around his chest, his body was tightly bound to the back of a chair with dull silver duct tape. His right arm, the hand propped on his left shoulder, was also secured to his torso. The binding made it difficult to breathe deeply, and he noticed a sharp pain in his right side when he drew in air.

His left arm, however, was not tied.

That's odd, he thought, inspecting the blood on his fingers from his head wound. *Why would he leave one hand free to move?*

At the table to his right he sensed a brooding presence.

"I see you've decided I still have some value," he muttered wryly. His eyes were not focusing, and he strained to make out details in the dim light of the rustic cabin. He opened and closed his free hand, flexing his swollen fingers to restore the circulation.

There was a wooden plank floor and a stone fireplace, the logs burned down to glowing red coals, the heat mitigated by the chill of the room.

Brackett had removed the shoes from the lawyer's feet, and his ankles were wrapped securely and separately to two different legs of the chair using layers of the same duct tape that was on his chest. Thomas was glad he still had on his socks. His feet were cold, and he couldn't reach them.

On a rickety wooden side table at his left elbow was a tin cup of what might have been coffee at one point. He eyed it suspiciously and decided if Brackett wanted to kill him, poison was probably not high on the list.

Thomas's mind worked methodically through what he knew, which wasn't much. He had been taken from the office on his way out of town. It would be a while before anyone noticed he wasn't in Savannah. He hadn't called Ben—but as long as he could keep his captor present with him, Cora was safe.

All he had to do was bide his time and keep Brackett talking. If he could distract him long enough from doing anything else, then Susan would certainly go back to the office. She'd notice immediately that something was off.

She would call Ben. Ben would come looking for him. More importantly, Ben would take care of Cora.

He licked his dry lips and reached for the cup. He took a tentative swallow of the bitter liquid before he put the cup back down, addressing his captor with his most professional tone.

"So," the lawyer said, his mind doggedly on the task ahead of him. "What's on the syllabus, professor?"

"You are rather chatty," Brackett said, poking absently at the fire with a stick of kindling wood. "Doesn't your head hurt?"

"No worse than your conscience," he said, venturing another touch at the back of his head with the tips of his fingers. "Assuming, of course, that you have one."

"Ah, clever man," Brackett said approvingly. "But you shouldn't lie to me."

"It takes too much effort to lie," Thomas said, returning his hand to his lap and noting that most of the blood was dark and clotted droplets.

Old, he thought. *It's already been a while. Surely Susan's back at the office by now.*

"You were saying," Brackett prodded. "Something about lying."

"All those details to remember." He moved his head as far as he dared before pain shot through his temples. "Personally, I need a notebook to keep up with the facts I'm told, and I certainly don't have enough paper to write down all the fiction."

Brackett rubbed the stubble on his chin with an irritated swipe of his broad hand and twisted in his chair, his tone flat and disinterested.

"Maybe you're naturally boring," he said thickly. "You're a lawyer, right? I'd have thought lying was an integral part of your training. I was led to expect clever repartee. Charlie's more fun than you are."

Thomas sighed, his head throbbing as though a marching band had taken up residence between his ears. He could tell from the blurry vision in his right eye and the radiating pain from his jaw that the right side of his face was swollen. He didn't know if he'd hit his head when he fell or if Brackett had struck him after he lost consciousness, but how it had happened didn't matter.

He struggled to keep his thoughts organized through the pain. He needed an opening, a chink in Brackett's armor. A weakness in mind or body.

He shook his hammering head.

"Maybe you'd like to explain the chess pieces you sent to my office," he offered. Talking seemed to ease the tension he felt in his upper body and took his mind off Cora and his present dilemma.

Pretend it's a courtroom, he thought. *Prepare the opening argument. Present the facts. Interrogate the witnesses on the stand. Respond to the prosecutor's points. You know how to do this.*

"I've heard you're something of a chess master."

Brackett cackled.

"Now, don't go hurting yourself trying to think."

The figure shifted, and Thomas caught the steel gray glint of a gun tucked into the man's ample waistband.

"I'm just interested in this game you're playing," Thomas countered, willing himself into the conversation. "Seems to me it's a little like being in a courtroom. The back and forth. Give and take. Question and answer. Someone's going to miss me, don't you think?"

"Already thought of that," Brackett said.

He removed a cell phone from his pocket, playing absently with the glassy black rectangle, holding it up for Thomas to see the screen.

Thomas recognized a candid picture of Solomon napping on the foot of a bed. His and Cora's bed.

"Did you know you can open the face recognition on a cell phone even when the person has his eyes closed?" he said. "You really should talk to Charlie about upgrading your security. I know all kind of things I didn't know before! You and Cora have been keeping quite the secret. A baby—congratulations!"

The shocked look Thomas could not hide sent the professor off into a gale of demented glee that ended in a coughing fit, stopping almost as suddenly as it had begun.

"Oh, no," he insisted, sobering and wiping the tears of triumph from his eyes. "No one is going to find you until we've done what we've come here to do, and then—"

He paused threateningly and leaned closer, his hot breath inches from the lawyer's bloody right ear.

"Then," he continued with a sneer, "then everyone will know where you are because I want them to know. Do you hear? They will know when I want them to know."

Thomas wished the pain in his head would stop a minute so he could think clearly. A thin shaft of light darted through the curtains at his back, and he turned his head much too quickly to look at the source.

Night already and there's some sort of porch light on the cabin outside, he thought, his neck strained and sore. *What message had Brackett sent to Cora that would satisfy her curiosity? I told her I wasn't going to call until tomorrow, but what happens then?*

He said a prayer for strength. He'd given his feelings away too clearly. Willing the exhausted muscles in his free arm to move, he lifted the cup and took another swallow of the bitter black liquid.

An unexpected dizziness came over him followed by a wave of nausea, not only from the pain of his head but also, he realized too late, the effect of whatever drug had been put into the coffee.

I am definitely not thinking clearly, he chided himself. *I should've seen that coming—especially since he didn't tie one of my arms. Easier if I just poison myself.*

And Thomas lost consciousness to the sound of raucous snickering and the thud of another log being thrown on the fire behind him.

Chapter 51

The Fourth Day: Thursday

Cora opened her eyes to the semidarkness and remembered the smell.

The recollection was faint and fleeting, but she knew with absolute certainty that she had been here before.

She was in the house where she'd been buried.

The house where Lonora died, only this wasn't the basement. This was the room upstairs where she'd come inside.

The dream was as real as the memory.

Late afternoon, just as the sun was setting. A hazy, dying light glowed through the dingy curtains and onto a faded square of cheap woven carpet. There was a fireplace at one end with the remains of what seemed to be burned papers, the acrid scent heavy and the ashes heaped in a smoking mound.

Cora saw the mismatched furniture scattered about the room—a lumpy sofa, a well-worn kitchen table with two wooden chairs, and a cast-iron daybed pushed to one side against the rough plank walls.

A tweed-covered armchair sat near the hearth, a side table with a dusty coal oil lamp at the side.

All covered deeply in the dust of abandonment.

As Cora's eyes adjusted to the gathering darkness, a quivering voice came from a doorway to the right of the fireplace.

"Do you know where you are?" the girl said, stepping onto the square of carpet and into the lighted space. "Do you remember me?"

Cora frowned, still trying to orient herself to the surroundings and searching for some sliver of memory she could use. She'd been in such a hurry that day. Distracted by the pregnancy and Lonora's impending birth. She hadn't paid much attention when she entered the house. She'd been too careless.

Cora shook her head.

"I suppose I should be glad you don't," the girl continued, playing absently with the zipper of her hooded jacket, sliding it up and down with nail-bitten fingers. "I guess that should make me feel better about what happened, but it doesn't."

Cora breathed in deeply, filling her lungs with musty air.

"I understand why you're puzzled," the young woman said. "We only met once—no, twice." She corrected herself nervously and moved to the tweed chair where she stopped. Her fingers left the zipper on her clothing and began to rub absently against the top edge of the deteriorating cotton fabric.

"I remember you very well. You and that detective were in the professor's office asking him questions when I came in to bring some essays I'd graded for the freshman lit class. . . . You were pregnant then too."

Her words were hesitant, her voice so soft that Cora found herself leaning in to hear, struggling to identify the distinctive accent—French and yet not quite Parisian. Cajun? That was it. Cajun French.

Yes, Cora thought. *You were the voice on the phone. You're the one who called me that day to come.*

"You weren't paying much attention to me that day at LSU," the girl said. "Neither was that detective with you. The professor said it was good that you ignored me. That you'd never suspect I was the one."

Brackett. Of course, Cora thought. *You're right. I didn't remember you.*

"You were one of the graduate assistants?" Cora asked. "Were you at the trial? I don't remember your testimony."

"Professor Brackett didn't want me to come," she said. "He said he had a plan for something I should do if everything went wrong, and it would be better for me if no one associated us."

"You mean a plan if he went to jail," Cora said. "You got involved because he went to jail. Is that what happened?"

A thrust of wrenching nausea rose in Cora's chest. She imagined for a wild moment she was about to throw up. This girl was nothing more than a child, how could she be involved with Brackett? She seemed so sweet. So innocent.

"You're remembering now," the girl said sympathetically. "I can see it on your face."

"Why are you here now?" Cora said, swallowing the torrent of emotions—fear, anger, horror, regret. Her hands trembled, and her body shook almost uncontrollably.

Wasn't the nightmare of losing my baby enough? Why am I remembering all this now? Why dig up a memory so awful? What is there here that I need to know?

"I was a little surprised that you came alone," the girl continued, the glimmer of tears in the corners of her eyes, her breathing shallow and labored. "But he was right. Professor Brackett said you would. He said you wouldn't be afraid of another woman. That you were an altruistic do-gooder at heart. You trusted me."

"I almost didn't come," Cora said, fighting the painful memories trickling into her subconscious. "You said you needed help. You sounded so sincere—and so afraid."

The girl looked away, her shoulders suddenly slumped, twisting her hands together and shifting her sneakered feet. She took a finger and wiped at the corner of her mouth.

"He made me promise. Said the time was coming when it needed to be done, and I was the only one who could do it. That I owed it to him."

"The only one who could do it . . ." Cora repeated. She had caught the rhythm of the girl's Cajun accent, deceptively gentle and full of remorse—the sound of the words in sharp juxtaposition to their meaning. "You mean, the only one who could kill me?"

"Yes," the girl said bluntly. "He said the rest of the pieces were already off the board. That I was the only piece left who could remove you from the game."

"Pieces on the board?" Cora asked. That sounded like Brackett. "Chess pieces?"

"Everything was about chess to him," she said. "I knew what he meant. He liked to plan ahead. Anticipate the moves of his opponent."

"But the game was over," Cora said. "He'd lost. Was it only about revenge?"

"He said he was setting up for another match," she said, taking a seat in the creaking chair, looking out the window as though talking to herself. "The professor was always setting up for another game. He thought that since he'd never killed anyone himself, that would save him from prison. He was afraid of you. He didn't count on you."

"Did he explain what he meant?"

"You and that detective were going to make the case against him. He knew it was going to happen from that first day you visited his office. He knew he had to have a plan to get rid of you."

The girl gazed wistfully at the peeling paint on the windowsill, her words flowing from her like dripping cold December rain. "He said he'd seen your kind before. He was sure you wouldn't give up until you'd tied him to the crimes. He was afraid you would outmaneuver him, so he took out an insurance policy."

"So it *was* revenge."

"Oh, more than that," she said, waving her graceful hand, shining particles of dust making patterns in the thick air. "He planned to appeal the decision and didn't want you around to testify against him again. He knew if you died during the trial, all the suspicion would be on him. He needed an ironclad alibi. Once he was in prison, no one would suspect that he had planned the whole thing."

The girl turned in the chair to face Cora and turbulent blue eyes met serene gray.

"The only time I ever saw him afraid was when he talked about you," she said. "He was terrified. The professor said you could look right through into his soul."

What am I supposed to do with that information? Cora thought. *How does that help me? What kind of clues are you giving me—and why?*

"Tell me how you came to be involved with Brackett," Cora said. She pulled out a chair from the table and lowered herself cautiously onto the cane bottom, the instinct to counsel overpowering all her other emotions.

"I'd finished my undergraduate in fine arts and was floundering," the girl began. "I tried getting a job, but the only thing I was good at was going to school. I felt so broken. Like there was an important piece still missing—and I didn't know where I'd left it, or when, or how long it had been gone."

She began to play with the zipper on her hoodie again.

"Then you met Ed Brackett," Cora prompted.

"I'd never taken any of his classes. They were mostly upper level except for a couple of freshman 101s, and he didn't bother much with those. He lectured, but he always had a graduate assistant to grade the papers. A friend suggested that I apply. I fell apart during the interview. Told him all about what was going on in my life. I thought he cared about helping me find myself—at least, that's what I thought he was doing. I can see now that he was looking for his own broken pieces. He used pieces of me to fill his life, and the glue he used was guilt and pain."

"He manipulated you," Cora said flatly. "He used his power and position."

"Yes," the girl admitted. "I saw how he used the people around him as pawns. I saw what he did. I thought I mattered more than that, but I was wrong. I'm sorry about your baby. I'll be eternally sorry for what I did to you both. He was afraid of you—and like a child, I was afraid of displeasing him."

"I'm not sure that it matters," Cora said, struggling to keep the bitterness from her voice. "He appealed his sentence anyway. I didn't die, and he's still out of prison. It's been too long. No one cares about what I think anymore. My testimony wouldn't have stopped the appeal one way or another."

"He didn't know that. I told you. You frightened him. But that's why I'm here," she said, standing and brushing at the legs of her jeans, another cloud of dust in the stagnant air. "Because he's out of prison."

"I don't understand."

"Ed Brackett *is* guilty of murder."

"I didn't die," Cora repeated, confused. "My baby died, but you said yourself—Ed Brackett never committed murder himself."

"No," the girl corrected her. "He *did* commit murder. Ed Brackett murdered *me* . . . and I'm going to show you and your detective how to prove it."

Cora's senses went spinning again, still searching for the missing clue when her eyes came to rest on the table beside the armchair.

In the center lay three white chess pieces—a knight, a bishop, and a pawn.

Beside the knight was a half-eaten candy bar, the wrapper pulled back and tucked under the sides.

And Cora was awake.

Chapter 52

The blinking light on the post office answering machine and the whiny predawn messages from the recently hired postal workers were the last straw that broke Quincy's harried patience.

The first message insisted that the caller was still suffering the effects of the autumn onslaught of pollen and informed the grizzled supervisor that the speaker was taking extended leave time through the weekend. The other was an outright verbal note of rude resignation.

Apparently there were higher paying, less stress-inducing jobs to be found in nearby Griffith.

Quincy had a fleeting moment of temptation to call in sick himself, but the sight of his poor, widowed postal assistant hobbling up the front steps to the post office, cane in hand, gave him pause. There were other people on the potential worker hiring list, and he would call them before the end of the day. He was sure one of them would work.

But that didn't help in the moment, and as much as he disliked making the downtown delivery rounds, he simply could not ask the aged Widow Emerson to do it for him. Not that she wouldn't make a valiant effort, but the backlash from the community and his own personal code of conduct stood firmly in the way of any such rash decision.

The other loyal veteran postal worker, also an octogenarian, had arrived much earlier and was happily sorting the day's mail into the post office lock boxes. By eight o'clock, he would be taking one of the two postal trucks out for the rural deliveries.

A disgruntled Quincy drank a third cup of lukewarm coffee and resigned himself to the walk through Balfour proper, dangling the prospect of a late lunch at Sam's in front of his waning enthusiasm for his job.

Mercifully, the bulk of the third-class mail and circulars were not due for delivery until the next Wednesday, so the mail sack was lighter than he expected. There were the standard end-of-the-month bills and invoices for the businesses on the edges of the town square, but little personal mail except for one large manila envelope addressed to Cora Stone.

Quincy, as he often did, inspected the return address with some interest and was bored to find that the material came from a publishing house in Tennessee.

Probably a contract for one of those books Cora writes, he thought sullenly. *As if she needs another excuse not to come out of the house and mingle with the rest of us.*

Not that he was judgmental, but five years was a long time to be cooped up in a house, any house. And like many of Balfour's residents, he wondered from time to time why Thomas had married someone so obviously antisocial.

Maybe he felt sorry for her, Quincy thought as he sorted and bundled the small stacks of envelopes, organizing them by delivery addresses and tucking them neatly in order into the satchel.

She was pretty enough. He'd caught a glimpse of her once or twice down the dimly lit hallway when he'd delivered a package to the front door to the housekeeper, Marjorie O'Quinn.

There were visitors who sometimes came and went during the week, and Quincy knew she had townsfolk who saw her on a regular basis for what he assumed to be counseling sessions—Katy Wilton, Harry Halstein, and that little girl, Jane, who lived with her now.

Except for the unspoken cloud of gossip that swirled around Charlie Abbott's periodic comings and goings, no one brought up the mystery of Cora's hermit-like existence or her lawyer husband's devoted defense of her privacy.

The manila envelope was the last item he placed in the postal bag.

After lunch at Sam's, the mailman decided firmly. *All the regular mail first, and then visiting the enigmatic Cora Stone will be a well-earned dessert.*

Chapter 53

The noises coming from the kitchen were mildly unnerving.

Ginny did not for a moment doubt her husband's ability, nor his determination, to make breakfast for her. On the other hand, she also did not underestimate his habit of making a mess of her highly organized kitchen.

Andy had so little time outside his commitments to the ministry that she'd taken over all the cooking and cleaning for the majority of their married life. He helped, of course, and did whatever she asked him to do with a cheerful spirit.

Even in the darkest days of her cancer, when she didn't have the strength to do what needed doing, Deborah's Daughters intervened on her behalf. The meals were prepared and delivered, the house routinely swept, the clothes washed and folded, with little fuss or fanfare—leaving Andrew Evans free to attend exclusively to the needs of his wife.

This morning, however, her doting husband had decided to

prepare food, his well-intentioned efforts audible through their closed bedroom door.

Ginny propped herself up against the pillows, waiting for the inevitable.

There was an eerie silence for five minutes or so before the door swung open and a disheveled Andy appeared carrying a wooden tray, which he set on the bench at the foot of their bed.

"I cooked breakfast," he announced proudly. "Earl Grey tea, toast, grits, a well-poached egg, and orange juice."

"Thank you, dear," she said sweetly. A faint whiff of burnt had followed her husband as he entered, and she looked expectantly at the tray. "It all looks delicious."

"It took me a minute to get the setting right on the toaster," he said, adjusting a pillow across her lap and settling the tray down on her upper thighs. "I only burned one piece of bread. I'll clean up the kitchen before I go to the church."

"Nonsense," Ginny said, lifting the scalding, strong tea to take a sip. "You don't need to do that. I'm sure I need to get out of bed at some point today and take a shower and dress. I can take care of it then."

"Why would you get up?" he said. "The more you rest, the quicker you'll get better."

"I'm not so sure the doctors would agree with you."

She picked up a triangle of toast, smeared with a thick portion of homemade blackberry jam, and took a bite, the seeds crunching as she chewed.

Her husband continued to hover.

"This is wonderful," she said, smiling up at him. "You were very kind to make me breakfast, dear, but just look at the time. It's already well past nine, and there are things to do at the church before Sunday services. Alice and Donna need you there."

"I suppose," he said hesitantly. "I don't like leaving you alone."

"Well, I don't like leaving the secretaries in the lurch with all the planning that needs to be done for the fall festival either."

She put the last corner of toast into her mouth and took a swallow of the orange juice, swishing the seeds from between the crevices in her teeth.

"So, it's settled," she said, picking up the spoon and dipping into the lump of rapidly cooling grits. "Your khaki pants are hanging on the closet door, and any of the darker polo shirts will match nicely. I'll tell you if there's a problem with the colors."

He knew he could count on her not to let him embarrass himself in public.

"Yes, dearest," he said quietly. "And socks?"

"Darker should do for those too, but I'll double check after you shave and shower. As long as they are the same color, it shouldn't matter." She tasted the grits. They needed salt and a pat of butter, but she took a second spoonful.

"This is quite lovely," she said. "Now you hurry along and get dressed while I finish my meal. I'm feeling better already."

Chapter 54

For Cora, the previous night had passed in a muddled blur, interrupted by fits of wakefulness and brief sleepwalking trips to use the bathroom.

She'd fallen asleep in her favorite oversized den chair with the lamp on, reading Jane's great-grandmother's transcribed diary and making detailed notes in the margins of the transcript—questions and comments she had for Thomas as well as highlighting items of special interest.

She'd found a few enlightening entries, and she had intended to read until she was finished, but her physical and emotional fatigue were too much, and—to Solomon's delight—she'd drifted off a little after midnight and stopped moving around.

When she woke around three a.m. from her dream, the manuscript was in her lap, folded back to the place she'd left off reading, and the ink pen and highlighter were nestled in the crease of the stapled pages.

Solomon had moved from the love seat and was snoozing just under her elbow, against her side and on top of the blanket, his whiskers twitching and a rumbling purr coming from deep inside his hairy chest.

Anticipating a nocturnal visit from James, she'd moved her private journal from her office to the side table when she curled up to read. She didn't want to disturb the cat too much when she wrote down the details for Charlie, fearing that the finicky animal might take offense and decide to sleep elsewhere in the house if she moved around too much to suit him.

She exchanged the journal for the manuscript in her lap.

Mercifully, taking notes took little effort and made almost no noise.

After she finished, she was able to wobble to her feet and down the hallway to the half bath with Solomon none the wiser. She had a crazy thought about calling Charlie, but three in the morning was absolutely too early without crucial information.

At least, she couldn't see how any of what she had been told would help Charlie convict Ed Brackett of murder and send him back to prison.

The baby, too, was restless, so Cora detoured wordlessly into the kitchen to make a quick cup of herbal tea and eat several pieces of fresh fruit that Marjorie had sliced and left in the refrigerator.

The chunks of cold, sweet peaches reminded her of Thomas, but she resisted a second urge to call someone in the middle of the night. There was no sense in waking everyone just because she was having trouble sleeping soundly.

He'd texted her a heart emoji, and that would have to be enough for now.

Eventually the unborn infant settled and an exhausted Cora slipped back into the chair without waking Solomon, drifting off into fitful, dreamless sleep.

Hours later she woke with the early morning light warming the sunroom and the bright shafts shooting through the kitchen windows. She rolled over and rose.

A slight wave of nausea slipped up her throat as she moved the dream journal to the side table along with the pen.

Might as well call Charlie, she thought, pushing herself up from the depths of the chair cushions and picking up her empty tea cup, waddling to the sink. She put the cup and saucer down without washing them.

Thomas won't call until he has news, and Marjorie's busy with Jane. I shouldn't have slept in the chair, but I suppose my body didn't care and needed the rest. I could go back to bed right now.

Solomon's plaintive yowl rose from the depths of the afghan.

"Oh, good morning," she said to the annoyed tom, who seemed quite irritated that his warm sleeping buddy had moved and he'd been left alone. "I suppose you'd like breakfast before I take my shower?"

The black cat's furry head emerged from the edge of the blanket binding as his four long legs shot out in all directions, uncurling his substantial body in a graceful feline ballet. His six-toed feet spread themselves in the air, his whiskers twitching as his mouth opened and exposed a curling pink tongue and two rows of pearl-white teeth.

"Come on then," she urged, reaching down to refill his cut-glass water bowl, a mismatched piece that Marcie had found at a yard sale and had given to Marjorie for a candy dish. "Just because I don't feel like eating doesn't mean I won't feed you."

He rolled from the chair with a graceful plop and made a leisurely stroll to where she stood, his black feathery tail sweeping across the tiles.

You're just as cute as you were when you were a kitten, Cora thought. *I'm so glad you were with me last night.*

She opened a lower cabinet and selected one of the single-serving pouches of soft food along with the plastic container of dry cat kibbles. Marjorie had thoroughly spoiled him with daily treats interspersed with her own smelly concoction of wet and dry food spooned into the feline's personalized food dish.

Solomon was one hundred percent Cora's cat, but when he was hungry, his loyalty was to his next meal and whoever responded to his feline needs.

Moments later, gagging at the strong smell of raw fish and liver on her hands, Cora was on her way upstairs to take a shower.

Charlie will just have to wait, she thought. *It's not like he's going to be glad to hear from me anyway.*

Chapter 55

Charlie didn't want to admit how impressed he was to find Jim alert and ready in the breakfast area of the hotel lobby after the late night they'd had at the station going over the Brackett files.

As he had predicted, Jim's winning smile persuaded the moon-struck clerk to send for the boxes of paperwork, which arrived shortly after they got back with the pizza.

Hours of pouring over the files brought no new insight, and around eleven they decided to break and resume again the next morning.

Jim took the meager remains of the pizza for a late-night snack and meandered back to his hotel, took a hot shower, and fell gratefully onto the bleach-scented sheets, where he snored contentedly until the shrill alarm on his cell phone sounded before the sun rose.

Charlie arrived at the Drury twenty minutes early and entered the breakfast area from the outdoor patio just as Jim was polishing off his second plate of waffles and crispy pork sausage.

Jim wiped a smudge of maple syrup from the corner of his chin with a paper napkin and frowned at the unexpected intruder.

"Am I late or are you early?" he said, checking his watch almost apologetically. "I brought my backpack down so we could leave from here and I wouldn't waste your time going back to the room, but I thought we'd agreed on seven thirty."

Charlie ignored the question, absently scanning the expansive food bar and warming table over the other man's shoulder.

"You're awfully cheerful for someone who probably didn't get into bed until after midnight," the detective said. "What's for breakfast?"

Jim's frown deepened.

"You aren't a guest of the hotel," he said, brandishing his fork and knife. "I like it here. Don't get me in trouble."

"Me?" Charlie said innocently, pushing his baseball cap away from his forehead, still eyeing the buffet. "Would I cause you problems?"

Jim snorted.

"I'm getting an orange juice to go and we can leave," he said, picking up his plate and silverware. "I've been thinking about those files from last night, and I'm ready to get back to work."

Charlie's stomach growled, and he looked hopefully around the room.

From her serving position in the far corner, a uniform-clad attendant had been watching the detective with open suspicion. In an act of casual defiance, he strode to the bowl of assorted fruit and took the smallest of the Red Delicious apples, polishing the already shiny skin absently against his jacket sleeve.

Then, in a further act of impudence, he gave her a boyish wink.

The matronly attendant was anything but amused. She lowered

her head with the tenacity of an angry bull and made a beeline through the crowded tables.

Jim, who had deposited his dishes into the black plastic bin, turned just as the woman reached Charlie, who held up the apple in a muted appeal for mercy.

But the outraged matron dropped her spray bottle of disinfectant on the nearest table, followed by a cleaning cloth, and reached to snatch the prize from Charlie's hand.

Jim stepped nimbly between the two, reached into his back pocket for his wallet, extracted a five-dollar bill, and tucked it into the woman's outstretched hand.

"Thank you for breakfast," Jim said, lowering his voice. "I appreciate what you do. Please excuse my rude friend. We're still in the process of crate training, and, as you can see, he isn't the best pupil."

"You're welcome, sir," she said stiffly, slipping the money into her apron and picking up the bottle to spritz the table. "Thank *you* very much."

Jim returned his wallet to his pocket and turned to Charlie.

"I'm ready," he said with the tone of a stern father to a disobedient child. "Is this place we're going on the way to the precinct?"

Charlie tossed the apple in the air and deftly caught it.

"Why?" the detective said, bantering. "Don't tell me you're hungry again already. You just ate."

"I *did* eat," Jim said. He watched the busy hotel worker wiping down the tables until he caught her eye, making certain his words carried loudly enough for her to hear. "But this is a buffet for hotel guests only. I'm a hotel guest. If you'll remember, we were supposed to meet at seven thirty. You're early, and I'm not really finished."

"Well," Charlie said, stuffing the apple into his coat pocket and his hands into the pockets of his jeans, "I'm sorry you didn't have enough breakfast buffet."

"It's okay," Jim said, striding toward the exit as he grasped Charlie's upper arm with brotherly determination. "I was doing just fine until you decided to call time on me. Wherever we're going now, it's on your tab and out of your pocket. I can finish filling up there—right?"

He stopped in the doorway to thrust Charlie out the sliding doors before him.

"See you in the morning," Jim called back to the attendant, but she didn't answer.

The woman had hidden her face in the sleeve of her uniform, hiding what might have been a chuckle into her elbow.

Chapter 56

Susan was shocked to find the front door to the office unlocked when she got to work just after nine thirty.

Without the usual pressure to be there ahead of Thomas, she'd taken her time and given her disgruntled Siamese extra attention before she left home. She'd also called Harry, who was out of town, and they'd had a leisurely discussion about a trip to Arizona at Christmas for him to meet her daughter's family.

Now the unlocked door sent panicked alarm bells sounding in her mind, and she chided herself for not coming in at her regular time.

She knew Thomas had been in a hurry to leave for Savannah, but no matter the rush she couldn't imagine that her methodical boss would be so careless as to forget to secure the building.

Swallowing her initial fear that some dangerous intruder might still be lurking inside, she pushed open the door, leaving it ajar, and bravely stepped inside.

She placed her oversized purse gingerly in the center of her desk and looked around the room for anything that might signify a break-in or theft.

You don't need to call the police yet. You're being paranoid, she told herself. *You're not some helpless woman who's afraid of your own shadow.*

After a moment, she realized that the three chess pieces she'd left sitting on the corner of her desk were missing.

Maybe Thomas moved them, she thought. *But why? Surely he didn't take them with him to Savannah. That doesn't make any sense at all.*

She swept the room again, more critically, and realized that the inner door to the office was standing ajar. Through the half-open doorway, she could see that the green glass banker's lamp on his desk was shining down in a bright rectangle of light.

There was something in the middle of the desk on the blotter, but, not willing to move from her relatively safe spot, she couldn't determine what it might be.

Okay, she thought, *that's enough. I'm officially spooked. Thomas never leaves the lights on—and he never leaves his door open either. I've seen all I need to see.*

She grabbed her cell phone from her bag and went back outside to call Ben Taylor from inside her car in the parking lot.

She was sitting there trying to decide whether or not to call Thomas too when the Chief arrived fifteen minutes later.

"Thank you for coming," she said, wiping the perspiration from her hands against the sleeves of her cotton sweater, gracefully avoiding the sequined design. "I hate to bother you, but there's just something not quite right about the office this morning."

Taylor respectfully removed his cap, giving her a perfunctory nod before he stepped inside the building. He was having a frustrating and rather typical morning himself.

Burton and Dalton had been summoned to Griffith on a jewelry store burglary, griping and complaining all the way out of the station about the shortage of qualified officers to respond to calls. Perkins was whining about filling out the forms for the last batch of traffic speeding tickets, balking over the added work that would have fallen equally on both his and Jim's shoulders.

And Jennifer, God bless her heart, abruptly announced for the third time in a month that she was done with all the complaining and fussing and that she intended to go back to the local community college to study cosmetology as soon as she saved up the first semester's tuition.

The Chief was sorely missing Jim's dependable, willing attitude and dreading the thought of interviewing, hiring, and training new recruits.

The call from Susan had been a welcome reprieve, although Ben felt fairly certain that there was nothing criminal going on.

"I was thinking about calling Thomas and letting him know," Susan said, standing close to the open outer door and speaking into the Chief's broad back. "I decided to wait to see what you think—if I should bother him."

"He's in Savannah, right?" Ben said calmly, hands on hips as he pivoted to survey the room for himself. "If he's there on business, he's probably turned off his cell phone. Let's see if there's probable cause."

Susan shook her head vigorously, pursing her brightly painted lips in disapproval.

This was exactly what she'd feared. The Chief wasn't taking her seriously.

Ben *was* having problems. He'd seen too many hysterical

women—and men, for that matter—with overactive imaginations. Her appearance didn't help his impression of her either. Her hair looked like a dancing bleached baby porcupine, her fingernails were enameled swords, and her clothing looked like a Las Vegas dancer had a garage sale on sequins.

"So why don't you tell me what's really concerning you," he said patiently. He lowered his considerable frame onto the corner of her desk, wishing for a cup of coffee.

"To begin with," she said, holding her temper in check, "there were three chess pieces that came in the mail yesterday."

"Hold on," he corrected her. "Back up. You called me about the *office*. Let's take first things first."

"Yes," she said, throwing herself into her own desk chair in resignation. "I left yesterday before Thomas. He doesn't usually do the locking up, but he insisted. I came in later than usual this morning, and the door wasn't locked."

"So you entered the building anyway?"

"Yes," she repeated. "I wanted to make sure there was a reason to call you, so I came inside to see if anything was out of place."

"And was anything out of place?"

"Do you know that you sound incredibly patronizing?" she said sharply.

"So I've been told," he said, tilting down his sunglasses to look over the rim. He kept his gaze on her eyes and avoided the distractions her bleached hair and glaring sequined sweater presented. "Please go on."

Susan resisted the urge to roll her eyes, indicating a brown wrapper in the trash can beside where the Chief sat.

"Thomas was going to call you when he got back from his trip and see what you thought," she said. "Beyond an open invitation for vagrants to come inside, the chess pieces that came in the mail yesterday were the main things out of the ordinary. Mailed from New Orleans."

"Where did you say you left the pieces?"

"Right here on the corner of my desk," she said, rolling her chair back. "Where you're sitting, actually. There were three of them, and now they're not here. Thomas had no reason to move them."

The legal assistant pointed past the Chief into the open door of the inner office.

"That door's not supposed to be open either," she said accusingly. "I haven't lost my mind. Something's going on."

"Thomas could have left it open himself," he said, trying to hide his skepticism and the growing tension at the base of his spine. Even he didn't believe what he was saying.

Susan shook her spikey head more aggressively, fluffing at the roots with her brightly painted fingertips.

"Thomas insists on keeping the office door closed," she said, her irritated attitude intensifying. "I've *never* seen it standing open like that—and he had no reason to move the chess pieces or leave the lamp on no matter how distracted you may think he was. Thomas isn't like that. I'm telling you, there's something wrong!"

Ben tossed his cap on the desk beside her purse and rose.

"Well then, let's just have a look in there and see," he said, stepping briskly across the room. Susan followed, bumping into him when he abruptly stopped. She peered over his right shoulder and gripped his collarbone, sending a stab of pain up the side of his neck.

"Ouch," he complained. "Those things hurt."

"Look," she said, ignoring his whining, "in the middle of his desk blotter—under the light."

Ben had never noticed quite how much a woman's painted fingernails could feel like tiny claws until she dug them into his uniform. He removed her hand and put an arm out to keep her from continuing into the room, trying to block her view, but she'd already seen the same thing he saw.

Chess pieces.

The knight was lying on its side in the center in a dark puddle of what looked like blood. The bishop, a few drops of crimson staining the top and sides, stood on the outer edge of light, separated from the fallen horseman by a few scant inches.

Between them on the blotter lay a crumpled once-white washcloth, soaked in red.

And though Ben called Perkins immediately and sealed off the office with crime scene tape, and Burton and Dalton thoroughly searched and dusted for fingerprints for the next two hours, the pawn that Susan insisted had been the third piece was nowhere to be found.

And Ben Taylor had discovered a newfound respect for Thomas Stone's legal assistant and a growing concern for the man who'd been smart enough to hire her.

Chapter 57

Vicki had just finished arranging a fall display of chrysanthemums and pumpkins for the front window of the shop when she saw Andrew Evans approaching on the sidewalk.

She'd called to check on his wife before she'd opened up shop, and Ginny had suggested that her husband might be coming by to buy flowers.

"I know all the signs," Ginny had said. "He started talking about how the room needed 'cheering up.' And then he made some lame excuse about needing to go out for milk and bread. He's so sweetly transparent. He says the same thing every time he wants to surprise me."

Not that Vicki necessarily needed a warning, but she did appreciate the heads-up. She wasn't a regular member of the Emmanuel congregation, and as much as she'd spent time with Ginny, she knew little or nothing negative about the preacher from his long-suffering spouse. She had, however, heard from other people that he could be a bit headstrong and opinionated.

Translated, Vicki thought, *that means, "Please don't be overly offended by anything he does or says." Ginny loves him, and that's enough to cover a multitude of sins.*

So the florist pretended to be suitably surprised when Evans came in, the tinkling bells on the doorframe announcing his entrance.

"Good morning," Vicki said pleasantly, giving him a moment to take in her flowing scarlet caftan, crimson talons of fingernails, and exotic purple eye makeup. She tilted her head to emphasize the dangling gold chains dripping from her ear lobes and down the sides of her slender neck.

"Good morning," Andrew managed. He was almost thankful that he couldn't see the color in the woman's ensemble. The sheer visual of her costume in black and white was heart-stopping enough.

"I'm Vicki," she said, extending a graceful, dark hand. "How can I help you today?"

"I'm Andrew Evans," he said, giving her hand a firm shake and wondering if he should add that he was the pastor of Emmanuel. He'd never lived in such a small town before, and he didn't know if he should simply expect her to know who he was—or if that would be presumptuous.

This is harder than I expected it to be, he thought, releasing her hand and picking up the nearest object, a ceramic container filled with violets. *I really should get out more into the community. Outside the circle of regular church members. I've been too dependent on Ginny to make all our social commitments.*

"Virginia's husband," Vicki said, sweeping herself behind the counter and giving him some space as her clothing danced around her agile form. "Of course. We were so sorry to hear about her automobile accident. I hope she'd doing better."

"Thank you," he said, carefully replacing the potted plant. "She's resting at home today. She speaks very highly of you, and I thought you might help me find something special for her."

"But of course," the florist said sweetly, her Cajun accent adding to the exotic nature of her appearance. "Did you have something particular in mind? Cut flowers? A growing plant of some sort?"

"She's always been easy to please," he offered. "And she loves variety."

Vicki nodded.

Yes, she thought, *that's one of the best descriptions of Ginny I've ever heard. She loves everyone, and I've never met anyone so at peace in every situation.*

"I have some quite lovely lilac plants that came in this morning," she said. "Or roses are always a good choice. I have some sweetheart pink ones, and I could do an arrangement with baby's breath and ribbons."

When she saw the look of confusion on his face, she realized she'd forgotten about his color blindness.

"Maybe you're more interested in their fragrance," she said helpfully. "Perhaps you'd like to smell some of the choices and make a decision based on the aroma."

It was more a suggestion than a question.

"Yes," Andrew said with a sigh of relief. "That would be a good idea—but I'm allergic to pollen, so you'll have to forgive me if I sneeze."

"Ah," Vicki said, finally understanding how to please her customer, "then there are several varieties we can choose from that have been specially bred for just that problem—tropical hibiscus, asters, impatiens, sunflowers, English lavender. You are not alone in your suffering, *mon amie*! You will trust me, please! We will find something extra special for your lovely wife that will please both of you. This I promise!"

Chapter 58

Cora had taken her time showering and dressed in another of her husband's oversized shirts. With no one to fuss over her food choices, she'd eaten a small bowl of peach slices and made herself a cup of green tea to fortify herself for the call to Charlie with her latest nocturnal clues from a long-dead graduate assistant.

She was in no particular hurry to tell her ex-husband that he needed to solve another murder, and that the only clues she could offer for the five-year-old homicide were three chess pieces and a candy bar.

She wanted him to have time for his second cup of coffee and a beignet or two before she went wading into that alligator-infested swamp with him.

Solomon had moved himself to the floor of the sunroom and was taking his second nap of the morning, annoyed with her abandonment and, she supposed, missing the company of his tiny human.

She had finally made up her mind to call Charlie when her cell phone began vibrating in her pocket.

Who could possibly be calling? she thought absently.

She didn't recognize the number, and she considered not answering at all, except for a sudden premonition followed by her unborn child's sharp kick to her left kidney.

While she was considering what to do, the vibrating stopped for several seconds before it resumed with the same unknown caller.

Maybe it's a wrong number, she thought. *This could go on all day.*

"Yes," she said. "Who's calling, please?"

"How polite you are." The husky masculine voice was eerily familiar. "I'm hurt that you didn't recognize the number from yesterday, Cora. You knew I'd call back, didn't you? After all that time you spent rummaging around inside my head, there's a whole room filled with furniture and furnishings you left behind."

Her unborn child kicked again and rolled.

Brackett. Her lungs burned as she struggled for air, a panicked dread threatening to close off her airways.

This isn't the office phone where he called yesterday, she thought. *No wonder I didn't recognize the number on my cell phone.*

"Was there something you wanted to say?" she said, regaining a limited sense of control and refusing to give him the satisfaction of hearing fear in her voice.

"Of course," he said. "Quite a few things, actually. I've begun looking forward to our little chats. You weren't busy, were you? Not with a patient?"

She cradled her swollen belly and moved onto the sofa where she had more room. Her senses screamed at her to hang up the phone, but her fingers refused and simply gripped more tightly.

This monster had called for a reason, and she needed to know what that was. Charlie needed to know.

Maybe it's a good thing I haven't called Charlie yet, she thought.

For a fleeting moment, she was glad Thomas wasn't there to fret over her. If he knew she was getting these calls, he would never leave for the office again, much less go to Savannah.

"I'm listening, Professor Brackett," she said, her hands trembling as she reached for her notebook to take notes.

"Pleasantries first," he said. "I'm enjoying this glorious fall weather. Mountains splashed with color and early frost, a roaring fireplace in the cabin. A new friend."

New friend? Cora thought, writing quickly. *His words sound slimy, aggressive. Another victim?*

She had no time to formulate a question or interrupt his monologue.

"Aren't you the least bit curious?" he continued with a sinister, patronizing sneer. "Where I am? Who I'm with? That's not like you, Cora. You were always so inquisitive. So curious."

She knew she should keep him talking to gather information and clues, and yet she realized that she was afraid to discover what he might say.

While she hesitated, he resumed talking, without passion or feeling, as though he were lecturing a class of disinterested undergraduates.

"Ah," he said, "does that black cat have your tongue? You still have Solomon, do you not? He was only a kitten, but as I recall from my conversation with your husband—well, ex-husband now I suppose—anyway, he had enormous paws and a sixth toe on each foot. I always wondered about that. Charlie hated him, you know."

Where is this going? she thought. *Why in the world would he bring up my cat? How would he remember? Should I just let him ramble?*

"He hated the cat because of the chess pieces," Brackett droned on. "Come along, you *must* remember. That's why I remember. Charlie told me all about him the first time we met. In my office at LSU, I had a chess set in the corner of the room, near the window. Charlie said he had a chess set himself. That he would set up the board to play and the cat would rearrange the pieces. Charlie was very specific."

Cora vaguely remembered the conversation. She'd been busy watching Brackett for telltale behavioral signs, and Charlie had distracted the man with idle chitchat about chess—and their new kitten.

They had gotten Solomon, a six-month-old rescue, from the local shelter. Cora fell in love with the furry black ball of trouble on sight. Charlie said she needed company while he was at work, but he didn't tell her that he didn't especially like cats and had hoped to find a dog she wanted instead. But she was set on the kitten.

Solomon was playful, and he *did* get into everything, but Charlie insisted he didn't regret getting him. When Charlie brought Cora to Balfour, Solomon slept in a carrier under her feet and, until he adopted Jane as his bedfellow, had always slept like a sentry at the foot of Cora's bed.

She'd asked Charlie afterward why he'd lied about having a chess set, and he said he was only putting Brackett at ease. Trying to make conversation. Throwing him off guard. Giving her time to evaluate.

"Kittens are mischievous," she conceded, realizing that Brackett had stopped talking. Bewildered by the topic of cats and chess, she needed to say something or he might stop talking altogether.

"Ah," the man said. "I was afraid you'd fallen asleep. So you *are* still listening."

"I'm here," she said quietly. "You were talking about Solomon.

He made quite an impression, it seems."

"And Charlie," Brackett added. "Charlie said the kitten was especially fond of knocking over the pawns. Sliding them around the board and onto the floor—under the sofa and the bed. They'd go missing, then poor Charlie had to go looking for them. I suppose a detective *would* like his pieces where he can see them all the time, lined up along the edge of the board like soldiers preparing for battle, especially the horsemen. Charlie did love the horsemen. How do you feel about knights, Cora?"

Cora's mind went blank, and she could think of nothing to say. She couldn't recall any of the details that Brackett was spouting.

Charlie tended to elaborate his stories, and she'd been too busy observing the professor's behavior to care about her then-husband's fanciful fabrications.

"Never mind," Brackett said suddenly, interrupting her reflections. "I've been too thoughtless to chatter on like this. You're probably tired—with the pregnancy and all. I've kept you on the phone when you're going to need your rest for the game, little bishop. Can't have you exhausted before we've even begun."

And a bewildered Cora was left staring at the silent cell phone in her hand.

Chapter 59

Charlie never liked to analyze his feelings, but today was different.

Today he was remarkably introspective.

Maybe because he was back in New Orleans, strolling familiar streets on his way to the precinct he knew so well and had grown to call home. Maybe because Cora's dreams—and the recent fight with Thomas—seemed distant and removed from this part of the world. Maybe it was the unexpected but welcome sight of Jim Smith with his warm, homespun demeanor and methodical ways.

But even the Rookie had changed. He was more independent and assertive since he'd last seen him.

Maybe that's what hanging out with the FBI does for you, Charlie thought. *Maybe he's finally found who he is. That can't be a bad thing in the long run.*

Whatever was going on, Charlie found his mind seemed much clearer and he could think without all the burdensome emotions of the last three days.

Even the four file boxes, brimming with the evidence, photographs, and folders from the Brackett trial—now scattered across one of the interrogation room tables—looked more like old friends and less menacing than they had when he and Jim first opened the containers the night before.

Maybe it was last night's pizza too. Watching the Rookie scarf down an entire supreme while he sorted and sifted through unfamiliar territory brought a welcome sense of camaraderie.

Or the beignets and expresso he had introduced to Jim at his second breakfast.

No wonder Inola Walker wanted the young officer for her FBI team. He might eat like a herd of Clydesdales, but the man's work ethic and attitude were worth their weight in pure gold—and his skills were without question.

Whatever the reasons, Charlie was ready for Cora's call when it came to his cell phone a little after ten o'clock in the morning.

He was even, he tried to tell himself, prepared for whatever she had to tell him.

He didn't even try to hide, taking the call in the interrogation room while Jim worked at the table. There was no need for privacy. The Rookie was absorbed in the multitude of photographs that had been taken during the investigation, sorting pictures into various stacks, his open sketchbook and his colored pencils at his elbow.

Charlie had no idea what the man was looking for, but whatever it was, Jim and his magnifying glass were apparently determined to find it.

As he listened to Cora and watched Jim work, Charlie realized that there were so many details about the case that he'd tried to forget. So many he'd pushed down into the darkest part of his memory that he'd hoped would never again see the light of day.

"No, Cora," he said when she had finished speaking, "I don't remember a candy bar, and I certainly don't remember any girl. You said *you* remember her?"

He struggled to keep his doubt out of his tone, but nothing he could think to say about her present state of mind was complimentary or kind.

"I'm pretty sure I do," she said. She'd left the sofa and really wanted to go out and sit on the porch swing, to feel the fresh air and cool breeze. But after the phone call from Brackett she felt vaguely uncomfortable with unlocking the front door when she was all alone in the house, so she'd settled for the bench in the sunroom.

Solomon had apparently forgiven her and was napping on the stone floor like a guard dog on her bare feet, the random rumbling of his purrs warming her toes.

"You weren't yourself," he offered lamely. "Neither of us were at our best. But I don't see what your dream has to do with Brackett's release from prison. Are you sure that's what she said? That she worked for Brackett? He'd been behind bars for two weeks before you got the call that morning. We didn't see any connection then, and I don't see a connection now."

She felt the sting of his words, although she was positive he didn't mean to be cruel or unfeeling. She knew he'd taken the blame all these years for Lonora's death, but the bitter truth was that she could have been more careful. She could have listened when he told her not to take reckless chances.

She'd been naive and trusting. She'd left the house that day. She'd known better.

"Charlie," she said softly. "I know that it's been five years in actual time, but in my dream it seemed like only yesterday. Brackett's arrest. The trial. Testifying. The morning when I got the phone call. Going to the abandoned house."

She readjusted herself on the bench as the baby inside kicked and squirmed.

"You're right," she continued. "I was preoccupied and seriously overconfident after the trial. Brackett was in prison. We were on the front page of every newspaper and featured on every newscast across the Southeast. I felt invincible when I got a vague call that promised a tip on one of our cold cases."

"You felt you needed to go," he finished her sentence for her. "We've been over all this, Cora. You weren't sure at the time who called you to the abandoned house, and we couldn't link any of it to any case we were investigating, cold or not. I tried."

"I know you did," she said. "You turned over every stone."

I quarried most of south Louisiana, he thought bitterly. *No fingerprints or any evidence at the scene. Nothing to link what happened to any criminal we'd investigated—together or apart. The case crumbled after you left. Your lack of memory didn't help. That psychiatrist—Ted Floyd—he said you had a kind of amnesia caused by severe trauma. He also said the psychotic break meant you might never remember.*

"But there *was* a graduate assistant when we went to talk to Brackett," Cora insisted. "I'm sure there was. I didn't pay any attention to her at the time."

"Well, I didn't either, Cora," he said. His jaw had begun to ache from holding his gum securely against his molars in an effort not to make chewing sounds in her ear. "You were never able to give us any details about what happened, and I really don't remember her."

"What about the candy bar?"

He looked up to find that Jim was holding a photograph to the light, eyeing it intently under the magnifying glass in his hand.

"No," Charlie said. "I can't say that I remember any candy bar either. I'm sorry, Cora. The house where we found you was on private land. I can go out there and look again, but I don't know what that will accomplish."

Cora closed her eyes. In her mind, the graduate assistant was watching her. A sweet, determined smile of encouragement and sadness rested on the young woman's face.

"One more thing," she said. "Brackett called me again this morning on my cell. I have no idea how he got the number. He rambled on and on about Solomon and how you never liked the cat because he played with your chess pieces."

Cora left out the detail about Brackett mentioning her pregnancy. She didn't need Charlie getting distracted from what he needed to do in New Orleans—at least not until she decided how she felt about the detail herself.

"He must be losing what's left of his mind," Charlie said. "He's going to muck up his legal case against you if he keeps harassing you on the phone."

"Nevertheless, you need to find out what happened to the young woman who worked for him five years ago," she said firmly. "And then you need to look for evidence of a candy bar."

Charlie sighed, releasing the gum from the tightening grip of his molars.

"I'll call when I've got something," he said. "And I'll make a note that he called you again and talked about black cats."

He laid the cell phone down and fished in his pocket for a fresh piece of gum.

"Candy bars and graduate assistants?" Jim asked, shifting his athletic body in the metal office chair and leaning back, a single photograph in one hand and the magnifying glass in the other.

He saw a look of mild surprise on Charlie's face.

"I figured if you didn't want me to hear what you said, you'd go into the hall or another room," the officer said easily. "I mean, I could pretend I don't know what's going on—but that seems like a waste of valuable time."

Charlie grimaced. He'd opened the proverbial front door, and Jim had sauntered into his personal business.

"Fair enough," the detective said, depositing his used gum in the wrapper and popping in another stick. "Cora says there was a female graduate assistant working for Brackett in the LSU English department during the trial. We need to investigate what happened to her."

"What's her name?"

"I don't know," the detective admitted, chewing. "I don't remember her."

"But Cora does." Jim rubbed his chin thoughtfully. "Do you think she would be able to describe her to me?"

"Why would we do that?" Charlie said, trying to keep the sarcasm from his tone.

Talk about a waste of time. He was already feeling frustrated about the files. As far as he was concerned, Cora's clues were getting crazier by the minute and this pregnancy of hers must be affecting her mind.

"We'd have more luck finding clues," he added, "with that photo you've been staring at for the last twenty minutes."

"Hmm," Jim said, scratching his chin. "You're in a mood. We

could start with the fact that as of right now, you're fresh out of leads. But, since you brought up this picture, take a look at what I've found."

Charlie shrugged.

"It's a photograph of Brackett's office," the detective said, waving it away with the back of his hand. "Cora asked one of the FBI crime scene photographers to make a set so she could prepare for the trial. There are more than a dozen of them from all different angles. It's some profiler thing she does—she studies the suspect's surroundings for clues to behavioral patterns."

"Makes sense to me," Jim said. "You can learn a lot about people from the way they live and work."

"Spit it out," Charlie said. "What are you trying to say?"

Jim handed him the magnifying glass and laid the photograph on the table.

"Look at the corner of the desk and around the trash can on the floor," he said. "Ignore the books, the stacks of papers, and the chess pieces. What do you see?"

Wordlessly, Charlie picked up the picture and looked.

"Do you see them?" Jim asked quietly as Charlie's pupils widened and the detective gave a long, low whistle of discovery. "There's a jar stuffed full, right there in plain sight on the desk. Must be at least four or five different kinds of bars. The trash is overflowing, and empty wrappers have scattered all over the floor. Somebody had a serious sweet tooth."

Charlie picked up his phone and dialed Cora's number.

"Hello, Charlie," she said, taken aback. "Didn't we just talk?"

"We did," he said, avoiding Jim's knowing look. "I had one more question. Any particular brand of candy bar I'm looking for?"

He could hear her swift intake of breath.

"I don't think so," she said, startled by the rapid return call. "Just a candy bar. I can't tell you the color of the wrapper so I can't give you a clue about the brand—"

"Because you don't see color in the dreams," Charlie finished her sentence for her. "I know."

Jim reached out his hand.

"I've got an idea," he said. "Can I talk to Cora, please?"

Charlie laid his cell phone in the Rookie's broad palm.

"Hello, Cora. Jim Smith here with Charlie," the Rookie said. "I'm not sure how well this will work, but can you describe this graduate assistant? I understand there's no color—but I can do a detailed drawing with the right information."

He separated the softer black B, H, and F from the colored pencils, arranging them in alphabetical order as he waited for the psychologist to answer. When Cora agreed, Jim's mood visibly lifted.

"Good. Well, it's a little unorthodox," he went on cheerfully, "and it might take a while, but I can draw and then text you a photo. We can go back and forth until you're satisfied."

The officer selected one of the harder graphite pencils, inspecting the sharp point.

"Great," he said, nodding enthusiastically to himself. "Let's get started."

"I'm going to take a break and go next door to Café Beignet to get fresh coffee and a bag of beignets," Charlie offered. "You want anything?"

But Jim Smith was hyper-focused on his appointed mission. He'd propped the cell in the middle of the table on speakerphone, flipped to a clean page in the sketchbook, and had already begun to draw delicate gray curves against the stark white of the paper.

Chapter 60

The air was chilled and heavy, the room unfamiliar and bathed in the shadows of the daylight sifting through the half-drawn curtains and the surrounding woods.

"Ah," a deep voice drifted out of the fog in his aching head, "there you are, Mr. Stone. And with impeccable timing too. I've made you a fresh cup of coffee. Sorry I didn't bring food for two. You'll need to make do."

Thomas fought back the stabbing pain at the base of his neck and the back of his head, his mind determined to rise above the confusion.

Brackett, he thought, his senses reorienting. *What's the last thing I remember? He's got my phone. He went through it. He knows Cora is pregnant. Did he call Cora? What did he say?*

Thomas tried to keep calm. He reminded himself that Cora wouldn't do anything foolish. Not with Marjorie and Jane there with her.

The lawyer dragged open his heavy lids and allowed his pupils to adjust to the growing sunlight in the rustic room. The smell of burning wood from the smoldering fireplace stung his nostrils, and the bitter taste of stale coffee coated the surface of his tongue. A sooty ceramic teapot sat on the hearth alongside a battered spoon and a glass jar of instant coffee.

"I would ask how you are feeling," the other man continued, as though they were old friends who'd met on a street corner and were reminiscing after years of separation, "but the simple truth is that, of course, I don't really care. I'm just bored with waiting."

"Honesty," Thomas quipped, trying not to wince when he flexed his lower jaw to speak. "As a lawyer I can appreciate the rarity of that trait in a convicted murderer."

"Tsk, tsk," Brackett clucked. "You of all people should know better than to level unproven accusations. I've never been convicted of being a murderer."

Brackett slid his chair back and stood, the screeching noise sending waves of agony into the lawyer's eardrums.

"Attempted murder, then," Thomas said, squinting against the increasing light and flexing his aching muscles under his blood-stained suit jacket. "Past. Present. Future. Let's not quibble."

Multiple haphazard thoughts were darting in and out of his poor addled brain. He was fighting to stay alert while avoiding thoughts about his present condition—held captive by a crazed man with a gun and a grudge.

He looked down at his chest. He was wearing one of his more expensive suits. He'd bought several when he worked in Atlanta, but he seldom had reason to wear them anymore. They seemed ostentatious in a church like Emmanuel or with his everyday clients, but Cora agreed that meeting with a federal judge in Savannah to discuss

Jane's adoption warranted his best. The habits and conventions of all the years in a courtroom and dressing for success and to impress were difficult to overcome.

He didn't really regret that the suit was ruined, but his favorite tie from Cora was still neatly tied around his neck, a bit loosened and spattered with what he surmised were bloodstains from his head wound.

Darn, he thought, illogically distracted from his injuries and groggy from the influence of the drugged coffee on an empty stomach. *I hope those stains come out. I really do like this tie. Maybe Cora can order me another one.*

"No snappy comeback?" Brackett said, moving toward the window and peeking out between the simple muslin curtains. "That's not very sociable of you. Even Charlie does better than that."

"Maybe later," Thomas said, lifting his left hand to tentatively investigate his wounded scalp again. "When my head clears."

His torso was still aching, and his right hand and arm had gone numb from lack of circulation. Nausea rose in his throat, and his whole face felt battered.

"Well, I suppose that will have to do." Brackett casually resumed his seat across from the lawyer. "I hope you don't mind if I babble a bit, though. Solitary confinement takes its toll on a man's mind."

Thomas blinked his swollen eyes and held his temper and his tongue. The coffee mug from yesterday still sat on the table beside him, but from the level of liquid and a faint heat coming from the sides, Thomas thought it must have been refilled.

More drugs, he thought. *I won't drink if I can help it. Brackett's clever to leave one arm free to take a swallow whenever I want.*

Thomas lifted his chin defiantly, the rest of his body lethargic and weak.

"So much learning comes from listening," the professor said, settling into the chair and removing a cell phone from his jacket pocket with a flourish. He held the phone up to the light, waving it absently in the air like a magic wand. "I listened in prison, you know. Amazing the odd facts and beneficial information that the incarcerated carry around just itching to share."

Thomas closed his eyes against the light.

"For example," the professor lectured on.

Thomas licked his dry lips and listened, willing himself to pay attention.

"I know better than to call Cora from your phone," Brackett continued. "But your phone *was* rather useful for collecting numbers to put in my burner phone. And then I turned it off. Burner phone is such an odd name, don't you think? I should research why they call them that. Who knew they were so easy to use and so difficult to trace?"

Thomas groaned, rolling his head stiffly around his shoulders.

"I'm sorry," the lawyer said. The bands of tape around his torso felt as though they had shrunk overnight, and his breathing was shallow and painful. "I keep drifting off in the middle of the lecture. Did you have a point?"

Brackett snickered.

"Now, that's what I'm looking for!" he said gleefully. "I knew eventually you would prove a worthy student. That's excellent, Mr. Stone. Yes, I did have a point."

He waited until he had the lawyer's groggy attention.

"I only mention all this because I'm rather pleased that I was able to talk to your lovely wife again this morning on her *personal* cell phone number rather than the office number," he said. "I'd have woken you to share the news, but you were sleeping so peacefully, I hated to disturb you."

Cora, Thomas thought, rocking the chair slightly, struggling as he made a vain attempt to free his bonds, his hands clenched in frustration. *Dear Lord, help me hold it together until they find me. I don't care what happens to me—help Cora and our baby.*

"You look tired," Brackett continued, mocking. "You can't escape, so don't try. You'll only injure yourself further. Take another swallow or two of your coffee there. I've made it special for you. You should rest while you can. There's more to come in our little chess match, and you'll need your strength. Yes, indeed. You are going to need your strength."

Chapter 61

After the other detectives and officers had arrived and processed the crime scene, Ben dismissed them to the station and sat down with Susan at her desk to begin his own formal inquiries.

Susan began with the unsolicited advice that, for the time being, they should keep the disturbing information about Thomas away from the pregnant Cora Stone.

She hadn't wanted to tell him about Cora's condition, or that she only had another month before the baby would be born, but it was hard to ignore the fact that losing a baby was what had brought the woman to Balfour in the first place.

Ben didn't understand the problem even when Susan tried to explain.

He thought the whole town probably knew about the upcoming baby anyway. There had been suspicions and rumors circulating, but Thomas was tight-lipped and everyone respected his right to privacy, even though most, including Ben, did not understand the why.

"I'm not sure why you think she's so fragile," Ben said, regretting his words when he saw the look on Susan's face but unable to control his responses. "She's bound to notice her husband's missing sooner or later."

"You're such a man," Susan sputtered.

He'd heard that from Marcie more than once, but Susan made it sound more like an insult than a friendly jab at his lack of sensitivity.

Ben didn't care one way or the other about other people's secrets, except when they interfered with fulfilling his responsibility to the community.

"For the record," he said, stung by her criticism, "I've got a job to do, and I intend to do it—with or without your permission."

"Aren't you supposed to wait at least twenty-four hours?" she said. "What if he turns up and wants to know why you panicked his wife?"

Ben couldn't imagine that scenario at all, but she did have a point.

"When was the last time you tried to call Thomas?" he said gruffly.

"I called about a half-hour ago," she said. "Then I called Judge Mayer's office and they said they hadn't heard from Thomas this morning. I don't know if he planned on going there first, or if he was going to talk to the police chief in Savannah beforehand."

"Give me the police chief's number," Ben said politely.

Susan opened the Rolodex and handed him the card.

Mack Maclin, his veteran police instinct alerted, was much more concerned than the judge's office with the news that the Balfour police were trying to find Stone.

"Of course you've put an APB on his car," Maclin said. "When did he leave Balfour? Is there any reason to believe he might have changed his plans?"

"*Yes* to the first," Ben said, "*don't know* to the second, and *no* to the third."

"Does his wife have any ideas?"

Ben hesitated.

"We're playing this pretty close to the chest right now," he offered, knowing full well that explanation was not going to satisfy the other officer. It certainly wouldn't have satisfied him either if the circumstances were reversed.

"I suppose you know what you're doing," Maclin said skeptically. "What else do you need from me?"

Ben considered his limited options.

"We're short-staffed at the moment," he admitted. "Any search you can man from there would be helpful. Stone's assistant talked to Judge Mayer's office. If you know of anyone else that Stone might be meeting or any place he'd planned to go while he was in Savannah, I'd appreciate a list."

"There's a law firm here that I know he was working with," Maclin said. "And a private detective who did some follow-up after the initial investigation during the Chen murders. I can give them a call to see if Stone's been in touch with them in the last twenty-four hours."

"Thanks," Ben said. "Updates appreciated."

"Likewise," Maclin countered and hung up.

Susan sat, her hands uncharacteristically folded in her lap and her sequined sweater buttoned primly to the top. To Ben, she looked like a sparkling snow leopard about to pounce on unsuspecting prey.

"Well," she said, almost purring, "what's the next step?"

Ben wanted to tell her to go home, but the look on her face and the glint in her heavily shadowed eyes told him that would be a foolish idea.

"Susan . . ." he began cautiously, but she put up a hand and stopped him.

"Don't you dare pick a fight with me, Ben Taylor," she said. "I may not be one of your deputized minions, but I know Thomas better than anyone else, and if he's missing, I'm the best chance of helping you find him. Period."

"Okay," Ben said. "We're waiting on lab results for the, uh—"

"Blood," she interjected. "You can say the word blood. I'm not a child."

"With Lisa out of town I had to send the sample to the lab in Griffith," he said. "It will be later this afternoon before they can type it and crossmatch to the donor files so we know if the blood belongs to Thomas."

"Okay," she said. "There's that. What about his Honda?"

"I put out an APB with the Georgia State Patrol," he said. "If it's on the highway or an interstate, they'll find it, but you know what the north Georgia countryside is like. Too many local backroads and fire lanes, not to mention how easy it would be to cross state lines and head into the mountains of Tennessee or South Carolina."

"So you're telling me it's hopeless."

"I'm telling you to be patient," he said. "These things take time. We don't even know exactly what time he left yesterday or who was with him. We don't know if he moved the chess pieces as a clue for whoever found them, or if someone else moved them for him. We don't know what we don't know."

You're trying to suggest that I'm overreacting, Susan thought. *Trying to lower expectations and soften the worst-case scenario. You don't seem to know Thomas very well, and you don't know me at all.*

"What about the fingerprints?" she said. "Surely those will help."

"They're working on that now back at the station," he said. "This is a busy office, but we'll know soon enough who has been here."

Susan's cell phone began to vibrate on the desk.

"It's Harry," she said. "He's been in Memphis for the past week."

"You should take the call," Ben said, standing. "I'll give you some privacy. I know I don't need to tell you we shouldn't mention any of this until we have definitive news, although I *am* going to talk to Cora. She has every right to know."

Susan tried not to take offense. She didn't like being told what to do, but as much as Ben irritated her, she believed he meant well.

"Hello, Harry," she said as the police chief made his way to the outer door and slammed it firmly behind him. "Am I still meeting your plane at Anson's on Saturday night at six? I'm looking forward to seeing you. Tell me all about your trip so far."

Chapter 62

Inola Walker answered almost before Charlie had time to spit out his gum.

"Why, Detective Abbott," she said, "I've been waiting to hear from you."

"I sent a fax to the Memphis office about twenty minutes ago," Charlie said. "It's a sketch that Smith drew from a firsthand witness. I need for you to run it through your infamous databases."

"I got your fax," Inola said evenly. "What I didn't get was an explanation for why you're treating me like your errand girl. What are you working on?"

Charlie considered his options. Walker had told him to stay in New Orleans and not to do anything, and yet here he was investigating a new angle.

"I got a lead on a case, but I could really use your help."

"Do you have a name? Fingerprints? DNA?" she asked skeptically. "We can do a comprehensive search of photographs, but you've given me precious little if all you have is a sketch, even one of Officer Smith's."

"There's more," Charlie said. "The young woman was a graduate assistant in the English department at LSU when Brackett began his sentence at Angola."

There was a moment of charged silence before the FBI agent responded.

"I thought I told you *not* to do anything. This feels like you doing something."

"I know," Charlie countered. "I really do. If this pans out, it could mean you can put Brackett back behind bars. Maybe for longer than five years."

"Interesting. What's her connection to Brackett, other than working in the English department? Was she a witness during the trial?"

"Not to my knowledge," he said. "She was on the peripheral, and we didn't see a connection at the time. We interviewed several other grad students and professors, but Brackett didn't have any character witnesses to defend him in court. Not much character to defend."

"Then explain why we are looking for her," Walker said.

Charlie swallowed hard. He hoped his silence would be enough to convey where he got his lead from.

"Okay," she said finally. "Is there anything else I need to know?"

He thought about Cora's insistence on the candy bar, but he refused to risk sharing such a ridiculous clue without more investigation into the glass jar on Brackett's desk. That still seemed like a long shot at best.

"Not yet," he said. "Just need an ID on the girl."

"Point made," she said. "I'll get an agent to crosscheck the roster of graduate assistants in the yearbook with the sketch for the year of Brackett's trial. There can't be that many young women in that category."

Charlie made a noise of agreement and put another stick of gum into his mouth. He was feeling restless and rather subservient as well as hungry and annoyed.

"On a more pleasant note," Inola continued, "how's Officer Smith getting on?"

"Jim?" he said, looking up at the clock. He'd sent the Rookie on a well-earned break for a shrimp po-boy for lunch, and he wasn't due back for another fifteen minutes. "Why do you ask?"

"Don't be so defensive," she said. "I sent him to New Orleans to help. He's on my payroll. I'm allowed to ask questions."

Payroll my hind parts, he thought sourly. *He's here to babysit and bodyguard is what you mean.*

"He's Jim," Charlie said aloud. "I'm feeding him, if that's what you're asking . . . and getting him to bed at a reasonable hour, Mom."

"You can't answer a straightforward question, can you?"

"Nope." He began to smack his gum noisily. "Have you *met* me?"

The door opened.

Jim was back early, several fragrant take-out bags clutched against his broad chest and a plastic convenience store bag slung on his forearm.

Charlie swept the papers on the table to one side along with his cell phone.

Agent Walker had hung up in his ear without saying goodbye.

Chapter 63

Cora remade her makeshift bed in the den, folding the blanket and stacking the pillow on top and to one side on the love seat. She fluffed the two throw pillows on the sofa and tossed them at either end. She left the afghans in her oversized chair alone, since Solomon had returned there to nap.

Then, having made her surroundings tidy, she set to work on the question that unexpectedly needed her full attention.

How does Brackett know I'm pregnant? Cora thought.

There was no easy answer.

The last time she was pregnant, her hormones and emotions had led her to make foolish choices and decisions. She was determined not to repeat the experience and was trying vainly not to be disturbed by Brackett's calls.

It was obvious Brackett wanted her to feel intimidated and insecure ahead of whatever legal maneuvers he had planned. He had now called twice, making sure to drop in the detail of her pregnancy, a fact he shouldn't have known since he'd been in prison. Why did her pregnancy matter to him? Because it was a secret?

She turned over the list of names of people who knew.

Thomas. Marjorie. Lisa. Katy. Susan. Jane.

None of them had any contact with Brackett.

Charlie.

She dismissed it as soon as the thought came to mind—she knew Charlie would never have shared something so private, especially not with Brackett.

The only other possibility was that Brackett's attorneys had somehow dug it up in the course of their preparation for suing her and had shared that information with their client.

In fact, it was the only possibility that made sense.

She made the hard decision to let it go. Charlie said that Brackett was a chess master who played mind games, so this must be one of those.

Master of mind games, she thought. *I won't let you get to me. Not this time.*

Thomas had been concerned about leaving her alone, and she didn't want to give him a reason to doubt her when he called.

Food seemed the next normal step.

She decided she shouldn't wait until she actually wanted to eat. She'd put off lunch too long already—it was past noon.

Taking the Tupperware container of Marjorie's homemade chicken salad from the refrigerator, she put a generous scoop in the center of a round bowl, then lined the outer edges with saltine crackers.

That should be sufficient, she thought. *Even Marjorie couldn't complain about that portion size, and it looks appetizing—she does make excellent chicken salad.*

Solomon appeared in the kitchen as soon as he heard the refrigerator door open, planting himself at her feet and gazing up at her longingly with his sleepy almond eyes, but she filled her glass with tap water and ignored his petition for food.

"No, sweetheart," she said, shaking her head. "Go back to your nap. Marjorie puts sweet pickles and dried cranberries in her salad. You know you wouldn't eat pickles or cranberries even if you were starving. Don't beg."

She took out a fork from the silverware drawer and carried her plate into the den.

The determined cat followed, jumping up on the oversized chair before she could sit, curling himself into a defiant puddle of black fur.

"Smarty pants," she laughed. "You enjoy your afghan. I'll sit on the sofa."

The doorbell rang just as she put the second bite into her mouth.

"Oh, darn," she mumbled through the cracker, crumbs falling lightly onto her shirt front. "Who can that possibly be in the middle of the day? Do you think they'll leave if I don't go answer the door?"

Solomon blinked and twitched his ears.

"I don't think so either," she said, struggling to get up. "I'm putting my plate on the counter. Don't you dare touch it."

The doorbell rang twice more before she made it down the hallway and peered through the decorative frosted oval in the center of the door.

A manila envelope was pressed firmly against the glass.

"Won't that fit in the mailbox?" she said, debating with herself about opening the door to someone she didn't know. "You can leave it on the table on the porch."

The manila envelope dropped out of sight and was replaced by a wizened face encircled by a snowy white beard and bushy eyebrows, the pupils squinting in an attempt to see into the house.

Oh, goodness! Cora thought. *Santa Claus is outside my house delivering mail!*

"It's Quincy, the postmaster," the man announced. "Sorry, but I need a signature. Is Marjorie home? She's signed before."

That's what I get for hiding in here for so long, Cora thought. *I've gotten much too dependent on other people to do the simple things for me. I bet I wouldn't know half of the residents of Balfour if they appeared on my front step.*

"Okay," she said cautiously. "Do you have an ink pen, or should I get one?"

He took a pen from his shirt pocket and tapped it on the glass.

Cora decided she was acting like a bashful child. Surely this grumpy looking Santa didn't pose a threat. She unlocked the deadbolt and, opening the door a scant few inches, reached through for the envelope and the pen.

To her relief, after the man delivered the mail he put his hands into his pockets and took a wide step back, waiting patiently while she signed on the line and tore off the receipt.

"There," she said, embracing the envelope and poking the pen and paper back at him. "Thank you."

"You're welcome," he said, but he didn't move, looking absently around at the porch swing with its floral pillows, taking in the scent of the climbing white roses on the railing before returning his attention to the half-hidden sight of the diminutive woman in front of him.

She's not what I expected, he thought suddenly. *She's not what I expected at all. I mean, we've all heard stories, but she looks so fragile, like a porcelain doll.*

He scratched at his whiskers, searching for something else to say before she closed the door and he lost the opportunity to speak to a near celebrity that most of the people in Balfour had never seen.

"Nice to finally meet you," he said gravely, tipping his postal cap and adding a tiny bow from the waist.

Cora tried not to laugh at his elegant, turn-of-the-century manners. He seemed so kind, so sincere, so interesting.

"I'm not sure this qualifies as a meeting," she said, a foot still pressed against the bottom of the door as if that might somehow prevent the elderly man from entering if he wanted to do that. "But it's nice to meet you, Quincy. I'm glad to meet you too."

Chapter 64

Cora immersed herself in writing her last notes on the journal after she ate her own lunch and pacified Solomon with a handful of smelly treats.

Marjorie had sent a brief text to let her know that she would call around four or so to chat and let Jane talk. Her sister-in-law had been so excited that both of them had finally come to visit that she insisted on taking them out to explore for the afternoon.

Cora was glad they were having a good time and a little guilty for feeling relieved to be in the house alone.

The late afternoon air was warm and unmoving, and she was feeling lethargic and more than a little sleep-deprived.

The dreams were tiring enough under normal circumstances, but in her present pregnant state, she was exhausted. She was also a bit bored from reading and a little concerned about how to tell Thomas the truth about the journal.

It wasn't what she thought it would be at all.

When he asked, she would be forced to admit that the gems of discovery she'd expected were instead a boring narrative of daily life in the Chen household.

A private woman, Madame Chen, Jane's great-grandmother, had written very little about her feelings or the emotions she must have felt leaving Taiwan and coming to America after her husband's death. There was no breathtaking story about the origin of the priceless alexandrite necklace that had been smuggled from Russia through mainland China. Not even a footnote. Even a mention of the dragon ring that had been passed down from mother to daughter was nowhere to be found among the pages.

There *were* copious journal entries with names and dates that related to the import and export business, notes about buying and selling of properties, and a veritable logbook of all their employees and their job descriptions written in alphabetical order and without elaboration.

There were the usual records of signed contracts and bills of sale, including for the priceless antiques that once filled the house in Savannah and now resided in long-term storage for Jane's future use.

Madame Chen had a separate section of the journal where she had dutifully recorded the birth dates of her children, followed by the names of all the schools they attended and any degrees and honors they had earned. The most interesting part of that was that she had also included a family tree that listed relatives going back almost two centuries.

Amazing to Cora was the absence of personal comments concerning Madame Chen's grandchildren. Her grandson, the son of her elder son, was mentioned in a casual line at the bottom of a page. An asterisk to her life that did not warrant so much as a paragraph of celebration. The boy's mother, along with her birth and death dates, was noted as having died during childbirth. There was nothing else about her.

The birth of Jane's mother was equally dispassionate and lacking in detail.

Under the woman's name was written the single word *Jun* with the word *daughter* in parentheses. The date was September 5.

Cora tried to feel grateful that at least there were dates beside the names, which she assumed to be birthdays, but she was puzzled by the name Jun. She made a note to see if the word had any significance in Mandarin, and why it might be associated with Jane. She wasn't sure how someone could have mistaken Jane's name, but she had to entertain the possibility.

There were a few pages about the attic room, mostly in the form of an inventory of furnishings moved from the main area of the house into the secluded space. Cora also found a list of classic children's books and educational toys, the dollhouse among them, apparently purchased by others and delivered to the home.

At the back of the journal, Madame Chen had made yet another list, this time of family jewelry—minus the necklace and the dragon ring—and an extensive catalogue of the artwork, vases, and sculptures that decorated the elaborate rooms.

She'd collected many priceless imported antiques over the years, and Cora's heart was sad that those possessions seemed to warrant considerably more attention and detailed description than the human beings who had lived under Madame Chen's roof.

Thomas had seen to it that all the items had been specially secured in a guarded warehouse and appropriately insured for their full value. These, plus the furniture and property, were Jane's legacy, and he had worked to preserve them for her when she was twenty-one and old enough to assume that responsibility.

Cora knew that Thomas would certainly appreciate the attention to detail, but all in all the journal was not what she had hoped to find in a family history. She had hoped for more personal stories about the aging dowager whose life had been full of adventure and advantages. But, much like the ancient woman in Cora's dream about Savannah, the real Madame Chen was equally cold and uncommunicative in life as she was in death.

What was abundantly clear to Cora was that both Jane and her mother must have lived lives of isolation, devoid of what she would have called grandmotherly affection. There were no keepsakes. No tokens of affection. No birthday or Christmas cards. No pictures—other than the ones that had adorned Madame Chen's dressing table. No anecdotes, no stories, no warmth.

Nothing to show that the illegitimate mother and daughter had ever been any more than an embarrassment to the matriarchal ruler who governed her home with an iron fist encased in a velvet glove.

The attic room was theirs, and from the list of furnishings, unlike the rest of the mansion. A sanctuary and refuge, a secret place they shared.

Thomas had the movers pack those precious things too. Those boxes, the ones the child would know best, waited while little Jane's heart healed.

Cora had no idea what memories the rocking chair and the quilted beds would evoke in Jane. No clue how she might respond to seeing the dollhouse or the books.

And as she read the journal, Cora wiped away tears from her own eyes.

She had chosen to confine herself, much like Jane and her mother had been confined, in Charlie's grandparents' house. She had locked herself away from a world that she avoided as she watched the rest of humanity come and go outside her front porch windows.

Was she really the best mother for Jane if she herself couldn't venture outside her own front door? How could she possibly help a child when she herself was almost paralyzed by dread?

Had her years of experience in psychology taught her nothing?

Marjorie was a blessing in her life, and Thomas was a dedicated, devoted man—but what kind of mother would she be not only to Jane but to the new baby if she couldn't free herself from her own past?

Cora's head had begun to ache and she closed her eyes, intending to rest for only a few moments.

But within a minute, her body grew heavy and she sank into the cushions, fast asleep on the den sofa in the middle of the afternoon.

Chapter 65

Cora looked down at the unfamiliar coffee mug and realized that something was terribly wrong. She was dreaming—alone and seated at a strange dining table, not standing at a sink and certainly not in her grandmother's kitchen.

Her intuition was on fire with dread, hanging in the air around her like a blanket of pine-scented smoke. Something serious had happened. She knew it. Something life-threatening and unexpected—and personal. Very, very personal.

She could almost smell the sickening-sweet odors of blood and death mixed with the scent of burning wood. A fear she did not quite recognize rose into her throat as she fought a natural inclination to panic.

A chill of hard, cold air brushed across her bare face, and she turned to look at the curtained windows.

There was no sign of light. Predawn. The empty hours before day began.

Where am I? she thought. *What am I supposed to see?*

The sturdy wooden chair across from her was at an angle, pushed away from the edge as though someone had suddenly gotten up and left the room. A used spoon, a circle of what smelled like coffee staining the inside, lay to one side of the mug.

Cora looked closer.

Her own floral cup sat in front of her, quite full, untouched and icy cold, an iridescent sheen on the top of the black liquid.

How long has that been poured? she thought. *Was someone expecting me?*

She reached across and picked up the other mug and lifted it closer. Inside, an inch or so layer of thick liquid coated the bottom. Undissolved grains of a lighter powder formed a crusty ring above the top of the liquid, and the whole solution had a bitter odor.

She took a sharp breath, put the mug back down, and closed her eyes.

From the recesses of her mind, an image of Charlie appeared, almost as though he were seated in the chair beside her.

The irritable, childishly frustrating version of her ex-husband with that smirk on his face she knew so well. Watching her expectantly for a clue she didn't have.

She opened her eyes and looked around for him, but he was gone.

Is this his mug? she thought wildly. *Is that why I feel panicked and unsettled? Has he been poisoned? Is he dead or dying? Is that why this place feels so personal?*

No, she chided herself firmly.

If Charlie *were* dead and had something to tell her, he would have shown up himself, even more impatient and annoying in death than he was in life. Besides, he would never have sent a half-empty coffee mug to do his talking for him.

Charlie didn't understand the meaning of the word subtlety.

That thought made her smile for a split second before she sobered and realized that one feeling was true—she *should* be looking for clues. There must be something she was supposed to find. Something to see.

There had to be more than just an irrational feeling of anxiety.

But what and where? And more importantly, who was involved?

She rotated herself slowly and studied her surroundings.

A striped silk tie, devoid of color, was hanging on the back of the chair beside her.

Thomas, her mind screamed. *That tie belongs to Thomas!*

Trembling, she reached out, but before she could close her fingers, the image slipped away and onto the floor where it disappeared like a vapor.

Straightening, she saw another object in the semidarkness, perched beside the floral cup.

A solitary chess piece. A riderless horse. A pale knight.

And Cora woke from her nap, cold chills of fear running up and down her spine, the sound of the office telephone ringing insistently from down the hall.

Chapter 66

Ben did his best to put the sight of the red-stained knight and the washcloth drenched in blood out of his mind, but no matter what he did to distract himself, the image returned.

Watching the second hand tick from minute to minute was excruciating.

When Perkins finally came into the office with the forensic report, he knew before he opened the envelope what the results were going to be. And he knew exactly what he needed to do.

If anyone had advice about finding Thomas Stone, it was Charlie Abbott.

Charlie had been the answer to too many unsolvable mysteries over the past year to keep him out of the loop. How Charlie always seemed to know when to show up in town or what leads to pursue, Ben didn't know. But right now, one of his own was missing and he would take all the help he could get.

The detective answered his cell phone on the first ring.

"Hello, Chief," Charlie said. "What's up?"

Ben leaned back in his chair and considered his empty coffee mug. "I've got some news" he said.

"News?" Charlie said, standing and stretching. He and Jim were almost finished sifting through the files from the Brackett case in the multiple storage boxes. They'd narrowed the photographs they needed to a select few and were waiting on a call from Walker about the identity of the graduate assistant.

Jim looked up from the sketch he was redrawing and tilted his head expectantly. Then he pointed to himself and the door as if to ask if Charlie wanted him to leave the room, but the detective shook his head and motioned for Jim to remain seated.

"Go on, Chief," Charlie said. "I'm listening."

"Thomas was supposed to drive to Savannah yesterday," Ben began, "but Susan found the office unlocked this morning, and there were bloody chess pieces in the center of the desk in Thomas's office."

Charlie sat down hard.

"Come again?" he said. "Whose blood?"

"Forensics just came back," Ben said. "We found Thomas's blood on two chess pieces and a washcloth in the middle of his desk, and there's a faint trail of blood drops out the doorway and into the parking lot."

"Have you found his car?"

"No," Ben said. "And he's made no contact with anyone in Savannah. We've issued an APB, notified the GBI, and Mark Maclin's got his men working from that end."

Silence. Ben waited and silently prayed Charlie knew something he didn't.

"I'm in New Orleans, Chief," Charlie said quietly, breaking the silence. *Where I've been told to be.* "What do you want me to do?"

Then a horrific thought hit Charlie squarely in the chest.

Chess pieces. Dreams. Cora. Brackett.

"Have you talked to Cora?" he asked. "What did she say? Did she tell you to call me?"

"Well," Ben said uncomfortably, "no, I haven't talked to her yet."

Charlie sensed that there was a great deal more the Chief wanted to say, so he waited, dread running rampant through his mind. When the Chief didn't speak, Charlie pushed ahead.

"It's not like you to break protocol," Charlie said, struggling to maintain his resolve. "Why now?"

Ben sighed and opted for the truth.

"I've done all I can do for now, and I was hoping you might have some ideas."

Why does everyone expect me to know how to solve their problems? Charlie thought.

Cora had given him a job to do here, and he had to see it through. She *told* him the dreams said she should handle the professor on her own. She *told* him the girl was important.

Thomas was important too. But so was following the clues Cora had laid out for him. Charlie felt the discomfort of being stretched in too many directions.

"You need to notify next of kin," he said. "Now."

Ben regretted his decision to call Charlie. He should have known better. The wild card detective had helped the Balfour PD more times than Ben wanted to admit or even allow, but Charlie was his own man. He'd do what he wanted when he wanted. No more and no less.

And apparently this time Charlie didn't want to help.

"Thanks, Charlie, I'll do that," Ben replied curtly.

"Anytime," Charlie said. The cell phone began to buzz in his ear with another call. "Wish I could do something, but I can't. I've got to go."

He disconnected Ben and took the second call.

"Hello, Agent Walker," he said, taking out his pen and notepad as he listened and then scribbled a name. "Thanks. Later."

Jim had busied himself quietly replacing all his art supplies in his backpack and cleared the table, stacking the evidence boxes neatly in the corner of the room. Only a handful of photographs in a clear evidence bag remained on the top of his own bag.

"I need a change of scenery," Charlie said, slipping his cell phone into his back pocket and throwing his jacket over his shoulder. "Not sure how productive it's going to be, but I'm going stir crazy in this room. Grab your things. We'll get snacks on the way."

Chapter 67

For a fleeting moment, as Cora snatched the phone from its cradle, she hoped that the call on her office phone was Thomas, reassuring her that she had been foolish to worry about him. That he'd just been busy with talking to people and overseeing the adoption. Logically she knew if he called, he'd call on her cell phone and not the office—but she hoped anyway.

Instead she was greeted with the unexpected concern of her former psychiatrist, Ted Floyd, and his strident, nasal whine.

She was irrationally both calmed and distracted by the sound of his voice.

"I've been meaning to call you for several weeks now," he said, sounding to Cora as though somehow he thought it was her fault that he hadn't called. He seemed to bring out that reaction in her. Sessions with him had made her feel like a small child, although she could never quite pinpoint what it was that made her respond that way. It was just his method of analysis, and she disliked it immensely.

She felt that he dismissed her feelings in favor of his opinions. Her sessions with him often left her more depressed than healed, and she was relieved when Marjorie came into her life. Marjorie had helped her find peace away from Floyd's unrelenting desire to push her into medicating the depression away.

Not that she minded taking prescriptions when she needed them. She simply wanted to be consulted about her condition rather than treated like a rebellious child who wouldn't eat her vegetables.

Cora could picture him in his expansive sixth-floor office, seated in one of the two massive black leather chairs on either side of the picture window, looking out over the treetops toward the Atlanta skyline. There would be a cup of Earl Grey tea on the side table at his elbow and an iPad in his lap as he prepared to take notes on their conversation.

Floyd was a weasel-faced little man, and although Cora respected the numerous framed credentials that littered his walls and admired him as a noted psychiatrist, she didn't like him as a person.

"Hello, Dr. Floyd," Cora said, her heartbeat pounding in her ears. "Did you call about something specific?"

"I heard on the news last night that Ed Brackett has been released from prison in Louisiana," he said, the s's in his words hissing through the space between his front teeth. "You worked with the FBI on that. How do you feel about the fact that he only served half his sentence?"

I'm not your patient anymore, Cora thought. *My well-being is not your business. We parted ways when you persisted in giving me unwanted advice and you were angry when I wouldn't do what you told me to do.*

"I thought you might be calling because you'd read my latest book on childhood trauma," she said, lowering herself slowly into her own office chair and propping up her swollen feet as she regained her composure. "I was hoping you'd have a view of the treatment options in Chapter 3, or maybe offer to write a review for *Psychology Today*."

"Cora," he said sternly. "You are deflecting."

Then his voice uncharacteristically softened.

"The book is excellent," he said. "I read it when you published last month, and I found your views fresh and innovative. There are a number of my colleagues who agree that you are rapidly rising as one of the preeminent authorities in the field. Now, not discounting your abilities, I am still your psychiatrist, and I haven't heard from you in almost a year. I wanted to touch base with you and see how you are doing in light of recent events."

She had no idea if Brackett's release was the only recent event that Floyd meant. She doubted he knew about her pregnancy or about the recent spate of dreams with James and working with Charlie, and she felt disinclined to share personal details.

Her private life was her own, and she liked it that way.

"Did you really have a reason to call?" she said.

As she waited, Cora could picture Floyd taking off his glasses, tapping one of the legs on his hairy chin, and considering how to answer her. He'd always said she asked more questions than he did, and he didn't like that at all. He preferred to ask the questions.

"I keep up with the news," he said smugly. "The Brackett trial made the major networks when he was convicted. You had a crucial role in his incarceration. The local stations in Atlanta have all covered his recent release—and speculation is high that he is looking for legal retribution. That would involve you."

So you're calling because you think I might need you again? Cora thought. *I'm not sure you're that self-serving. Are you really concerned about my welfare?*

"I can hear you thinking," Floyd said confidently. "Dredging up the Brackett trial is bound to evoke deep emotions. I wanted you to know that I'm available if you need me."

"That's considerate of you," Cora said politely.

When pigs fly and fish dance and the cows come home singing, she thought. *I'd rather sit down with a copperhead over coffee and discuss the meaning of life.*

It was Cora's turn to hear Floyd thinking.

"You've heard from Brackett, haven't you?" he said. "You didn't want to tell me."

She knew he was only guessing, but she also knew that Floyd would be able to tell if she lied to him. Maybe he understood Brackett's true nature more than he could understand hers.

"Yes," Cora said. "He's called me."

"Well," he said, his self-important tone grating on her last nerve, "I'm sure you know who you're dealing with. All the same, I'm going to give you a piece of advice. A reminder. You might find that Brackett's release stirs up old emotions for you and brings you back to that time in your life. But you aren't a victim, Cora. You're a survivor. Don't let Brackett or any legal action he might take derail your progress. You've already given in to fear too much."

She knew Floyd was harping about her refusal to leave the house. Again. He'd brought it up often enough in their early sessions. In his defense, he didn't know that things were different. He didn't know that she was pregnant and she had a baby to protect. It wasn't just about her anymore.

But she wasn't going to tell him any of that. He didn't need to know.

"I can handle Ed Brackett," she said.

"And I don't doubt it," he said. "When you make up your mind, Cora, you can do anything you want to do."

Something about the tone in his voice was vaguely reassuring—and surprising.

"Thank you," she said sincerely.

"Not at all," he said brusquely.

She could imagine him putting his horn-rimmed glasses back on and pushing them up his pointed nose to glance suggestively at his Rolex watch, about to point out that they were out of time and her session was over.

There was an awkward pause.

"Cora," he said, "call if you need anything. I mean it. Please call."

"Thank you," she said again. "Thank you, Dr. Floyd."

Chapter 68

Marjorie went out on her sister-in-law's back porch and settled in one of the cushioned rocking chairs to call Cora, but she hesitated. She'd taken out her cell phone when a curious, unsettled feeling of dread came over her for which she had no reasonable explanation.

The afternoon had gone beautifully.

Griffith was a friendly, bustling town with sprawling modern shopping areas full of interesting places to explore. Her sister-in-law had given considerable thought to what might please Jane—a corner ice cream shop with a mind-boggling assortment of frozen treats, a light lunch with child-sized portions of food at adorable tables under striped outdoor umbrellas, and an elaborate park playground with a separate section exclusively for toddlers and smaller children.

The log cabin playhouse in the children's section fascinated the little girl, who found two other children with whom to play. To the entertainment of the hawkeyed adults, all three seemed to fall in together in a game of make-believe that resulted in giggles and copious conversation. They climbed in and out of the doors and windows, up and over the slides, and around the porches and cubbyholes until all three were worn out and ready to climb into the laps of their caregivers.

Once back at the house, Jane washed her face and hands and obediently crawled onto the ruffled daybed in the sunroom, the cat sisters tucked in her tiny arms.

Marjorie and her sister-in-law made cups of tea and settled themselves in the living room to catch up before Evie excused herself to begin preparations for supper.

And that's when Marjorie went on the back porch to call Cora.

The housekeeper knew from the moment Cora answered the phone that her feelings of dread were justified. Something seemed off and out of the ordinary.

Cora's voice was unemotional and detached. Almost cool.

"Cora," Marjorie began, "what's going on? Is it the baby? We can pack up and be home in about an hour if you aren't feeling well."

"I'm fine," Cora fibbed, justifying herself for not telling the whole truth.

Marjorie and Jane both deserved time for themselves away from the confines of the house. Besides, the dream list said they were supposed to go. Just like Charlie was supposed to go. She was supposed to handle Brackett alone.

James said so.

"I was up late last night reading Madame Chen's journal and I'm just a bit sleepy, that's all. But I've been eating the chicken salad and fresh fruit. Thank you for taking care of everything here so well."

"Have you heard from Thomas?"

Cora checked her watch, considered her recent disturbing

dream, and was glad she didn't have to fib again.

"No," she said. "He sent a heart emoji last night, but I'm not expecting him to call until he's had an opportunity to talk to everyone in Savannah. He told me up front that he might be gone for two days. Judge Mayer is a busy man, and the appointment to see him was only tentative. I know Thomas wanted to review all the security measures for the storage unit with Mark Maclin and also go by the mansion to talk to the administrator there. There are so many details, and he wants to be certain everything is above board before we proceed with the finer points of Jane's adoption."

"I can't imagine anyone suspecting you or Thomas of being underhanded with Jane's inheritance," Marjorie said, glad that Cora had opened up and was sounding more like herself. "That's ridiculous."

"Still," Cora said, "you know how detailed Thomas is."

"Yes," the housekeeper agreed reluctantly. "He is at that. But are you sure you're okay? When is Lisa coming by to check on you?"

"Well, I did sleep downstairs in my chair with Solomon," Cora confessed, hoping that would satisfy her friend. "And he and I had a nap about an hour ago and we just woke up. Lisa said Casey would be by tomorrow for the weekly visit. Seriously, Marjorie, I would feel awful if you and Jane cut your visit short because of me."

"I can still be concerned," Marjorie said doubtfully.

"You can be as concerned as you like, as long as you do it from Griffith."

Cora forced herself to add a light laugh to her declaration. The last thing she wanted was for Marjorie and Jane to come home and find themselves in the middle of upheaval and uncertainty. Besides, the dream could mean anything. She couldn't upset Marjorie and especially not little Jane until there were more definitive answers.

There was a sharp knock at Cora's front door.

"I'm feeling a bit sleepy again," Cora said, cupping her hand over the receiver and wondering who could possibly be knocking. After the postman's visit she could imagine all sorts of potential guests. "Could you call me back after you've had your dinner? I'd love to talk to Jane before she goes to bed tonight."

"Of course," the housekeeper agreed. "Get some rest and drink plenty of water."

"I will," Cora said and hung up quickly, padding down the dim hallway to see who was waiting on her front porch now.

Chapter 69

Ben gripped his police cap in his sweaty hands and waited on Cora's front porch until he could see her shadow on the inside of the glass oval in the door.

"It's Ben Taylor," he announced. "Chief Ben Taylor. Could I please speak to you, Mrs. Stone?"

Cora peeked through the frosted glass. She had no way of knowing that the man was who he said he was, except that he was wearing a uniform and he did vaguely seem to fit the description she'd once heard from Charlie.

"Good afternoon," she said, opening the door a crack. "What can I do for you?"

"I'd like to talk to you, if I may," he said, taking a wide step back to give her ample room to feel comfortable with his presence. The sight of her tiny frame in its pregnant form was unnerving. "Maybe you'd rather I stay out here on the porch."

For the third time in as many days he wished Jim Smith was here in Balfour instead of off with that FBI agent in Memphis. Jim would have been the perfect person to talk to this woman. Jim would have known what to say. She'd have been at ease with the gentle giant and his friendly demeanor.

"Mrs. Stone?" he said. "It's really important. I talked to Charlie."

Poor man, Cora thought instinctively. *This must be serious. This must be about the dream about Thomas.*

"Of course," she said, refusing to allow herself to speculate, smoothing the front of her shirt over her belly nervously. "Could I bring you out a glass of sweet tea or lemonade?"

"I'm fine, thank you," he said. "I'll just mosey over to the swing and sit, if that's okay with you."

"Yes, of course," Cora said, watching him as he walked across the wooden planks and settled himself on the edge of the cushions.

She stepped out to get a better look at him, although she remained leaning against the frame of the open door, one hand on the knob and the other resting on her swollen abdomen.

"It feels wrong to sit while you're standing," he said, beginning to rise, but she waved him down.

"I appreciate that," she said, "but when you're as far along as I am, there's really no position that doesn't feel awkward—sitting, standing, reclining—they're all the same at this point. One of us should be comfortable."

Ben didn't know whether she was making a joke or not, but she wasn't smiling. He couldn't remember the last time he'd had to give a pregnant woman bad news or he'd been seated instead of standing in the presence of a woman. But his knees felt a little watery, and he decided it was better to stay put than stand up and have to sit right back down.

"You said you talked to Charlie . . ." Cora said helpfully.

Ben ran a thick hand around the inside of his collar, rubbing the back of his neck and anticipating the migraine he knew was about to erupt at his temples.

"When was the last time you saw your husband?" he said, taking out his notebook and pen, balancing and bearing down on his thigh as he wrote.

Cora felt the blood drain from her hands and feet, leaving her icy cold, unsteady, and quite dizzy. Her stomach lurched violently.

"Thomas left the house yesterday afternoon," she said, twisting the gold feather-and-ruby ring on her finger. "He said he was going by the office to pick up some papers, and then he'd be leaving for appointments in Savannah. What's going on?"

"Did you hear from him last night?"

"Just an emoji from his cell phone," she said. "I assumed it was his way of telling me he'd arrived safely at his hotel."

"Was that something normal for him?"

Cora thought for a moment. It hadn't seemed odd at the time, but they'd never been apart like that. She was embarrassed that she didn't know the answer.

"Chief Taylor," she said, "please be honest with me. Why are you here?"

"I got a call from your husband's secretary this morning," he began. This was the part he always dreaded.

"Susan," Cora corrected him gently. "She's a legal assistant, not a secretary."

"Yes, Susan," he repeated. "The legal assistant. Anyway, she found the office unlocked when she went in this morning and there were chess pieces with blood on them, mailed from New Orleans."

Cora's pulse began to throb and her heart pounded against her rib cage. The blood that had left her extremities flooded back with a vengeance. She could feel the nausea rising in her throat as the baby shifted inside, pressing against her aching spine.

She stared at the Chief, realizing that he looked almost as distraught on the outside as she felt on the inside.

Was this my dream? About a tie and a chess piece? How can I know for certain? Who can I tell? They'll all think I'm crazy.

"Mrs. Stone," he said carefully. "Do you have any reason to think that your husband didn't make it to Savannah?"

"Does the blood belong to Thomas?"

Ben twisted his hat in his hands.

"Yes," he said, marveling at the apparent calm of the young woman in the face of his disturbing news. "We're treating this as a missing person investigation as of now. I'm very sorry. Is there something I can do? Someone I can call to come and stay with you?"

"That isn't necessary," she said. "What are you doing to find my husband?"

"We've put out bulletins, and we contacted the GBI. Maclin in Savannah has got his men investigating from there, and he's reaching out to one of their local investigators who worked for Thomas."

Ben stopped to wipe the sweat from his neck again.

"We're doing all we can, but we don't know what we don't know at this point. I'm shorthanded, so it's counterproductive to send men out to do random searches when we may need them here."

Cora nodded and smoothed her shirt down, fingering the buttons absently.

"What about DNA from the office?" she said quietly. "Other people who might have been there when Thomas was there."

She's worked with the police before, Ben thought. *She knows the questions to ask. She knows the drill. Maybe that's why she's not in a heap on the floor.*

"Results aren't back yet," he said. "It's a busy office, and we're doing exclusion prints."

"But you'll let me know what you find out, right?" she asked, her mouth dry.

"It's an ongoing investigation," he said. "I wish you'd tell me who I can call to come and sit with you. This is shocking news, and you shouldn't be alone. Why don't I have an officer do an hourly drive-by?"

Cora shook her head. The bachelor police chief's suggestions were kind, but she'd seen his type before both on the force and in the military—strong men who never really seemed to know what to do with a pregnant woman.

Cora was beginning to think that Ben was going to insist that she have a babysitter for the night.

"Just keep me informed," she said, shifting from one foot to the other, the baby inside beginning to roll and kick. "I appreciate that you came in person, Chief Taylor. Both my husband and Charlie hold you in high regard."

Ben stood respectfully.

"And I'm going to try to live up to that, Mrs. Stone," he said. "You can count on the Balfour Police Department. I'll be in touch as soon as we have any word at all about Thomas. And you let me know if there's anything else I can do for you."

Chapter 70

The remainder of the afternoon passed quickly in the small town.

Once Ben let the rest of the department know he'd spoken to Cora, word of Thomas Stone's disappearance spread from shop to shop and person to person like an outbreak of a rare, feverish disease on a preschool playground.

Simmons' Restaurant was abuzz with speculation, and even stoic Bill came out of the kitchen more than once to deliver plates to crowded tables and booths, listening attentively to the gossip and rumor that passed among the patrons.

Sam, ironically, did not seem to be enjoying the rampant conjectures.

She called in one of the standby servers to help with the lunch crowd and spent most of the day in solitary, hovering around the cash register, brooding and considering her most recent conversation with Charlie.

Wondering if he knew his best friend was missing and whether or not he'd made his peace with Thomas before he'd gone back to New Orleans.

She'd picked up the phone once or twice to call him, but she put it down just as quickly. Cora knew Charlie better than anyone else, except maybe Thomas. If Cora had news, she could call her ex-husband and tell him what was going on.

Down the street at the B&B, Darcie had heard the news from one of her regular guests who was spending the weekend in town on his way to North Carolina on a business trip. He'd taken a late lunch at Sam's and overheard a discussion that he felt compelled to share with his hostess.

Darcie called Marcie, who did not let her baby sister know that she already knew what was going on. There was a time and a place for sibling bragging, and this was neither the time nor the place.

After calling her sister, Darcie called the Senator on his personal cell phone. Normally she would not have taken such a presumption, but Thomas Stone was one of the most important men in Balfour. If he was missing, then the Senator needed to know.

Stewart Wilton could be high-handed, arrogant, and ego-driven, but he had resources no one else could match. If anyone had the ways and means to find the missing lawyer, it was the prominent senator.

Wilton promised Darcie he would finalize business for the week and take his private plane back to Balfour by tomorrow afternoon to see what he could accomplish.

Marcie, for her part, did not call Marjorie, knowing, as she did, that Jane was with the doting housekeeper in Griffith. No sense stirring a pot that was already boiling. She knew if Cora wanted Marjorie to know, she'd tell her. Little Jane certainly didn't need to be dragged into an emotional mess, and Marjorie didn't need her attention divided in two places right now.

The owner of the Piney Woods did, however, consider calling Charlie, but she decided that that call, too, fell to Cora Stone. So Marcie spent the afternoon muttering to Elvira and cleaning out the storage shed at the back of the property.

Ginny, homebound and impatiently resting in bed, received two phone calls—one from Vicki at the florist shop and then another from Alice at the church office. Both women hoped Ginny would offer some suggestion about what Deborah's Daughters could do for Cora.

Ginny called Katy Wilton, which is how Katy found herself standing on Cora's porch just after six o'clock and knocking on the front door, a small overnight bag at her feet.

"I've come to spend the night," Katy announced cheerfully, seeing the surprised look on Cora's face. "I've already eaten, so you don't have to be concerned about that."

Cora embraced the younger woman in a long, warm hug, tears of gratitude slipping down her cheeks.

"You didn't have to come," Cora said, sniffling. "I'm just fine."

Katy closed and bolted the door behind her, picking up her bag and depositing it by the foot of the staircase.

"You never believed me when I said that," she said kindly. "I don't know why you'd think I would believe you when you say it either."

"Katy," Cora began, but the other woman strode past her down the hallway and into the kitchen, carefully avoiding the curious Solomon who'd followed the pregnant woman when she'd gotten up from her seat in the den.

"Let's have some tea," Katy said. "I know Marjorie doesn't like people puttering around in her territory, but she'll forgive me this once, I'm sure. Have you eaten yet? I'm not much good at fancy cooking, but even Lizzy likes my omelets."

"Katy," Cora tried again. Solomon added a muted meow.

"Lizzy is spending the night with Amy and the baby," Katy continued, opening cabinets and filling a pot with cold water from the faucet to put on the stove. "Hannah's clucking over all three of them like a mother hen with a brood of newly hatched chicks. They don't even know I'm gone."

"Katy," Cora said, sitting on a stool at the kitchen island and leaning over to prop herself up on her elbows. "You don't have to be here, but I do appreciate your concern."

"This isn't concern," Katy said, taking down several boxes of tea and lining them up on the countertop. "This is caring. Caring has feet and hands. More than half the town is concerned—I'm here because they'd like to care and don't know how."

Cora found herself unable and unwilling to argue with the energetic, bustling woman, so she watched as Katy washed up the few dirty dishes in the sink and placed them on the rack to dry.

"I'm happy you can see my point," Katy said, wiping her hands on a dishcloth. "Now, tell me what tea appeals to you, and I'll check the refrigerator for something for your supper. I'm sure Marjorie left you amply supplied, but my omelet offer stands. You don't know what you're missing until you've eaten my eggs with cheddar cheese."

Chapter 71

Thomas sat, still tightly bound to the chair, drifting in and out of consciousness, his head bowed and his stiff lips moving silently but deliberately.

Brackett turned from the cabin window, letting the curtain fall back in place.

"Praying, lawyer?" he said sarcastically. "Don't get your hopes up. Even your God can't save you now."

Thomas licked at the corner of his dry mouth, the bitter taste of the tainted coffee thickening his speech.

"Oh, I'm okay," he said softly. "I was actually praying for you."

A heavy hand swung out and struck him across the side of his already swollen face, and Thomas felt his teeth bite sharply into the inside of his cheek.

A fresh trickle of warm blood escaped from his mouth as he flexed his jaw.

"Clever," Brackett spat. "But that's not what your piece does.

You're the knight. The white knight guarding the king and his castle. And doing a poor job of it, I might say. Oh, you might fancy yourself a crusader, but you're not. Your little wife's the bishop. She's the religious one. Didn't you know that?"

"I know chess is the oldest game of skill in the world," Thomas replied, tentatively touching the side of his mouth with his one free hand and checking for chips in his teeth with the tip of his tongue. "A game of war and strategy."

Nothing broken, he thought. *That's a blessing. Keep him talking. The longer he talks, the more time they have to search. I know they're searching. They have to be.*

"Why don't you enlighten me on the finer points of the game," Thomas said, shifting as much as the constraints would allow, sharp pain shooting through his limbs.

"It's been a long time since I've played, and I was never very good."

Brackett eyed him suspiciously.

"I suppose we have time," he said, "before I decide to call and tell Cora how to find you. I want her to suffer through the night first. A night or two alone, trapped in the consequences of her choices. Not much compensation for all those years I spent in a cell, waiting for release, but it will have to do."

"You're going to call Cora again?" Thomas said. He didn't like saying her name out loud. It brought up too many images, but he needed to know the plan. Understand what he was up against. Decide what needed to be done and what he could do.

"Tomorrow." Brackett lowered himself carefully onto the bench as it creaked. "I'll call her in the morning. We'll talk a bit, and I'll explain the situation to her. And she will agree to come to meet us here. She won't have a choice. She's the bishop, you know. The third most powerful piece on the board. The bishop represents the church."

"The church?" he said, feeling his lip begin to swell. "Is this about religion?"

"Oh, you'd like to make it about that, wouldn't you?" Brackett sneered. "Your morality and self-righteous superiority. I thought you people believed all sins were somehow equal in the eyes of your God. How do you think He feels about your sin—that you married another man's wife?"

"Well," Thomas said, fully expecting another blow for his retort, "she wasn't another man's wife when I married her."

Brackett threw back his head and laughed—an ugly, nasty laugh.

"You *are* a lawyer!" he bellowed. "An answer for every question! If I'm not careful, white knight, I could begin to like you."

"So," Thomas said, remembering the three pieces mailed to his office, "Cora's a bishop and I'm a white knight—who's the pawn?"

Brackett's eyelids narrowed.

"Pawns are disposable pieces," he said. "They come in all varieties. They can be foot soldiers or peasants. The first line of sacrifice and defense. The ones who make the first move in the game."

"I thought knights could make the first move too," Thomas said. "Just hop over the pawns and take the field."

Brackett's eyes narrowed, his forehead wrinkling.

"You remember well for someone who hasn't played recently."

The bench groaned under Brackett's weight as he shifted and balanced his elbows on his knees, the gun cradled between his hands.

"You haven't answered my question," Thomas insisted. "Who's the pawn?"

"I'm tired of being cross-examined, lawyer," he said, smothering a yawn. "You're beginning to sound like one of my former failing students, haggling for the answers to the exam."

Thomas looked away to the window, a sliver of orange, glowing light glimmering between the sparse curtains.

Looks like the sun is going down, he thought, dropping his chin to his chest in a vain attempt to lessen the pressure on his skull. *I've been here, what, two days? What chance do I have if they come in the dark? Cora wouldn't really come, would she? Not alone. Would she bring Charlie? No. If she asked Charlie to help, then he'd keep her away. Charlie would come on his own, and then Brackett would shoot them both and go after Cora.*

Beads of cold sweat broke out like a rash on his forehead and battered cheeks. His glazed eyes rolled back in his head.

Don't be stupid, Charlie, Thomas thought wearily. *Call Ben. Call your FBI friends. Lock Cora in a closet somewhere and come with an army. Don't take chances.*

"Tsk, tsk," Brackett said. "Thinking again. Shame on you. We can't have that."

And before Thomas could protest, another blow to his temple sent him plunging into dark and splintered oblivion.

Chapter 72

A refreshing breeze was blowing in Jackson Square and had begun to clear the cobwebs from his mind when Charlie saw the name on the caller ID.

He took a breath to consider how he should play things.

This is either about Thomas or about the girl and the candy bar, he thought. *And on both accounts, I don't have answers.*

He and Jim had gotten word from Agent Walker about the name of the graduate student, and they were pursuing what felt like a half-lead on the candy bar, but they didn't know what to do with that yet.

It didn't matter. Though everything in him wanted to avoid it, he dutifully answered his ex-wife.

"Hey, Cora—" he began, but she cut him off.

"Charlie," she said, barely managing to hide the quivering in her voice. "Thomas is missing. I think he's with Brackett. Ben came by and talked to me. He's checking for blood matches and prints."

"Cora—"

"There was blood on a chess piece in the office. Thomas doesn't have a chess set at the office that I know of, and Susan says he received a package of chess pieces from New Orleans. It all points to Brackett," she said, choosing not to mention her dream to Charlie just yet. "Tell me the truth. You know Brackett better than anyone. If he does have Thomas, do you think he plans to kill him?"

"Cora," he repeated, trying to calm her but knowing there was nothing he could do. Not without abandoning the job she'd sent him back to New Orleans to finish. Not when he was so close to finding the person responsible for burying her and baby Lonora.

"Charlie, I had another dream," Cora said. "Nothing definitive. Nothing for sure. But there was a tie of Thomas's and a chess piece."

Charlie weighed her words carefully, pausing before he spoke. He had to be careful—his greatest desire was to comfort Cora in her moment of need, but he couldn't deny the facts.

"As far as we know, Brackett is just an instigator, the head of the snake. He's a chess master, not a murderer. He's an academic, not an assassin. We don't know enough yet to jump to conclusions."

"I don't know what to think," she said. "I'm so confused."

"Okay," he said, trying to get her mind back on track to a solution and away from speculation. "You said you talked to Ben."

"He came by this afternoon."

She had walked out into the backyard to call him and to feel the coolness of the grass beneath her bare, swollen feet. The line of pines in the backyard swayed with the light breeze. The fall vegetable garden was still green and growing. The mixed hardwoods—oak, cherry, hemlock, and elm—were shedding their leaves in a rain of color.

She'd reluctantly left Katy cleaning up the dishes from supper.

"'Ben said he's done everything he can for now," she said. "He's put out the standard APB and contacted GBI. Ben said he even called Maclin, and they're searching Savannah."

"Ben Taylor knows how to do his job," Charlie said.

"I know," she agreed, patting her unborn child and looking over her shoulder at the sunroom windows. There was no sign of Katy.

"What does Marjorie say?"

"She doesn't know. I sent Jane with her to visit Marshall's sister," she admitted. "I'm not alone, Charlie. Katy Wilton's here with me."

"Katy's a good person," he said. "I get it about Marjorie. She'd come straight to you and bring Jane. Then she'd fuss over you and sing every song in her repertoire—twice—until you sent Katy out for earplugs."

He was trying to make her laugh, making silly jokes. He understood Cora—she didn't need him to add to her fears.

"What do you want me to do, Cora?" he said kindly. "You told me I needed to leave. Are you asking me to come back?"

"No," she said firmly. "I was right the first time—you shouldn't come back. You haven't found what you're looking for. There's an order to things. *I know* there is."

"I could get Walker and the FBI involved," he offered, "but Ben might take offense at going over his head. If you're sure about your dreams, then confide in Ben. He'll listen."

She knew he was right, but that didn't make her feel any better.

"Those are the least reassuring things you have ever said to me," she said.

"I know." His voice went flat. She'd tied his hands and sent him away. What did she expect him to do?

Jim was sitting patiently on the other end of the park bench, his pad propped on his knee, sketching the drifting bystanders. He seemed to relish the atmosphere of Jackson Square as it swirled around him, busy, bustling, and full of lively visitors and entertainers who strolled the sidewalks—street performers, acrobats, and countless other artists.

Charlie envied the man's ability to adjust to every situation with the same even calm and composure. No wonder the FBI wanted him.

There was nothing else to say to Cora, and the silence had dragged out far too long. He didn't want to start an argument with her. He had his own puzzle to solve.

The puzzle she'd dropped in his lap.

"Call me if you need me," he said.

And he hung up the phone.

Chapter 73

Of all the limited number of places Jim Smith had ever seen, he decided that Jackson Square had the most fascinating collection of individuals he'd ever seen in one location.

Still, he reminded himself, he wasn't on vacation. There was work to be done and he was trying not to be too distracted by his surroundings—or his present company.

"Tell me again what Cora said," he said as he surreptitiously doodled one of the street vendors, his hands demanding that he busy himself with something besides the never-ending snacks that Charlie pushed at him. For the first time since he'd had the flu last September, he was regretting what he'd eaten and wished he didn't have access to unlimited food.

"I've told you three times already," Charlie snapped, running a hand through his curly hair and tucking his pen behind his ear.

He'd been doing his own doodling of a sort on a yellow legal pad, trying to make sense of the craziness. But nothing was any clearer than two hours ago.

The change of scenery wasn't doing his thought processes or his attitude any good at all.

Walker had given him little else besides a name for the graduate assistant—Michele Hirsch. That and the fact that she was dead. The FBI were sending a copy of her driver's license with her photo, but Charlie didn't know how much use that would be.

She'd died in a head-on collision with an eighteen-wheeler five years or so ago.

And he certainly didn't know what to do with a handful of photographs of the corner of Brackett's desk proudly displaying a glass jar full of assorted candy bars.

Or a trash can overflowing with wrappers.

He'd found the clues Cora told him to find, and they were doing precious little to solve anything that needed solving.

Now it seemed that Brackett wasn't in New Orleans at all. That he'd somehow made it to Balfour and kidnapped Thomas Stone, leaving bloody clues.

Jim reached for a water bottle in his backpack.

"You look really angry," the Rookie said, taking a generous swallow. "I mean, you look like a thundercloud just before a storm."

Charlie pulled a box of mini-Moon Pies from the plastic grocery bag on the bench.

"Have something else to eat," he suggested, smacking his gum a little louder than usual. "I'm busy."

Jim carefully took the box and put it back into the bag.

"If I eat another Moon Pie," he said, trying not to belch, "there are going to be marshmallows coming out my ears."

"That's disgusting," Charlie said. "Thanks for the visual."

Jim leaned back on the bench.

"This is a great place to spend an afternoon," he said agreeably, "and I know investigations are sometimes a lot of hurry up and wait—but what exactly are we waiting for?"

"Forensics is what it is," Charlie said, staring at his own scribbled notes. "Ben's checking fingerprints from the office in Balfour, and he's sent DNA samples to Memphis. Walker's sending us a fax of a driver's license for Michele Hirsch along with anything else the agents can scrounge up. We've got pictures of a jar of assorted candy bars on Brackett's desk. Believe me, Rookie, if I knew what to do with all the pieces, we'd have a masterpiece."

"I'd have thought a big city would go faster," Jim said.

"Testing can take anywhere from thirty minutes to two days," Charlie said. "You know that. Even with the FBI's help and Inola's nagging, the techs can only do what they can do with what we gave them."

"Doesn't it bother you?"

Charlie knew the Rookie wasn't just talking about the forensics. He was talking about Cora's phone call.

"I'm not in Balfour, and I can't do a damn thing about Cora from here," he said bluntly. "Or Thomas either."

"Wow," Jim said, closing up his sketchpad. "Maybe you're the one who needs to eat something besides sugar. I've got another bottle of water. It's cold."

Charlie stood up abruptly.

He wasn't used to explaining himself to anyone or getting along with anyone. He hadn't had a partner in years, and Jim was just too agreeable and easy to get along with. The man's inability to be offended was maddening.

"I didn't mean to push your buttons," Jim said, taking another drink of water.

"Buttons?" Charlie said, thrusting his hands into his jeans pockets. "I don't have buttons. My nerves are a seven-octave keyboard, and everyone I know is taking a turn at *Chopsticks*. Some of them are playing duets. Right now, you're the worst."

"Yeah," Jim agreed. "Sorry about that."

He glanced over at the diagram that Charlie had been drawing on the yellow legal pad. Multiple circles scattered around the horizontal page, connected by lines, and all strewn with names, dates, and phrases written in the detective's unique script.

"Did you come up with anything?" he said, attempting to read upside down.

"No," Charlie said. "I need forensics to tell me something I don't already know. I need for the phone to ring with some answers."

I need to avoid thinking about Cora and stay on task here, he thought. *Rookie, you have no idea how difficult that is when every time I look up and see your face, I think of Balfour.*

"I need a fresh pack of gum," Charlie said. "I'll be back in fifteen minutes."

Jim knew Charlie wasn't asking his permission or asking him to come along.

When Charlie strode off into the crowd, the Rookie took a Moon Pie out of the cardboard box and popped open the cellophane wrapper with a sigh.

Not that a beignet wouldn't be delicious, but right now he was missing home.

Chapter 74

The Fifth Day: Friday

Cora opened her eyes and saw James sitting at the table, one hand on the open Bible before him and the other on the handle of his steaming coffee mug.

Her usual chair was pushed back as if waiting for her, and her grandmother's flowered cup sat at her place, wisps of vapor rising from the rim.

She looked down and realized that she was fully dressed—maternity jeans and a sweatshirt pulled over her bulging middle. On her usually bare feet were ankle socks and tennis shoes. Her hair was pulled back from her face in a tight bun. She reached up and realized that she was wearing a knitted cap over the top of her head.

"James?" she said, so many questions crowding her mind that she had difficulty prioritizing all but one. "Where is Thomas?"

"Come sit down, Cora," he said patiently. "All good things . . ."

But she interrupted him, refusing to move and having none of his platitudes.

"Tell me now," she snapped. "Where is my husband, and why am I dressed like this?"

"Do you want answers," he said softly, "or do you want to vent?"

"Both," she said, crossing her arms defiantly and fighting back the urge to grip her dead friend by the shoulders and shake him until he told her what she wanted to know.

The impulse both horrified and astonished her, although from the expression she saw on the preacher's face, she could tell he knew exactly what she was thinking and he was neither horrified nor astonished.

"Your tea is getting cold." He waved his hand, inviting her to sit. "We need to talk, and you need to focus."

"You are exasperating!" she said. "Do you have any idea how I feel?"

"You're a psychologist, Cora," he smiled. "Do *you* know how you feel?"

"Let's get this over with," she said, ignoring his jab. She strode to the table, still refusing to surrender to the chair and looming over him. "Where is Thomas?"

"We need to talk first."

"I'm not sure I'm interested in anything you have to say until you tell me how to find my husband."

"Cora," he said, rising and taking her elbow, "telling you where to find Thomas won't help until I tell you how to save him."

"If I know where he is," she said, "I'll just call Ben Taylor or Inola Walker and they can help me."

"Are you sure?"

The question hung in the air, searching for the answer.

"Are you so sure, Cora?" he repeated. "I told you that you would have to handle this yourself—are you so sure I'm wrong?"

She thought about how many times he had been right. How many mysteries had been solved through the dreams. How many paths that had become clear once she had taken the first step.

Reluctantly, unwillingly, she let go of the rebellion in her heart and lowered herself awkwardly, cradling her swollen middle section.

"I feel helpless," she said, her fight replaced with fear. Her lips felt dry, and her throat was tight with tension. "Please don't tell me that I'm going to lose him, James."

He covered her hand with his.

"That's not up to me," he said, "but you already know that, don't you?"

"Is he with Brackett?"

"Yes."

She jerked her hand away and covered her mouth, stifling a sob.

"You won't be any good to him if you panic," the preacher said. "You aren't the type to panic though, are you, dear girl? You can keep your head about you. You've had faith before."

"Then you're going to tell me where he is?"

"Someone else will tell you soon enough," James corrected her. "I'm going to tell you who to take with you when you go."

"Who to take with me? Isn't that obvious?"

"Since when is anything we talk about ever obvious?"

He peeked over the top of his glasses, his eyes crinkling with amusement.

She tried to tell herself that the situation couldn't be as bad as she thought it was if he could laugh. The baby inside pressed outward as if in agreement.

"Is that why I'm dressed like this? I'm supposed to take someone with me and leave the house to find him? What then?"

"One question at a time," he chided her, picking up his coffee cup. "Have a sip of tea. Calms the nerves."

She knew he wouldn't move on until she did what he asked. She picked up the cup and took a tentative swallow before replacing the delicate china into the saucer. As she leaned away, her eyes wandered around the room and came to rest on the open Bible.

"That's not yours," she said, allowing herself to be momentarily distracted. "But it looks familiar."

"It should," he said. "You know who owns it. I brought it with me once when we talked, almost a year ago. His name is engraved on the cover."

Andrew Evans, she thought. *What does he have to do with any of this? That's all I need, another preacher bossing me around and giving me advice.*

"Nevertheless," James said, reading her thoughts, "ask Evans to come with you. He won't want to at first, but you'll know what to say to persuade him."

"I will?" she said, bewildered. "How will I know?"

"You'll say what I told you before," he said.

"You've said a great many things over the past year."

The old preacher tilted his head and adjusted his glasses.

"Tell him that he's not the only one with dreams," he said, tapping the Bible lightly. "He'll know exactly what you mean."

"Yes," Cora said impatiently, "I do remember that you said that—but I didn't know what you meant. Why would I think you were talking about the town preacher?"

"He's wanted to talk to you about his dreams since the first time you met in your den," James said. "He didn't know how to ask for your help. And now you need his."

"I'm not following you at all," she said.

James paused, as if considering her complaint, before charging ahead.

"You're right. There's no time to be cryptic. You're also going to need Quincy," the preacher went on, ignoring her protests. "He'll volunteer to come. Katy will take care of that."

"The postman?" Cora was incredulous. "I'm supposed to tell Katy?"

James had told her some ridiculous things in the past, but they'd always involved her ex-husband. She had no idea how she was supposed to rescue Thomas on her own with a preacher and a mail carrier.

"Are you sure?"

"I'm quite certain," he said, adjusting the lapels of his suit coat. Cora had the sudden impression that he was coming to the end of their conversation, and she was still without vital information or any sense of purpose.

"Surely there's someone else?" Cora prodded. "Ben? The FBI? The police?"

She almost said Charlie—but James had told her to send him back to New Orleans. She wasn't used to depending on other people like this.

"Well," he conceded, "there *is* one more person. He is crucial."

James paused and looked directly into her eyes, unsmiling. He took one of her hands in his and squeezed her fingers.

"Casey," he said. "You must take Casey with you when he comes tomorrow."

"You have *got* to be kidding!" Cora's patience was all but gone.

"The paramedic? That's horrible, James. You aren't funny. A man's life is at stake, and what you've given me sounds like the punchline to a ridiculous joke."

The old preacher laughed, more softly this time, but the grip on her hand had begun to sting.

"I hadn't thought about it that way," he mused. "I did always like to start the sermons with a touch of humor. How would I begin? I know—a preacher, a postman, and a paramedic follow a pregnant woman into the woods."

"Stop it!" She leaned into his face, closer to losing control than she'd ever been with him, and pulled her arm away. "What am I supposed to *do*?"

"You'll know when the time comes," the preacher said cryptically. "Katy will help you find the answers. You'll know, Cora. You always do."

And Cora was awake.

Chapter 75

The black dog tags tapped soundlessly against each other, dangling from the chain around his neck. He felt for the second chain, running his hand around the back of his neck to relieve the pressure, but there was no relief from the agony of expectation.

He was in the dream.

He looked down at his hands.

Odd. He was wearing a wedding ring.

How could that be?

He found himself sweating from the heat of the desert, the perspiration dripping from under the edge of his Army helmet, plastering his hair to his scalp.

The sounds of combat echoed around where he lay prone on the ground, half-hidden in the moonlight. Waiting.

They would send for him soon. He knew it. That was how the dream always played out. His turn would come, and he'd be expected to pick up his rifle and follow a soldier into the darkness.

Expected to do what he was good at doing.

No, he corrected himself. *What I am the best at doing.*

To his immediate left, a shadow crept closer to where he lay, and he caught the faintest whiff of something unexpected. Unfamiliar.

Apples, he thought suddenly. *A fresh sort of green apple scent in the air amid the odor of war. And chocolate. Odd combination.*

A lithe form dropped beside him, crouching, balancing gracefully on the balls of her booted feet, hands on her fatigue-clad knees.

"Hello, Ranger Evans," the young woman said quietly. "Are you ready?"

He studied her face in the dim light, her pale hair pulled back. Wide, innocent eyes held a spark of intelligence. He didn't know her. He was sure of it. Knew he had never seen her before in all his times dreaming the same dream.

The messenger had always been a man. The same male soldier.

Evans had even imagined once that he was an angel.

Where had she come from? She was so young. Too young.

"What unit are you with?" he said. "I'm with the Seventy-Fifth out of Fort Benning, Georgia."

"I know," she smiled. "You're not supposed to be here."

He stood up, his knees protesting and creaking, and she put out a strong hand to steady him.

What's wrong with my legs? he thought.

He dusted the front of his uniform and brushed his hands against each other in a silent clap. He couldn't quite make out the insignia on her uniform.

He was sure it wasn't regulation.

"But I'm the sniper," he said, confused as much by her appearance as her attitude.

"I know," she repeated, "and I've come for you. You aren't supposed to be here."

Evans lifted his rifle into his arms, balancing it in the crook of his elbow, barrel down, before realizing that it was not his gun.

It was a well-worn hunting rifle with a scope. Someone else's gun.

But this felt right somehow, the weapon familiar.

"You keep saying that," he said, puzzled. "If I'm not supposed to be here, then where *am* I supposed to be?"

"Ask Cora Stone," she said. "She knows. She can tell you."

From behind her came the sound of exploding munitions and a flash of white-hot light, shooting out like a thousand stars.

And Andrew Evans was awake.

Chapter 76

Katy stretched her arms and rolled over on the love seat, several small square throw pillows at her feet dropping to the floor as she kicked them off to make more room. She fluffed the pillow under her head with one hand and pulled the afghan over her thin shoulders. The love seat had been comfortable enough for a spontaneous one-night sleepover, but her body was stiff from missing her own bed.

She missed Lizzy too, but she didn't regret spending the night keeping Cora company.

Some choices were worth making.

Strange, she thought, *how just a year ago I was in the middle of the worst crisis of my life—my life in shambles, no idea where I was going. I knew Thomas as a lawyer, but I'd never even met Cora. Now look at me. Sending lavender envelopes and managing the Wilton House with Amy. Life certainly is full of surprises.*

There was a crisp, early morning chill in the air, and she was glad she'd brought a long-sleeved T-shirt and leggings for sleeping.

On the nearby oversized cushioned chair, Cora lay curled in a semifetal position under a cotton blanket, her head propped on the broad arm of the chair, her half-closed lids gazing out into space.

The lashes slowly blinked, and Katy realized that Cora was awake.

Katy had convinced the pregnant woman that she should take a warm, relaxing bath before they had a late-night snack of fruit and settled into their respective spots for the night. Then Katy, with a devotional book she'd been reading, and Cora, with her notes on Madame Chen, each read until around midnight when they both drifted off to sleep.

Solomon had expressed his distaste for the intruder by retreating up the stairs just after the women had made their makeshift beds and refused to share their peach slices. When she went up to check on him later, Cora found him keeping sentry at the foot of Jane's bed, pouting amid the stuffed animals and toys.

Curled and purring, the feline showed no inclination to follow Cora back down the stairs, although she knew he'd come running quickly enough when she opened his food container in the morning.

She scratched him between the ears and forgave his grumpy mood.

After all, she thought, *he's missing Jane and Marjorie too. I'm a poor substitute for blind adoration and stinky cat treats.*

The two women were lying there in companionable silence when Cora's cell phone blared out shrilly from its charger on the side table.

"Hello," Cora said, without checking the caller ID. She pushed her dangling dark hair out of her face and struggled to sit up. "Hello?"

Katy didn't want Cora to think she was eavesdropping, so she wrapped herself in the afghan and went into the kitchen to put on the teapot.

When she returned with cups of steaming herbal tea, she could see that Cora was quite clearly disturbed.

"Do you want to talk about it?" Katy said, placing the floral cup carefully on the table at the older woman's elbow. "It's none of my business, of course."

Cora fought back tears as she considered her options.

There were precious few people with whom she had ever shared her dreams.

Charlie, Thomas, Marjorie. And Dr. Floyd, the only one who had ridiculed them for what Cora knew they were. For what Inola Walker knew they were.

Walker was a gifted profiler too. A woman who had been able to connect the dots between Charlie's ability to solve impossible crimes and Cora's visions. A woman who understood about faith and the gift of sight—and had pledged herself to keep Cora's secrets from being exploited and misused.

Last night James told her what to do. To trust others. Trust Katy. She took a breath and decided.

"That was Ed Brackett," Cora said simply. "He's kidnapped Thomas, and he's holding him until I come to him."

Katy sat down on the edge of the love seat and folded her quivering hands.

"Ed Brackett? Who is he?" she said.

"Someone I helped put away years ago. I think he wants to kill us both," Cora said plainly. There was no reason to pull any punches with Katy. "He told me that they were in a place where he could see me coming—and if I come with anyone, he'll kill Thomas as soon as he sees us."

"Do you believe him?"

"Yes," Cora said, swallowing her fear. "I believe he will do what he says."

"Then we need to call Ben."

Katy tried to reach for her phone, but Cora stopped her hand.

Here's the part where I trust you, she thought. *Here's where I confirm the rumors and invite you into my deepest secrets.*

"Katy," she said, "there's more. I need to tell you something you may not accept and you certainly won't understand—but I need your help, and I need you to trust that I know what I'm doing."

Katy squeezed Cora's hand in return.

"Of course," she said bravely. "That's why I came. Tell me exactly what you want me to do."

Chapter 77

A little over five hundred miles away, Charlie's faded blue Volkswagen was making a final turn down the gravel driveway to his most infamous former crime scene.

Jim, perspiration gathering on his forehead both from the increasing heat and the confines of the front passenger seat, was oddly composed.

Jim got up extra early to enjoy the breakfast buffet to its fullest. Charlie had shown up right on time without attempting to help himself to the fruit bowl. Everyone was satisfied, including the watchful attendant.

"Where are we going?" Jim asked pleasantly, adjusting his sunglasses. His cell phone had dropped to two bars, and it seemed like hours since they left New Orleans and headed north into the sparsely populated countryside.

"It's an old homestead," Charlie explained. "Past Algonac State Park and the St. Clair River. The house is condemned. All the value is in the land. Acres of land."

"Is that where—"

"Where Cora was buried," Charlie finished, rolling his shoulders to release the pent-up tension. "In the basement of the dilapidated house."

"I didn't think there were basements around here, what with the water table and all. Isn't there a danger of flooding?"

Charlie nodded. *Trust the Rookie to do his homework.*

"It's uncommon to dig basements, but it does happen. Some turn-of-the-century houses have unfinished areas under the main floor, mostly dirt and used for storage. Chance of flooding, so there was never a question of anyone living down there or finishing it for human habitation. The bare floor made it easier to dig the shallow grave. Only about four feet or so deep. Cora fell down the stairs and someone rolled her into a makeshift coffin—a wooden packing crate lined with blankets to keep out the dirt."

Jim couldn't think of anything to say. He'd never seen Charlie quite so willing to talk about himself, or Cora. Listening seemed like a golden opportunity to hear a story he might never have the chance to hear again, although he did feel a bit like he was eavesdropping on a private conversation.

"She got the call in the middle of the afternoon," Charlie continued, his voice fading and far away. He set the brake on the Volkswagen and stared out the window at the yard around the house.

As he talked, Jim's mind began to wander. Despite his best intentions, the gloom and foreboding of his surroundings filled his mind with his own fears distinctly apart from the narrative he was hearing.

There were a number of stark trees, unkempt evergreens and

scrub oaks, along with some pecan, mimosa, and chinaberry, that encircled the main building. The roof was high-pitched in the center with two narrow windows like gaping eye sockets.

The longer ground floor base extended out past the slope of the roof on either side with a door at each end and two smaller windows between them.

There were three or four narrow wooden steps, crooked and rotted, going up to the left door and a simple stone landing outside the right.

Behind the main building were two ramshackle sheds that might once have been storage for tools or firewood. Their windows, like the ones in the house, were broken and edged with jagged, dirty glass. The roofs, where they weren't damaged and shingles missing, were laden with fallen branches, drifts of pine straw, and multicolored leaves.

The whole area was neglected and long ago abandoned. The scene a setting for some low-budget horror movie or eerie Southern gothic suspense film.

Toward the middle of the equally forsaken yard, Jim saw an old-fashioned water pump, the slender pipe rising from the well and the graceful, paint-chipped handle draped uselessly to the side. Nearby was a rusted metal bucket lying sideways on the ground and a handmade pine bench covered at the base with a bouquet of black-eyed Susan and milkweed. The yard itself was a crazy quilt of colors and textures. Clumps of assorted grasses were interspersed with a generous dash of dandelions.

Jim was visually overwhelmed, his first thought that this was the perfect habitat for copperheads and moccasins. And once past the dangers outside, the house inside would be full of brown recluse spiders and their sisters the black widows.

He stared at the windows and imagined that they were covered with lacy cobweb curtains, the arachnids in the corners and the reptiles lurking beneath the floorboards, all ready to strike at the first sound of an intruder.

He swallowed his churning apprehension and looked over at a quizzical Charlie.

"When did you stop listening to me?" the detective said, a hint of unexpected amusement in his voice. "Or were you listening to me at all?"

"Are we going in there?" Jim said, ignoring the obvious criticism. He was only slightly ashamed of his inattention. He tried to tell himself that as much as he wanted to know, he had also been completely unprepared for such unabashed sharing from the avowed loner or for the sinking feeling in the pit of his ample stomach at the sight of the former crime scene.

The reality of the location, intermixed with the gruesome story, was a bit much.

"*You* don't have to go with me," Charlie said, reaching for the door handle. "I'd roll down the window, though. Mosquito season is pretty much over, so you're safe from them, but it's still hot and sticky for October. It's going to be stuffy in the car. I won't be too long."

Jim reached for his own door handle.

"If you're going, I'm going," he said, remembering the Savannah mansion and its bizarre portrait, mahogany staircase, crystal chandelier, multiple rooms, and the hidden steps that led into the secluded attic. "This isn't actually the creepiest place we've ever been, so I'll manage. What are we looking for?"

"I don't know," Charlie said flatly. "I'm stumped without more information. Going forward isn't working, so we're going backward."

More than five years ago, he'd combed every single rotting plank in the main building for clues—any indication for why Cora had come to this place or whom she had met.

Who had buried her and left her for dead.

Forensics teams came too.

But there was nothing of any consequence. At least not out in the open.

The vibration of Charlie's cell phone startled them both.

"Hello," Charlie said. "What's up?"

Chapter 78

Casey arrived on the front porch of Cora's house a few minutes before ten o'clock in the morning. Lisa had told him that it wasn't necessary to call ahead. That Marjorie would likely be there and Cora would be expecting him.

Either way, there would be a friendly greeting and an invitation to lunch, or at the very least one of Marjorie's famous homemade cookies.

He'd gotten off the third shift late, run by the apartment to shower and put on a fresh T-shirt and jeans, then grabbed a quick cup of extra-caffeinated coffee from the shop where Jack was working.

Casey loved his work, but he was tired—physically and mentally.

The Griffith ER had been relatively quiet for the night. Nothing life-threatening or critical. Concerned young parents came in bringing their firstborn—a fussy toddler with a high fever. An adventurous teenager was sneaking out of his second-floor bedroom after midnight to meet his friends to party and fell off the roof and broke his arm. His worried mom was more upset than her son and twice as vocal.

And a man in his mid-sixties with mild chest pains was dragged in by his overly concerned and appropriately smothering wife.

Everyone was treated in a reasonable time and sent home with instructions, admonitions, and the appropriate medications.

The toddler was treated for a double ear infection. The teenager had a clean break and was rewarded with several stern lectures and a colorful cast. And several tests later, the man with chest pains was diagnosed with severe indigestion, probably from a third generous helping of his wife's spicy homemade tacos.

Casey was still worn out despite the relative lack of activity.

Dealing with the emotional issues of his patients and their families was almost more exhausting than treating the injuries themselves.

He adjusted his medical backpack over his shoulder, his mind wandering to Ellie as he waited for someone to answer his knock.

He wished she could be there with him as he met Cora for the first time. He'd heard some pretty crazy rumors, and, not that he took any stock in rumors, he'd had just about as much of the extraordinary as he could handle for one day.

Ellie was grounded. Logical. Normal.

To Casey's mind, those were the highest compliments.

She'd been helping him get to know people in the community and make connections. Not that he couldn't have done that on his own, but being engaged to the daughter of a civic and business leader made him high-profile. Everyone seemed to know his name, and he needed a crash course to try to keep up.

He'd parked his car at the fire department just behind the police station and walked the short distance to Cora's house, hoping the brisk air would help shake any cobwebs from his head after the sleepless shift.

He was still standing on the porch admiring the climbing vines of white roses when he saw a car pull into the driveway and park. A distinguished-looking man in khaki slacks and a sport jacket got out and started up the walkway.

"Good morning," Casey said. He recognized Jack's father immediately, although he hadn't expected to see him in Cora Stone's driveway.

Andrew Evans strode deliberately up the steps.

"Good morning, Casey," the preacher said, extending his hand for a firm shake. "Didn't expect to see you."

"Same here, sir," Casey said. "I'm subbing for the doc today. She's out of town in Atlanta at a convention."

Evans looked mildly puzzled, but Cora's appearance at the front door forestalled any more explanations. He was overwhelmed by the change in her appearance from their first and only other meeting. The sight of her tiny form swollen out of proportion with pregnancy left him almost speechless.

"Good morning, Preacher," the young woman said, opening the door and ushering them inside with a wave of her delicate hand. "I'm glad you called."

She turned to the paramedic, who also seemed to be a bit taken aback by her appearance, although he was hiding it a bit better than the preacher.

"Hello, you must be Casey," she said. "I'm Cora. There's coffee in the kitchen. Katy's making a call. Come along and have a cup, then we can all sit down and talk."

Chapter 79

"I don't think I heard you right," Quincy said, holding the phone slightly away from his face. "You want me to do *what*?"

"I want you to meet me at Cora Stone's house," Katy repeated patiently. "I want you to drop everything. It's important."

The grizzled postman looked around the vacant mailroom and scratched his bearded chin, searching for any reason to refuse. The day's mail had been sorted and bagged, his two new hires already out the door and on their way. There was literally nothing left for him to do unless he wanted to send his only other employee home and tend the front window himself.

The idea of selling stamps and listening to trivial conversation for the whole of the afternoon did not appeal to him, but he also didn't know what to think about this high-handed call from Katy Wilton demanding a command appearance.

It seemed somehow disrespectful and presumptuous.

"Katy," he said in his most dignified voice, "I cannot abandon my duty and responsibilities as a postman on a whim."

"Well," she said, matching his tenor, "we've found ourselves in a situation that could really use your expertise. Would you really leave us in our hour of need?"

Quincy didn't like the sound of that either. Or Katy's matronly attitude of authority.

Her words triggered a memory of Charlie's demand that he bring his lock-picking tools and open a hundred-year-old chest. He knew then that Cora was involved. Maybe this was something like that. Maybe it had to do with Cora—and Thomas.

"Do I need to bring anything with me?" he said.

"Not just yet," Katy said. "And don't tell anyone where you're going."

Fifteen minutes later, Cora greeted the postman at her front door, but this time she didn't hesitate to open it all the way, giving him full view of her bulging midsection.

"We're all in the kitchen," she said, waving him inside and waddling down the hallway. "Thank you for coming."

He didn't pause to consider who the *we* might be.

The sunlight in the kitchen was full and warm, cutting across the room in diagonal stripes from the window over the sink. Andrew and Casey were seated on stools on the same side of the island facing the doorway. They were deep into animated discussion that did not stop when the postman entered the room.

Quincy pulled up a stool across from the two men and politely made himself at home.

Cora rejoined Katy, who was making sandwiches at the counter.

"So," the preacher said, nodding an acknowledgment of greeting toward the postman as he continued his conversation with Casey,

"Jack said you're an EMT."

"I'm a paramedic," Casey corrected him politely. "It can be confusing. All EMTs are not paramedics, but all paramedics are EMTs. I'm fourth level—EMTP. I can push IVs, administer drugs, and perform invasive interventions."

Andrew's face clouded over as pieces of information began to come together in his mind. He glanced over at Cora and saw that she was watching him.

While Katy had given Casey coffee in the kitchen, Andrew had followed Cora into her office. He opened his mouth to explain why he had called her and the dam broke, his words flooding the room. When the water leveled off, he realized that she knew exactly what he was talking about. They were kindred spirits with a common bond.

She was afraid, and he could help. He intended to help.

Andrew realized the room had gone silent and that it was his turn to say something.

"Jack said you did a couple of tours in the military," Andrew said. "What branch?"

"Navy," Casey said. "I already had my basic EMT when I enlisted, then I took further training. Marines don't have medics. Medics for Marines are Navy."

Quincy leaned forward, interrupting, interested and engaged in the dialogue.

"So, were you blue or green?" the postman asked.

Casey turned and faced Quincy.

"Green," he said, admiration in his voice. "Military?"

Quincy nodded, unbuttoning his cuff as he pushed up his right sleeve, pointing to a tattoo almost hidden beneath the mass of curly white hair that covered his forearm. A faded bald eagle, its wings spread protectively around a flag-draped globe, its sharp talons gripping a banner that read simply *Duty First.*

"Master sergeant, Vietnam," he said. "Army. First Infantry. The Big Red One."

Quincy paused as Casey offered his own forearm for inspection—a tattoo of a caduceus whose base was an anchor, twin snakes twisted together looking up at a pair of wings on top.

"Son," he said, "I've got the greatest respect for you. Docs and the rescue pilots make the difference."

They both saw the curious look on Cora's face.

"Blue medics serve on the ships," Casey explained. "Green medics are combat, the battlefield. In the thick of things on the ground. Either way, it's immensely satisfying to be called Doc by a grateful soldier when you've given him a chance to survive."

"True words," Quincy agreed, remembering his final bitter return from war and the harsh reception he received, even at the hands of those he knew well.

"And sometimes," the old man added, "the only satisfaction that soldier has is his gun and knowing that some people are alive because of it."

For a moment the room grew uncomfortably silent.

"So, Quincy, is Balfour your hometown?" Andrew asked.

"All my life," Quincy replied testily, tugging down the brim of his uniform cap. "And at least three generations that came before."

Katy, like the rest of the room, hesitated to ask anything else that might upset the elderly man. They needed him, but she couldn't help but be touched by the sadness and disappointment on his face. She was too young to remember Vietnam, but she had heard disturbing stories about how the returning soldiers had been treated. She couldn't imagine how it must have felt to feel betrayed by the country he had sacrificed to serve.

He thinks he's lost his purpose, she thought. *We're a ragtag group of volunteers, about to take an enormous leap of faith. What are we thinking?*

She reached around him, brushing his shoulder, and placed the tray of assorted sandwiches in the middle of the island. Cora slid a plate and a glass of lemonade in front of each of the men.

Solomon, miffed that there were so many inattentive adults in his personal space and attracted by the smell of chicken salad, complained loudly from the French doors in the sunroom. No one seemed to notice or care.

The postman himself finally broke the increasing tension.

"Can we take family histories later?" Quincy complained gruffly, embarrassed that he'd become the center of attention and perhaps even an object of pity. "I'd like to know what kind of mess I've just stepped into here."

"We're here to help Cora," Casey said quietly. "Preacher Evans and I were just getting to know each other while we waited for you. Thomas has been kidnapped. We plan to help get him back."

"Isn't that a job for the police?" Quincy said, unconvinced. "I heard the rumors, but I mean, you're a doc and I'm an old soldier. And Evans over there is a preacher. I don't quite see how we're going to be particularly helpful unless this is a prayer meeting—and believe me, I won't be too useful at that either."

Katy gently touched his forearm, covering the tattooed globe with her warm hand.

"I think you'll be more useful than you think," she said. "Just think of this as a very important lavender envelope."

"Well, this sounds like a sight more than baking a cake, delivering a bouquet to the nursing home, or making a fancy dress," he said, picking up a half-sandwich. "Little lady, going after an armed kidnapper is serious business."

"And we're taking it very seriously," Andrew said. "Cora's received instructions and asked the three of us to help."

"You've agreed to this?" Quincy said, disbelieving, lowering the sandwich without taking a bite. "Instructions from who? How do you even know where Thomas is?"

"The kidnapper called me this morning," Cora said. "He told me where he's holding Thomas, and he's demanding that I come or he will kill Thomas."

"This is crazy!" Quincy jumped up suddenly, tossing the sandwich back onto his plate and knocking the stool to the floor, bringing another sharp yowl of complaint from Solomon. "You can't go by yourself!"

"That's what I told him," she said, more calmly than she felt. "I said that I didn't have a car and that I haven't driven in years. That a friend was staying with me and that she'd have to bring me."

"Well, you and Katy can't go," Quincy said firmly, righting the stool with a sharp thud against the floor. "And that's that."

Katy placed an arm around Cora's shoulders.

"We *are* going," she said firmly. "We were waiting on you."

Quincy turned on the women.

"What are the two of you thinking?" he bellowed. "Even if we're crazy enough to go along with this plan, this isn't a job for civilians. We aren't the police. We aren't armed. We'd need someone who can shoot in case it comes to that. Do you know what will happen if something goes wrong?"

"That's why I called you," Katy said quietly. "That's part of the plan."

"Well, I can't shoot worth a flip!" Quincy said, looking around the island at the other faces. "I'm no marksman! We can't go in firing willy-nilly. Someone is going to get seriously hurt, maybe even Thomas. What makes you think I'm right for this?"

"Because you're here," Katy said. "I'm going to drive Cora in my SUV. You're going to hide in the back with Pastor Evans and Casey. We'll make a quick stop for you to get one of your hunting rifles with a scope."

"What do any of you know about hunting rifles?" he scoffed.

"Nothing," Cora said, "but Pastor Evans does."

Quincy dropped his arms to his side and sat back down on the stool.

"Preacher," he asked, "what is she talking about?"

"Master Sergeant Quincy," Casey said, his voice level and steady, "meet Army Ranger Andrew Evans."

The deep lines in Andrew's face flooded with color, his tired eyes closed against Quincy's stare of skepticism and doubt.

This was his worst nightmare come to life. But he'd finally done as Ginny had suggested for so long. He'd come to talk to Cora Stone, and the brief conversation had taken a wild, unexpected turn.

She had convinced him—persuaded him that her husband's life depended on him and the skills he had put aside.

They'd called for the sniper, and he'd answered.

The others could do what they pleased. He was going to do what he needed to do to save Thomas and Cora Stone if he had to take Quincy's rifle and go alone. Cora's voice echoed in his ears.

You aren't the only one with dreams.

Chapter 80

It's all just a game, Brackett thought, watching as his bound, bloody prey slept the restless slumber of drugs and desperate exhaustion from pain. *Experience is the best teacher. A limited number of moves and countermoves that can be made—and players of my caliber can predict what another player will do.*

He was certain he knew what Cora would do. She was transparent and afraid.

She'd do what she was told. Like she did before.

And if she did decide to bring anyone with her, then he was ready for that too.

No one could get near the cabin without being seen. No one.

Not even a white bishop could checkmate his king now, and the white knight's sacrifice would be in vain.

He distained the amateurs and the lesser opponents who sat across from him on any given day. Those who were incapable of seeing the pattern right in front of them, refusing to plot the path ahead while he was anticipating moves and gaining strength.

They had no idea that once he set the strategy in motion, there was little they could do to change the ultimate result.

He parted the curtained window and looked out at the wooded gravel lane.

She'll be here shortly, he thought. *And she won't be a problem to anyone else, not ever again. It's a pity she's bringing a pawn and that she'll have to die too. But I didn't put more pieces on the board—Cora did.*

The first pawn—that simpering graduate assistant who had been sacrificed, well, she had been *his* piece. He'd intended for her to die. To disappear.

No one ever had to know about her.

And Ed Brackett was right about one thing.

Cora *had* put more pieces on the board. Several more.

But what he could not see and would not understand was that those pieces had never played chess and did not know the rules of the game.

Instead, they had every intention of sweeping each and every piece to the floor before they tossed the board against the nearest wall to declare victory.

Chapter 81

Ellie Sanderson had spent all morning anticipating her one o'clock appointment at the florist's shop to discuss her wedding flowers.

Her usual taciturn nature had grown more and more enthusiastic as the day wore on, fueled by the avid attention of her coworkers at Beulah Land as well as the socially deprived patients who had nothing better than the weekly Bingo game on their minds.

Even the crotchety business manager wished her well and told her she could leave as soon as Ellie had finished her rounds for the morning.

Everyone, it seemed, was thrilled about a wedding. Not just a local wedding, but the wedding of the only child of one of the most prominent citizens of Balfour, as well as the first local nuptials to be held at the prestigious Wilton House Estate.

Or, at least, the reception would be held at the newest venue. The wedding ceremony itself would be held at Emmanuel Baptist Church, but there was no amount of persuasion that was going to allow dancing in that hallowed fellowship hall, so the matter was settled almost before it had time to gather controversy.

Sanderson had declared he wanted only one thing if they expected him to walk his beloved daughter into the church and let her leave a married woman—he wanted to dance with Ellie on her wedding day.

Not only that, but everyone in Balfour was invited to eat cake and dance too.

"And that," Ellie's mother had said sagely, "is that."

From that point on, the entire community became involved in the planning and considered themselves honored guests if not outright distant relatives.

Which is why, almost a half hour after their scheduled appointment time, Ellie was concerned that Casey had not yet arrived to meet her.

Everyone else is so excited, she thought, trying not to be critical. *I wonder what in the world is keeping Casey.*

"It really isn't like him to be late," she said, taking out her cell phone and checking for the fourth time for a message, trying not to sound as worried as she felt. "He usually takes a minute to call if he gets caught up in an emergency at the hospital."

Vicki fluttered her orange-tipped fingernails and made sympathetic clucking sounds.

"You must not worry, *cherie,*" she said consolingly. "He has, I am certain, a good reason for being late. He is a handsome and kind young man. We must be patient, little one."

Ellie nodded, mildly distracted by the thin gold wire vines covered with tiny leaves that dangled from Vicki's earlobes, brushing against the florist's neck as she spoke.

Everything about Vicki was animated—her artfully painted eyes and lips, her dark arched brows, her enthusiastic gestures. Even her slight body seemed to be in a constant state of motion beneath the elaborate flowing caftan.

For a moment Ellie pictured a dynamic Vicki, dancing at the wedding, wearing some elegantly tailored new caftan with matching jewelry, enjoying herself immensely to the wonder of all the other guests.

Her cell phone vibrated and the image was gone.

"See," Vicki said encouragingly. "This is your young man, yes?"

Ellie stared down at the screen.

"He said something important came up," she said blankly. "No explanation. He said he'd call me later."

The young woman was still looking vacantly at her cell phone when Ginny Evans opened the door to the florist's shop. She was pale, and Vicki thought she looked ill.

"*Ma cher*!" Vicki began, dancing around the counter. "Give me your hands!"

She rubbed the other woman's fingers briskly.

"You are very cold," she observed. "Should you be out of bed?"

"Hello, Ellie," the preacher's wife said, pulling back her hands and tucking her purse closer to her chest. "It's my first time out since the car accident, and I was coming to order flowers for the shut-ins and this week's hospital patients. Andy insisted on meeting me here to help carry everything."

"When is he supposed to meet you?" Vicki asked.

"That's just it," Ginny said. "He just sent the most cryptic message. I guess I'm on my own here."

"It's none of my business," Ellie spoke up, "but do you mind telling me what he said? I mean, exactly what he said."

Ginny looked puzzled, but the question seemed harmless enough. "He said something important came up and he'd call me later."

Ellie and Vicki exchanged pointed glances.

"Funny," Ellie said thoughtfully. "That's exactly the text I just received from Casey. He's supposed to meet me here too."

"There is no such thing as a coincidence," the florist declared, her arms sweeping the air. She looked like a winged bird about to take flight. "There is something strange, no doubt. We must discover what it is."

"Vicki," Ginny chided her. "You sound downright superstitious. Let's not read into this more than there is. I'm sure Andy must have a really good reason."

"All the same," Vicki said, refusing to be placated. "Where there are questions there must also be answers, no?"

"What kind of questions?" Ellie said, leaning against the counter and sliding her hands into her scrub pockets along with her cell phone. She was suddenly not in the mood to talk about flowers.

Vicki arched her eyebrows and folded her arms, the soft fabric bunching around her elbows.

"When did you last speak to your young man?" she said. "Before this message."

"He called before I went to work," Ellie said. "He said that he'd meet me here around one. That he'd be over this way because Dr. Lisa had asked for a favor."

"A favor?"

"Something about checking in on one of her patients," she said. "He said he'd be in Balfour anyway so he'd be glad to help—"

"Did he say which patient he was checking on?" Ginny interrupted.

"No," Ellie said, turning to the older woman. "He just said it wouldn't take long and he'd have plenty of time to get here afterward."

Vicki turned her attention to the shop window, readjusting the fall display. Her dark face was furrowed with deep lines of concern and concentration.

"When was the last time you spoke to Andrew, Ginny?" she said, the vines of her earrings dancing above her shoulders. "Where was he going today?"

Ginny hesitated. Andy was so private. She hated to talk about him, but there was a deep foreboding in the pit of her stomach she could not ignore.

Maybe it's only Vicki's superstitions, she thought. *Or maybe she's right . . . and it's something more.*

"When I last talked to him, he was going to see Cora Stone," she said, hoping it sounded like a routine visit from the preacher to a regular member of the church.

Except that Cora Stone was anything but a regular member of Emmanuel, and they all knew it.

"Do you know why?" Vicki said.

"No," Ginny lied. There was only so much she could share without Andrew's express permission. "What are you thinking, Vicki?"

"At this moment," the Cajun woman said, "I am not thinking, *cher*—I am *feeling*."

Well, you're certainly giving me the heebie-jeebies, Ellie thought.

The outer door to the shop opened and Allison breezed in, slamming the door roughly behind her.

"Oh, my!" Vicki exclaimed. "Are you in a mood today too, *ma petite cher*? Did you go by the post office to pick up the ribbons we ordered? They were there, no?"

"They were certainly not there—no," the teenager said petulantly. "Or if they were there, no one knew where they were."

"No one?" Vicki said, picking up the phone on the countertop and looking around for the sheet of local numbers she kept for just such an emergency. "Surely you aren't telling me that the postmaster doesn't know! Did he lose the order? I'm calling now."

"Won't do you any good," Allison said defiantly. "He left for the day."

"What does that mean?" Vicki said. "Isn't he working?"

"You'd think so," Allison said, "but the woman who works the counter said he'd left a message. He said something important came up and he'd call her later."

Chapter 82

Quincy was still objecting strenuously to the entire crazy scheme even as he got his rifle and handed it off to Andrew.

He'd complained on the entire bumpy ride and up to the point where he and the other two men had left to hide in the woods while Katy drove on with Cora.

His insistence that the group call Ben to handle things might have persuaded someone with less confidence in his ability than Andrew Evans. In the brief span of time since he'd spoken to Cora Stone, his entire demeanor had changed. He seemed a different man.

Casey recognized the stern set of the Army Ranger's jaw, the squared shoulders, the steady hands. All the signs of a highly skilled sniper. A marksman.

He'd trusted his life many times on the battlefield to men just like Andrew Evans. He would do it again. But that was not why he'd joined the group.

His first responsibility was to Cora and her unborn child.

When Cora made it clear that she was going whether they came along or not, his decision was made for him. He'd gone into heavy enemy fire on foreign soil to rescue wounded soldiers. He wasn't about to let a pregnant woman traipse off into the Georgia woods to be executed by a crazed killer.

Not on his watch.

He could never look Ellie Sanderson in the eyes again if he didn't do what he had been trained to do.

Even if Quincy had won out and they had called Ben, Casey knew he would still be part of the rescue mission. Just a different team of individuals, that's all. They'd need a medic because when guns are involved, sooner or later someone gets shot.

So that left Quincy.

Andrew said they'd do without him if he wanted to stay back, but that was gasoline to the brush fire.

"You don't know these woods!" the postman raved. "And you aren't walking off with my best rifle either. Dang fool womenfolk. What makes Cora think she can pull this off? Who does she think she is?"

"As I understand it," Andrew said quietly, "she hasn't left her home in almost five years. She's been living under a cloud of fear, isolation, and debilitating depression. That dang fool woman has decided she is willing to exchange her life for her husband's and I, for one, will not stand by and watch her die."

Quincy's bearded jaw dropped open.

"Kindly shut your mouth or start walking back to town," the preacher added. "I've got no patience for whiners. I need to concentrate."

Casey slid his medic backpack from his shoulder and placed it on the ground at his feet. He'd already decided he was staying, although he did think Evans's speech was one of the best sermons he'd heard in a long time.

Quincy, with an olive-green ammo can in one hand and a dark green blanket in the other, took a sulking stance at the base of a nearby scrub oak, dropping the can and spreading the blanket on the straw-covered earth.

Andrew—cradling Quincy's Mossberg bolt-action rifle in his arms like a colicky baby—leaned against a pine tree as his stomach rose into the back of his parched throat.

He recognized the familiar feeling of dread mixed with adrenaline.

The tips of his fingers tingled and his mind, though troubled, was clear with the necessary calculations—wind speed and direction, target distance, weapon prep.

Faces flitted through his memory in rapid succession, filling his scope with the eyes of every kill shot he'd ever taken.

Did they deserve to die? His mind was awash with regret and remorse. The old emotions were back and threatening his resolve.

But this time is different, he reminded himself. *No one can take the shot I can take. There isn't time to explain to the police. Cora made it clear. If this madman sees anyone, he will kill her husband. A shot like this—at this distance through the woods—it's going to take everything I've got.*

Casey reached over and put a hand firmly on the sniper's shoulder.

"You okay? Do I need to take your vitals?" he said, a furrow of concern deepening in his forehead.

"Second thoughts?" Quincy scoffed. "Make up your mind before we let Cora walk into a killer's sights. Rather botch this up myself than watch you do it, preacher."

"It's been a long time," Andrew said. "But I remember what to do. I've had a lot of practice lately remembering what to do."

"You know what they say," Quincy said, squinting through the foliage and the dense thicket, surveying the cabin in the clearing just beyond them and the SUV. "Like riding a bicycle. Once you've learned, you never really forget."

You have no idea how much I've tried to forget, Andrew thought. *You have no idea at all.*

Chapter 83

Jim didn't know if he was relieved or only confused when Charlie told him that they weren't going into the house after all.

Inola Walker's research had uncovered the name of the graduate assistant from Cora's dream, the address of her apartment near Louisiana State University in Baton Rouge, and a former landlady with a cooperative streak.

Only another forty-five minutes or so away from where they were.

"We can always come back here if we need to," Charlie said, shifting the audible gears and gently cursing the clutch. "This place isn't going anywhere."

"Better to follow an active lead than a dead end," Jim offered, folding his broad hands and once more settling himself into the cramped, uncomfortable passenger seat, uncomplaining and cooperative as always.

Whether it was a sign of guilt or growing camaraderie, Charlie stopped at the first respectable-looking convenience store of sufficient size and bought gas to top off the tank. He came out with the receipt in one hand and a bulging plastic bag in the other.

He tossed the offering into Jim's lap.

"You're looking a bit peaked," he said, climbing in and stuffing the receipt into a manila envelope under the driver's seat. "Thought you could use a snack."

Jim took out one of the three Yoo-hoos, dripping with condensation, and opened the bottle with a metallic click.

"Thanks," he said sincerely, downing the drink with one continuous swallow and re-capping the empty bottle.

He hesitated for a moment and then tucked the container neatly between his feet on the floorboard of the car.

"You can feel free to eat the barbeque pork rinds too," Charlie said, manhandling the stick and getting back onto the near-empty highway. "I won't complain about the smell—well, not much. Maybe you should roll down the window just in case."

"Thanks," Jim said again, popping open the bag and reaching in. He strongly suspected that the food was only a convenient way to keep him from talking and asking questions the detective was not ready to answer.

But the officer had a personal policy against refusing pork rinds and anything chocolate, so he crunched contentedly, his face pointed out the open window until they reached their destination.

The campus housing units were familiar—what Jim expected and remembered from his college days. Faded bricks. Concrete walkways. Monotonous, nondescript doorways. Dingy windows, heavily curtained. Here and there a random flowering weed had struggled up between the cracks in the sidewalk and in the crumbling mortar of the walls.

The apartments seemed tiny from the outside, so he could only imagine how small and restrictive they must be on the inside.

Charlie knocked on the landlady's door and she opened it immediately, her round, friendly face alight with a cheerfulness in sharp contrast to her somber surroundings.

Her ample form was draped in a tent-sized faded purple-and-gold LSU jersey over baggy jeans, and a pair of scuffed once-white tennis shoes.

"Detective Charlie Abbott," he said, "This is Officer James Smith."

Being called by his given name startled the Rookie, and he took a polite step backward, almost tripping on the edge of the narrow walkway.

"Waguespack," she returned, extending a plump, age-spotted hand in greeting. "Agnes Waguespack. I can spell it if you like."

Charlie smiled and shook her hand, impressed to find a grip that matched his own in spite of the obvious difference in their ages.

"Thanks," he said. "I've got it. Work with a Bryan Waguespack, Precinct Eight, New Orleans. Big guy. Heads the canine unit."

"I've got cousins on the force in New Orleans," she said. "There's lots of us Waguespack's littered all over Cajun country. All related, you know how it goes."

"Yes, indeed." Charlie took out his pad and pen. "We're here about a former tenant. A graduate student named Michele Hirsch."

"That's what the lady said." Agnes stepped out onto the sidewalk and pulled the door shut behind her, inserting a key from an immense ring of keys into the lock and twisting it. "She said you'd be coming by today and that I should cooperate."

"Agent Walker," Charlie said. "Special Agent Inola Walker."

"I guess so. She said you'd know who she was." Agnes started down the sidewalk at an energetic clip. "Too many names for me. Pretty sure she said FBI out of Memphis."

The landlady turned the corner at the end of the building before the two men could catch up with her.

"Wait," Charlie called out, rounding the building and almost colliding with the woman, who had stopped and was opening what looked like just another door.

"Watch it, cowboy," she cautioned. "I don't need a fall at my time in life. Imagine me explaining how I got run over by a handsome detective on my own sidewalk."

She chuckled to herself at the image in her mind.

"Sorry," Charlie said, folding his arms as he waited patiently for her to continue.

"I guess you want what she left behind." She pocketed her keys.

"Left behind?" Jim said, towering over the detective's shoulder.

"I keep it all," she said, flipping on a light switch, illuminating a windowless storage room with a yellow glow. "Not forever, mind you, just until I'm sure no one's coming back. The furniture, the big things, they're gone. Donated. Someone else could use them, you know. But the personal things, someone's only treasures, those I keep until I see if a next of kin ever shows up."

Charlie peered into the dimly lit room. There were floor-to-ceiling shelves, the cheap cream-colored plastic snap-together kind from the local Walmart. Every shelf sagged with the weight of someone's unclaimed treasure—book bags, laundry baskets, duffels, small cloth suitcases and their larger counterpart trunks in assorted colors and patterns.

Then there were the brown cardboard boxes—labeled with names.

"Give me a minute to look," Agnes said, an optimistic lilt to her voice. "It was five years ago or so. The older stuff gets pushed to the back, and I'll need to sift through a bit before I get there."

Charlie leaned against the doorframe.

Several dusty minutes later, Agnes emerged from the crowded shelves with an oversized olive-green backpack.

She held it out to the detective and smiled.

Attached to the top with a white zip tie was a cardboard tag with the name *Michele Hirsch* printed in neat Sharpie marker.

"Is that all?" Jim said. He couldn't help but feel disappointed. Had they really gone through all this just for a book bag? What could possibly be inside?

"What the officer means," Charlie said, "is thank you very much for going to all this trouble for us. We really appreciate it."

"Sure," Jim corrected himself quickly. "That's exactly what I meant to say."

"You're welcome," Agnes said. "Just glad to see something leave the room."

She lifted the bag into Charlie's hands with a kind of reluctant reverence, then turned and gave the shelves a final glance.

"I'd be glad if everything left the room," she added. "It's sad to come in here, you know. I hate looking at what's here. Broken promises. Forgotten dreams. Lost hopes."

Charlie handed the book bag to Jim as the woman turned off the light, plunging the storage room into darkness again.

Then she turned the key in the lock and disappeared around the corner of the building without another word.

Chapter 84

"How are you two holding up?" Casey said quietly. "I've got a bottled water."

Andrew shook his head and checked the scope again, listening for the sound of the wind through the branches, his mind on what he knew needed to be done.

"I'm okay," he said through stiff lips. "Who's got the time?"

Quincy pulled his cell phone from a front overall pocket.

"Ten till one," the postman growled. "You losing your nerve, preacher?"

"Lighten up, Quincy," Casey said.

The old man bristled at the reprimand.

"I've met Army Rangers before," Quincy snapped, "and none of them resembled preachers."

"And I met ordinary men in Afghanistan," Casey said, "and not many considered themselves heroes until the shooting started. Judging is a dangerous business, master sergeant. You should know that better than most."

"You don't look that old, son," Andrew said. "You must have been very young."

"My dad didn't think so," Casey countered. "He was eighteen when he enlisted. My grandfather was younger than either of us, but he lied about his age."

Andrew lowered the gun to his side.

"Quincy," he offered sincerely, "would you rather take the shot? I haven't done this in years, and you go hunting all the time."

The postman's face reddened and he looked away.

"Never much of a marksman," he mumbled. "Damn poor now that I've got arthritis and cataracts. Truth be told, I can't scare a squirrel out of a pine at twenty feet. I might miss and hit Thomas."

The door to the SUV abruptly opened and Cora slowly emerged.

"Then it's settled," Casey said. "Preacher, it's up to you."

Chapter 85

Charlie put the multipocketed canvas backpack on the table and took two pairs of blue gloves from his pockets. He handed a pair to Jim and put on the other himself.

"What are you thinking?" Jim asked, tugging gently at the edge of the vinyl, forcing it to fit his oversized fingers.

What I'm always thinking, Charlie thought. *What have Cora and that dream preacher gotten me into now? But I can't say that to you. I can't even say that out loud to myself.*

"Let's dump everything on the table and see what we've got," he said. "If there's anything that can link all the pieces together—Cora's burial, Brackett's trial, Michele Hirsch. Anything at all."

The detective unzipped the main portion of the bag and began to remove the contents. A three-ring binder with dividers filled with notebook paper. A purple pencil case with assorted ink pens and mechanical pencils and a large pink eraser. Some loose paper clips, a half-used lip gloss tube, and several black ponytail holders.

at the bottom. Two textbooks, their pages brightly highlighted with yellow, blue, and orange, and a spiral-bound flowered planner, its edges littered with protruding sticky notes.

Nothing out of the ordinary.

No laptop. No cell phone. No electronics at all.

"Here," Charlie said, holding out the planner. "Check the entries around the date of the trial and see if there's anything significant."

Jim sat down at the table and flipped through the pages methodically.

"Did Agent Walker tell you what happened to Michele Hirsch?" Jim asked.

"She was driving in the pouring rain. Early hours of the morning. Hit head-on by a semitruck on Interstate 10. Died at the scene. Driver of the truck escaped with minor injuries."

Charlie looked up from the textbook in his hand before continuing.

"Once we knew who we were looking for, Inola pulled her usual strings and had the report sent over from the state troopers who worked the accident. Happened at about two in the morning. The driver said the car was traveling the wrong way and ploughed into him. He didn't think she saw him. He didn't see her until it was too late."

"No autopsy?"

"No real reason. No relatives to push for answers. Seemed pretty cut-and-dried. College-aged girl. Moonless night and raining. They assumed she was sleep-deprived, drunk, or high."

"Seems a little callous."

"I guess," Charlie agreed. "But this isn't a small town, Rookie. Michele Hirsch was dead. I mean, what else were they going to do for her?"

"What happened to her body?"

"Someone at Catholic services put her in a pauper's grave. There's a section set aside in the cemetery at St. John the Evangelist. I guess since she was so young they hoped someone would come looking for her eventually."

"And here we are looking for her."

Jim held up a photograph that had been sandwiched between the pages of the planner. The photo revealed a brooding young woman leaning awkwardly against a heavyset man. He looked distinctly uncomfortable. She looked sad, her eyes empty and her cheeks hollow and unsmiling.

Behind them there were shelves of books and a desk, also covered with stacks of books and papers.

"Is this Ed Brackett?" Jim asked.

"Yes," Charlie said. "And that must be Michele Hirsch."

He took the photograph between his gloved fingers and inspected it more carefully, his face wrinkling in concentration.

"Do you remember her?"

Charlie shook his head.

"No," he said. "I wish all this brought back some magic flood of memories, but it doesn't. I don't remember her, and even if I did I don't know how that helps us now."

There was a long pause while Charlie turned the bag upside down and shook it over the table, a few bits of paper and stale crumbs from some long-ago snack drifting down like a brief cold rain.

"I want to nail him to the wall," Charlie said quietly. "If he hurt Cora, if he had any part in the death of my baby and this young woman, I don't ever want him to walk in the sunshine again. I want to prove that. I want evidence that proves what happened without a shadow of a doubt."

There was a knock at the door, and it opened.

"Abbott, there's a call for you," the officer said. "Said she's from some place called Balfour, Georgia, and that you'd want to take her call. Her name's Vicki."

"Sure," Charlie said. "I think we're almost done here."

He turned the bag right side up and passed it across the table to Jim, who slid his hand absently along the side.

"Wait a minute," the Rookie said. "Here's a zipper pocket we didn't open."

Without waiting for an acknowledgment, he jerked the tab down, exposing the exterior compartment, and shook the bag once again over the tabletop.

A partially eaten candy bar, the covering torn to expose the top but still wrapped around the base, landed on the table with a soft thud.

Chapter 86

Flanked by the crouching paramedic on his right and the brooding sergeant on his left, Pastor Andrew Evans adjusted the gun against his shoulder and fervently prayed.

The pine straw beneath their feet was soft, cushioning their silent stance. The density of the undergrowth provided cover for their presence.

The men had stopped all conversation as soon as Cora left Katy sitting in the SUV and approached the isolated cabin. They had silently adapted their positions, moving only to make certain that there was a clear view to the porch and the front door.

The ranger pressed his left eye against the lens of the scope and took a deep breath, the butt of the rifle driven deep into his shoulder, the barrel braced where two branches of the scrub oak met and divided, shoulder-high.

The adrenaline had kicked in, and Andrew felt a surge of reflex and muscle memory. His years of training took command. There was no thought in his mind but the mission, the purpose, the target.

Cora had taken her stand at the foot of the cabin steps, waiting. Her hands hung limply at her sides, her body rigid.

Andy heard her call out to Brackett. He sensed the men on either side of him tense, but he could not afford the luxury of feelings or distractions.

The door to the cabin swung open, and about six feet inside in the semidarkness he could make out the lawyer's body tied to a chair, the man's face bloody and his head bowed. Brackett's face appeared just over the man's shoulder, using his captive as a human shield.

Stand up taller, Andy thought. *I need a clean shot. Stand up! A little to the side.*

He prayed Cora would remain still. Follow the plan. Do what he'd told her to do.

He'd never seen anyone quite so brave. So determined.

Move to the left! his mind shouted at his target. *Left!*

And, as if the sniper's command had been audible, Brackett straightened himself, leaned out to the left, and raised his arm toward Cora.

In that split second, the sniper saw the handgun, and a fraction of that later, he himself fired.

The crack momentarily deafened him, but he ignored the temporary pain. He held the Mossberg out, and Quincy took it as the preacher bolted toward Cora on the heels of the racing paramedic.

Casey reached the downed man first and kicked away the gun that had fallen outward from the shooter's wounded grasp. Blood poured from the man's shoulder as the paramedic jerked open his medic bag.

Brackett had landed face-first on the threshold of the doorway, writhing in pain, his bloodstained hand gripping the wound in his upper shoulder and moans coming from his contorted mouth.

"I've got him!" Casey shouted at Andrew, who had stopped long enough to grip Cora's arm as she stumbled up the steps. The preacher guided her around the pair and into the dark cabin to her injured husband.

"You shot me!" Brackett screamed to no one in particular. "You were supposed to come alone!"

The paramedic roughly rolled the man over onto his back, pulling a thick gauze pad from his kit and ripping the sterile package open. He pushed the struggling man down with one unflinching thrust, straddling his torso as he covered the bullet hole and applied heavy pressure to stem the tide of blood.

Casey removed another stack of gauze from his bag and pressed a knee into Brackett's shoulder.

"That hurts!" the man screamed. "Get off my chest! You're hurting me!"

"I'm saving your life," Casey said matter-of-factly. "You're lucky it's a through and through. He missed your carotid. Stop moving around and lie still."

Brackett groaned and lay still.

"Once the bleeding's under control," Casey said, addressing the inside of the cabin, "I'll check on Thomas. Preacher, have him lie down until I get in there."

Quincy stomped up the steps, his white hair flowing from under his baseball cap and his rifle tucked into his elbow.

"You calling an ambulance?" Casey asked cheerfully.

"Already on it," Quincy said calmly, the phone to his ear. "He's lost his shooting arm so he's not much of a danger—if he ever was."

"Shut up, you old coot!" Brackett screamed.

"Old coot?" Quincy ran a hand down his beard, shifting his weight and balancing the weapon easily, pointed downward and away but ready at a moment's notice. "Old coot with a Mossberg. Don't you forget that, you fool."

"Quincy," Casey cautioned. "He needs to lie still."

"Humph," Quincy said. "He'll lie even more still if'n I shoot him again."

Casey shook his head.

"You hear him?" he said to the wounded man. "I'd lie really still if I were you."

Quincy lowered the cell phone, dialed, and pressed the phone against his ear for a second time, his eyes never leaving Brackett's face.

"Ben," he began, but that was all he said. He listened carefully and, after a long moment, slid the phone into the pocket of his overalls and readjusted the rifle.

"Good news," he announced to Casey. "Apparently the womenfolk already alerted Ben that there was trouble. He was ready, and he's following the ambulance with a posse."

Brackett protested weakly and tried to sit up. Casey tightened the grip with his knees and the pressure on the wound.

"Wouldn't do that if I were you," Quincy warned the man. "Settle down. They're bringing a meat wagon, and we'll have you patched up and back to that comfy, safe cell in no time at all."

The sound of the fire department ambulance echoed from the main road, mixed with the blare of a patrol car's siren and the stampeding of multiple cars.

"See," Quincy continued pleasantly, "ain't technology grand?

Those GPS things are really handy in a pinch. The cavalry's almost here."

"Casey!" Andrew called from inside the cabin. "In here!"

"I got him," Quincy said, shifting his stance. "If he decides to get up and run, I know where to shoot him so he won't lose much more blood. Check on Thomas."

Casey stripped off his blue gloves and tossed them down, grabbing a fresh pair as he rose from Brackett's body to pick up his bag. He gave Quincy a questioning look.

"He won't go anywhere," Quincy assured him. "Help Thomas."

The paramedic's eyes adjusted rapidly to the dim light, assessing the situation.

Thomas, his head crusted with blood and his face battered, was seated on the floor beside a prone Cora. Andrew Evans had backed away from the couple, standing awkwardly in the corner of the room by the window.

"I'll make myself useful outside," the preacher said, moving to the sunlit porch.

"Where are you hurt?" Casey said, pulling on his gloves and kneeling beside the lawyer. He gripped the man's damaged wrist, searching for a pulse to take his vitals as he began taking inventory of the man's injuries—dilated pupils, a two-inch forehead gash, copious amounts of blood on his clothing, and darkening bruises on his cheekbones and chin.

Thomas decisively pushed the paramedic's hand away.

"I'll be fine," he said, his voice choking with emotion as he cradled his wife's head in his lap. "Help Cora. Her water broke. She says the baby's coming."

Cora heaved a ragged breath, exhaling a sharp cry of agreement.

"Ambulance is on its way," Casey said reassuringly, feeling a surge of hope and gratification. "No worries. Let me clean up your face a bit before they get here, and then we'll take care of your wife. We're all going to be just fine."

Chapter 87

Jim had returned the file boxes to the records clerk, and there was nothing to do now but wait in the empty interrogation room for the results of the DNA and content composition tests from the candy bar. Between the waiting and the news of Cora's confrontation with Brackett in Balfour, Jim was feeling a strange sense of satisfaction.

He'd taken up a position in the corner of the room, his chair leaned back diagonally against the wall, his arms crossed against his broad chest.

Charlie had wandered in and out of the room several times in the last hour, each time with another bottle of soda or a snack from the vending machines—offerings for Jim that he humbly accepted and stuffed into his already overflowing backpack.

Finally Charlie came in with coffee and a bag of beignets from Café Beignet next door and placed them in the middle of the table.

"You really don't have to do that," Jim protested. "I feel like a newborn at a two-a.m. feeding. I don't actually eat every hour on the hour."

"Results are back," Charlie said, pulling out a chair. He removed a piece of paper from the inside of his jacket and scanned the contents.

"Michele Hirsch died in an automobile accident almost two weeks after Brackett was incarcerated and the night Cora was found at the abandoned house," he began. "She crossed the double lines and hit an eighteen-wheeler head-on. The car she was driving caught fire, and investigators assumed she fell asleep. Walker is working on an order to exhume her body."

"Really?" Jim said, bringing his chair to the table and picking up one of the coffee cups. "On what grounds?"

"The half-eaten candy bar contained a dose of arsenic," he said. "And the only fingerprints on the wrapper are hers and Brackett's."

Jim was incredulous.

"You think Brackett meant to poison her after she tried to bury Cora? To get rid of any traces that he was connected?" he said. "But how could he be sure she wouldn't eat the candy bar until afterward? That sounds pretty risky to me."

"I don't know how he managed it," Charlie conceded. "Maybe it was her favorite kind. Maybe he'd told her that it was a reward for a job well done and not to eat it until she was finished. She was willing to kill for him, why wouldn't she do exactly what she was told to do?"

Jim opened the bag of beignets.

"What does Walker think?" he said.

"Our friendly FBI special agent thinks that there was just enough poison in the candy to cause a serious reaction as well as impair judgment. That she took several bites of the candy, realized something was wrong, and tried to drive herself to get help."

"Would arsenic do that—I mean, could she still drive?"

"It's nasty stuff. She would have been in pain and probably vomiting. Combined with her state of mind, realizing she'd killed another human being for someone who had betrayed her, she wasn't thinking clearly. It was late at night and raining."

Jim put the beignet back into the bag.

"Is that enough to convict Brackett of intent to commit murder?"

"That's Walker's job," Charlie said, sipping at his coffee. "We've done the legwork. The FBI can take it from here."

All I know is that Cora was right . . . again, he thought, *sending me off on a wild goose chase around the South looking for candy bars and long-dead graduate assistants. Apparently, the ghosts of the past don't have an expiration date. They can skip into the present whenever they darn well please and muck up the future.*

"Where do we go from here?" Jim said, wiping the powdered sugar from his fingers with a napkin.

"Brackett's in custody in Balfour," Charlie said. "They'll extradite him as soon as federal agents can get there to bring him back to stand trial for Michele Hirsch's death."

"But what about the kidnapping and attempted murder charges in Georgia?"

"They'll have to take a number and get in line."

Charlie looked at his watch.

"We've got just enough time to get you back to your hotel so you can pack and be on the next plane back to Atlanta."

The detective clearly didn't want to discuss anything further, but the officer wasn't ready to end the discussion.

"But," he began, "I was hoping—"

"Listen, Jim," Charlie said. His face went hard and every wrinkle and crease appeared deeper, making him look even older than his nearly forty years. "You've got a job waiting at the FBI, and I've got work to get back to here."

"Oh, I understand," Jim said, his words forceful, contradicting the serenity of his dark face. "You're Charlie Abbott, and you work alone."

Charlie stood up.

"I don't want to talk about it," he said. "I'm tired. The case is over."

Jim stood up, overshadowing the detective like an offensive lineman facing off against the opposing team's quarterback. Charlie had the distinct impression it was the final seconds of the game and he was about to be tackled to the ground. Jim clearly had been preparing to say something, and that something was going to hurt.

Jim knew he was going to Memphis to join the FBI. Knew the likelihood he would ever have this opportunity again was slim. He'd held it in until the fourth quarter, and what he had to say was now or never.

"I *do* want to talk about it," Jim said, glowering. "Sit down, detective."

Charlie turned the chair around defiantly and straddled it.

"Okay then," he said. "I guess I owe you. Let me have it."

Jim sat on the edge of the table.

"I've learned a few things in life," he said, "and not just from this last year working with you. I've learned the best lessons, the important ones, come from broken people—honest people who know they've been broken. People who aren't afraid."

"That sounds like a ton of horse manure to me," Charlie said, trying to lighten the mood, but he stopped when Jim raised his hand for silence.

"That's my limit," he said. "I've listened to several truckloads of your particular brand of horse manure, and it's time *you* listened for a change, so close your donut-crusted, gum-popping mouth."

"I'm listening, Jim," he said. Charlie had no idea where this was going. He hadn't been lectured like this since Ben took him aside in high school and threatened to tell his grandfather if he caught him causing trouble again.

"I don't think you understand who you are," Jim said. "I mean, in God's eyes."

"So now you're telling me you can see through God's eyes—"

Jim's hand came down much too hard on the detective's shoulder, and he winced in pain.

"I swear," Jim said. "If you don't close your mouth—"

His broad hand squeezed into Charlie's collarbone with a crushing promise.

"Don't you dare mock me," he warned. "You act like you're a tough guy, walling yourself up, cutting yourself off. I've been there, and I tried it too. Being judged sucks. I was a tank. An empty-headed bruiser. My size doesn't help with first impression, but I'd begun to work at changing. You gave me a chance. You didn't have to do that, but you did—and I'm grateful."

Charlie opened his mouth, but Jim's hand increased the pressure and what came out was a squeak of pain instead of words.

"I told you," Jim said. "I've been saving up for this, and you're going to hear the whole lecture to the bitter end, if I have to break some bones in the process."

The detective nodded, squirming uncomfortably.

"Good," Jim said. "Bad habits are hard to break—but that's what friends are for. You helped me become a better person, and

I'm here to return the favor."

Jim paused for a moment and stared at the blank wall. For a split second, Charlie thought he might be finished, but then he realized that was overly optimistic.

"Where was I before you decided to disrespect me?" the massive man said quietly. "Never mind—I remember. We were talking about what God knows."

Charlie heard the sound of the air-conditioning unit kick on somewhere past the vents in the wall. Outside the window the wind rustled an oak tree, and he could hear the whisper of the dead leaves crackling as they let go and surrendered to the ground, already littered with a thousand more. In the next room, someone's cell phone played an annoying jingle that was gone as quickly as it began.

Jim loomed over him, and for the first time in a very long time Charlie was at peace. He felt a warm, relaxed feeling like a weighted blanket on a frosty night.

It's okay, Charlie thought. *He's right, I haven't been okay—but I will be. It might just be time to hear this . . . and make some changes.*

"Go on, Jim," he said. "I'm ready."

Jim turned his own chair and sat.

"You're the most honest man I know," Jim said. "You're also the best liar. The problem is, you've been busy lying to yourself too. All that garbage that you throw at people—that ego you project. It's a cover-up, friend."

"Are we friends?"

"Shut up, I'm still talking. I'll let you know when I'm finished."

Charlie shrugged his shoulders, a crooked grin stealing over his face.

"Sure, whatever you say."

"It's about time that sentence came out of your mouth," Jim said, shifting himself so the chair complained under his weight. "Stop pretending you're some smart-aleck jerk who has to go through life fighting the villains all alone and then ride into the sunset on your trusty horse Miata with your loyal dog at your side."

"I don't know how to take what you're telling me," Charlie ventured.

"You think you're being yourself, but you aren't," Jim said, pretending he hadn't been interrupted. "The real Charlie Abbott is a brilliant, gifted investigator with an inferiority complex—a man who is so afraid that no one will like him that he makes himself unlikeable on purpose."

"Is this supposed to hurt my feelings?" Charlie said. "Because it's working."

"Don't worry," Jim said. "It can be your secret from the world if you want, but just stop lying to yourself—that's all. And for goodness' sake, stop lying to me."

Jim shook Charlie's shoulder until it began to throb.

"Just one more thing," he said, releasing his grip and standing. "I'm going to be your friend and your any-time, part-time partner no matter what you do. No matter what you say. Whether you like it or not. So if you think you're going to get away with this attitude with me anymore, you've got another think coming."

Charlie waited, expecting more.

"That's it. I'm done now," Jim said, irritated but glad to have his thoughts off his chest.

"Thanks, Jim," Charlie said, standing and extending his hand.

"That's enough of that," Jim said. "I'm hungry, and I want some real food before we get on the road back."

"What are you talking about?" he said. "I wasn't going—"

He stopped abruptly.

"Sure you were going home," Jim said, finishing the sentence. "Brackett kidnapped your best friend and tried to kill your pregnant ex-wife. They'll be in the hospital for the next few days. Don't tell me you don't care enough to look them both in the eye."

"You're a pain in the butt, Rookie."

"Happens every time I spend time with you, detective," he said. "Won't take me a minute to throw my things together. It's been a while since I drove a stick, but we could be halfway there in the time it will take us to get to the airport and take a plane, not to mention having to get a rental on the other end."

Charlie considered his battered Volkswagen.

"If you're game to spend eight hours in the front seat," he said reluctantly.

Jim shrugged.

"I've been in worse and survived," he said, visions of a cramped Mitsubishi in his head and the smell of barbecue pork rinds in his nostrils. "Besides, have you seen the skimpy snacks on planes? A man could starve between airports."

Charlie slid his chair back under the table and picked up his sport jacket.

"We've got several hours of daylight if we leave in the next hour," he said, fishing his keys from his pocket. "Promise me you're done talking for at least a hundred miles."

Right, Jim thought. *I remember. You hate the chatter.*

"Sure," he said agreeably. "Maybe even two hundred, if I get sleepy. I'll grab my backpack. Let's get this show on the road."

Chapter 88

The Sixth Day: Saturday

An uneventful fourteen hours and innumerable rest stops later, the Volkswagen rolled into Balfour. Jim asked politely to be dropped off at the station so he could pick up his truck and drive himself home.

Charlie had plenty of time to decide what to do on the way home, so he made a quick unscheduled stop before he drove to Griffith. Then he stopped at a pharmacy to buy a gift bag and tissue before sitting in the parking lot of Griffith Memorial for almost an hour, gathering the courage to go inside to the third-floor maternity wing.

Once inside, he waited again in the hallway outside Cora's room, inspecting her name on the sign affixed to the wall, wondering about HIPAA laws and privacy notices and why the door wasn't closed instead of standing open for the world to stop and stare the way he was staring.

Legalities that, to Charlie's mind, should have concerned Thomas—if he hadn't been so totally engaged in holding little Jane in his arms and gazing down at his wife and new son in the hospital bed as though he'd never seen a newborn in his entire life. Thomas's entire face was glowing with radiant awe and love.

Charlie could certainly empathize with his oldest friend's obsession and wonder, considering how little contact either of them had ever had with babies.

And Charlie's mind went back to the only newborn the detective had ever seen close-up—Lonora. They tried to convince him not to see the body, but he insisted. He climbed into the back of the ambulance and pushed the EMT aside. Cora was still heavily sedated, strapped to the gurney, and he wanted to see his wife first. But he needed to see his dead child too.

He remembered telling them that there was no one else who cared—at least, not the way a father cared. That they couldn't keep him out.

He'd picked his daughter up from the plexiglass tray where one of them had been working on her until they both turned their attention to Cora. As he cradled the loosely wrapped infant, he turned to his motionless wife—the IV taped to her bruised hand, an oxygen mask covering her pale nose and mouth, the blood pressure cuff still wrapped around her too-thin arm. Her black hair twisted up and around her head.

Her shallow breathing comforted him.

She didn't know yet. She couldn't hold their child. Didn't know she'd never hold her child. Their child. But someone needed to hold the baby. Someone needed to say goodbye.

Charlie wanted to scream at them to try again. To keep trying. But he'd seen it before—the sadness on their dedicated, stoic faces. They'd accepted what he couldn't. They'd done all they could.

He thought the blanket they'd wrapped her in wasn't soft enough, but that wasn't their fault either. He couldn't tear his eyes away from Lonora's tiny head, covered with matted hair, her eyes closed, skin translucent, her expression so incredibly serene.

Perfect. She was perfect.

Charlie didn't know what he expected to happen. What he'd expected to see or feel. She looked like a doll except for the bits of blood and the sticky white substance that looked like smeared petroleum jelly, partially wiped away by experienced, kind, dedicated hands.

He was both moved and horrified.

Charlie wasn't sure how long they let him stand there, blocking their access, the anger building inside. And then he heard them talking.

From far away and yet just over his shoulder he heard a paramedic telling him quietly, firmly, that he needed to get out of the ambulance so they could take Cora to the hospital.

That his wife was stabilized but she needed to get to the hospital emergency room. That someone would bring him in a patrol car and follow.

Someone tenderly took his daughter out of his hands, and he never saw Lonora's face again. Along the way, another one of the nameless somebodies pressed a pen into his hand and he signed for the body to be cremated. It seemed like the right thing to do at the time. He still thought so.

Sometimes the whole twenty-four hours after it happened were a total blur—and other times, like now, the memory was as clear and cold as ice. A dagger of ice.

"Charlie!" Jane's voice called out from across the room, her enthusiastic shout breaking through his excruciating memories. "Come see my brother, Charlie!"

The detective's feet felt glued to the floor. The gift bag in his hands suddenly felt like a ten-pound weight, and he couldn't imagine why he'd thought coming to see Cora was a good idea. Why he'd been persuaded by the Rookie's advice.

Jane wiggled in her daddy's arms, insisting that Thomas put her down. Once free, she ran to grab Charlie's hand, pulling him a half-dozen steps closer to the bed.

"He's so beautiful," she said, her child's voice full of pride and awe. "He's ours. We get to take him home."

Charlie's eyes met Cora's, expecting to find pity—but there was none. What he saw was something else entirely.

She extended her hand and reached for him.

"Charlie," she said. "We're so glad you've come."

The detective looked uncertainly from Cora to Thomas, but his old friend was smiling too, nodding and beaming like a man who'd won the lottery.

And Charlie knew he had.

Leaning down, the detective carefully picked up Jane, her arms hugging him tightly as he balanced her on his hip and held the shiny blue gift bag to his side.

Reluctantly, he took the last few steps to his ex-wife's side and stopped.

"What's that?" Jane said, twisting around his chest and indicating the blue bag. "Is that a present for my brother?"

Charlie gingerly returned the little girl to Thomas, passing her carefully over the foot of the bed, and set the gift bag on the cotton hospital blanket beside Cora.

"Yes, it's a present for your brother," he said. "Is that okay?"

"Is it another cat?" Jane persisted, straining forward and attempting to look over the top and through the mass of curling ribbon securing the sides. "Is it a cat daddy?"

"Good guess," Charlie said, a blushing color creeping up his neck and spreading across his jaw. "But no."

His intense gaze met Cora's.

"The holidays are coming up soon," he said quietly, "and the start of a new year. I don't know how much I'll be coming back to Balfour, so I decided I'd give you something that would remind you of me in a different way."

He lifted the bag over Cora and the baby, pushing it into Jane's reach.

"Since he's too little to open presents," he said, "how about you open the present for him?"

Jane cheerfully leaned out and grabbed the bag, tearing the paper away and tossing the variegated blue sheets of crumpled tissue that hid the treasure to the floor. Thomas pulled the bag back and away from Cora and the baby as Jane's tiny hands dug, emerging with a large, bright blue sock monkey.

The little girl's mouth flew open and a giggle escaped, followed by another in a waterfall of delight.

"He is a daddy—he's a daddy monkey!" she exclaimed, poking happily at his black felt eyes and tracing the curve of red thread that created his traditional grin. "He looks like my baby monkeys, only he's bigger."

"It's one of Linda's," Charlie said lamely. "I hope you don't mind Linda said that Jane had some smaller ones, so I just thought . . ."

"Thank you," Cora said. "That's very sweet of you."

"Yes," Thomas said. "That's very thoughtful, Charlie. Thank you."

The infant lying in Cora's arms squeaked a tiny noise of protest accompanied by a wiggle and a stretch beneath his swaddle.

"He's—"

Charlie searched for a word that might be appropriate. All he could see was the little boy's face, and that was a sliver of wrinkled reddish skin between the edge of the pink-and-blue striped blanket, snug around his neck, and the matching knit cap pulled down low over his forehead and ears. The newborn yawned to reveal a toothless mouth under squinting eyes, fighting to open in the dim light of the room.

So like Lonora. So unlike Lonora.

"Yes," Cora said helpfully, finishing his sentence. "He's handsome, isn't he?"

"Absolutely," the detective agreed, almost too quickly. "Handsome—that's the word I was looking for. He looks just like you, Thomas."

"I like the monkey," Jane said, her dark, waist-length pigtails dancing as she pressed the cartoonish, handmade stuffed primate to her chest. "He has big ears and big eyes—"

"And a big grin," Charlie finished, waving his hand. "I get it, Cherry Blossom. You think he looks like me."

"I like you, Charlie," Jane said, her tiny voice suddenly trembling with memory. "You took the blue-eyed man away. He isn't going to bother me anymore."

Charlie tried to ignore the look of gratitude that passed between Cora and Thomas and landed squarely on him. He shifted his weight from one foot to the other and dug into his pockets for a pack of gum, about to announce he had to go when a stern-faced nurse poked her head around the semiclosed door.

"Visiting hours are almost over," she said sweetly. "Someone's little brother is going home tomorrow, and someone's mommy needs to get a good night's rest."

"Me," Jane giggled happily, the monkey's long tail swinging from her embrace. "She means me."

"Indeed she does," Charlie agreed.

The cell phone in his jacket began to vibrate and he took it out, glancing down at the caller ID.

"Sorry to leave you with the monkey and run, but I've got to take this call."

Charlie extended his hand toward Thomas, but the lawyer set Jane and the monkey gently on the end of the bed and walked around directly to his friend. Pushing Charlie's hand aside, he put his arms around the other man's shoulders in a bear-hugging embrace that took Charlie completely off guard.

"You've always been my best friend," Thomas said, slapping Charlie on the back as he had in the days when they played football together, when the friendship was new and their history together short. "You'll always be my best friend. Don't forget that."

The detective bit his lip, holding back the emotions that threatened to betray him.

"For a lawyer," Charlie quipped, "you're really a terrible judge of character. No wonder you gave up criminal law for this one-horse town."

Cora's voice called him from behind her husband, and Thomas stepped back out of the way. Her hand was extended as it had been when the detective came into the room, but this time he took it.

"I don't want to keep you," she said, feeling the chill on his skin where she had half-expected warmth. "I thought you had to take the call."

"I did say that," he said, trying to pull away while she held fast. "But it's Inola. If I answer her the first time, she gets all big-headed, thinking I don't have anything else to do but wait for her calls. Then she starts ordering me around. She'll leave a message."

"Well then," Cora said, her eyes misting over. "We certainly can't have just anyone ordering you around now, can we?"

"No," Charlie said lightly. "We can't have that."

"Take care of yourself," she said, squeezing his hand before reluctantly releasing his fingers. "Until next time."

"Sure," Charlie said. "Sure thing."

The cell phone began to vibrate again.

He turned and strode to the doorway and down the hall without looking back.

When the elevator doors closed behind him, Charlie Abbott was cracking jokes in Inola Walker's exasperated ear, but for some strange reason, his eyes were stinging and his cheeks were wet with tears.

Chapter 89

Homecoming Day

The ride home from Griffith Memorial Hospital was unexpectedly normal.

Jane chirped happily from her car seat in the back, and baby Tom slept, nestled deeply into his infant carrier, gurgling contented noises from time to time in his sleep. His big sister had helped dress him in a special blue-and-white-checked footed sleeper, and the ordeal had thrilled the elder and thoroughly exhausted the younger.

Cora felt a bit exhausted herself, and Thomas wisely left her to her own thoughts, concentrating on driving the rain-slick roads. He wondered idly if his Honda would be big enough for them now, and whether or not he should consider buying something larger and more family friendly. If maybe Cora would want to go shopping for cars in a few weeks and they could make a day of the trip and Marjorie could watch the children.

There were so many restaurants in Atlanta that he thought Cora might enjoy. So many places that he wanted to take her, show her.

He knew he was being overly optimistic, but he could hope.

He could always ask. They could talk. There were so many things to talk about.

When he stopped at a red light on Highway 19, he took the opportunity to reach over and gently squeeze one of his wife's hands, and she responded with a smile. She tried not to notice the red rings still visible around his wrist where the tape had chaffed and cut into his skin. Tried not to think about what might have happened. He had conceded to an antibiotic cream but drew the line at the gauze one of the nurses tried to wrap around under the cuffs of his shirt.

"I'm not bleeding," he said shortly. "I'm fine. Please don't bother."

The matronly nurse, accustomed to men who refused to take medical directions, walked away and left him praying at his wife's bedside. She knew when her actual patient awoke from her fitful sleep, she could persuade him to be treated for his injuries.

But the nurses didn't argue when the newborn son was brought to the room from an overnight stay in the NICU for observation and Thomas insisted on sleeping in the chair in the corner of his wife's room. In spite of all his own injuries, he steadfastly refused to leave her side.

Cora ran a light index finger over the angry marks before the light turned green, and Thomas half-heartedly put his hand back on the steering wheel.

Those are going to be scars, Cora thought to herself, marveling at the man beside her and his stoic faith. *Reminders of horrors we can never forget. Horrors he can never forget and will probably never share with me.*

Yet oddly enough, she found that the fear she had been carrying for so long was gone, and she had no idea at all when her spirit had been liberated. She glanced over her shoulder at her children and then at her husband's profile, refusing to think more deeply about anything for the time being.

Unwilling to be drawn back into the past and relishing the present.

Drizzling rain had begun to fall, spattering the windows with misty droplets that mixed with the clinging pine needles and leaves. Enough moisture to make them stick more closely to the exterior of the car without dislodging them.

The trees, shedding the last of their brilliant autumn colors, looked sparse and chilled in the damp air. The leaves, mottled yellow, red, and brown, were piled around on the soaked earth like abandoned confetti.

What had been crisp and vibrant only a week ago was now soggy and fading.

Winter was coming.

Cora hugged herself a little tighter under the oversized blue sweater Marjorie had brought her when she dropped off Jane.

The same sweater she'd worn that day she'd gone to the law office. The day she'd left the house so many months ago to tell Thomas that she loved him more than life itself. That he was the center of her world and she loved him, needed him, cherished him.

A strong gust of wind blew across the driveway, and they were finally home.

Chapter 90

The Last Dream

Cora was unsettled as she stood at the kitchen sink and stared down at her hands. Her skin was warm and soft, the nails closely clipped and clean. There was a dishpan of soapy water in the left side of the enamel double sink and another matching dishpan of hot water for rinsing on the right. To the far right was the drainboard.

She realized from the fact that the dishes and silverware overflowed that she must have been washing dishes for quite some time before the dream began. Her hands still felt the sensation of the water.

From her far left, she felt a warm flow of heat from the stove, but the burners were off and there was no evidence of pots or pans.

Not even the enamel coffee pot.

Turning around completely, she became aware that she was alone. The ladder-back chairs around the table were empty and pushed under. The oilcloth appeared slightly damp from a recent wiping.

There was no light from the windows. Instead, a single coal oil lamp sat in the center of the table, creating a faint circle of light in the dusky darkness of the room and filling the air with the musty smell of burning oil.

The dream confused her. Something didn't seem quite right. Something seemed finished. Over. But there was no satisfaction at the conclusion.

Only confusion. And clean hands.

Cora stared down at her ringless hands and saw that she was holding a dishrag. For a moment, she concentrated on the cloth.

Along the edges, in a faded pattern of embroidery, was a double vine of tiny leaves and flowers. There were no colors, of course, but the threads were worn. The cloth had apparently been much loved and much used over the years.

Cora pulled the softened, damp cotton through her fingers, letting the bumpy threads of the stitched pattern rub against her sensitive skin.

Quite unexpectedly, a feeling of peace flowed over her, weakening her knees so that she dropped down to the linoleum floor. In her confusion, she gripped the cloth closely over her pounding heart and tried to make some sense of what was happening and why.

Then she was awake.

In her own bed, in her own room. Beside her, her husband snored contentedly. At the foot of their bed was a bassinet, and in it their infant son slept soundly. In the room across the hall, their daughter was dreaming of tea parties and kittens, a watchful Maine coon cat on guard.

And Cora knew she'd cleaned the kitchen. She'd finished the dishes.

Everything was put away and in its proper place.

She had wiped away the traces of the past.

The time for dreams was over, and a new day was coming—and she was ready at last.

Epilogue

Saturday . . . Six Months Later . . .

The spring air was as cool and fresh as no other day had been in a long, long time. At least, that's how Ellie Sanderson saw this particular morning.

She'd woken far earlier than her customary crack of dawn to count her blessings and begin marking off the items on the extensive checklist for her wedding day.

Her parents were also bustling around the house, preparing themselves in much the same way they had prepared years ago for the birth of their one and only child.

Expectant. Hopeful. Anticipating a momentous change between the world they knew and the one that was about to be thrust upon them.

Pastor Andrew Evans, assisted by Ginny, had also gotten up especially early, dressed more carefully than usual, and met the bridal party at the side doors to Emmanuel for the first of many formal photographs for the day and a special breakfast catered by

Sam and Bill in the fellowship hall.

Ginny, with her own brand of quiet confidence, assumed the role of director, managing the bridal party with patient experience, offering suggestions and giving soothing reminders to keep everyone on task and on time.

The ceremony itself, attended by a small percentage of the community who had been specially invited, went off without a single hiccup.

Unless, of course, anyone counted the stern looks from Mr. Sanderson as he met his new son-in-law at the altar to surrender Ellie, and Mrs. Sanderson's obvious sobbing as the preacher invited the same young man to kiss the bride.

An hour and a half later, the group from the church had been joined by the remainder of the town, and the Wilton House erupted in merriment.

Vicki, with Allison's increasingly agreeable assistance, had moved the more significant of the flowers from the church to the estate. Not that the additional flowers were necessary with the gardens in full bloom, but the bridesmaids' bouquets of violets, yellow rosebuds, and daisies made lovely centerpieces for the outside tables.

Ellie's elegant bouquet of yellow roses, daisies, and violets with varied shades of purple ribbons found its home on the table with the wedding cake, and the groomsmen's rosebud and daisy boutonnieres formed a half-circle around the dark chocolate groom's cake.

Everyone insisted that Vicki had outdone herself this time.

Katy Wilton had offered the servers a choice of a sunshine yellow or royal purple T-shirt, to be worn with black slacks and crisp white aprons. She'd also ordered candies wrapped in yellow and purple cellophane to be placed in crystal bowls, flanked by fat yellow and purple candles, scattered for decoration on the tables around the house.

All in all, the wedding and the reception following were everything Ellie had imagined, including totally unexpected changes in the attitudes of some of Balfour's most cantankerous citizens.

Quincy showed up in a pristine white shirt and modest purple striped tie, his flowing white hair combed back over his broad shoulders and his beard neatly trimmed. A half smile peeked out from under the outer corners of his mustache. He dutifully took the place beside the front door, taking charge, from all appearances, as the designated doorman and potential bouncer. No one knew why, and no one dared ask.

Vicki's envious teenage assistant, Allison, who had spent the week complaining about the additional work, also found reason to be happy.

The teenager arrived at the florist's shop to find a white dress box with a gorgeous gossamer seafoam formal gown wrapped in tissue paper. Tucked into a corner at the bottom of the box, she found a dyed-to-match pair of slippers.

Vicki feigned surprise and instructed her helper to bring the dress and shoes so she could change clothes at the Wilton House after her duties were complete moving flowers from the church to the reception area.

Yet another scowling guest, Zedekiah Balfour, dressed in his finest suit and tie, was perched on the stone wall nearest the garden exit to the parking lot, watching his daughter Naomi as she skipped happily among the various groups. Naomi had been asked to serve the groom's cake and was taking her duties quite seriously, darting back and forth between her parent and her post at the table placating her father with smiles and hugs.

Zedekiah secretly loved that she had found a place to be valued, to have an outlet for her burgeoning creative spirit. His only complaint was that she insisted on dragging him in her wake to mingle with the overly friendly Balfour townsfolk—people who persisted in greeting him as though he were a long lost relative and thanking him repeatedly for sharing his daughter as well as his talents and his cabin with the community.

Confound Katy Wilton and her meddling, he thought sourly, as yet another roving server asked him if he'd like a refill on his pink lemonade or a fancy hors d'oeuvre from a silver tray. *Double confound this whole town and every cheerful soul in it.*

On the patio, Darcie Jones was fluttering about making her own effort to be one of the cheerful souls that Zedekiah despised. Her opportunity came when she spotted the reporter from the Griffith Historical Society ineffectively hiding behind one of the potted palms.

"Daryl?" Darcie gushed. "Is that you with a fern in your face?"

The man coughed uncomfortably, embarrassed to be called out by name.

Darcie came close to saying that she almost hadn't recognized him without his gaudy suit and mustache, but she bit her tongue.

At least he's dressed like your average human being in that brown suit and striped tie, she thought generously. *Maybe he's learned a lesson or two.*

"Vicki said it was okay if I came," he said defensively. "I'm not taking pictures or anything. She said no one would mind one extra person."

"Of course," Darcie said, idly wondering about the friendship that had developed between the flamboyant florist and the weasel-faced historian. "The Sandersons invited everyone. Vicki was right."

Turning enemies into friends, Darcie thought with admiration, *and great publicity with the Historical Society for the Wilton House venue at the same time. Clever girl.*

A passing server paused with a tray of lemonade cups, each containing a clear cube of ice with a frozen cherry in the center. Darcie took one for herself and put another in Daryl's empty, pudgy hand.

"Thank you, dear," she said, nodding at the teenager, who moved on to the next group of partygoers.

"Now, drink up, Daryl," she said firmly. "And you march yourself right out there into the garden and have a big piece of wedding cake too."

He gave her a quizzical look, his jaw hanging open slightly, unable to speak.

"Yes," she insisted, patting his face with her free hand. "And if anyone asks, you can add my name to Vicki's and say that I told you."

In the elegant foyer of the Wilton House, Ben Taylor was about to usher his most dependable officer out of town.

Jim Smith, dressed in a tailored suit instead of his usual police uniform, was finding himself unexpectedly emotional about leaving.

"It's all right son," Ben said. "I knew the minute you came back from Savannah with Charlie that you'd caught the wanderlust. Charlie's a carrier. We all know it."

"Chief—" he began, but Ben cut him off decisively.

"Don't you dare try to talk yourself out of taking this job," the man said. "I'm not going to try to keep you here, and I'm certainly not going to let you go and sabotage the opportunity of a lifetime."

Neither man noticed the arrival of Katy Wilton, who had crept up behind them.

"Officer Smith," she began, "did I hear that you're leaving us for Memphis?"

"The FBI," Ben interjected proudly, slapping Jim on the back. "Special Agent Walker wants him on her team."

"That's wonderful!" Katy said. "I know you'll do a great job."

"And I heard congratulations are appropriate for you too," Ben said. "Aren't you taking over the executive management of the Wilton House?"

Katy straightened her shoulders.

"Amy and I are co-directors," she said. "I'll be working with the personnel, and she'll be handling the day-to-day, vendors, and scheduling events. Darcie Jones is the financial director, and, of course, Ginny Evans and Linda Candler are on the board along with the Senator."

Ben looked around the elegant entrance to the house and the massive staircase up to the second floor.

"Well, you've all done an excellent job," he said. "Who would've thought all this was even possible?"

From the top of the staircase, a glowing Ellie appeared, followed by her mother and an array of attentive bridesmaids and aunts. She'd changed from her wedding dress into a more practical blouse, cardigan, and slacks with flat shoes.

"Are you leaving so soon?" Katy said. "I didn't think the plane left until six."

"Casey's concerned about the traffic on I-285," the bride said. "The car's packed. We've got our passports ready, but TSA could take longer than we expect."

"Don't want to miss the plane," her mother added tearfully, one hand protectively on her daughter's shoulder. "Casey's thinking ahead."

Ellie stopped on the staircase and embraced her mom.

"I'll call as soon as we land at Heathrow," she said. "I promise."

"Is everyone leaving?" Stewart Wilton's voice rang out from the patio doors. "I thought we came for a party."

"Oh, the party's going on until all the food's been eaten," Ellie said, laughing. "Just ask my parents!"

Word passed rapidly through the crowd that the bride and groom were leaving, and the foyer spontaneously filled with relatives and well-wishers who spilled out onto the driveway at the front of the house, tossing handfuls of birdseed and shouting their farewells

When the hoopla concluded, the celebration indeed went on.

Ellie's parents insisted.

The food table groaned under the weight of culinary delights the garden band played requests, and everyone danced as though no one was holding a camera.

The guests filled the patio and the surrounding tables well into dusk.

Darcie danced several times with the Senator, much to Katy and Amy's delight. As he twirled the matron around the floor, he whispered in her ear. No one knew what he said, but Darcie blushed to the roots of her bleached hair. When they left the dance floor, they were holding hands.

Zedekiah was persuaded—or perhaps threatened—by Naomi to come in from the parking lot and join the other guests. Once there she dragged him protesting onto the dance floor. Between each song, she loudly and quite publicly hugged his neck and called him

Daddy until she coaxed a laugh from him and a promise to stay until the band stopped making music.

Even Daryl danced with the energetic Vicki, although their version of dancing was a bit like watching an exercise video from the 1970s—highly entertaining in its own quirky way.

Ben and Marcie drank lemonade and sat, Jim Smith between them, at a table under the trees as they snacked and plied the officer with questions about the FBI and his plans for the future.

Even Andrew and Ginny Evans, followed closely by a dignified Judge and Linda Candler, managed to find a slow dance to share before blending back into the crowd and making their way home earlier than most.

Amid the merrymakers, Cora sat quietly at a table with baby Tom cooing in her lap. A bashful Jane stood beside her, tucked securely under Cora's arm and hiding her face from anyone she didn't immediately recognize. The frothy white shawl Thomas remembered from Easter morning was wrapped around his wife's upper arms over a blue silk dress embroidered with tiny pink rose-buds. The blue of the dress matched Tom's practical cotton onesie, and Jane's pale pink dress was decorated with the same tiny flowers as her mother's.

Thomas had cheerfully agreed to complete the photo-perfect family wearing a blue dress shirt and a pink-and-blue striped tie. The scars on his face, except for a pale line across his forehead, had all faded into memory.

Marjorie had eyed him skeptically as he adjusted his coat in the hall mirror, waiting for everyone else to come down the stairs to leave.

"If it makes Cora happy," he said, shrugging at her, "then that's all that matters."

At the edge of the gravel parking lot, Charlie Abbott could hear the music, but his feet wouldn't take him any closer. He was absently pacing back and forth, considering whether or not to put in an appearance at the reception.

As he ruminated, Inola Walker drove up in an impressive black Mercedes SUV.

She, too, hesitated at the edge of the gravel parking lot.

"You were invited?" he said, surprised.

"You weren't?" she countered smartly, tugging down her gray suit jacket.

A shadow of raw emotion flitted over the detective's face, and Inola decided she might have gone too far. "I'm here to pick up Jim Smith," she said, looking over his shoulder at the sound of the music. "There's a flight out of Hartsfield tonight."

"Never really saw you as an Uber driver," he quipped. "Are you afraid he'll change his mind?"

"It's need to know, Detective Abbott," she said, lowering her voice. "We aren't going to Memphis."

Charlie stuffed his hand into his jeans pocket and pulled out his keys.

"So that's the way we're going to leave it?" he said with a grin. "Secrets?"

"Apparently so," she said, pivoting and heading toward the patio, her sturdy shoes crunching the gravel as she walked. "Works for me, cowboy."

Charlie watched her disappear into the house.

Change isn't always a bad thing, he thought, ambling toward his battered blue Volkswagen. *Sometimes change can be a good thing. Even a very good thing.*

He turned the ignition and shifted the stubborn stick shift into reverse.

I'm pretty sure I've had enough changes in my life to hold me for a while.

He rolled down the driver's window as the sounds of music and laughter from the party drifted in, but Charlie didn't hear. He'd already turned up the crackling radio and left the parking lot, headed south toward Highway 19 and home to New Orleans, with a quick stop along the way for a Yoo-Hoo and maybe some barbecue pork rinds, for an old friend's sake.

His heart was at peace, his soul at rest, and deep down he knew that no matter where he went, he was only a dream away from Balfour and the people he loved.

to Harry's Farm
Balfour Clinic
to Zeke's Cabin
rows of houses
Police Station
Cora's House
Simmon's Restaurant
Courthouse
N
W
E
S
Dragon's Breath
Dragon's Breath Bookstore
Town Square
COPPERFIELD'S
Copperfield's
To Highway 19
Bakery
Tipton's Service Station
Bakery
Balfour B&B
ACE
Ace Hardware
Holiday Inn Express
Sanderson's piggly wiggly
to Atlanta
Sanderson's piggly wiggly

to Wilton Estate

Shetland Lake

to Piney Woods

Miss Bessie's House

United Methodist Church

Cemetery

Hanson's

Hanson's Pharmacy

Emmanuel Baptist Church

Cemetery

Florist's Shop

Florist's Shop

Park & Playground

Parson's Funeral Home

Balfour Elementary School

Nursing Home

Stone Law Firm

POST OFFICE

Post Office

Balfour, GA

est. 1818

to Anson's

ABOUT THE AUTHOR

KC Pearcey has spent much of her life traveling from state to state, but home for her has always been her grandmother's house down a dusty road in a small country town deep in the South.

There the magnolias, pines, and scrub oaks dotted the rolling landscape while a pair of front-porch rocking chairs and a wooden porch swing had the best view in the known universe.

Dreams are often born from memories, and the dream of writing a novel was born on that front porch with the kindest, most intelligent person she ever knew over a cup of coffee in the predawn hours of an autumn morning.

The house is no longer there, but five years and five books later the dream has become reality and the time has come to move along to other places.

She's looking forward to meeting you there.

Just saying . . .

Made in the USA
Columbia, SC
02 July 2024